HER
BILLIONAIRES

THE COLLECTION

BY JULIA KENT

Copyright © 2013 by Julia Kent

ALL RIGHTS RESERVED. This book contains material protected under International and Federal Copyright Laws and Treaties. Any unauthorized reprint or use of this material is prohibited. No part of this book may be reproduced or transmitted in any form or by any means, electronic or mechanical, including photocopying, recording, or by any information storage and retrieval system without express written permission from the author / publisher.

Sign up for my New Releases and Sales email list at my blog to get the latest scoop on new eBooks, freebies and more:
http://jkentauthor.com

Table of Contents

Author's Note...iv
Her First Billionaire..5
Her Second Billionaire...67
Her Two Billionaires...131
Her Two Billionaires and a Baby..................................207
    Chapter One..209
    Chapter Two..247
    Chapter Three..267
    Chapter Four..301
    Chapter Five...357
    Chapter Six...373
    Chapter Seven..403
    Chapter Eight...411
    Chapter Nine..427
Other Books by Julia Kent..455
About the Author...457

Author's Note

This book was originally published as four connected novellas:
- Her First Billionaire,
- Her Second Billionaire,
- Her Two Billionaires, and
- Her Two Billionaires and a Baby.

The reading order for the entire series is:
- Her Billionaires (this book);
- It's Complicated;
- Completely Complicated (contains the novellas Complete Abandon, Complete Harmony, Complete Bliss and Complete We);
- It's Always Complicated.

Thank you for reading. ;)

Her First Billionaire

HER FIRST BILLIONAIRE

"Hot, luscious piece of ass who can suck a golf ball through forty feet of garden hose seeks rippling-ab'd firefighter who has a tongue that thrums like a hummingbird and enjoys painting my toenails and eating Ben & Jerry's out of the carton while watching Orange is the New Black."

Laura Michaels stared at the online dating site's registration screen and frowned. That's what she really wanted to write. Here was the truth:

"Needy, insecure, overweight twenty-nine-year-old financial analyst with three cats, a corporate job with pension and no debt seeks Mr. Impossible for way more than friendship and lots of ice cream. I'm desperate for some physical affection and oral sex with a guy who doesn't view it as a favor, and then expects to be praised like he cleaned my toilet. One night stands are better than nothing as long as you brush your teeth. Call me!"

Her best friend, Josie Mendham, punched her in the bicep.

"You can't say either of those!"

Josie was Laura's opposite. Where Laura was 5'6", Josie was barely tall enough to ride roller coasters. Remove the 1 from Laura's size and you still had to subtract a few to get Josie's size 2. Where Laura had long, curly blonde hair and bright green eyes, Josie was chocolate all around.

"Mutt and Jeff" her mom had called them, and they'd been besties forever.

Which meant Josie knew Laura too well. "You are going to do this, damn it," she said, wagging a finger in front of Laura's face. "No trying to be perfect. Perfect is the enemy of good enough."

"I haven't even found Mr. Good Enough!"

"That's because hundreds of Mr. Good Enoughs have walked past you, Laura, and you're blind to them."

Josie nudged Laura aside and started typing, her long nails burning up the keyboard. How did she do that? Typing on the pads of her fingers seemed impossible, but Josie did it, keeping her manicure intact, little replicas of the famous grey necktie from *Fifty Shades of Grey* on each nail.

The two had been out at a club the night before and Josie had slept over, waking up chipper and springing this online dating thing on Laura before she'd even had her first cup of coffee. As the machine gurgled and burbled, Laura willed it to hurry. Weighing out her entire dating future in a half-zombie state was not good.

Laura knew she had to lie, but how much was acceptable? Could she shave off a few sizes, or would she need to hack off an imaginary arm and leg to make herself seem "fit" and "athletic"? The drop-down box with its built in descriptors seemed like judgmental torment. No choices were there for "zaftig" or "juicy" or "full figure."

Being a size eighteen with F-cup breasts wasn't a crime, she knew. In real life, she was fashionable and flowing, plump and pleasing, and could arm wrestle most guys into submission, but reducing her accomplishments, personality and, yes, *body* into a vocabulary designed by some Internet start-up team of nineteen-year-old dropouts from Stanford and Carnegie Mellon made her irrationally angry.

No—*rationally* angry.

Seeing little choice, she pointed to the boxes on the screen and told Josie, "Pick the word 'fit.' I can deadlift

HER FIRST BILLIONAIRE

105 pounds. Which is," she said as she eyed Josie, "more than you weigh."

Josie pointedly ignored her, biting her lower lip and deep in concentration. "Voila!" she shouted, her hands spread wide in a grandiose gesture. "There's your ad."

She announced:

"Luscious, curvy financial analyst seeks friendship and more. Financially independent and self-assured, I'm a fit woman who wants a man (or, more than one! YOLO!) for stimulating conversation...er, yeah. Conversation. Message me (or massage me!)."

"I can't write that!" Laura groaned. "It makes me look like I want an orgy!" She squinted at the screen. "And what the hell is 'YOLO'?"

"Who doesn't want an orgy?" Josie wiggled her eyebrows lasciviously and stuck out her tongue, waggling it in a very bad imitation of oral sex. "And YOLO stands for 'you only live once.'"

"Cut it out. You're turning me on. It's been *that* long since I got some, and the last guy used his tongue like he was a Roto-Rooter man. Like that." She pointed at Josie's tongue and bent over, laughing.

And then Josie, with a flourish, pressed the Submit button.

"Thank you for joining—your profile is now live!" the screen read.

"Oh, no, Josie, did you really just do that?" Laura sputtered as she grabbed the mouse.

"What?" Josie batted her eyelashes. "Live a little. See who replies!"

She grabbed her heavy, over-full Vera Bradley purse that they had discovered at a local thrift shop for $3.99

and fingered her car keys. "Gotta go, Laura. And don't you dare delete that."

Laura laughed. "You know me too well."

"No kidding," Josie muttered. Her face turned serious. "Really, Laura. You need to get out there. Some guy is being deprived of your awesomeness. And besides, your budget needs the break."

"My budget?"

"Yeah. What are you spending on batteries for Bob?"

Confused, Laura shook her head. It was like Josie spoke a foreign language sometimes. "Huh?"

"Your battery-operated boyfriend. You know—BOB."

And with that she snickered, running for the door as Laura threw a section of a fashion magazine at her. Josie's evil laughter filled the apartment as she ran down the hallway, the sound fading once she hit the stairwell. "Have a good day at work!" she hollered from the street.

The coffee machine gave its death-rattle gasp that signaled the pot was done, and Laura went to drink it greedily, needing sustenance to kick her brain into gear. With enough caffeine, she could date anyone. Hmm, maybe she should do a search for baristas on that site. Free lattes would be a nice perk.

* * *

Dylan Stanwyck couldn't believe what he saw when he logged into the online dating site. Four months of weeding through so many crappy profiles had jaded him. Finding the right woman would be like coming across the proverbial needle in a haystack, but in this case he didn't want to face any pricks.

And yes, women could be pricks. So far he had been inundated with requests to chat, and he knew exactly why. Being a firefighter who competed in weightlifting competitions for fun, along with the occasional mini triathlon, made his pictures look quite nice.

The problem with the women who were responding to him was that they were also the type to be drawn to appearances only. It seemed so shallow of him to think it, but sometimes being built the way he was could be a curse.

Curse of the Jersey Shore chicks. Because that was the type who seemed to seek him out, like moths to a flame. A trashy, Snooki-like flame of ho-dom. When he met up with these women he found himself in some alternate universe, where they licked their lips and offered themselves up in the alley behind the nice tapas restaurant where he liked to take dates. A few goat-cheese stuffed dates and pitchers of sangria later and he was being humped up against a slimy brick wall next to the trash cans.

And when he turned them down...

He still had scars from one woman's long, overdone nails raking his neck as she screeched, "You don't know me!" over and over, as passersby gawked, took pictures they probably uploaded to Reddit, and mercifully called 911 when it became evident he required police assistance.

So when this new profile for Laura appeared, he peered at the description and leaned back in his chair, taking a deep breath. Cute. But not too cute. A little sassy. He liked sassy. He ran a hand through his thick, wavy hair. *Time to get a haircut, dude. You look like a survivalist. And smell like one, too*, he thought as he studied her picture and caught a whiff of himself. His morning run was done -- 3.8 miles logged on his online fitness program -- and he reeked.

She looked like a 1940s pinup girl. A little plumper, with soft curves to her shoulders, and a fuzzy, lime-green sweater accentuating her breasts. Her jaw line seemed firm and gentle all at once, and what appeared to be naturally-blonde hair was swept up off her face in a pony tail.

His mom would call her a "corn-fed farm girl" and those lips— lush and grinning a half smile that seemed to say "Kiss me, Dylan."

Smart, too. A financial analyst? Sounded suitably bland and yet signaled she was smart enough to carry her own in a conversation about something other than Kim Kardashian or *Fifty Shades of Grey* (Really—why had every date for the past two months mentioned it?). A real woman. What a refreshing change.

So he continued reading:

"Luscious, curvy financial analyst seeks friendship and more. Financially independent and self-assured, I'm a fit woman who wants a man (or, more than one! YOLO!) for stimulating conversation...er, yeah. Conversation. Message me (or massage me!)."

Something fierce and hot inside him came to life. From that description it sounded like she...seriously? No way.

"Mike! Hey, Mike! Get in here!" If there were a chance— any chance at all, here, then he had to act fast. Someone this amazing was about to get inundated by messages from needy weirdos.

And he needed to be the first.

His roommate wandered in. Where Dylan was all muscle and brawn, Mike Pine was tall and sleek, a marathoner's body of long, lean tissue. Dylan's dark, thick, Italian, looks made him popular with women, but Mike was the golden boy, with blonde hair and blue eyes—the long-distance runner with a soft heart, the guy women turned to and poured their hearts out, Mr. Sensitive to Dylan's Mr. Conquest.

Dylan tapped the screen. "Take a look at her."

He smiled smugly as Mike's eyes raced across the screen. They'd been waiting for a long time. Too long. His roommate's expression told him everything he needed to know. Score! It might finally be time.

"Do you really think that's a code for being up for a threesome?" Mike asked, eyebrows arched. "I don't know, Dyl...I think it's a joke she's making. You know how nervous and weird people can be when they try to distill their entire life into a few sentences."

Dylan chewed on the inside of his cheek. Bad habit. "Good point. Well, even if she isn't into a nice ménage arrangement, she is one fine woman." A low whistle escaped from his lips. "I have a project on my hands now, don't I?"

Mike nodded, peering at the screen, eyes lingering. "You are going to have a lot of competition."

Dylan snorted. "Like I care. May the best man win."

Mike went silent, then grinned, his fresh-faced boy-next-door look morphing into a Wall Street trader's predatory smile that made Dylan suddenly uncomfortable for no reason he could pinpoint.

"Yeah. I hope he does."

* * *

Ding! The little chat box on the online dating site lit up like a Christmas tree. Laura sucked the last mouthful of her coffee and gaped at the screen. *You have got to be kidding me*, Laura thought. Already? She clicked and read a message from "9inluvr":

Hey, babe. I live in the city and so do you, so let's hook up for some FWB action.

She snorted. Oh, sure. Just like that. *Yer a catch, Bud. A real romantic.*

Ding! This one was from some guy named Dylan. Before she read the chat she looked at his profile.

Well hellooooo there, Mr. Firefighter.

A thin line of drool formed at the corner of her mouth, an instant response to the picture before her. It was a professional picture, the guy wearing no shirt, a fireman's hat perched at a jaunty tilt. Like a stripper's picture in a firefighter's role.

Oh, God. I can't date a stripper, she thought. *He'd have nicer g-strings than mine.*

But no—he was a real firefighter. The picture, he explained in his profile, came from a charity bachelor auction he had been in. Bachelor auction? How much had he gone for?

As she studied the picture she guessed a solid four figures. She was already primed to empty her life savings for a night with this guy.

On a whim she Googled "Dylan charity bachelor auction firefighter" and her drool increased so much she would soon need a bucket.

Oh, holy hell. The image search showed the same man, whose name was Dylan Stanwyck, in firefighter's pants, boots, a fireman's hat and suspenders, perched on the floor of a fire station right next to the pole. He was leaning on one elbow and had smears of soot on him, with well-oiled muscles and a smug-ass grin.

Her First Billionaire

Whoever set up that photograph needed to be recruited for her company's marketing department because damn—she was ready to use up every available dollar on her credit cards to get a night with him.

Maybe she could save a bunch of money and just set herself on fire. Or her car. It probably wasn't worth much, but if she found out his schedule and whether he'd be the one responding...

And *he* was pinging *her* on the dating site?

She dropped her coffee and scrambled to write back in the chat room.

"*Hi,*" she said, all inspiration and creativity vanishing as the heat forming between her legs apparently melted her brain.

Hi. I'm Dylan. Nice to "meet" you. :)

Think, Laura. Think. Man, where was Josie? Of all the times for that girl to be on time to go to work. She needed help figuring out something witty to say.

Hi. I'm Laura. Nice to "meet" you, too!

She wrote back. Then he answered:

I was hoping you might be interested in going out? We can do coffee, maybe? Or go to a nice tapas bar?

Tapas! Her favorite. But wait—Josie always said any guy who likes tapas must be gay. Laura checked the photo again. No way. And even if Dylan was gay, she would still sleep with him. Cute, polite, and loves tapas?

Tapas sounds great! When?

Damn it. Now she sounded too eager. She waited. And waited. No reply.

Maybe he was having second thoughts. Or she sounded like a moron. Or he realized he didn't like tapas after all. Or he really was gay. Or this was his cat impersonating him.

She began to pace, willing the chat bar to ping. If she stared hard enough...

Finally:

Uh, this might seem too eager, but I don't care. I am free tonight. I work a 24 tomorrow, so this is my last chance for a few days. I don't mean to be rude, asking you on short notice, but...please tell me you're free tonight.

Yes! Yes, yes, yes, she wanted to write. But she needed to play that stupid game, the dance of meeting someone new. Her turn to wait. She reread his message. What was a 24?

She puzzled over that one as she chewed on her cuticle, pulling on it until it bled. Brilliant! Screw up your manicure when you have a hot date tonight, Laura.

Might have. *Might* have. Don't put the cart before the horse.

I am free. Prince William is now taken and so I have an opening in my busy social schedule.

She hit Send before she could change her mind. Too cheesy?

LOL. Sounds great. Meet me at Tempo Bistro after work. At 6?

Tempo Bistro? The most expensive, chi-chi restaurant in town? Not tapas, either—something she couldn't quite remember. Asian fusion? How on earth could a firefighter afford that?

Not your problem, Laura. And she was making terrible assumptions. She needed to assume they were going dutch. Good thing she was a careful saver.

'lo?

The chat window pinged. *Geez, Laura. Get out of your head.* She typed furiously:

Sounds even better. I'll see you there and you know what I look like.

And he replied:

Oh, yes. :P

What was that supposed to mean? Her eyes swept over the clock—now she had eight minutes to shower. Damn. Laura shook her head and walked to the bathroom, stripping naked by the time she crossed the threshold and turned on the hot water.

Sliding under the spray was bliss, the beads of water trailing their way down her body, her hair wet and ropy within seconds, the curl relaxed and the strands stretching long enough to tickle the top of her sacrum. Eh—why not leave the ad up? Who knew. Maybe she'd attract a better breed of guy. Or, at least, a different kind. She eyed the showerhead—did she have time? Eight minutes?

More than enough for the last guy she dated.

Just enough time for some intimate attention from Mr. Showerhead, though. Josie was wrong. It wasn't her battery bill that was getting expensive.

Her water bill, on the other hand...

Good thing her vibrator was waterproof. As she soaped up she was cognizant of the time, knowing she had minutes to finish. Pulling up the old standby fantasy always worked. Two men, luscious and thickly-muscled, both in the shower with her. *Mmmm...*

The extra tip of her vibrator slid along the soft, sensitive skin of her clit as she perched one foot on the tub, opening up for access to slide in her fantasy lover, who was soaping her body with his sculpted, large hands, hands that smoothed over her curves, cupping her ass to pull him toward her, sliding his enormity into her while the other nameless, faceless lover kissed her, hard, his tongue lashing against her and exploring as the spray rolled down in rivulets between them, gathering at her folds and adding to the tease.

Her passage tightened as she imagined him bending down, onto his knees, his tongue now lapping where the vibrator's little antennae tweaked her—not her own hands moving the thick shaft in and out but the lovers', four hands at once on her as one mouth descended on her eager, red nub, the other man thrusting her up against the shower's wall, her body ready for more.

She tensed, knowing she was so close, craving all these hands, more than enough for two men who wanted and needed her, the familiar muscled cresting of her climax so innate she barely cried out, the release perfunctory but oh, so welcome.

And, now, the guilt. Because how could a "normal" woman really want two men at once? As she absent-mindedly rushed through the rest of the shower, quickly washing off her trusty toy, a persistent voice said, *You, Laura. You.*

She really did. Some wishes were never meant to be, she told herself, drying her hair and rushing to get dressed.

Just a fantasy that got her off.

HER FIRST BILLIONAIRE

* * *

"I don't think I can do this, Josie," she said that night as she prepared for the actual date. Dylan had picked out a nice restaurant in a part of town that was above her pay grade. She wondered how on earth he could afford it on a firefighter's salary. Laura wasn't going to question it because maybe she had finally found somebody who was going to treat her properly. The way she had always dreamed of being treated—and not like a booty call or a person you'd settle for when you really want something more but settle for "good enough."

It didn't help that Laura felt a huge discrepancy between what she saw in herself, what she saw in the pictures of Dylan, and what she found when she did a search for him online. This guy was a catch; not just a catch, but a *catch*. Like, the difference between catching a good-sized bass in a Great Lake versus catching a giant, enormous marlin. He was outstanding. There was no other term for it.

He looked like something that had been sculpted by an artist.

"You're more than ready and you know it, Laura. It's about time you found some guy who..." Josie looked at the screen again. "I don't think I remember what I was about to say because I'm about to burst into flames if I look at that guy one more time."

"He's mine," said Laura, baring her teeth in a fake show of territoriality. It wasn't that fake, though. Some part of her meant it.

"I can look. I know I can't touch, but I know I *can* look," Josie joked.

Laura had picked out three different sets of clothes, being as meticulous as possible today, trying so hard to cover what she felt were definitely deficits. Big, enormous deficits. Calling her a fluffy woman would be a perfectly nice euphemism, if you didn't prefer the term fat.

Not fat in a derogatory way. Just fat as a practical, pragmatic way of describing how she was. It's not like you get to be a size eighteen by meticulously eating seven hundred calories a day and never, ever doing anything wrong in terms of what you put in your mouth. She couldn't stand it when people would claim that they're fat because of their genes, they're fat because they have a thyroid problem, they're fat because—*because, because, because*.

She owned it. She was fat because she put too much unhealthy—and even healthy—stuff in her mouth. Laura liked food. She really, *really* liked food. Enjoyed it. Savored it. Pleasured it. Found it to be a joy in her life.

And she paid the price with the extra pounds, the *padding*—what a lovely euphemism that was, too. She liked her curves. The curves made her feel normal, gentle, open, emotional—*bare*. You couldn't hide from a curve. You couldn't hide from a love handle or from a padded hip or from a booty that made enough men blush and drool. She knew it was an asset (pun intended) to some guys.

What she *deeply* hoped was that she could beat the odds and find in him someone who really valued someone like her. So far that hadn't been the case. Online dating had turned out to be a giant nightmare of electrons that didn't line up exactly the way that anybody had planned. She seemed to photograph well because she got an awful lot of come-ons and she figured maybe there was something to that.

Her First Billionaire

She was blonde, with a healthy glow in her face and a pretty decent smile with two dimples that appeared when she laughed hard enough. Her shoulders carried some of her weight, but it made her look bosomy and big-chested. If she picked the right form-fitting sweater she could come across a good twenty pounds lighter than she really was.

That may have been part of the problem, though, because it was always that look that the guys gave her when she walked into the bar, the coffee shop, the plaza, the restaurant—whatever public place that they had planned to meet.

It was that look. That fucking *look*.

It was a look of surprise—and not of good surprise. It was the look of, oh, you're not what I was looking for. Oh, you're not what you look like in your picture.

Oh, you're a fat chick.

Oh.

Sometimes they had the decency to tell her the truth and to say those thoughts aloud. Yeah, really—the decency. It was better to hear it up front, to her face, *in* her face even, than to sit down with that type of guy, to try to read the signals, the tilt of the face, the grin, the look in his eyes, the *lack* of a look in his eyes if he glanced away. All of the little tells, the way he held his hand, the way he fidgeted, the way he reached for his phone for a text that didn't really exist.

All of those sights and sounds and movements that added up to one thing.

Rejection.

So far, she had had a few one night stands, a few guys who were willing to fuck the fat chick. She didn't turn them down because the offers were few and far between. At first, it wasn't obvious that these were pity fucks—until it was glaringly, painfully, heartbreakingly obvious.

Most recently, like she had told Josie, she was sick of it. Just *sick* of it. This last ditch attempt at online dating really was the final attempt.

And Dylan seemed too good to be true.

Here she stood in front of Tempo Bistro at six p.m. sharp wearing a pencil skirt, really nice high heels, and a mohair sweater, the same one she had worn in the dating site picture, so she could—in her own head—not consider herself to have been falsely advertising. What he would see in a minute was exactly what she had shown online.

No less.

No more.

Her hair was pulled back in the same funny little ponytail and her eyes were sparkling with hope that she dredged up from deep, deep inside.

Laura was about to plunk her hope down in front of him, ready to try once more.

* * *

Getting ready for this first date with Laura had turned out to be more complicated than it had any right to be. First of all, it turned out he got his dates wrong. His twenty-four-hour shift was actually tonight. He'd had to change shifts with Murphy, who wasn't know for granting favors easily. He not only extracted another twenty-four-hour shift out of him, but also convinced him to give up his beloved Red Sox tickets for the next game.

Dylan hoped like hell that this date was worth it, hating the sly grin on Murphy's face.

Her First Billionaire

Four different clothing changes later, he finally settled on something that he hoped resembled "business casual" in the corporate world. She worked as a financial analyst for some large nameless, faceless corporation and that meant that she probably had an expectation about what a guy would look like. Dylan's generally preferred state of dress was some old concert t-shirt from the 90's, a pair of ripped up jeans and whatever pair of shoes were comfortable enough to pass muster.

Wearing business casual pants, a buttoned-down shirt, and—tie or no tie? He had finally settled on no tie. He felt like a fraud. If he added some penny loafers and a loose cotton V-neck that showed the top of his chest he would look like something out of a Macy's ad, which actually would've been possible ten years ago when he'd dipped his toe into the world of modeling before realizing that most of the people in that business were douchebags and he couldn't stand it.

"Who died? You look like you're going to a funeral, man," said Mike, walking into the room looking pretty natty himself in a similar outfit, just without the black pants. Mike was wearing khakis and some kind of boat shoes that Dylan thought had gone out of fashion back in the 80's, when he was a kid. The guy managed to make Superman look puny. He could have been a stunt man for *The Avengers*, minus the confidence. For whatever reason, Mike was a man without swagger. He just *was*, a steady presence that made Dylan feel complete.

"What about you, man?" he challenged. "Why are you all dressed up? You got a hot date, too?"

He narrowed his eyes and peered at his roommate, wondering. Nah, no way—he didn't. Mike hadn't gone out in eighteen months, not since Jill died.

Mike grinned. "I wish. Meeting at the ski resort."

"It's July!"

"I know, but we start getting ready now, believe it or not. Some people actually plan out processes and don't always fly by the seat of their pants." He muttered the last sentence under his breath but clearly meant for Dylan to hear every word.

Dylan shook his head and said, "I like being a pantser." Big grin. "Have fun."

"I'd rather be doing what you're doing," Mike replied, then paused, seeming to think over what he'd just said.

"Me too," Dylan laughed, grabbing his keys. "Don't wait up for me."

"I'm staying overnight at my cabin, so no worries. You have the place to yourself. I hope things work out with Laura. That," he paused, brow furrowed, "could really benefit everybody, huh?"

Mike winked and the two hugged, Dylan forced to reach up to the only person in his life taller than himself. And broader.

"Something like that," Dylan said, shaking his head.

"Are you going to tell her about the money?"

Mike's voice was more defiant than usual, as if challenging Dylan to a battle he didn't even know was on the horizon. Dylan knew that the tone in Mike's voice was as much about his own demons; neither had ever expected this kind of surprise from Jill's death. They would both gladly give it all up to have her back. Barring that, though, the inheritance from their dead partner was certainly a welcome, if perplexing, change in their lives.

It meant nothing and it meant everything. Neither had said a word to anyone they had dated. Not a word to their friends or coworkers. Mike had quietly purchased the ski resort where he worked; it had been up for sale for a long time and was on the brink of financial collapse due to inept management and an owner who viewed it as a losing business. Mike would change that, Dylan knew.

Having the money to buy the ski resort and one of the nicest cabins on the mountain had blown some life back into his partner. Too bad they didn't have the third who would complete them, taking a dull dyad and turning it into a robust triad.

Maybe Laura would...ah, who knew?

"No, of course I'm not going to tell her about the money." Dylan turned away from Mike and finished pulling on his sweater. "Can you imagine that scene? 'Oh, hi, I'm Dylan and I am a billionaire.'"

He choked on the word, his face flushing and going cold at once, the syllables so fake. So *poseur*. Like a little kid dressing up in Dad's dress shoes, or a teen trying on personalities to find the right fit. Except he had no choice here. Jill had left them this fortune and it was theirs. No trying anything on for size. This was serious money and Dylan and Mike had been catapulted from working class stiffs to billionaire bachelors.

"Billionaire." Mike lifted his chin, as if sniffing something. "It does roll off the tongue nicely."

"Mike Pine, billionaire," Dylan announced grandly, jumping on the bed and bouncing like a mad monkey. His hair flopped in his eyes and he watched Mike plant his hands on his hips, shaking his head, as if faced with a recalcitrant, hyperactive eight year old.

"You are such a child."

"Yes, but I am a wealthy child!" *Bounce bounce bounce— boom!*

Dylan jumped off the bed and bounded onto the floor next to Mike, like a superhero landing. Mike's eyes went from amused to pained, then his shoulders slumped forward. Dylan rubbed the soft spot between his shoulder blades and they both stared at a spot on the wall that seemed to contain everything they yearned for.

"She left us all this money, Dyl. We had no idea."

Dylan shifted uncomfortably and said nothing.

Mike picked up on his change, though, and turned to him with an accusing look. "You knew?"

Dylan dropped his hand from Mike's back and sighed. "No. I didn't know she was a billionaire! But I figured out pretty early on that she had money. We were in college, Mike. The dot com boom hadn't happened, and she claimed to make money off 'websites.' How do you think she could afford to spot us on all those trips we took?"

"We camped and kept it cheap," Mike sputtered. "She didn't live like a crazy-rich person."

Blinking hard, Mike started to say more but turned toward the dresser where Dylan kept a picture of Jill. The three of them on Cape Cod, at First Encounter Beach, the green marsh grasses so thick that hundreds of thousands of minnows lived in the shallow waters there, almost giving the water a viscosity of live, teeming fish.

The ocean had been perfect, the water warm though thrashing for the bay that day, and the three of them peered into the sun, some random stranger stopped and asked to take a pic.

A pic taken a month before they knew Jill had lymphoma.

For the month after that trip she'd been fatigued. Not herself. Quiet. Waving away their concerns, she

HER FIRST BILLIONAIRE

had trudged on, working on her "websites" and going for long runs that turned into long walks and that, finally, turned into a leisurely stroll during which she'd collapsed. Mike had been with her and carried her three city blocks to the emergency room of a hospital. The next few days were a blur Dylan couldn't let himself resurrect.

Not now. Not as he prepared to go out with someone new. Someone vibrant.

Someone alive.

"Yeah, Jill kept a lot of secrets from us, Mike."

His partner bristled; the wound was still too fresh.

"Let's continue her legacy, then, and keep the money a secret."

"For now, sure. When the time's right, we can talk about it."

"Jesus." Mike ran a shaking hand through his hair and stared out the window at the city below. "What a fucking curse."

"And a blessing."

Angry eyes met Dylan's as Mike spun around. "Call it whatever you want."

"It's both," Dylan conceded.

"It just is— you're right. It's both."

"You get to save the ski resort. You know Jill would have been happy."

"Then why didn't *she* save it? Why didn't she tell us she had all this money? I mean, damn! It's not something you casually forget to mention. 'Oh! That's right! I'm part of the richest point-whatever-oh-one percent in the world. While you were complaining about your ski mountain going under, did that slip my mind? Oops!'"

The sneer in Mike's voice was utterly uncharacteristic and made Dylan recoil. Dude was pissed.

The anger, Dylan knew, was really a form of mourning.

"Tell it to Jill, Mike."

The words took the winds out of the larger man's sails, his body literally shrinking before Dylan's eyes. Jill's ashes were on that very mountain Mike had just bought—a big reason for his purchase. Now he could have her forever, safe and sound and secure.

But still dead.

Mike bit his upper lip and nodded. "Yeah. I will."

Dylan was running late for his date and slipped out the door quietly. He was ready to move forward, to move on, to continue past the past. Someday—soon—he hoped Mike could join him.

He looked at his smart phone. Already running late. No way he was going to blow this by making Laura think he was standing her up. A quick look in the mirror again, a little bit more cologne. A final check of his smile in the mirror and he walked out of the apartment and into what he hoped would be a part of his future.

Mike could stew in the past.

* * *

Laura wasn't quite sure what to make of this as she paced a safe distance from the restaurant, trying to leave herself an out if she needed to save face and just disappear. A sink hole might have been better, but she couldn't conjure one at will. Running away in shame, though, she was familiar with—so she skulked three storefronts from the entrance.

Her First Billionaire

He had said 6:00 and it was 6:07. Seven minutes normally meant nothing in terms of the wheel of life. Right now, each second felt like torture and four hundred and twenty tortures were adding up to to one big ball of fear. It all rested right in her gut where desire and happiness should be right now, where joy and, well—not quite love, but at least lust should be residing.

Not this pit of despair.

It's only seven minutes, she said to herself. The seconds ticked on until her smart phone clicked over and now it was eight minutes.

It's only eight minutes. A thin bead of sweat burst under her lip, and on her cheeks, in that valley between her breasts in a way that only the cold irrational anxiety of dating could bring out in her.

Oh, fuck this, she said to herself. *I don't think I can do this anymore. Even Mr. Hotty Hot Hot Firefighter isn't worth this. I'm just going to go home and have a date with Ben and Jerry. That's my comfort zone, right there baby. Maybe the most dependable men on Earth because this, this is bullshit.*

Zzzz. The phone buzzed suddenly. She had it on vibrate. Laura startled and it fell out of her hands, clattering to the ground.

"Damn," she shouted, reaching down, scrambling after it, hoping that the screen hadn't broken. Luckily, she had a protective case on it, and grabbed it and slid her finger across the screen to answer the call.

"Hello? Hello?" she said, trying desperately to keep her eagerness out of her voice.

"Hello." A deep man's baritone greeted her, with a friendliness that he had no right to offer her—yet she was so glad he did. "Uh," he hesitated, "is this Laura?"

"Yes, it is," she answered brightly, her voice a little too high-pitched, her anxiety a little too intense right now, but she trudged on.

"Yeah, really?" The voice stammered. "This is Dylan. I am so sorry," he said, and she hoped that the sincerity was true. Needed it to be true with a part of her that knew that there was no way of knowing.

"I'm so sorry. I'm running late. I am walking down Twelfth Avenue right now. In fact, I can see the entrance to the restaurant and, wait a minute. Hmmm. I don't know." A low wolf whistle. "I don't know if I'm going to be able to make it."

"What? What? What did you say?"

"There is this gorgeous woman just standing out there wearing a fuzzy sweater and a damn fine gray pencil skirt and heels that make her legs go on forever. Laura, I may have to date *her* tonight instead of you."

She nearly dropped her phone again. *Oh, my God*, her brain burned, her internal voice screaming like a rat stuck in a cage with Napalm all over it and lit on fire.

And then she got it, calming down instantly. *Oh.* He was complimenting her.

He was joking. He liked her.

Who *was* this guy?

Now she could see him. *Deep breaths, Laura,* she told herself.

He was joking around. Being playful, not mean. He was a block and a half away, walking toward her with a swagger, with a confidence she didn't see in many men. One hand in his pocket, marching down the street like he had all the time in the world.

And boy, were his eyes eating her up. She could feel it.

And she was giving it right back.

Her First Billionaire

Her heart was beating a million times a minute from the fear about his joke, and the anxiety that the joke had triggered. But now—it was like the electrons were playing banjo between them. Molecules were flying millions and millions of miles a second. She wasn't sure what she was going to do when they actually stood two feet from each other, because she was ready to take him right there, on the street, public indecency be damned.

Seconds later, he was down to a block, half a block, and he took his hand out of his pocket, giving her a wave.

He had been talking to her the entire time and she had no idea what he was saying.

* * *

"Laura? Laura? Hello—are you there? I can see you and you're standing there. I am waving at you right now. Laura, have I mistaken you for a human being or are you a really hot store mannequin?"

He heard her laugh. Aha. *Keep going,* Dylan told himself. Recover from the terrible joke.

"Or part of some performance art thing like that guys like me don't understand? Were you Andy Warhol's protégé? Is this a flash mob set-up and nineteen naked members of the Pirate Party are about to appear and don Mickey Mouse masks in some geopolitical protest?"

She suddenly folded and bent over laughing.

He breathed a sigh of relief. *Sweet!*

She was forcing him to use all his remaining brain cells to process basic bodily functions as every red blood cell rushed to his groin. He couldn't stop raking her body with his eyes. He couldn't stop eating her with his retinas. She was some kind of Dylan magnet.

Her entire appearance was luscious and her eyes—as he got closer he saw the kindness, the sweetness in them. There was a beauty, a full-bodied, full-fledged gorgeousness about her that made him hard instantly.

"Stupid business casual," he muttered to himself, mouth tilted away from his phone. He was wearing the kind of pants where his arousal could become very obvious.

No more than a foot and a half separating them, he felt like the biggest idiot on the planet for even joking about not dating her. She was stunning, all curves and woman and he wanted to smell her, bury his face in that sweet neck, feel her in his arms and listen to her breath as he made her happy.

What did her cries of ecstasy sound like? Would she turn her face away? Bite the pillow? Rake lines of ownership into his back with those glossy nails?

Later.

Later, he would find out. The same confidence that had always been there for him told him so. Like a second person living in his head, it just knew. She was his, and she didn't know it yet. But she would, and he had all the time in the world to teach her that.

With his tongue.

He stood there and stared at her, not knowing what to say. He couldn't recite what went through his head as his eyes roamed over the perfect topography of her body. She stared back and didn't seem to know what to say, either.

This silent dance needed a better beat.

One he could drive home with his cock.

Finally, she pointed to the door and said, "Great restaurant you picked," her voice as breathless as he felt. Except she was actually talking and he was standing there looking like a fish out of water, his mouth opening and closing as he tried desperately to get something like a linear thought going.

Where the hell was that confidence now? He wasn't awkward or worried or any of those namby-pamby feelings Mike always described having. It was more that his brain had gone blank at the sight of her and everything but his arousal went into hibernate mode.

She smiled and seemed to expect something intelligible to come out of his mouth. First, he had to dig his way out of the enormous, gaping hole of lust he'd just tripped into.

How in the hell was she still single? Why hadn't someone snatched her up?

"It's this whole Asian fusion thing. My friend told me it would be a good idea to bring a first date here and it might be a place to impress somebody." *And the food is supposed to be amazing, but that's secondary.* She seemed so nervous, those glittering eyes wary, already on guard from his lame attempt at humor on the phone.

He felt like an ass. He could sense he was losing her. His charm system went into overdrive, not the shallow Dylan so used to getting a woman to step out of her pants within an hour of their first drink in a bar, but the slower burning Dylan who stumbled across Jill in college years ago and who felt sucker punched and euphoric all at once.

"Impressing me is more important than the food?" Laura laughed and looked at him with an uncertain caution in her eyes, a hesitation that spoke of something he couldn't put his finger on.

"Yeah," he said, a slow grin stretching over his face, the word more a promise than an answer.

"I don't think you have to worry about someone like me," she replied, looking away with a bashful smile, her blond ponytail sliding down the side of her creamy neck as if guarding her, creating a safe barrier and holding her in place.

He cocked his head, looked her over again and wondered what on earth was she was talking about. Standing outside the restaurant babbling like an idiot wasn't exactly his idea of a good date, though, so he motioned her toward the door and said "Shall we?"

As she walked past him, impulse took over and he put one hand on the small of her back as the maitre d' held the door open. The connection to her soft skin was so strong that he grew harder, which he didn't think was possible.

Even if this dinner was going to cost him half of an entire paycheck, he did not care.

Oh—that's right.

He wasn't relying on his paycheck anyhow these days, he reminded himself. Finances had changed radically months ago, a surprise that he and Mike still tried to assimilate.

Stop it, Dylan. Stop thinking about Jill, he told himself. None of that should enter into the calculation of the emotional side of this.

Tonight is about Laura.

As they were led to their table in a smoky-grey environment, with a giant twenty-foot golden Buddha lit up in the corner and a small fountain bubbling at its feet, all he could do was stare at her ass, trying to to figure out how not to sound like another one of those guys who is desperate enough to go on an online dating site and find somebody to fuck.

Her First Billionaire

Neither of them seemed to know what to say, so he figured, being the guy, he would take the lead.

That's how it would work in bed, right? His mind went blank at the flash of a vision of his face buried between Laura's soft thighs.

He practically threw the folded napkin in his lap to hide what he thought must be the tallest raging hard-on ever.

Dylan coughed. "Your profile said you're from the west coast, but you moved here to the east coast. Who do you work for?"

Just then, the waitress interrupted as if on cue and asked them if they wanted a drink. Laura ordered a sake.

"Make it two," he added. If she was going to go for the harder stuff, so would he. Boy, this could end up being a much more interesting date than he ever expected.

* * *

She felt like she had lost her entire vocabulary all in the past three minutes. This guy was incredible. He had taken her to the hottest place in town. Granted, his friend had recommended it, but who cared if that was the main reason why?

Dylan seemed to care, to take the time to make a good first impression, and she loved his sense of humor even if it did nearly lead to her early demise from a heart attack via misunderstanding. She had never been taken anywhere so nice. Of course, she could never tell him that.

Most of the guys who dated her took her to a restaurant that had fifty-inch plasma televisions blasting five different sporting events all at once, and the most gourmet item on the menu was fried mozzarella sticks.

She blanked when the waitress asked her what she wanted to drink, so she blurted out sake, because it was the one drink she had ever had in an Asian restaurant years ago, when her mother had taken her to a Hibachi place for her twenty-first birthday. She figured one shot would loosen her up and then she could show more of herself. With Dylan requesting the same, she knew she'd ordered appropriately for this type of restaurant and began to let herself unclench a little.

She glanced at the table and saw that she was revealing more of herself already. Her sweater had dipped down a little too much to show the black lace of her bra. When she looked up, she found that she did not meet Dylan's eyes with her own, but that he was staring at the same spot she had just been looking at.

Apparently, he was not enough of a gentleman to pretend that he wasn't staring—until he cut his eyes away abruptly. He threw his napkin in his lap, looked down at the menu, and said "I have no idea what any of this stuff is." Then he turned and craned his head to watch one of the servers take a tray over to a nearby table. "Whatever it is, though, it smells incredible."

That loosened her up more, her nervous laughter shifting into something more genuine. These startlingly special few minutes felt like they had already altered reality for her. She couldn't quite put her finger on it, but was trying very, *very* hard not to make more meaning out of these few perfect moments with Dylan.

A giddiness, unfamiliar and *not* fleeting (to her utter shock), filled her skin and her thoughts as she shyly caught his eye and let it settle, not looking away. Their stare deepened into something more primal, more knowing, and her insecurity faded as they communicated without words.

Interrupted by the waitress, she pulled her eyes away with regret as the woman brought their drinks.

Dylan held his up in a toast and said, "To...financial analyzing!"

She nodded acknowledgment, and answered, "To firefighting," clinking glasses before they drank and put down the empty shot glasses. She fingered the rim of her glass and then they both leaned forward on the table with great expectation.

Finally, she realized he expected her to answer the question he had asked what felt like hours ago, and she said, "I work for Stohlman Industries."

"Stohlman?" His expression showed he was impressed.

That pleased Laura—it *was* impressive. Stohlman was known for being very, very competitive for jobs, and it had been hard to break in to the world's third largest media company.

"I've been there since I graduated college."

"Really? What is your degree, then?"

"IT—Information Technology."

"But you're a financial analyst?"

"I work with the tech side of things."

He leaned back in his chair, folded his arms, clearly making himself comfortable, and gave her a mirthful look. "So what do you *do*?"

And she laughed, her face relaxing, her cheeks spreading and matching his mirth. "Do you really want to know? 'Cause it's awfully technical."

He leaned forward on his elbows, propped his chin in one hand and said, "Yeah, I do want to know."

She studied his eyes. He meant it—he really *meant* it. Oh, man, was this really the whole package? Did she really get a gorgeous, ripped firefighter who gave a damn about what she did for a living as a financial analyst for some mega corporation? If so, she didn't want to pinch herself cause this might be a dream.

Then again, there were parts of her that she certainly wanted him to pinch.

"I work in healthcare IT, and what I do right now is work on a large project for military healthcare."

He nodded. Made an expression with his mouth that indicated that it was interesting.

She said, "Enough about my job. You're a firefighter, right? You save damsels in distress from burning buildings and rescue cats out of trees. I don't have to really know more than that," she teased.

He laughed, bright teeth gleaming, straight and perfect, speaking to orthodontia decades ago. His eyes twinkled a bit as he fingered his empty sake glass and said "It's a little more complicated than that, but you got the gist of it."

"Aw, come on. Tell me more. How is it more complicated? Are there, like, different levels of fire fighting?"

The words came out of her mouth and she felt a slow, electric feeling creep up her spine as his fingers crossed the table and reached for hers, his fingers clasping hers, the warmth shaking her, going all the way up her neck, through her hips, into her belly.

Rendering her completely speechless once again.

"Well," he said, peering down at her hands and then looking at her with raised eyebrows that asked an obvious question. She grinned back. He softened and clenched her hand just slightly more, and the added pressure was like having her hand turn into one giant, throbbing clitoris.

"I do plenty of shifts where I rescue cats from burning buildings and help damsels in distress out of trees," he joked, "but mostly, I'm in charge of fire management safety protocols for large corporations like yours."

"Really?"

"Pretty much. After 9/11, we had to tighten up on how you empty out a thirty or forty floor building, especially in the face of a disaster."

The blood drained out of her face. He had just, without knowing, dredged up her biggest fear. Something in his expression said that he knew it.

"Oh, no, I am so sorry, really, I didn't mean to upset you. Did you lose someone in 9/11?"

She shook her head. "No, no, actually I, it's just that..." She took a deep breath. *In through the nose, out through the mouth.* "It's one of my biggest fears. I've always been afraid of a fire in my building, and I work on the thirty-second floor."

He took his hand away from hers and whacked his forehead repeatedly, shaking his head now. "I just picked the worst possible thing I could bring up during a first date, didn't I?"

Her heart rate resumed a normal beat. She took a risk and reached across the table to retrieve his hand.

"No, it's fine, if nothing else it's interesting that you managed to tap into that about me, after having only known me for..." She glanced at her smart phone "...for fifteen minutes."

"It's amazing what Google will help you figure out."

If she had had a drink in her mouth, she would have spit it all over him. Did he Google her? It was only fair—she had Googled him. Did he know that she had Googled him? Was there some way he could have known?

"Laura?" He reached out and touched her chin, tipping it up to catch her eyes. "That was a joke."

* * *

By the time the waitress brought his meal, something he couldn't pronounce and definitely couldn't identify by sight, he felt like he was losing her.

Idiot, idiot, idiot!

How could he have brought up the burning building scenario on a first date? Within fifteen minutes, no less? God, the look on her face. It was like something collapsed. There was more to it than she was sharing. He could see that, and it left him with too many questions, inquiries he couldn't make right now because he was being too stupid for words.

Yet here he was, babbling on about it like it was no big deal, and that's what he did for a living, and *ha ha ha*, and here she was, you know, in charge of giant health insurance systems.

She began to eat her meal. He dug into his. Even though he didn't like it, he welcomed the silence, perplexed by the contradiction. Lately, his entire life seemed to be one big steaming pile of complexity. He watched her. He took the dinner as an opportunity to just keep an eye on her. To see what she was like. To see what her body language would give away.

She kept pulling on the shoulder of her sweater, correcting everything so that the edge of her black silk bra wouldn't show, and every time she did it, a little part of him tugged. Mostly in the crotch area. But also in his heart.

Because, man, was he *lovin'* that little piece of black lace right now.

He forced a mouthful of something that he was afraid might still be half alive in between his teeth.

"*Mmmm!*" he groaned. "This is incredible."

"Mine's luscious."

So are you, he thought, spearing a piece of fish and holding out his fork. "Do you want a bite of mine?"

He held the fork out for her and she looked at him in a certain way, eyes narrowing a bit while cocking her head, one little curl floating out of her ponytail as she tucked it behind her ear and leaned forward. Her lips enveloped the fork, her mouth tugging at the piece of food as he reluctantly pulled the fork away, those lips closing over the fork.

He wanted part of *him* to be that fork. A very big, throbbing part of him that no napkin was capable of covering now.

Chewing, she groaned with pleasure. It was the sound he wanted to hear later at night in his bed or in hers or on somebody's couch or *hell*—in the alley by the parking lot at this point. He wasn't picky. Dylan's cock strained against his trousers, more aroused then he ever imagined possible, just from watching her eat that scrumptious piece of God knows what.

"Isn't it incredible?" he asked.

"That's perfection. Where does it comes from?" she asked.

He glanced over at the menu and replied, "Malaysia and Tibet."

"A Malaysian, Tibetan piece of perfection," she said, then crinkled her brow with a bemused look. "Fishing in Tibet?"

He shrugged. "The monks have to do something." A diner at one table over frowned at them and Dylan let it roll off.

Laura speared something else on her plate and lifted the fork to him. He took it greedily, eating something he didn't even understand. Watching her, his eyes boring into hers, he realized that this meal was the appetizer and he was going to have the main course later on.

In bed.

* * *

She'd never been treated like this before in her entire life. In fact, she was a bit concerned that she was leaving a wet spot on the upholstered bench. It felt like she had soaked completely through not only her thong, but also her pencil skirt, the outer layer of the bench's covering, the pad, and into whatever store was beneath this restaurant because this guy was not just hot, he was flaming and how appropriate that he was a *firefighter*.

She could see it in his eyes, too. Whatever was going on, there was a kismet here that really shouldn't be happening. After they exchanged their bites, like a cross between *Lady and the Tramp* and a porno movie, she knew that she was going to go home with this guy.

Laura was going to sleep with him and she was going to *like* it.

From the look in his eyes, he was in the same place mentally. Hopefully physically, too. They both seemed to hurry through their meal. The conversation finally resumed after they had finished eating.

"Do you want another drink?" he asked, reaching for her hand again, now that it was free from eating dinner.

Her First Billionaire

She wiped her mouth with the napkin using her other hand, set it down, and said, "I'm still too full. Maybe we could go for a walk?"

"Actually," he said, looking away, "I had planned something else if you don't mind."

"Oh, really? What's that?" *Breakfast?*

She stifled the thought, terrified she had actually blurted that aloud.

"Turns out there's a really a nice cruise here in town that I was hoping we could go on."

"Oh." She looked at her watch, trying to hide her churning emotions. It was already late. A cruise. She did some quick mental math. A couple of hours on a cruise meant there was going to be no down time—she had to work, had to get up at six a.m., and that meant blowing out the whole night. First date.

Calm down Laura, don't be a slut, don't be a slut, don't be a slut, she told herself.

Don't sleep with him on the first date, don't sleep with him on the first date if you want a second date, said Josie's voice. *Don't do it, don't do it, don't do it.*

Unless he's incredibly hot.

Josie never was much help.

She had this entire conversation in a period of about three seconds with herself, with Dylan looking at her with a very puzzled expression. Angel Josie and Devil Laura argued inside her head until she realized she needed to respond to Dylan's comment.

"Okay, yeah, sure! A cruise sounds great. Did you already get tickets?"

He squinted and furrowed his brow, confused. And then his face went neutral.

"Oh, no, actually, not yet. I just figured we'd go there, and, you know, climb on."

You can climb on me, she thought. Her eyes widened. Hopefully, those words hadn't actually come out of her mouth, because at this point, she didn't know what she was thinking as she squirmed and straightened her shirt again. The black lace popped out like an erection. If she could see his package from across the table, she suspected that he had his own little version of the black lace pokin' out going on somewhere in his pants.

The waitress brought the check. She had that internal dialogue that all single women have when going out on new dates. *Do I offer to pick up the check? Do I offer to go halfsies? Do I...*

He didn't give her a chance. Dylan grabbed the check, handed a credit card to the woman, and waved it off. Turned to Lura, he reached for her hand, and said, "Thank you for a lovely date. Or, thank you for a lovely meal."

"My goodness!" she said, a little taken aback that she didn't even have an opportunity to fight for the check. "Thank you so much! I mean, I, really, I, can I, I'd like to offer to pay the..."

He nodded. "You can get the next date."

"Oh! *Oh!*" She said, his words sinking in, finally. "Right. The next date."

* * *

He couldn't read her. It was driving him nuts. He just couldn't read her. Had he gone too far with the 'next date' thing? Was she offended that he was implying that she should pay for the next date? You never knew exactly how to handle the awkwardness of who paid for first dates.

When he was taking women on dates, he had more than enough money these days now that he had come into his trust fund, which he had always viewed as a bit of a curse—but now he viewed as one hell of a blessing, because if it meant that he could treat a woman like Laura right, then maybe he could have the future that he had hoped for, and then it wasn't just a blessing.

It was everything.

Discomfort gnawed away at him. How he had come into his trust fund was an issue he had not begun to explore, he and Mike the recipients of an annual income equal to approximately 2.7 percent of the $2.2 billion in the massive trust, split in half.

The trust manager had laid it out in such clinical terms that Dylan had nearly vomited on the spot, the words *twenty-nine million and change per year for life*, minus management fees, pinging around his skull like a racquetball that never stops.

And that was two months ago. He still drove the same car, still worked his full shifts at the station, but splurged in little ways, the enormity of his new-found fortune not quite sinking in.

Mike had bought a cabin on the slopes. *Cabin* wasn't quite the right word. *Haven* was more like it, a four bedroom ski palace that he knew would keep Mike happy for the rest of his life. The ski resort, too—which had been almost an after thought.

Oh, yeah, I can save the struggling ski mountain I love, because I have more money than God now. Well, almost.

As Dylan caught Laura stealing shy looks at him, his money problems (*twenty nine million of them per year*) faded and he started to wonder if she could keep them happy for the rest of their lives.

"Dylan? Ready to go?"

The waitress had taken the check, cleared the table, and was practically pulling out the vacuum to clean their spot.

The meal paid for, they stood and he put his arm around her waist. She leaned into him just enough to finally send him a signal that told him, *Oh, yeah*, and off they went outside. He reached for her hand, intertwining his fingers in hers. As they walked toward the boardwalk, he realized they weren't going on that cruise.

No way.

Her scent was intoxicating. He couldn't believe that her unique mixture of perfume, musk, and soap fused together to produce this. Even better—he knew that there were other scents, other tastes that would be even more divine if he could get there tonight.

Dylan stopped, finally, bursting at the seams with his own internal dialogue, his own body's cravings, and just looked at her. In that moment, he decided that he needed to be as forthright with her as he had been with most people throughout his life, because these games weren't cutting it anymore.

Time to make his move.

He leaned down, caressed her jawline with his right hand, and brought his lips to hers. She responded, pressing her body against his until everything, from breast to hip, was his, pushed into him, and anything he felt for her was extremely obvious right now.

They were definitely *not* going on that cruise.

* * *

Cruise? What cruise? She had no intentions of going on a cruise. As his kiss deepened, lips parted, as their tongues danced, she found herself roiling in ecstasy inside, going so far as to be twisted into a cliché, one leg lifting up as she stood on her tiptoes, even in high heels, to match him in his kiss.

His hands roamed her back. She returned the motion, her fingers splayed across the broad, muscular expanse of his shoulders, his hands cupping her jaw now, pushing, needing, craving....

"Ah," he said, his voice gravelly and thick with desire, "Can we take a pass on that cruise?"

She dipped her head down and laughed softly. "Good thing you didn't buy those tickets after all."

Cocking his head, he looked at her with smoky eyes and asked, "Do you have a car parked nearby?"

She knew what he was asking, his words code for *Can I take you home and fuck you without worrying about your car getting ticketed or towed?*

How sweet. Most guys didn't care.

"No car. I took the train today."

Nodding, his smile widened. "I drove, so let's take my car to my place? For drinks?"

Laura swallowed hard, knowing that this was really it. He wanted to sleep with her, was inviting her back to his place for it, and she ran through her mental inventory.

Clean lingerie? Yes.

Shaved legs? Yes—she'd been optimistic.

No car? Yes.

Birth control?

Oh, shit. She was on the pill, but had forgotten to take it a few days ago. Missing one day shouldn't hurt, right?

Hopefully he had a condom.

His puzzled look told her she was taking too long to think. "I would love a drink," she declared.

Dylan leaned in for another kiss, the move more certain now, his hands on her more demanding and visceral, claiming her and marking her arms, her neck, her lips and ass with his hands, his touch, his caress.

She was his tonight, and that had to be enough for her. He was hers for whatever he gave, and as the kiss heated she felt her core warm, clit throbbing and eager for what his tongue was promising right now, exploring her as his hands roamed her back and neck.

People were staring openly. As she opened her eyes, the onlookers tittered. She pulled back and wiped her mouth, embarrassed.

Dylan just grinned, leaned in and said, "Let's stop giving the jealous bastards a show."

Her laughter rang down the street to the parking lot where his Audi sat.

When she climbed in it smelled like a campfire.

Blasting the local 80's station on the radio, they rode back to his place in silence, his hand planted on her knee whenever he wasn't shifting, the fingers playing a melody of lust and creeping higher up her thigh until they arrived at his apartment complex. It was a skyscraper made of glass and steel and screamed *money*.

How in the hell did a firefighter afford this?

As if he heard her thoughts, Dylan muttered, "I have a roommate."

"Oh." Disappointment flooded her. Maybe he really did just want to have drinks? No guy ever, *ever* invited her to his place to share some vodka and Coke, though. Not even the true assholes who beer goggled their way to fucking a fat chick they despised in the morning.

Relief took over her disappointment when he smiled a wicked grin and said, "But he's gone for the night."

Getting out of the car, walking up two flights of stairs and wandering down Dylan's hallway was a blur. Laura vaguely heard his keys rattling and then a fierce, hot mouth was on hers, Dylan's thick forearms scraping her shoulders as his hands slid up her jawline, behind her ears, fingers nestling in her hair and pulling her blond curls loose.

His tongue explored her mouth with such precision and his hips pressed into hers with intent. Gasping, she inhaled sharply as he pushed her up against his open door and took her mouth greedily.

Without another word, he maneuvered their entangled bodies, closed the front door, tossed his keys on the floor and had her in his bedroom in seconds.

No complaints here, Laura thought, and that was the last rational idea she had as he went straight for her clit.

No pretense, no artsy coyness.

"What are you—?" she gasped. And then he went right for the center of her heat, the briefest of touches so profound she nearly came all over his lips in an instant. Her thong slid down her legs as if an unseen force stripped it off and then—

"Ahhhhhh," she groaned, practiced arms reaching under her hips, establishing his power. Using his forearms, he guided himself to her clit, freeing one hand to touch her there, slipping a finger into her pussy and caressing so that it set off unexpected waves of pleasure.

It was like a dream come true. She had resigned herself to guys who went down on her like their Novocaine was wearing off. Lips flapping and trying to do one thing but accomplishing nothing more than drooling.

Who was this man? *This?* This was like being made love to by a silk mouth.

Her body flushed red and hot, the fire focused on her hot nub as he teased it, slowly growing the release within, entering and pulling back with two perfect fingers. Her thighs twitched and shook, and she knew she would come like a freight train soon. She buried her fingers in his hair, sinking her hands into him, pushing his face in tandem with her need to strum her to the next level.

"Oh, Dylan!" she murmured, fucking his tongue, which licked her, hard, dead center on her nub. His tongue opened up, hot flesh on hers, as he gave her focused and expansive flesh play. Two different sensations tipped her completely over as every muscle tensed, her dripping hole clinging to his finger, riding his face like a stallion, his tongue working hard to keep her frenzy going.

"There! Right there," she groaned, hands curling into fists of orgasm, body flailing as she murmured over and over, "Oh, God! Oh, God!"

She was self-conscious. Most guys didn't just do this. They might flirt a bit with the clit, but they didn't engage so fully. So, uh, *deeply*. He clearly *enjoyed* this. Reveled in it. And as he picked some perfect rhythm for making her come, she realized she was being played by a sex virtuoso.

Give in to it, Laura. Give in, she told herself, hoping he didn't care about her fleshy belly, her curvy ass. All worry faded as she came and realized she had never thought this was possible, had never been in the hands of a master like this. Keeping her pussy on his tongue, he maintained constant contact, tongue pushing and withdrawing, getting every last bit of her release as her muscles unclenched, her gasps subsiding, little sounds of exertion.

He looked up and grinned, sliding his hands up her body, following her curves. One hot kiss full of her taste geared her up again, her clit and pussy clenching so hard she climaxed yet again simply from the kiss, her hips pushing into him, her juices in her mouth, his mouth, the scent so arousing that she was actually coming from a *kiss*.

* * *

The taste of Laura was so much more delectable than anything they had just eaten at dinner.

Instinct drove him to kiss her again. As he was ready to make his next move, she surprised him by taking the lead. She reached for him with a familiarity, the skin on his aching cock so soft and eager, rising up to meet her. Laura deftly massaged his thigh with her other hand, cupping his balls, pressing against the base with her thumb, a deep groan growing out of him unbidden.

Oh, man, did this woman know how to touch him.

She licked her lips with intent, boldly maintaining eye contact, then looking down and drawing out the wait, making him hold his breath with the agony of anticipation.

She held the base of his cock with one hand and began licking him slowly, flicking the tip until he groaned again, hoping he could hold out until they were ready to make love, his body so ready to dive into her flesh, to grab those curves and to luxuriate in her body.

Taking him in inch by inch, she tongued him until he twitched. Licking the front of his cock below the head and then pulling him even deeper into her mouth, flicking her tongue against him, she made him tighten and release his breath, hips shifting as he moaned at the feel of her mouth around his cock.

Her hand gently masturbated him while sliding her mouth up on his cock, making sure he felt the inside of her cheek, her tongue and her lips, not really sucking but milking him. *Milking him.* At this rate he'd come in her mouth, and as seconds passed that idea became increasingly appealing...

One of his hands touched her head, stroking her hair encouragingly even as he struggled inside, fighting the pleasure she was draining from him, torn between wanting immediate release and craving the feeling of being in her.

Building up the speed with excruciating deliberation, she played him like a damned instrument, and as his fingers tightened in her hair, her silky locks felt like another layer of possibility, her hair casual and comforting and just right—like everything else this night.

She gently touched his balls and he felt his juices begin to ooze out into her mouth, so that she gasped even with his pole in her mouth, the combination of moist heat and cold, rushing air too much.

The sound of her voice vibrated his cock in her throat, her lips kissing her own thumb and forefinger, wrapped like a cock ring, as Dylan was completely enveloped by her. Nearly screaming, he sat up and grasped her head, grinding his hips in and out as she sucked hard, then let go, in rhythm to get him off. She completely covered his root with her lips. He panted, overtaken by this gem, his hands roaming over her gorgeous breasts, her hair falling in waves over her face as she mouth fucked him, and the better part of him stopped her, wanting to give her more.

But holy hell, she was a master at this.

Second date, Dylan, he told himself. *Second date.*

* * *

Am I really giving head on the first date? Laura wondered, her mouth working the magic she knew she possessed. She was good at this. *Really* good. A fleeting thought, *pretty girls don't need to do that*, shot through her mind and she willed it away. Giving a blow job wasn't about being pretty enough.

It was about control.

Until Dylan had stopped her, she had him completely in her spell. And liked it.

His fingers sought out her arousal, discovering her wetness. "I want you, Laura. I need to be in you," he murmured, her eyelids fluttering shut and her brain bending into a pretzel, twisted by a sudden lust, a lushness to his words, their presence, this *now* that made her want to immerse herself in Dylan forever.

You would think she would be sated from what he had done with that skilled tongue, but a new wave renewed within. She wanted every inch of him, however he was willing to give it. Laura needed to impale herself on him, to ride that shaft, to feel his body on top, to have his hands on her, in her, over her —*whatever* her—and she wanted to exert control once again, to be controlled, to just—

Have *more*.

Shoving him on the bed, she put her legs on either side of his hips, the rasp of leg hair and flesh like music to her ears, his mere touch connecting her to a confidence she enjoyed. Aiming him carefully, she hovered over him, savoring the seconds, his eyes locked with hers, the skin around them warm and inviting. She plunged herself directly over his gloriously-thick shaft. He was eager and pulsing, and she groaned when he went all the way in.

What she wanted to say was something profound, the right words to match what her body was screaming.

Instead, she sighed his name, for the feeling was indescribable, a denouement, emotional and psychological, all at once. Like a real hole being filled, finding a being strong enough to fill it.

As she stretched up to his tip, sliding up his pole was a sweet sensation, her body moving toward a screaming orgasm more amazing than any before. He licked one hand and stroked her nipple. Moving slightly, changing everything, Laura slid enough to make him beg, tightened her core, then plunged down again.

"You are so, so tight, so warm," he convulsed. She sighed, the feeling too intense. She didn't have a mind, just an ass he grabbed and nerve endings and her fullness.

Dylan took charge, both standing now, bending her over the bed, tummy down. One hand slid him in as he took her from behind, his other hand in her hair. She reached for her clit as he dove into her, face buried in the bed.

She thrust back against his cock, the pleasure so insane, the force of his tip against her cervix making her scream. She clenched the bedsheets, her fists tightening, her finger finding her clit a swollen, hot mess ready to explode.

"Ah, GOD!" She screamed and screamed and rutted, an animal of need as wetness hit her, knew she was spurting, felt him jerk and jizz as he filled her with his semen, as he shouted, too.

"Laura! Fuck...." He drew out the word with a groan, couldn't speak any longer, and she stopped thinking. Her body tried so much to come as hard as it could, her flesh determined to work with the magnitude of climax as his slickness and the power of his legs moving him in and out of her turned their coupling into a well-oiled machine.

He pounded and pounded, and she thrust back. Dylan stroked her belly, and created a tiny pain, the pain all blending with the creaming and the cum to split her voice into something fierce and low, until all that was left was a drained feeling, all sex and candy and heaven.

They came down, little aftershocks from the remainders of their sex, Dylan still in her, as he melted into her, trapping her, their wetness all she knew. She stopped thinking, her pussy done, her body relaxed, all sated.

Nothing but *now*.

"Oh, man..." he mumbled into her back, hot breath ticklish and sweet.

She turned around and pressed into him. "Oh, no. Oh, *woman*, " she replied, a wicked grin plastered across her face as she kissed him.

* * *

How long had they been asleep? Laura wondered as she peered into the grey darkness, Dylan's arm covering her bare breasts, the sheets tangled between them.

The post-coital haze lessened and reality sunk in. She realized that they were here in his apartment, and then it was—*Oh, no!*

When she checked her smart phone it read 3:22 a.m. What should she do? Should she stay? She looked down at this tender, precious, hot, naked man who had just devoured her in every way possible, and felt a rippling sense of guilt.

He seemed to be into her in this whole one-night-stand thing. She was accustomed to bringing the guy back to her place and then having the guy leave right after everything was over. This was new territory for her and she wasn't sure. Should she stay? Wake up early, make him breakfast?

Lifting his arm off her, she slowly stood, stretching and examining the room.

As she looked around his bedroom, she saw pictures. Pictures of Dylan with a woman on the beach holding surfboards, a woman in a stringed bikini, and then another picture of the same woman in a sport bikini playing beach volleyball.

And then *another* of what looked like the same woman standing at the ski slope along with a different man, his face covered by a balaclava and tick ski hood.

Yet another picture of the same woman on the snowboard doing a flip in mid air.

What the fuck? Her heart started to pound. Now she knew. This was just some one night-stand. Was that his wife? His girlfriend? Who?

Every insecurity flooded her, everything fearful poured into her, and here she stood completely naked standing in the moonlight, staring over this guy who had just given her the best four hours she had had in years.

It was all a lie. A big, *fat* lie.

She scrambled to find her thong, her skirt, her sweater, her bra—where was it? Found it somewhere across the room hanging off of a doorknob of a closet.

Had they really been that, uh, *acrobatic*? Apparently. As the feelings all merged into one big bundle of sheer fright, she found herself flooded with shame—shame and despair. And most of all, a massive adrenaline rush that just kept screaming, *Get out, get out, get out, get out, get out now*.

She tiptoed, holding on to the straps of her heels, making sure she had her purse, her scrunchie pulling her hair together quickly so she didn't look quite as ridiculous as she felt as she handled the walk of shame, clicking the door as quietly as possible.

The hallway was empty. She tread gingerly down the stairs in her stocking feet and then finally found herself outside in the cool night air, the streetlamps illuminating the path back home. Fortunately, there were cabs floating around at three in the morning and she grabbed one, completely ignoring every comment that the cabbie made, hoping like hell he could read the fact that she had leaned back against the backseat and closed her eyes, wanting to be left alone.

Alone was safer.

Laura used every spare molecule of energy and focus to still her heart, to calm it back down to where it belonged, in the normal, boring, slow pace she'd experienced before the whirlwind of Dylan. She should have known it was too good to be true. Every damn moment of it. He just wanted a piece of meat on the side.

A *big* piece of meat. A little variety was the spice of life, right? Her body was so different from his girlfriend's, a sleek, muscled, athletic sculpting she couldn't imagine.

Damn, damn, damn—here came the tears. They weren't the great big heaving sobs that she felt after dating someone for months and then realizing that it just wasn't working. These were the scalding tears of reproach, of the fact that she should have known better, -- and a bit of giddiness that she'd gotten something more than she'd expected out of the evening.

Dinner and mind-blowing sex was great, but apparently what she had just had with him was all she was going to have, because he was clearly involved with whoever that woman was and that woman had a bod that went on for miles. Damn, if she had ten percent body fat, Laura would be amazed. And if that was his type, what was Laura? Just some cow he decided he'd grab onto for the hell of it, trolling some dating site.

Whatever.

The screech of the cab's brakes told her it was time and then *boom*— the car jerked to a stop. She handed the cabbie enough of a tip to make herself feel good and to make him grin, and to wish her a good night. As she headed up to her apartment, her shoes vibrated like a gong, *click, click, click,* her legs propelling her on on very weak heels, very tired calves, very tired *everything*.

Mind, body and soul.

She peeled off her outfit, poured herself into her big oversized flannel pajamas, and just crawled into bed to sleep the slumber of the conflicted.

* * *

Dylan was accustomed to waking alone, Jill's side of the bed a cold place, a sexual Siberia, but he had hoped to find Laura there this morning. Making her breakfast and having her *be* his breakfast had been on his mind as he'd faded off to sleep, cradling her in his arms.

Hopefully, she'd left a note. Maybe she needed to rush off to work. He understood. It was hard to juggle shifts and bosses and—

His eyes stopped as they landed on a picture of Jill. Hawaii. About seven years ago. Her skin glistened in her wet suit and she grinned a relaxed, happy smile as the sun kissed her nose, Mike standing next to her, turned toward her and showing the camera only his profile, face largely hidden. He was a good foot taller than petite Jill. Their hair had lightened so much on that vacation, though Dylan's dark locks had stayed the same. By the end of the week Jill and Mike were hooked on surfing, while Dylan...

His thoughts faded as the enormity of Jill's death hit him. In some ways, her death was still striking blows. Good ones. More than fifty million blows a year.

He, unlike Laura, would never have to worry about getting to work on time again. Man, even letting himself think like that made him queasy. It was a sick, sick way to become rich—losing your soulmate—and he was still so angry at something—God? Cancer? Fate? His own helplessness?—that he just wouldn't quit the fire station, preferring to act like a working class slob because until two months ago, that's exactly what, and *who*, he had been.

The masquerade of normalcy was important. Necessary. Especially now that he was dating Laura. Until he knew she cared for him as the old Dylan—before the trust fund—he needed to play it cool.

Sitting up, he stretched his arms over his head, willing blood to flow into his biceps, triceps, popping his elbows and slowly stretching out his neck. His hips ached just a little, the good kind of ache from a nice, deep, intense session of lovemaking. He grinned, the smell of her still on his sheets, her soft skin nearly still there, as if brushing against his chest.

Laura was soft and sweet and sighed like it was all some kind of dream, as if his touch were new. He'd been tender with her, but detected a little something extra, a naughty streak. He'd been right and reveled in the discovery.

If he texted her now, would that be seen as too pushy? Too stalkerish?

Who cares?

Grabbing his phone, he dug out her number and texted: *So you went home and all I got was this morning boner.* ;)

Silence.

Give it five minutes, Dylan, he told himself. Standing, he let the sunlight stream in through the window and wash over him, his naked form tight with need. A bottle of lotion and a nice hot shower could kill off his arousal.

Even better, though, would be a date tonight.

Nothing. He knew it seemed way too desperate, but he looked up her number and dialed. No answer. Not even a voice mail message. That was supremely weird, because the only reason you couldn't leave a voice mail on someone's phone was if they blocked you.

Cold rushed through his body, his flesh covered with goosebumps in seconds. Blocked? Why would she block him? He took a really good look around the room and let himself inhale, then exhale, a few times. More centered now, he thought carefully through the last twenty-four hours.

He had found her online. Asked her out. Scheduled a dinner at the hottest restaurant in town. Found her attractive and the feeling mutual. Made a move, invited

Her First Billionaire

her over, had mind-blowing sex (*which he wanted more of*) and had fallen asleep, spooned with her in his bed.

Waking up, he was alone. He texted her. He called her—and now it appeared she had blocked him.

Blocked?

That had to be a mistake. He called again. It rang twenty-eight times before he hung up. Where was Mike?

Oh, that's right—at his cabin. He had decided to clear out so Dylan could have alone time with Laura. Except now Dylan had tons of alone time—with himself. Not the kind of private time he was hoping for.

He popped on the computer and opened a chat window at the dating site. She wasn't in his "Favorites" any more. Huh? He ran a search—no Laura Michaels. It was as if she had vanished.

Blocked?

* * *

Beep-beep-beep!

She whammed her hand on the alarm button, but it was elusive; a little too far out of her grasp, so instead, she whacked the heel of her hand on the corner of her end table and listened to her own yelp of protest.

"Damn it." She opened her eyes, giving the machine a glare meant to melt circuits. Six a.m.—time for work. Really? Had she really only gotten two and a half hours of sleep at best? Damn.

She stood up, forced herself to stretch and then wondered why she felt so sore, so sticky, so—

Oh.

Dylan's tongue on her clit, lapping in circles as his finger slid in and out, her legs on his shoulders and—

That's why.

She closed her eyes and sighed heavily, letting emotion wash over her and just feeling it, knowing that blocking it, denying it, or pushing it aside would do her no good.

Let it be and it would fade. Force it away and she'd carry the pain forever.

What she had thought might have been just wasn't meant to be, and she had to accept that. Too good to be true, really. He was way out of her league.

But that was okay. Today was a new day. She reached for her smart phone, confirming the time and then seeing that she had about twenty-seven texts from Josie. She'd have to answer those later. Josie would make her spill everything, tell all, and would congratulate her for refusing to accept second best.

Right now, though, Laura needed to wallow.

And that, like so much else, was okay as well.

Her coffeemaker gurgled, the tell-tale signs that the cup was just about finished. She had forgotten that before the date she'd set it all up just like she always did. Grateful for her past self's actions, she sloshed the coffee into her mug and sat down, booting up her computer to check email.

Dylan, Dylan, Dylan, Dylan, Dylan.

Laura logged on to her email, ignored a bunch of ads, found nothing of real value in there until suddenly she noticed that the online dating site had sent her a message.

"You have a new request to chat."

Her inbox was overflowing.

Seventeen new requests to chat. Yeah, right. Not chat requests -- fuck requests.

Thanks, guys, I'm all chatted out and my fuck request meter is broken.

She wanted more of last night. The magic. The thrill. Being charmed and charming someone back. Falling into that special knowing and feeling warm and safe and excited all at once, the heady passion of the new.

The pictures all over Dylan's room filled her brain —that woman, his girlfriend, his wife, his *whatever*. He didn't wear a ring, but that didn't mean anything. She had learned that within her second or third date after college. The married men always lied and they tended to be the slickest—and this guy was pretty slick.

Laura took a deep breath. His taste was in her, as if his scent had permeated her lungs, as if it coated her trachea, as if—

Inhale. Exhale.

She breathed in, she breathed out—breathed in sadness, breathed out happiness, breathed in sorrow, breathed out joy. No matter how hard she tried, though, it wasn't cutting it. Caffeine would have to do what meditation could not, no matter what her yoga teacher said about the evils of coffee.

You can pry my caffeine from my cold, dead, outstretched hand.

She sucked down the cup of coffee, poured herself another and thought, *What the hell?*

Laura clicked on one of those chat messages in email.

Some guy named Mike wanted to meet or wanted to chat with her.

Mike—thirty-two, 6'5", a runner. Online dating was devolving into ordering from a menu.

Would you like fries with that?

There it was: "Likes to run marathons and works at a ski resort."

Oh, dear— her idea of running was waving madly at the bus driver and sprinting when she was late for the morning bus, and skiing? Lodge. Hot toddy.

Not snow.

Deleting his message would have been the easiest thing in the world, and her finger even hovered over the button, but something stopped her. If Josie had been there and asked, Laura couldn't have explained it. She just...stopped.

Clicking his profile, she read up on him. He looked kind of like the opposite of Dylan. This guy had sandy blonde hair and Nordic features. Dylan was Italian and dark and swarthy. Mike looked long and lean with pictures of him riding a bike, shots of him crossing finish lines, and pictures of him camping.

Camping. She shuddered. Her idea of camping was no mint on the pillow. She wasn't sure this was going to work. She read his little intro about himself:

"Hi, my name is Mike Pine. I am thirty-two. I'm really new to this online dating thing. I'm very active and athletic, work at a ski resort, I teach skiing and also work on the first aid team. In my spare time, I like to run and camp and bike, and I'm looking for friendship or more, and would like to chat with other people who are interested in the same thing—"

Beep-blip! A little chat window popped up on her screen. Laura splashed coffee on her hand in surprise at the unexpected sound.

"Ow!" she shouted, grabbing a kitchen towel and shaking it out. "What the hell!?" She peered at the now lit-up screen, a familiar chat window open in the right lower-hand corner.

"Oh, geez," she sputtered, her words echoing through her empty apartment.

Marathon Mike himself.

Hi, there. Are you on right now?

She still had the smell of Dylan on her and now she had some new guy coming after her? What a slut she was. She thought about that for a second. The word *slut* didn't really apply to her, ever. It was more that she was trying on new behaviors.
Let's try this one on for size, she thought.

I'm just drinking my coffee and getting ready for work and I logged in and saw your message, so hi!

Oh, good morning! Yeah, I'm not really functional without two or three cups of coffee myself.

He added a little grin icon.

Hmph... yeah who isn't, she thought.

Laura chugged the rest of her mug's contents and typed, one-handed,

So I see you're Mr. Triathlon and ski dude. My idea of exercise is walking across the room to get the remote.

He wrote back several lines at once:

lolol, yeah don't be afraid, we could just go for a hike if you want.
Oh, I think I just asked you out.
Yeah I did.
?

"Oh, man," she muttered. She stared at the glowing screen, dumbfounded, her empty coffee mug dangling precariously off her right index finger as she absorbed this. What *was* this? Did she hit the good-looking guy lottery? She had just totally ditched Dylan in his bed last night, and now she had some guy who looked like a lankier version of the actor who played Thor hitting on her. Deep inside, she decided she was trying on this new life, and she would go for it.

Just go for it, Laura. What can it hurt?

A swell of physical memory from last night made her warm between her legs, made her skin flush with the recall of Dylan's hands. She wanted more. And if she couldn't have more of *him*, she might as well have some of *Mike*.

A hike, yeah, I'd like that. That sounds really cool.

She breathed in opportunity, and breathed out rejection, breathed in despondence, and exhaled chance.

Chance favors the prepared. Laura was more than ready.

At least, that's what she told herself.

Her Second Billionaire

Mike knew that there was absolutely no chance that she was going to answer his little chat outreach within the next twenty-four hours. He knew that Dylan had a date with her last night, but hoping against hope and because he was an eternal optimist, he logged in while drinking his morning cup of coffee.

He figured she was still in Dylan's bed, probably going on for round seven (knowing Dylan), and there wasn't a chance in hell that she would...

Wait, *what*?

He stared at his phone, where he'd logged into the app for the online dating site. Her little icon blinked rapidly—he'd subscribed to her and Laura's avatar had suddenly turned green.

Oh, holy hell, no!

Hell, yes!

Enough with the ridiculous self doubts—he had to grab his chance now. She was logged on to the dating site early in the morning after a date with Dylan. The implications stunned him. Made him smirk.

Mike took a swig of coffee and quickly tapped out:

Hi, there. Are you on right now?

She typed back:

I'm just drinking my coffee and getting ready for work and I logged in and saw your message, so hi!

Wait a minute. Back up for a second. If she was at home drinking her coffee, then that meant Dylan had struck out.

Ooh! That wasn't quite what he wanted. He'd hoped Dylan would have some success, but not hit a home run. It looked like maybe he'd hit a single? A double?

The app stared at him, as if it were alive. He quickly punched in:

Oh, good morning! Yeah, I'm not really functional without two or three cups of coffee myself

with a little grin icon.

See, now, this was the problem with trying to find the right women. He didn't want to be the sloppy second that the women settled for. He wanted someone both he and Dylan could share, equally. When it came to their limited experience trying to find the right woman, Dylan had always been the front man and Mike had been the wingman.

He was tired of being the wingman.

Maybe it was time for the best man to win. That comment to Dylan had most definitely not been just a joke—he'd been very, intensely serious.

And that man was stepping up to the plate now, ready for his turn at bat.

The app beeped as she replied with:

So I see you're Mr. Triathlon and ski dude, and my idea of exercise is walking across the room to get the remote.

Oh, man. She was chatting him up. There was a natural opportunity here and he couldn't blow it. He sat there in his boxer briefs, typing away with one finger on his ridiculous smart phone interface and noticed that the boxer briefs were getting awfully uncomfortable. As he typed, he stared at her little avatar with those sweet dimples, and that intelligent look on her face and decided that his body's response was telling him pretty much all he needed to know.

He typed out something that sounded good on the surface, and the second that he typed it—*augh!*—he wanted to take it back.

lolol, yeah don't be afraid, we could just go for a hike if you want.
Oh, I think I just asked you out.
Yeah I did.

and then he ended it with a question mark.

A hike? *A hike?* Could that be any lamer? Why couldn't you come up with something romantic? Beating himself up came naturally, and this time he had good cause—*a hike?*

Dylan had taken him up on his advice and taken Laura out to the fancy Asian fusion place that so many of the women they had dated loved to go to.

Then again, he could count "all of the women they dated" on one hand.

One hand that had turned into his girlfriend lately.

All of the women had also flatly and resoundingly rejected what they were offering, which was, he had to admit, pretty unique. However, settling for second best had left them both hollow and incomplete, and now they had an added complication. Two-point-two billion of them, to be exact.

A hike, yeah, I'd like that. That sounds really cool.

The words sat on the screen like fairy dust, as if some unseen spirit had conjured them from a mystical layer in the universe and plopped them on Mike's phone. Seriously? She said *yes*?

She liked the hike idea. Oh, my God. He sucked down more coffee, the hot liquid helping to regenerate his brain cells, making him come alive and *think think think* to say the right answer.

Which was...?

Smacking his forehead, he ran both hands over his scalp, twitchy fingers through his hair, his other palm grazing a day's growth on his chin. Jesus. She was saying yes! The coffee felt like a pool of hot lead in his gut as he raced to reply, typing out a response.

Breathe dude. Breathe, breathe, breathe. What could he say?

Keep it simple. With a shaking finger, he wrote:

OK. How about this afternoon. After work? You wanna do lunch and then go for hike? I know a great spot in this State Park, a nice easy trail, it won't be too hard on you.

He hit Enter and then realized that that was probably one of the stupidest things he could have said, his fingers itching to find some magical "retract" button, a switch he could flip to withdraw his words from cyberspace.

Fuck! He wasn't implying that she was out of the shape, he didn't mean to... damn it. He was so bad at this.

He buried his head in his hands and fully expected her little icon to go away and disappear, and for Laura to think he was just a double failure at this shit, to go running back to Dylan—who knew how to handle women. Then again, if he was that good, why was Laura chatting right now?

She replied:

Sounds good. I'll wear my hiking boots, don't worry. I have feet, I can walk, I can use them, I can even move them independently while chewing gum.

He laughed and wrote back:

OK, phew, good to know. I like bipeds

and typed his phone number.

Laura sent hers back and he realized that he needed to say something, yet had no idea what to say. This was the first time that he had actually found a woman, on his own, without Dylan.

Technically, Dylan had found her, but Dylan had no idea that Mike was independently pursuing Laura. The not-inconsequential fact that he had just sniped her couldn't be ignored, either.

Mike just stared at his smart phone, dumbfounded, willing away an erection that ignored the effort, with no hope that it was going to go away. He could tell as he stared at the blinking cursor.

Finally she wrote back,

Hello, hello. Are you there, Mike?

Oh, Jesus. He startled as he realized he needed to respond, and quickly typed back:

Yeah, sorry. Not enough coffee yet. So, great, it's a date? And thanks.

She wrote back a little smiley face, and he realized as he leaned back in the chair that he might have just made the biggest mistake of his life.

* * *

Had Laura really just made a date less than three hours after sneaking out of another guy's bed? She opened up one of the seventeen texts from Josie which, as she scrolled through them, appeared to all be variations of "Please tell me about the hot guy."

She finally decided to put Josie out of her misery and typed out, "*Hey. Awesome night. Will tell you the deets later*", hit Send, and almost instantly got back a response.

What do you mean later? Hell, no. I'm coming over.

She wrote back:

Can't. I'm late for work as it is. Let's just say I need a shower this morning.

and hit Send.

Squeeeee

was Josie's reply.

Do you have another date?

Do I have another date? Oh, yeah, Josie, I have another date. It's just not with the same guy.

Ugh. How was she going to tell her this? She needed *two* showers. One to wash off Dylan and the other one to wash off her own skank.

Laura replied:

There's a lot to this. Will write more later. Talk later.

She hit Send and turned her phone over, leaving Josie hanging, padding into the shower. Indeed, it was time to wash off Dylan and her own sense of ambiguity? Indecision? Disappointment?

Revelation?

For she had learned so much these past few days, mostly about herself. In some ways, she was surprised to realize that it didn't matter that Dylan was with someone else. In the past, that would have crushed her, but now—now she felt a renewed sense of power. Of strength.

Stripping down and turning up the temperature on the shower's spray, she felt her body melt into the hot water, the sting of the jets tearing her away from her looping thoughts, putting the focus back on her body. Rivulets of water streamed over her breasts, down her belly, with its gentle curves and lush skin, pooling at her V and sliding down her thighs, a familiar heat rushing into her womanhood.

It may have been only a few hours since she'd left his bed, but his mark really was on her. Closing her eyes, she remembered his touch and felt an incongruous sense of guilt. Guilt? He's the one who had a girlfriend or wife. Yet here she was, scheduling a date with a stranger hours after having Dylan in her. On her.

All over her.

The detachable shower head was about to earn its keep.

She knew exactly where to aim it, her hands practiced when it came to masturbating. All her normal fantasies, though, weren't cutting it—not the dream about Jake Gyllenhaal, or Matt Bomer, or even Zach Braff.

Instead, her mind drifted to Dylan. And Mike.

As she zeroed the jet spray on her clit, she fought the image of Dylan *and* Mike! Both? Yet nothing made it go away. Her body responded to the mere idea of it, of both of them at once, of four hands, two mouths, two cocks all focused on her. Laura. On her needs, on her pleasure, on her discovery. *Ahhhhh...*

This was crazy! She hadn't even met Mike yet. Had crawled out of Dylan's bed just a few hours ago, resolved never to see him again. Why was she letting them dominate her fantasies? She still had Dylan's juices in her, his saliva dried on her, his kiss and skin and lips.

As the water washed the night away, that wasn't really true any longer, but her neck tightened as her breasts swelled, her hands holding the shower spray in one hand, centered straight on her clit now, her other hand parting her lips and two fingers slowly entering her, the balance hard to achieve but easier as she propped one foot up on the edge of the tub and leaned back against the shower wall.

Her fingers encountered slightly sore flesh, her mouth spreading with an unexpected grin as she recognized why it hurt a bit, why the water's sting was so bittersweet. Dylan been thick and huge and gentle and rough all at once, knowing exactly how to press her skin, tweak her tight spots, play her body to perfect orgasm over and over with his tongue, his lips, his fingers, his hands, and that gorgeous, veined cock.

Now she had a face for her menage fantasies—Mike's. Why not? *Live a little, Laura.* No one knew what went on in the privacy of her own mind, her own shower, and as she sighed deeply, the pressure of everything vanquished, she felt a familiar heat and bliss rise up in her as the water pulsed its way into her soul, her clit crying out for more.

Her fingers slid in and out of her tight pussy -- not in a heated rush but, instead, slowly, stroking that spot on the top that always made her clench just a tad harder, made her breath hitch, made her imagine it was Mike's fingers in her, Dylan's tongue strumming her clit, both men eager and ready to enter her at once.

"Mmmmm," Mike moaned in her ear, his thick, wiry runner's body sliding next to hers in the shower, beads of water darkening that blonde hair, toned arms lifting her up and plunging her down on his ready shaft. And then—was that Dylan's mouth on her clit? Then gently parting her cheeks as Mike lifted her, had her straddle him across the waist as he effortlessly held her in place, strong legs bending slightly so Dylan could...

She snaked her pinkie finger down so it played with her puckered anus, the mere touch of her fingertip on her perineum enough to tip her over, imagining Dylan filling her, double entry almost too kinky to even let herself dream about.

"Ah, God, Laura, more," Dylan groaned behind her, his cock inching slowly inside her ass, Mike's tip pushing hard against her cervix, her body entombed between them as the water sprayed down. When Dylan's mouth found her earlobe she—

Exploded.

The shower head, her pinkie finger on her anus, her fingers exploring her g-spot, and her dream all combined to make her bend down and scream as a mad rush of orgasm pounded her instantly, no warning, no teasing, just a wall of everything that left her gaping, her mouth open and her throat hoarse as she let it all unleash, her shoulders twitching and bashing into the wall, her hands moving and milking this for everything she could find, her mind filled with images of Dylan and Mike simulfucking her, their faces strained and coming, too, all from her.

Her body, her presence—*her.*

And then—nothing. Like a switch flipped, she pulled her hands out of all her orifices, turned the shower head off, washed up fast and got ready for work. Sated, no longer distracted, she shifted from horny, bewildered single on the dating scene to financial analyst for the megacorporation.

That wouldn't last more than a few minutes, for she knew her mind would wander, soon. For now, though, it was a welcome and much-needed break.

* * *

When Laura had typed "Yes," he couldn't believe it — and panicked. Now he actually had to step forward. He had a date. That meant he had to put himself out there.

Dylan had always gone out and found the women and had been the one to find Jill, and no matter how desperately they both missed Jill, she was gone and they had to accept that.

Laura was pretty much the opposite of Jill, but he could see what Dylan saw in her. That was one sweet smile. She seemed accomplished, and there was something Mike couldn't put his finger on, a genuineness and authenticity, but he and Dylan were not exactly the most conventional package.

He worried that maybe a financial analyst at Stohlman Industries wasn't going to make the cut—or maybe he was more worried that *they* wouldn't make the cut with her. in his experience, the office cubicle type wasn't exactly eager to go out on the slopes or to even watch him at mile marker twenty during a marathon.

But Dylan was giving it a good try and Mike had to, too. The problem was that Mike had to do it in secret. He typed in a few more words, they scheduled the hike, and then she disappeared, off to whatever corporate job she had on whatever floor of whatever giant skyscraper downtown. That world was so alien to him. He worked at a ski resort, and in fact he was missing it already.

Her Second Billionaire

You don't just work there anymore, a voice inside him said. *You own it...*

The season hadn't started yet, but he looked forward to it. He always did every year and when he wasn't skiing, he was running. Between the two he kept his sanity somehow, for over the years he had learned that the endorphin kick that came from running and from the massive double diamond trails in the winter were what he needed most. Jill had fit in nicely with his life and with Dylan's life, spending time running with him. Man, was she an ace on the slopes, too.

She and Dylan had an affinity for action movies, for cooking and...he let himself get nostalgic, even let his eyes well up with tears. Letting the memories flood him was dangerous, his mind tipping over from nostalgia to deep grief, a mourning he'd only recently been able to emerge from, the slam of Jill's inheritance making him ache all over again.

His body was consumed suddenly by grief at her loss. It hadn't been running, it hadn't been skiing, it hadn't been any of Dylan's crazy antics like sky diving or parasailing that had killed Jill.

It had been one cell that mutated and mutated until finally it had taken over her body, the lymphoma wasting her away and neither of them had gotten over her death from eighteen months ago. In some ways Mike had gotten over Jill even faster than Dylan, though Dylan had been the first to go out and find somebody to sleep with. Mike hadn't gone out and broken that physical barrier yet, replacing the memory of Jill's body with someone else's— he just hadn't.

Couldn't.

Eighteen months, though. It had been a long dry spell and he was frustrated. Mike finally felt emotionally ready to at least give this a try, and he was *more* than physically ready. Who knew what the hike would bring? All he knew was that he had to try, and he had to try on his own. He couldn't be the tag along with Dylan. That had complicated their relationship with Jill for far too long.

It wasn't until it was too late that Mike realized that it actually hadn't mattered. He had loved Jill. Jill had loved him and they both loved Dylan. And the three of them had made it work, somehow, in their own crazy way.

Could the three of them— this time with Laura— make it work? He was getting ahead of himself. All that mattered was having *one* hike with the woman. He just needed to see if this could be his future—*their* future.

* * *

She had never gone on a date like this—hiking? Meeting Dylan last night had been a very public affair, even if it ended in the very private way. She thought about it and realized that she needed to call in some reinforcements, so she texted Josie:

Hey, Josie, I have a date tonight. Can you help me?

Josie texted back:

Oh, cool, the firefighter? Awesome.

Laura winced and answered:

Well, no, not the firefighter. Someone different.

What?

Yeah, it turns out I'm popular on that online dating site.

Her Second Billionaire

Josie texted:

Hold on, I'm five minutes away from your house—why didn't you tell me earlier? Thought you were late for work.

I am, but who cares. You have time?

There is no way you can have that kind of date like last night and now a new date and not give me the juicy details before work.

Laura walked over to the coffee maker, put the basket in, dumped in some grounds and started what she knew was going to be one of many cups of coffee today. As promised, Josie arrived within five minutes, barreling through the front door and plopping down her suitcase-sized purse on the kitchen table, eyes ablaze with curiosity.

"You slut!" Josie said it with a tone of admiration, not condemnation, and the expression on her face was so comical it made Laura burst into laughter.

"Thank you, I guess."

"No, no, I just mean—damn. So, how does this work? What the hell happened with the firefighter?"

"He's married. Or has a girlfriend."

Josie's face fell, shifting from eager curiosity to self-righteous anger on Laura's behalf. What a great friend. Laura almost laughed at how bulldoggish Josie looked.

"How do you know?"

"Because I woke up in his bed at three in the morning and there were pictures of her everywhere. It wasn't hard to figure out."

"Maybe it was his sister?" Josie asked, her voice going up high, as if hopeful and as if there were a snowball's chance in hell it was true.

"In a bikini at the beach? Being kissed by him? Uh, no. Unless she's Angelina Jolie and he routinely tongue-kisses his sister—"

"OK, ewww. Point taken. So the guy is a slimeball and took you home while his girlfriend's out of town. Fucker." She rubbed Laura's shoulder. "How did you handle it?"

"I woke up, saw the pictures, freaked out on the inside but stayed quiet, got dressed and almost cried in the cab." Laura gulped a hot mouthful of coffee down.

"You sneak home after ditching a guy in his bed, after sleeping with him within three hours, four—OK, *four* hours of knowing him. You find out he has a girlfriend, with pictures of her plastered all over his room, so you decide you're going to come home and write him off and...now you have a date with another guy?"

Josie's expression was, to say the least, comical. It was like a graphic of a "what the fuck" emoticon.

Only in real life.

"It is pretty freaking amazing," Laura agreed, nodding absentmindedly as she added two spoons of sugar to her coffee. She hadn't consumed coffee with sugar since tenth grade. Since returning home from her date, though, she'd been doing a lot of out-of-character things, including dating two men on the same day.

"Spill it."

"I woke up, was about to shower, and this guy IM'd me on the dating site. I had just blocked Dylan, actually, and made sure he wasn't in my 'Favorites' anymore. So then Mike—"

"Suddenly some guy pops up in the chat window on this website and asks you out?"

"Yes."

"Worth it?" That was code for whether he was attractive.

"He looks like that actor who played Thor in the movie."

Josie's jaw dropped. "Not fair! When do I get Captain America hitting on me?"

Laura laughed and dumped her coffee, pouring a fresh cup. She started to tremble inside, the urge uncontrollable. It was all too much, too intense, and spelling it out for her best friend was making it all too real.

"What's he do for a living?"

"Ski instructor," Laura mumbled as she hurried to fill her mouth with more coffee and delay the interrogation. Josie rolled her eyes.

Her friend poured herself another cup of coffee, glanced at the clock and said, "Oh shit, I'm late for work, but I don't care, this is, this is—this is awesome! Way, way better than any movie. Plus I have a front seat view!" They both winced at each other and Josie added, "Uh, you know what I mean. Not literally." She shuddered.

"I'm so glad that I'm meeting your entertainment needs."

"Come on, what kind of life do I have? I haven't had sex in seven months. I have to live vicariously through you."

Laura snorted. "It serves you right after all the years I lived vicariously through you having sex. It's only fair."

Josie hung her head in mock shame. "Fair enough, but lay off the years comment. I haven't gone through *that* many men."

"I beg to dif—"

"Shut your whore mouth!"

Josie threw half an English muffin at Laura's head and, with catlike precision, she dodged it, both women howling with laughter.

Laura paused, thought for a moment, and said, "You know, you can open your own profile and see what pops up. To solve that seven month problem you've got going on there." She gestured vaguely at Josie's torso.

"Oh, I've seen what pops up. You know the phrase, 'shit floats'?"

Laura just laughed. Ouch. Then again, Josie's last date had been from an online dating site. Turned out to be a sixty-year-old neocon Tea Party activist who used a Groupon for dinner and made Josie pay her half before the coupon. Capitalism at its best—he'd made money off their date. And all Josie had to remind her was a lovely restraining order when the guy wouldn't leave her alone.

"So when is the date?"

"Tonight."

"Tonight?"

"Right after work. Mike says there's enough daylight to make the climb in ninety minutes."

"The climb?"

"We're hiking. One of those hills at the state park outside of town."

If Josie rolled her eyes any harder they'd pop out and wander down the hallway out into the street.

"He hikes, too?"

"He's a triathlete." Laura coughed, the unveiling increasingly ridiculous. Was any of this really happening?

"Wait a minute. Mr. Ski Instructor Gorgeous Triathlete Thor Lookalike chats with you for a couple minutes this morning and already tonight, you, who are about as athletic as a slug, are going on a hike to the top of one of the biggest hills outside of the city where you will eaten to death by mosquitoes, you will become sweaty and ridiculously tired and then..."

"You're so flattering," Laura muttered.

"What? You're going to climb a mountain, Laura? You have a heart attack when you can't find the remote and have to actually stand up to change the channel."

That gave Laura reason to pause. What the hell was she going to do? By the time she met up with Mike it'd be six at night. He said it was a ninety minute climb to the top. Granted, it was summer so there was plenty of sunlight until nine or so. But what had she gotten herself into? Did she even own hiking boots?

Josie continued, "Do you even have any shoes that are going to work with any kind of an outfit for climbing a mountain?"

Laura stared at her as if she'd been reading her mind. "I guess I'll have to figure that out. All I know is I'm kind of in a super-emotional state right now, Josie. I got an unsolicited chat yesterday morning from a hot firefighter. Went out with him to one of the trendiest restaurants in town and ended up in his bed. When I woke up, I was surrounded with pictures of a woman who looked like she was a combination of a beach volleyball player and a surfer. Which *I'm* not. Ever. At all. It will take me four lifetimes to ever be like that. I slumped out of there and then—*boom!*— I come home and there's a chat from another guy. I don't even have time to think. I don't even know what I'm *supposed* to think. All I know is I'm just saying yes to it all. I'm saying yes to life, I'm saying no to doubt and I'm just grabbing the brass ring and—"

Josie interrupted her. "And you're throwing out the clichés, you're talking a mile a minute, you won't throw out the baby with the bath water, you aren't going to count your chickens before they've hatched, you're —"

"Oh, shut up."

Josie stopped and put her hand on Laura's arm. "Just be careful."

"Oh, no, it's fine. I've got birth control."

"No, that's not what I'm talking about. You...I just don't want your heart broken again. You deserve everything that's going on right now. You certainly deserve to be able to fuck two hot guys in twenty-four hours."

"I'm not going to do that."

"Well," Josie wiggled her eyebrows, "I would."

"I know *you* would."

"But I'm not you, Laura. And I'm just saying, be careful with that heart of yours. You know what I mean."

Laura sighed. "Yeah, I know what you mean." She squared her shoulders, took in a deep breath, let it out. A nice cleansing breath. "I'm saying yes. I'm saying *yes*."

"Great. Will you buy coffee this time on our way to work? I really need a triple latte."

"What?" Laura shook her head as if clearing it. What was Josie talking about?

"You said you're saying yes. Say yes to buying me an overpriced coffee. Say yesssssssss....."

She waved Josie off and got out of the chat window and did what every woman does in the twenty-first century after being contacted by a guy from an online dating website. She Googled him, just as she had Googled Dylan.

"What a strange set of results, Josie. Check this out."

Her friend craned over Laura's shoulder to see the screen. Mike's name appeared over and over, followed by a bunch of numbers. Times, like a race? Wait. The Tri-state Marathon. The Sunshine Regional Triathlon. Oh, my God. He wasn't kidding.

He really was a triathlete. More than that—he was a steady, longtime triathlete. This wasn't some guy who did it once for bragging rights.

She knew that guys could shine her on, that people lied in online dating sites and they often talked about being athletic—which was code for *I watch TV on Sundays when the football game is on as an excuse to eat wings*.

But this guy was the real deal. Page after page—she had to go twelve pages in before she found anything other than some race time. According to the dates, this guy had been doing this for at least the past ten years.

Then she found a ski resort page. He worked at the ski resort. That's what he told her, so he had been telling the truth. He was a ski instructor and first aid person. Interesting. That was as different from her life as you could possibly get. Same with Dylan.

She pushed aside thoughts of Dylan. Dylan was, as far as she was concerned, off her radar screen. He might still be lingering on her skin in that deep, sensitive part of her belly, and the scent of him might still be on her sweater—and maybe in the crook of her elbow, and behind her earlobe and—

Oh stop it, Laura, just stop it.

The guy had a girlfriend or wife. He was trolling the online dating sites, probably just to find a one-night stand or because he was a sex addict or—who knew? No more Dylan.

Mike, on the other hand—Mike was new. Fresh. Untainted. What could she learn from Mike?

Some protective voice inside her said, *Are you a complete and utter moron? You're going to go at twilight, during dusk, and walk a multi-mile trail in the woods with some guy you've never met yet— are you crazy?*

Josie knocked her out of her reverie. "He seems interesting. I'm trying to imagine you running a—" Josie gasped, "—marathon." Wheezy laughter. "Uh...I just can't."

"You just lost your free latte."

"You know me, I'm a fast metabolizer of caffeine— that's what my genetic testing showed me. You have to get me one! This—" she pointed to the cup of coffee Laura had just made her—"isn't enough!" She mooned a begging face.

"Did your genetic testing show that you consume enough caffeine to mimic a sun-addled mosquito on crack every day?"

"Yes."

"Really?"

"Yes, it did." Josie nodded soberly. "Therefore, that explains why I need you to buy me a triple latte, Miss I'm Going to Say Yes to Life." Josie frowned, "Was the sex any good last night?"

"What? Why are you asking me that?"

"We're talking about saying 'yes,' so it seemed like a natural segue..."

"Of course it was good." Laura rolled her eyes, her chest heaving a bit as she sighed deeply. "Too good."

"What do you mean, *too good*? Is that possible?"

"It's too good when it turns out he has a girlfriend. He was just, *whew*— oh boy, Josie."

"The best you've ever had?" Josie asked.

"Well," she sighed heavily. "Yeah."

"You're sure he has a girlfriend?"

"The pictures made it clear."

"Damn. Well, maybe you can say 'yes' to this guy you're seeing tonight."

"Yeah."

"*Yes*."

* * *

Huff, huff, huff.

Laura was more out of shape then she'd ever imagined. Her idea of exercise was lifting her hand from her mouth to the bag of Doritos or lifting the spoon out of the pint of Ben & Jerry's.

No, she chided herself, that wasn't really true. She took the stairs at work, and that wasn't a joke, considering the fact that she worked on the thirty-second floor. And she and Josie power walked around her neighborhood (Josie jokingly called it their Mugging Prevention Program), but this kind of sustained, prolonged effort that used muscles that involved the hard work of uneven terrain, hiking along the trails and the woods? *This* she wasn't used to.

And that was OK. Really. Mike was a sweetheart who slowed his pace down and who was absolutely, fantastically interesting. Talking about everything from books that Laura hadn't read since college, but had always loved, to movies—who knew he had a Christopher Guest obsession, too? She couldn't wait for a second date where they could sit and watch *Best in Show*, and she could enjoy having that someone finally who appreciated the humor.

Second date? She was getting ahead of herself.

And she really liked that.

"Laura, are you OK?" Mike asked, a look of concern covering his face as she wheezed slightly while rounding a bend and staring at the tall hill leading to the summit. Too tall. Too high. Too little air. Ah, hell. What had she agreed to?

Huff huff huff.

"Oh, I'm fine," she lied. "Just not used to these tall hills. I'm more accustomed to doing eleven street blocks downtown while carrying my morning latte. Not hiking up a steep mountain while carrying a stainless steel water bottle. I'm adjusting, though— I'll be good."

He smiled and stared at her. "You're a good sport, you know?"

"I have to be. I don't think I have the oxygen to run away."

They both laughed and Laura felt a warmth spreading through her. She couldn't quite believe the way that the past two days had gone. First, she'd had an absolutely amazing date with Dylan. She could still feel him on her skin, even though she had slunk out of his apartment like a sorority girl sophomore learning how to navigate the world of one-night stands. Then again, it wasn't exactly her fault that he had pictures of his girlfriend all over the place; funny how that killed the mood. All of that was (*hours*) behind her, for now here was this golden boy, smiling at her and standing there like Thor at the gates of Asgard, taking her on a hike.

Mike was about as opposite of Dylan as you could possibly get. Tall— if he was shorter than 6'5" she'd be surprised— blonde, maybe Danish, with piercing blue eyes and the lanky body of a thirty-something guy who walked like he was seventeen and still a little awkward. Just looking at his body told her he was a true athlete, and he was a ski instructor, so obviously he was coordinated, toned and balanced, and could move with fluidity and grace whether they were hiking, skiing, or...in bed?

She, on the other hand, felt like a giant cotton ball right now. A sweaty, huffing cotton ball. Who wanted nothing more than to relax in a hammock with a pitcher of sangrias.

And an oxygen tank.

Yet here she was, about a quarter mile from the summit of some crazy-ass hill that he wanted her to climb to the top of. She could expand her horizons. This was something new. He was sweet, quiet, kind of taciturn—but not in a bad way. Nothing was awkward. Nothing was uncomfortable. He was just a man who didn't talk too much.

He preferred, obviously, to act, to stretch, to move — to move up that damn hill. Which she now stared at as if she were looking at the top of Mount Everest.

"We're really going to climb up that?" she asked, trying to keep the skepticism out of her voice.

"We really are!" he grinned. "But," he patted the log next to him where he'd sat down, stretching out his long legs, his arms toned and golden, eyes kind and nervous. "We can take a short break."

"A *short* break?" Eek. She didn't mean to sound so overwhelmed, but if she paused, took a deep breath, and did an inner inventory, she had to admit that this hike was killing her. This may be her true walk of shame, especially if Mike had to call 911 and have her hauled down this mountain on a hand-held stretcher. With her luck, Dylan would be the paramedic on call.

Don't think about Dylan!

"OK, a long break." His hearty laugh put her at ease. What was most comfortable, though, was what he didn't say—how he just moved from laughter to quiet, the silence self-composed and genuine. He wasn't shifting around or twitching in his own skin. He just wasn't going to say anything if he didn't have anything to say, yet his nonverbal communication was calm and sweet. Mike was just there, with Laura, and the two were spending time together. That was enough.

She liked this. It was new. Time and space were enough, and as the seconds unfolded gradually into minutes, the minutes now more than an hour, she felt like she was spending time in a bubble with this new man, learning an entire new language of mindfulness.

"Whew," she said, collapsing on the log next to him, trying to suck in her belly at the same time as her hamstrings cried out in relief.

Laura suddenly felt like a complete ass, her calm focus from just seconds ago vanquished, replaced by a self-consciousness that was most unwelcome. Not exactly experienced with dates like this, she'd overdressed and now, many miles into this hike, she was dripping with sweat, her hair limp and plastered against the edges of her face, her body flushed with the heat and the exertion of this trek up this crazy tall hill.

She felt about as feminine as a wet tissue, and yet that kernel of woman in her did have a spark of femininity, because she was responding to Mike in ways that shocked her.

Her body should have been spent from the night with Dylan. Rather than finding herself halting or tentative, it was as if what she had done with Dylan the night before had opened her up like a flower blossoming, giving permission to show its true colors and to spread itself in full glory—and right now, Laura was ready to spread herself again.

Easy, girl, she told herself as she stole another look at Mike.

What was it about these two? Dylan was incredible last night, yet she'd already crossed him off her mental list of eligible partners because the guy obviously had a girlfriend—or, worse, a wife. Who keeps the pictures of some gorgeous woman all over the place in their bedroom otherwise? And now here she was, less than fifteen hours after sneaking out of Dylan's house and heading home for what she thought would be a nice, big cry and a pint of ice cream, finding herself with yet another incredibly hopeful relationship staring her in the face.

Literally. She looked up and realized that Mike was watching her, his head cocked to the side, a little half grin making him look boyish and absolutely adorable.

"What are you thinking, Laura?" he asked.

"Uh..." she stammered, completely unwilling to tell him what she was really thinking. "I was just marveling at how beautiful it is here."

"It's amazing isn't it?"

Was he staring at her to tell her that those words had a double meaning? She felt shy, suddenly, and tucked a clump of damp hair behind her ear, flushing with bashfulness. A rising heat between her legs didn't help, either. Her body was telling her that they were alone, out in the woods, he was gorgeous and attentive, and—

"So you work here?" She forced herself to ask the question, to break her thought loop out of its rush, because if she didn't, pretty soon she would just plain old jump him.

"In the winter, but I just thought I'd bring you up here on a hike right now, because the canyon looks so much better. Different—when it's not covered with snow and skiers. Actually, it's kind of nice to be here when I'm not on duty and worrying about some teenager who breaks a leg or some eight year old who can't grab the tow rope properly and gets dragged up the hill."

He chuckled and she joined him. That was the most she had heard out of his mouth in one continuous stretch since she'd met him.

Mike seemed so good-natured, didn't talk much, was kind of quiet— and she liked that more than she ever would have imagined. It was really different from Dylan, who was so gregarious, open and extroverted. There was a quiet depth to Mike that she found refreshing. Most guys she'd met on the dating site were either out for a piece of ass or to just sit there on a date and talk themselves up. Nobody had ever asked her out on a *hiking* date. This guy was special— and she hoped she was special enough for him.

"Shh!" he said, grabbing her arm suddenly, the pressure of his fingers more urgent than arousing. "Look!" he hissed, pointing into the woods.

She leaned into him, craning her head to see what he was pointing to, taking advantage of the moment to get that much closer, to cross the silent boundary between them, to bridge the gap in those first seconds of contact that you never get back.

She could smell him this close and he smelled like pine and sweat and something more— a sporty musk that turned on her inner sensors, making her instantly flushed, a lump forming in her throat that told her that there was definitely a spark of chemistry here.

An inner bliss poured into her veins, channeling through her, making every pore hum and relax as she reveled in the newness of Mike.

"What is it?" she asked.

"There —do you see it?" Two deer stood deep in the woods, munching on the bark of a tree. The mother perked her head up, turned to her fawn, and looked back at Laura and Mike with a precision only animals could possess. The doe nudged her baby and the two ran off into the woods, not so much scared as careful. You never know about humans; they're just as likely to be friend as foe, and Laura understood.

Goodbye, little Mama, she thought.

"That's really beautiful," Laura whispered.

A quick glance showed that Mike was watching the animals as intently as she was, yet also attuned to the tension between them, now shifting from the sheer simplicity of first contact to a journey of unspoken communication. Blood pulsed through her, beating a rhythm of questions she hoped he could feel and that, in turn, he could decipher.

I want you, it said, and the greatest hope inside her was that his return beat would be the message, *I want you, too*.

The pressure of his fingers lightened, shifting from a grab of urgency to a lingering touch that asked a question his mouth couldn't— or wouldn't—ask.

Two seconds, Laura, she told herself, two seconds to just start to breathe before turning and looking at him. Was that his return beat? The feel of his fingertips was agonizingly puzzling, for it could mean nothing or, if she was right, it could mean everything.

When she turned, body perked like the doe's, heightened by animal instinct, she saw it in his eyes, too, as Mike leaned down and took her lips with his.

* * *

Bringing Laura up here had been a dicey move. He hadn't really thought much about his request to make a first date out of a hike, but then again he wasn't exactly

Mr. Suave. This was his life, so sharing it with someone upfront made a certain kind of sense to him. Get reality out of the way and if the other person still wanted to see him, then great. If not, they didn't waste their time and could move on.

If only everything were so simple. Dating, so far, hadn't been, no matter how hard he tried to make it cut and dried.

He found solace, peace—*meaning* and fun and even excitement in the woods, on the slopes, on a long run. When he ran, his mind turned off and something deeper turned on. An awareness of just *being* that he only got from the pounding of his soles against the pavement, against the dirt, on the trail.

Most people didn't like the way he lived. It was too different, too quiet, too introspective and too focused on doing. Not focused enough on talking, posturing, obvious displays of status or of involvement in things that just didn't matter to him.

He wanted to move. He wanted to run. He wanted to ski. He wanted to help people. And to his surprise, as he'd reached adulthood, he'd found that there weren't that many women, or men for that matter, who valued that.

He watched Laura closely and had liked what he saw. She wasn't an outdoors type but she had gamely marching on up this hill. He could tell she wasn't a hiker. She wasn't the type who would, on her own, take the initiative and go for a long bike or a run or a swim. She certainly wasn't a triathlete, but she had a gentleness about her and an openness and a willingness to just *be* that he didn't find in many people.

He didn't find it in *any* people other than Dylan—and then in Jill. So when he leaned in to kiss Laura, he surprised himself; that was the last thing he expected he would do on a first date. He wasn't exactly the kind of guy who wined and dined women, and yet this felt right.

It felt perfect.

Something in him deepened as their mouths met, as he reached for her, as he claimed those curves for his own. In that moment, he rose up and a finesse, a sophistication that he knew was there but buried very deep, surged to the surface. This woman was his, in his arms as she softened, opening up to him, their tongues intertwining.

He would definitely not be just *sharing* this woman with Dylan. They would be *partners* with this woman.

Arousal burst through his veins, a pump turned on, a switch flipped, with a sudden explosion of want and need and lust. Hungry for more of her in his hands, on his lips, against his body, he searched her, like going on a journey through another person's land, and found that his need to explore was absolutely endless. His erection pressed against her leg as she leaned into him pushing, searching, wanting as well. The two joined in an obvious mutual exploration that made him wish he had asked her to his cabin for dinner so that a bed were handy.

And then his mind slipped into that place it went when he ran, when he skied, when he hiked. He had never been able to access that part of himself through anything but heavy exertion or laser-like focus on the kinesthetics of life, but here, *here,* he found himself shifting. A subtle yet dramatic movement from one layer of life to another.

As her hands roamed over his shoulders, roamed his back, tightened over his waist and went elsewhere, he filled with a warmth, with an urgency that eighteen months of grief, denial, restraint and constraint had allowed to grow into something so strong, so big that it was in their kiss, and her touch unleashed it, here and now.

It just *was*. Endless and timeless and present, exactly as it had been with Jill.

But more.

* * *

Oh, my God, what was she doing?

She still had Dylan's taste in the back of her throat, Dylan's scent on parts of her skin in spite of her thorough shower this morning, Dylan's essence deep inside her—and here she was in the arms of another man. A godlike, amazing, muscular man. She felt his warmth underneath his clothes and wanted desperately to feel his skin without the layer between them.

How could this be happening? How could two incredible men want her within twenty-four hours of each other? Her mind went blank as Mike probed her mouth, his tongue filled with more questions and answers, his hands thick and strong, grabbing and caressing and owning parts of her. Her own questions faded, melted into the warm wetness of his mouth and she knew, just *knew* on some deep level, some layer within herself that she didn't even know she had, that this was so much more than she ever anticipated when that little chat window had popped up this morning.

Thank whatever higher power she was supposed to thank for that little chat window.

His hot breath filled her, and then cool air touched her lips as he pulled away. The sound of his deep breath, an intentional, centering breath that she recognized instantly, filled her with uncertainty. Was he having second thoughts? All these extra curves weren't exactly accessories that were standard features on the women Mike normally dated. Those were the weekend yoga babes, the women who competed in mini-triathlons for fun and who went on 100-mile weekend bike rides just *because*. They were a different kind of woman than Laura.

Hell, they might as well have been a different *species*.

What would Mike want with her, with all her soft rolls and overflowing cups and dimples and apple cheeks and—

Her old insecurities flooded her as she tipped her head down, averting his eyes, his hand still on her shoulders, one trailing a lazy path down the side of her rib cage, brushing briefly against her breast.

He let go of her shoulder and reached up to her chin, tipping it, forcing her to meet his eyes. What she saw there told her everything she needed to know.

She laughed nervously, "I don't normally do this."

"Do what?" His voice was smoky with need. The affable, slightly awkward man she'd started this hike with had suddenly evolved into a determined, commanding, dominant man.

"I don't normally go on long hikes with guys and then kiss them before we reach the summit. Typically, I wait until we get to the top."

He smiled. "Then I have something to look forward to. Come on." He pointed to the trail head.

She groaned. "All right, if you insist."

He held his hand out in a gesture of chivalry, "Ladies first."

"Promise?" she asked, the word popping out of her mouth before she could take it back.

He cocked one eyebrow, shot her a lascivious look, and said, "You can count on it."

What was she doing? *Earth to Laura!* She had to laugh at herself on the inside, trying to hide the racing thoughts from Mike. The pounding of her inner voice was so strong, loud and pervasive, that she feared everything going on inside her head was so obvious that he could read her.

As he took her hand, intertwining their fingers, and they walked slowly at Laura's pace up to the top, she tipped over. This was new and good and she wasn't going to let that ridiculous doubting voice inside her ruin it.

With each step her energy rebounded, her heart rate steadying and her body finding equilibrium to keep pumping herself up, to manage the trail and to climb higher. Perhaps it was the excitement of Mike's kiss, his proximity, of the promise of something more when they reached their goal. Silly though it seemed, that made her live in the moment, and when they finally reached the end, the view really was otherworldly.

So was Mike's touch.

Just don't sleep with him, that little voice chided her. *Don't be that kind of woman. Wait one more date.* In some ways, she hated that voice, but this time it really was right. Sleeping with Mike this soon after Dylan would be crass. Over the top. Unfair to Mike.

Unfair to *her*.

She needed a few days off from everyone to just think this through. Of course, she'd never see Dylan again. That was a done deal. However, she still had unresolved feelings for him, and that meant clearing her mind. Couldn't do that with Mike's tongue in her mouth.

Or his dick in her—

"Hey? That's an interesting look. What's going on in that mind of yours?"

Talk about a loaded question. Laura struggled to answer. He peered at her, seemed to really study her, and it was as if he knew. Knew what she was thinking, understood the demons she wrestled with, and was being respectful—but still curious. If it weren't one-hundred-percent impossible for him to have any idea about her date with Dylan last night, she would have thought he was giving her space to think things through.

That was just crazy, though.

He reached for her, pulled her into his embrace, her back to his chest, and he settled in, holding her as if they'd done this a million times. Inhaling deeply, she relaxed into the hold, feeling like they had done this forever. How could this be? Why did she feel so settled with him already—and yet so excited to get to know him, all at the same time?

She examined his forearms, bare and wrapped around her ribs and chest. Light, sandy hair dotted the arms, which were deeply freckled, though the spots were light. A few scars, but nothing that spoke of severe trauma. No ring, and no tell-tale white skin where a ring normally resided. He did wear an old-fashioned friendship bracelet, the kind she hadn't seen since she was a young teen.

"What's that?" She fingered the thin, braided band, faded from red and blue to a pale pink and blah-ish gray color. Changing the subject might help her escape more scrutiny about her thoughts.

He tensed, his wrist starting to pull back, and then he paused, taking a deep breath that she felt against her back. *How rare*, she thought. A man who took the handful of seconds to consider his actions, to be deliberate. Whatever response he was about to give her, she knew, would be forthright and honest, coming from a deep center she wanted to touch.

"An old friend gave that to me."

She could feel him swallow, could sense the unspoken. Someone very, very special.

"It's been beaten up and seems to have gone through a lot, but looks well-loved."

"So was she."

Laura stopped breathing. His voice had gone quiet, the words a *whoosh* out of his lungs, like something he couldn't control but that he could barely stand to say. The mood had shifted abruptly, her innocent questions something she normally would wish she could take back, would normally berate herself for asking, for making everything awkward with one simple piece of chit chat.

Except she wasn't. Regretful, that is. Asking that question may damn well have been the best choice she'd made all day, because she got a glimpse into an intensely private man and his profound nature was revealed.

This was what she wanted.

And Dylan.

Go away, Dylan! she chided the voice in her head — as if he himself had invaded her thoughts. Why was she experiencing this strange duality, in Mike's arms and feeling his pain for someone he'd once loved all while thinking about a man she'd been with last night— one with a hidden significant other?

It was madness.

"I'm sorry," Mike said, stepping back and turning her around. His eyes were sincere and warm, tinged with nostalgia and troubled. "Mentioning her is the last thing I should do on dates. Talking about a past girlfriend isn't exactly part of the blueprint for a successful new relationship."

Relationship? Did he say *relationship?*

Laura's heart sang.

"It's fine," she assured him. "I understand. You loved her. You can't separate that from who you are and what you feel in any given moment."

He flinched but kept eye contact, obviously shocked by her words. His reaction surprised her, but she knew she hadn't said the wrong thing. Her usual insecurity was gone, replaced by a steadfast calm. Whatever she said, it had been from the heart, and that was all that really counted.

* * *

How could she read him so well? Freakishly well. He felt like an idiot for talking about Jill right now, and yet somehow Laura made it seem fine. Natural. Like another extension of himself, just a perfectly typical part of life.

Against all hope he had thought there might—just might—be a woman like this out there for him and Dylan. Someone sweet and nice and understanding and accepting. Not quite convinced she was out there, he had basically given up, and now Dylan had found her on a damn online dating site, of all places. The kind of place where men trolled for sex.

Dylan, though, had been seeking something more. And now here "more" was, standing before him, telling him that who he was was totally fine. That talking about his dead girlfriend was OK because it was how he felt.

What had he done to deserve this—and how could he keep it all going?

Pulling her into his arms, he kissed her again, this time with more urgency and a deeper acceptance. Less questioning, more certainty. Was he imagining that she felt it, too? Her lips were less tentative, more confident, as her tongue slipped in and did its own claiming, her hands pressing against his shoulder blades and pushing him into her, her hips lifting up against his.

She was shorter than he was used to, but her curves were addictive. His hands wanted to touch every inch of flesh, especially the expanse of softness from the spot where her ass met her thigh, up through to her breasts. Handfuls of Laura and her little sighs of pleasure made him harden even more—if that were possible—and by God, if they weren't heading toward dusk on a mountain where it wasn't safe to be unprotected at night, he'd have spent the next five hours devouring her, right here, right now.

However, if they stayed, the bears might very well do the devouring, so with great reluctance he pulled back, cradling her face in his hands, smiling down at her lovely, flushed cheeks, those eyes eager and bright.

"We need to go down the mountain now before it gets dark." He pressed his forehead against hers and closed his eyes, taking a deep breath. "I wish..." He couldn't finish his thought, too overwhelmed by the crushing chaos of turbulence inside him.

She nodded, making his head bob slightly, in turn triggering a grin on his lips.

"That would be an inauspicious first date. 'Woman eaten by bear.'"

"Why do you assume the bear would eat *you*?"

He laughed and opened his eyes.

She was looking at him with a half-smile.

"Because I have more body fat and you can run faster."

"I would help you climb a tree."

"Guys do that so they have an excuse to stare at our asses."

He craned his head behind her body and looked down. "I don't need an excuse."

She blushed and looked up, a tight, amused smile on her lips. Had he gone too far? "*First* date?" she asked. She seemed to force herself to make eye contact.

Puzzled, he frowned. "Uh, yes?"

"That implies there might..."

"...be a second?"

She nodded.

"That's up to you, Laura."

* * *

Not telling Dylan about Laura really was going to kill him, but he needed this second date to confirm his suspicions. When he came out of his bedroom and found Dylan hunched over his laptop, naked except for his boxer briefs, shoulders curled and face staring intently at the screen as he chowed down a bowl of cereal, Mike couldn't help himself. He snickered.

Dylan practically climbed the walls, startling, his face panicked and body spidery with a fight-or-flight stance.

"What the fuck, Mike? Why do you do that?"

"Do what?"

"Creep up on people like that!" He had one hand on his heart. "Fucking gave me a heart attack."

"Hey, I didn't do anything weird. I walked into my own kitchen to grab breakfast. You're the freak. Why are you in another world?" A quick glance at the screen gave him his answer: the online dating site.

With Laura's picture and profile.

Fuck. Suppressing his jealousy, Mike opened the fridge door and grabbed a half gallon of milk to pour a glass as he popped two pieces of bread in the toaster.

"I'm—ah, hell, I guess I'm stalking Laura."

A rush of protectiveness hit Mike in the solar plexus like a punch. He knew Dylan wasn't going to harm her. Knew it was just because Dylan was crazy about her. Knew all that.

Still reacted.

"I thought she blocked you?"

"She did. Wait—I told you that?"

"Yup."

"Well, I made a new account and I'm trying that way."

Mike blinked. The toast popped. Dylan returned his attention to the screen. As Mike grabbed peanut butter, he asked, "You created a new identity to try to trick her into talking to you?"

"No. My new account says it's me. I'm not that crazy."

Yes, you are, Mike thought. Almost said it. Held back. Smearing the peanut butter with too much force, he shredded the toast, collapsing the piece and sliming his hand and wrist with nut butter. What a mess.

Yeah. *What a mess.*

"Aren't you worried she'll be creeped out by you? I mean, she blocked you. Case closed. Move on."

Dylan shook his head and sighed, his six pack folding in and then out, the muscles rippling up through his chest. Mike admired it with a contentment, like looking at fine art. He didn't need to touch it; just seeing it was satisfying enough. Knowing it was there when he wanted it sufficed.

"Seriously, Dylan. Any woman would be freaked if some guy went around chasing her like this. You tried messages on her old account. She blocked you. You tried calling—same. Now you're getting unhinged."

Beep-blip!

"Woot!" Dylan shouted. "She's responding!"

Mike rushed across the room to see. A swirl of good and bad mixed within him, for if she wanted Dylan again, would she stop seeing Mike? Or, hope against hope, would she consider seeing them both?

Please leave me alone, she wrote.

Mike couldn't contain a snort of laughter. Dylan scowled.

"Fuck!"

Schadenfreude aside, Mike's inner thoughts mirrored Dylan's, because in the end while this was amusing watching Dylan twist in the wind, the fact that he wanted to share Laura meant that somehow he had to find a way to make her see his partner again, to clear up whatever misunderstanding had developed that one night they'd been together.

Of course, Dylan couldn't know that Mike was dating her—man, when had this become so complicated?

When you asked her out, dumbass.

Oh. Yeah.

"How many messages have you sent her?"

"Thirty-four."

"THIRTY-FOUR?" Mike howled with laughter now, unable to hold back, leaning against the counter and spilling the last bit of milk in the half gallon carton as it toppled over, sideways, then plummeted to the tiled floor. "Shit!" he shouted, grabbing a hand towel and bending down to clean it up.

"Is that a metaphor?" Dylan muttered, typing something in the chat window.

"What are you writing?" Mike split his attention between the milk mess and Dylan's mess.

"I'm asking her to meet me for coffee."

"No chianti and fava beans?"

"Shut up." Dylan's glare turned from simple annoyance to a simmering fury. OK. Mike knew when to let up. Half a minute later and the milk was cleaned up; time to get out of the house and let Dylan find his way through his heartache. He had a date tonight.

One that required some serious planning to pull off. What was Laura thinking right now, facing her own screen as Dylan tried again and again to talk to her? Was she scared? Intrigued? Pissed? She kept turning Dylan down, and that didn't bode well for a future triad.

All Mike could do now was "wow" her with tonight's date. He left Dylan half-naked and brooding, to find his way through her roadblocks, the man grousing about all the ways he might have screwed up on their date.

* * *

Same mountain, new date. Or, it *seemed* like the same mountain. They all seemed the same to Laura as her vision blurred, her veins unaccustomed to blood pumping this hard through her body for any reason other than sheer arousal.

Arousal was an issue here, though, too.

The view from the top of the mountain was breathtaking. Laura would've appreciated it more if her attention weren't completely focused on Mike. He was all she wanted to watch. He'd carried a back pack at his side through much of the walk. Not wearing— just carrying it.

Her Second Billionaire

And now like it was a magician's hat, he pulled out a blanket, two bottles of red wine, a couple of glasses, a container filled with five or six different kinds of cheese, most of them with names she couldn't pronounce, and a container of grapes and strawberries, a couple of them chocolate covered.

"What's this?" she said.

"I thought I'd surprise us with a light dinner." He smiled shyly. "I'm too much of a gentleman to take a woman out and not feed her at least something. I may have dragged you along for another crazy hike and ruin my chances at the third date, but at least you can't say we didn't have dinner."

She surveyed the layout before her. A camping blanket; thin, but well-worn. Actual stemware, wine glasses that he kept in a special case. And as he inserted the cork screw into the first bottle of wine, and very deftly opened it, she sampled one of the cheeses.

"Mmm, sheep's cheese?" she asked.

His eyes lit up. "Yes! You can tell from the taste?"

"Yeah," she said, "it's one of my favorites."

"Well, hot damn! Who knew I'd find someone who knows their fromage?" he said, biting his lower lip, and smiling and nodding at the same time, as if he quietly celebrated a minor success.

"Who knew?" she said quietly.

She felt she could breathe around him, that she could appreciate each breath. As he handed her the glass of red wine, she sniffed it, then took a sip. "This is good."

"Guess?"

"Guess what?" she asked.

"Guess what kind of wine this is."

She surveyed the bouquet, sniffing a couple of times, lapped at the red wine very ostentatiously, took a sip, and looked at him grandly, with as much pretension as she could muster, and declared, "It's red."

He burst into laughter. "How sophisticated."

She shrugged. "Sorry. I may know something about cheese, but I know nothing, absolutely nothing, about wine. But I like this." She reached for his hand as they stood and stared out at the valley. "I like this a lot."

His warm palm closed over her shoulder and he looked down at her, standing a full foot above her frame, his neck leaning toward her, his face an inch away. "Yeah. I like it a lot too."

Making love outside, in the fresh air, had never been part of her bucket list. In fact, it was more a part of her anti-bucket list; bright light, no covers, on the hard ground? Who would find that appealing?

Uh, *her*. Right here. Right now.

As Mike stared at her, eyes burning with an intensity she fell into, an abyss of wanting, she found herself startlingly interested in trying this new experience. Was this why he had gone to so much trouble—the wine, the special blanket, the fromagerie of cheeses and such? It dawned on her that he wasn't just being a sweetheart, giving her a lovely, gourmet picnic for their second date.

As a matter of fact, what they had eaten was just an appetizer.

She was the entree.

His kiss wasn't a surprise; what shocked her most was the preternatural urge that welled up, unbidden, as his hands seized her ass and hips, his body knowing exactly what—and who—it wanted. He shifted, like he had on their first date, from a mild-mannered, lanky, zen-like dude to a ferocious, sexual alpha male.

And she—*she*—had triggered all that. It excited her almost more than his touch, the way his tongue conquered hers, how his palms were greedy for so much of her skin, his chest pressed into hers, the thick outline of his erection in such stark relief against her navel she could probably sculpt it out of clay from memory. When he urged her, gently, to kneel, then recline, on the blanket, she knew her outdoor sex cherry was about to be popped. A thin membrane of restraint was about to give way to a burst of need that told her she was more than ready to bare all before nature.

"Mmm," she sighed. His mouth moved from hers, hands tracing patterns of lust on her breasts, as if he were memorizing the terrain, his flattened palm stealing down her ribcage as his lips caressed her neck. She had worn a skirt today, a *just in case* move that she was grateful for now, because the easy access meant that sex would be so much simpler, more direct, less complicated.

Like Mike.

And, thankfully, she had shaved. Landscaped, if you will. Going nearly bald had been a new experience, the little landing strip like a giant, glowing neon sign pointing to her clit. Would he like it? Hate it? Not care?

Barely functioning nerves kicked in and she couldn't turn off the lopping thoughts, the cluster of fears and insecurities, even with this gorgeous athlete's hands greedily touching every part of her, even as his lips brushed her abdomen, her hands in his hair and—*oh!*

The smooth, cold feeling of her skirt sliding up her thighs felt like butter melting on hot flesh as a light breeze blew up to her V, centered on the little bit of hair under her postage-stamp thong. She shivered and he nearly growled, his face about to descend on her womanhood, his eyelids heavy and his hands communicating his own, barely-controlled need. A deep sigh from him as his hands roamed up her torso told her more than words, that he was enjoying this, that her body was his, and fine, and enough.

As he slid the thin string of her thong down her legs she worried they were too plump, too full, too—and then he gently kissed her labia, a soft touch like a promise, so profound she nearly came in his mouth, the thought and feel of this giant, gentle man wanting her such a balm.

A quick flash of Dylan—*would he never leave her thoughts?*—nearly ruined the moment for her, but she pushed him away and let Mike continue, surrendered to what was before her.

A man who very much desired her—and who was showing it, touch by touch.

"Oh," she whispered, his hands slipping between her ass and the blanket, her naked bottom half exposed for the sun and clouds and sky to view unfettered. Modesty disappeared under the sun's rays in their secluded spot, and the knowledge that here, miles from anything that could judge her, they were just two people enjoying each others' bodies and minds.

Muscled arms pressed in the right places, his fingertips gently folding back her labia and his hot breath teasing her just before his tongue did its dance, flicking against the tender, red skin that craved his mouth so much.

She bloomed with lust, every pulse of energy focused on her womanhood as he sucked her clit, slowly extracting the release within, entering and pulling back with perfect fingers as he seemed to know exactly what to do to make her build to a climax.

This wasn't some shy guy who didn't know his way around a woman's body; she couldn't control her shaking legs, a sign she was getting so close and, moreso, that he was a master at triggering a woman's touch points, making the different parts fall into place for the grand finale.

Letting go was so hard, but at one point Mike's hand came up and touched her hip bone, the simple, non-sexual gesture a symbol of a bond here—that this wasn't just sex, but it was something more. A connection.

She looked down—something she never, ever did during oral sex—and her hands found their way into his hair again, her eyes wide open as she took in the cloud formations, the shine of sunlight on the side of the mountain, the lush greenery, the quality of the light and the chirping of birds. They were just mammals who were part of nature, yet so much more.

"Please, please!" The words came out of her so abruptly she nearly pulsated as she came, her pussy walls slamming against each other as the orgasm hit her without warning. She groaned, pelvis grinding into his mouth and tongue, which danced maddeningly right where she needed it most.

Then he lapped her, enlarging the surface area of his amazing tongue, changing between flat and pointed to tweak every pixel of flesh he could. Feeling both sensations led to a screaming rush as a huge, muscular wave tightened every part of her, clinging to his finger, riding his face, his tongue eagerly catching up to her clit.

"Keep going!" she hissed, hands curling into fists of orgasm, her pussy crammed into his tongue as she hissed, "You are so—oh, Mike!"

The vortex of lust, the churn of hope and disbelief and pleasure, didn't stop. Laura didn't think it was possible to feel so much so fast, his fingers strumming her and his tongue licking exactly what she wanted and where she needed, the blanket beneath her ass soaked, his breath coming in little pants now as she imagined he was ready to explode, too.

Mike maintained a steady pace, little laps followed by faster, eager strokes, tonguing her, working to extract every last bit as she came and came and came, comfortable enough to let her face contort and her body twist as she reveled in what he could do to her. One deep, full-body clench as she closed her eyes so hard she saw fireworks behind them and she was done, the peak ended, her prayers nearly silent, the breath leaving her body.

He grinned, then climbed up her body, his long, lanky runner's frame a muscled wall as he made his journey One hot kiss full of her taste made her red and engorged again, her clit tightening so much she came right there from just a kiss, her hips pushing into him, her own musk covering her lips, her nose, the intoxicating odor so powerful that she couldn't believe she was coming again. What kind of man could do this to her?

This kind.

Frantic hands that didn't feel like hers pulled at his waist. She wanted him in her *now*. Preliminaries first, of course—she had to give him some attention, too, as a wildflower patch mingled with a low breeze to send an incredible, heady rush of pollen and perfume their way.

Freeing him, she gasped. She looked down at his cock, pausing a moment to really appreciate it, rising up to meet her.

"Laura," he said, his voice gravelly and tight.

"Yes?"

Mike reached for her, and in one fluid movement stripped off her shirt, his eyes lighting up as her skin shone in the light. She hunched her shoulders forward, a bit embarrassed to be so exposed in bright, unrelenting sunshine.

"Don't," he said, his hands cupping her breasts, fingers playing with the light-pink lace at the top of her bra. "Don't do that."

"Do what?"

Alarm raced through her veins, mixing with the endorphins from the orgasms she'd just enjoyed, leaving her cotton-headed and puzzled.

"Don't hide yourself. Oh, Laura—you are so beautiful," he whispered in her ear as he leaned forward, unclasped her bra, and pulled off his own t-shirt. Within seconds he had unveiled himself completely, his body nude before her, and he gestured for her to do the same.

She had to stand to slide off her skirt and she sucked in her lower abdomen, wishing she'd spent more time on pilates than dead-lifting, the pain of each fat roll of excess ruining her arousal.

Until Mike said, "You're like a model in a Renaissance painting. Perfect and real." He pulled her hand and brought her down to the blanket, kissed the nape of her neck, and she melted.

She was *real*. He was making her more real.

As she grinned, she took one experienced hand, making sure she had his full, erect attention now. She ran her tongue over her lips, savoring the pleasure she was about to give, so the first touch would be perfect, not too dry or bothersome—and, of course, all-too real.

Julia Kent

She clutched his swollen rod in one hand and teased his tip with her tongue, ripples of muscle under his rib cage going crazy. Flicking the tip until he groaned, she perfected the friction level all the way down, completely aroused by his excitement. Thick runner's legs shifted, the hair against hair like the sound of light sandpaper, and his face was open, languid, even, as she touched him.

No one—not even Dylan—had made her feel this comfortable with her own sexuality. So pure. So real. So alive. Mike was present with his arousal, so into the moment of her hand, her mouth—*her*.

Returning her attention to the tip, firming her grip and tonguing the soft rim of his mushroom, she knew he was getting close. Her hand rubbed the base of his cock while she very gradually moved her mouth up and down on him, accentuating the sensation of the roof of her mouth, her tongue and her lips, pumping him with her hand and hoping that she could give him the same pleasure he'd so beautifully given her just moments ago.

One of his hands touched her head, stroking her hair encouragingly, the fingers trying to tell her something she already knew—this was good. Great.

Amazing.

She took her time to extend his pleasure, for making love on this blanket at the top of a mountain, jet trails above them the only testimony to civilization, was a once-in-a-lifetime event. She wanted to make it perfect.

She continued this motion, going gradually faster and faster as his fingers tightened in her hair. She gently touched his balls, knowing she was on the right track when she began to taste him as he released that little drop of fluid, and she groaned with enjoyment. Taking him into her mouth as far as she could, her fingers clutched the base of his cock while continuing to stroke it, his athlete's body tensing and clamping without regard for anything but the pending release.

Laura blew more air on the sensitive skin while milking him and he groaned, neck muscles tense with the agony of holding back. She was ready to give him the release he so desperately needed and licked her palm to get ready for more when a firm hand covered hers.

"No. Not like this. I want to be in you," he commanded.

It wasn't a request. Laura was more than ready to comply, but he beat her to it.

He searched for her clit, finding her willing again. "You make me want to take you right here, right now, in the wild open, Laura."

A completely new wave of arousal came out of nowhere, slamming her, making her want to make love with him for the rest of time.

Or, at least, for the next hour.

She wanted to straddle him, to ride him, to feel that Greek-God body on top of hers, to be together and come together and so much more.

"Climb on me, Laura. I want to touch you," he said, pulling her gently onto his hips.

She was so wet as she reached beneath her, straddling his hips now, the little scalloped edges of muscle where his abs met his hips too tempting not to touch. As her fingertips brushed there he shivered and nudged her just so—making the tip of him go in her. It felt like sinking into the perfect, hot bath, like the first bite of a chocolate torte in a cafe in Paris, like—so cliched!—like coming home.

To a home you didn't know you had.

JULIA KENT

He pulsated and she moaned with pleasure as her thighs hit his balls. "You are so amazing," she rasped.

Her entire body stretched up, catlike, her breasts thrusting forward and instantly covered with his enormous palms, the feeling of his fingers pinching her nipples like a direct, hot route to her clit. Something *zinged* on her arm, then again on her thigh, and she felt more inside her pussy walls, her body overcome with little zaps that hurt, then faded.

As she rocketed herself up to the mushroom cap, the friction made her shiver, growing an orgasm that felt like it might just very well be more supernova than any before. He licked one hand and stroked her nipple, then repeated on the other side, the pale pink skin pebbling at his touch, making her throat tighten and her passage wetter than she thought it could be. He was making her G-spot scream for attention.

She shifted, changing her weight distribution, then drew him all the way out to the tip, clamped her walls hard, then impaled herself.

"How did you—what are you doing?" he groaned. "Do more," he urged, his hips thrusting up to catch her now, the rhythm clear. He was close, and so was she.

She was at a loss, the feeling too intense.

Mike took charge, his hands on her ass, guiding her in rhythm as he used his glutes and thigh muscles to push up, then pull back. If he angled her hips just so, he could hit her—

"Ah, God, right there, Mike!" she gasped. She needed to touch herself as he widened her pleasure zone by stretching his legs open a bit. Sitting up, she gave herself access to her clit, but was a bit shy. Some guys didn't like it when she touched herself.

"Yes," he urged. "Take the pleasure you deserve, Laura," he added, kissing the hand that had just touched her clit. She grinned and parted the soft, thick skin of her mons, finding her clit standing at attention and ready for explosion. A few strokes down to her hot self, where Mike thrust in and out and moaned and clenched, and she had liquid to move and circle, to slide.

She ground into him, the feeling so maddening, pounding beautifully into her cervix. And then she just...tipped over.

The release was there with very little warning, her hitched breath and sudden clamping the only clue poor Mike had.

"Oooooohhhh!" she moaned. She hollered and wriggled and thrust back, hot cream and sex bursting as their juices flowed, gushing.

"The heat! You're so warm."

Fading out, Mike's voice disappeared but he bucked up, fucking her hard and fast as he drained himself of his orgasm, too, their bodies twitching and pushing against each other to use whatever the laws of physics would give them. Her body made her come repeatedly, her flesh too weak to manage anything but release.

He pounded and pounded, she slammed back, he stroked her belly, and took one hand to tweak her right nipple, the pain mixing with the thrusting and the explosion to make her scream an animal sound—and then it was just a tired feeling, all cock and slick and mouth.

They slowed, little clenches from the remainders of sex slowing down. The sounds of nature filled her ears, layer by layer—birds. A buzzing. A pinch. She smacked a mosquito off her shoulder and then relaxed. Laura was still full of him as Mike relaxed, trapping her, their wetness and his muscled body all she felt now. She had no thoughts, her body surrendered, everything good, all complete, all chaperoned by the winking sun.

Neither said a word. Not a single one. By the time Laura realized they needed to leave, the sun had begun to set. Had they really just relaxed there, naked as the day they were born, for hours— staring at each other, watching the clouds, feeling the wind whip their sated skin?

Time disappeared, and as they reluctantly dressed in the sunset's glow, she decided not to say anything until he did. Perhaps this was more spiritual than she knew possible, and speaking would end whatever this was.

Mike packed and carried all their gear in silence the entire walk down to the trailhead's parking lot, where both their cars sat, expectant and a bit miffed, like parents of children new to the dating scene.

Laura laughed at the sight of their abandoned cars, the only ones in the lot, and Mike just looked at her quizzically.

He remained silent, but stepped forward and kissed her cheek gently.

"Third date?" he whispered in her ear.

She grinned so widely her cheek hit his.

"I'll take that as a yes," he whispered, then strode to his car, popped the hatchback, carefully placed the backpack and picnic goods, closed the trunk door and climbed in his car, watching Laura carefully.

By the time they both pulled out of the parking lot and made their respective turns, Laura's face was covered with tears.

Her Second Billionaire

* * *

Some things were just too personal to share even with her best friend. Laura was going steadily mad and if the itching didn't stop she was going to scream. Rubbing her butt against her kitchen chair wasn't working, damn it. Why on earth had she ever bought vinyl covered seats? With good old upholstery at least she could have scratched her butt in a way that gave her some friction—and some relief.

This itching was slowly penetrating her every conscious move, making her one big, non-stop twitch, and she'd only been conscious for an hour. Two cups of coffee hadn't helped.

Finally Josie, who had finished four cups to Laura's two, cocked her head and asked, "What in the hell are you doing, Laura? You look like a nine-year-old boy who just had an ice cream fest and a few shots of espresso."

"I am just not comfortable." Understatement of the year.

Rub rub rub.

"Did you pick something up from one of the two guys you fucked within twenty-four hours?"

Ouch. "Oh please, it wasn't within twenty-four...and you can't get...oh, I don't even want to go there. Shut up, Josie." She reached behind and scratched her ass.

"You're scratching your ass in public. I mean, *man*—"

"We're not in public—we're in my apartment."

"I am *public*. I am a human being."

"No, you're not. You're my best friend."

"You...what is going on?"

Laura couldn't help herself, scratching her breast. Her nipple was throbbing with the hot, torturous itch that plagued her ass as well.

"Why on earth are you scratching your boob, Laura?"

"Because it itches."

"That's not what I meant." Josie's exasperation showed in her tone and, finally, Laura couldn't stand it anymore. She stood up, pulled her pants down, pulled down her underwear halfway and reached for the tube of hydrocortisone cream that she'd shoved in her purse to take to work.

"Laura, oh, my *God*."

"What?" Laura twisted around and stared at her own ass. Yup. It wasn't any better this morning. What had started out as a series of small mosquito bites was now a minefield of red, hot flesh, swollen up into these enormous hive-like bites. When she had returned home from her date with Mike, she'd realized pretty quickly what had happened. While making love outside in nature, on top of a mountain, with the most incredible view possible—both of nature and of Mike's body— had been earth shattering, quite literally, the reality of nature had set in.

On her butt.

She had about fifty mosquito bites all over her ass down her legs, up her chest, and one had managed to land on her left breast areola. Those zaps? Those *zings* of pleasure? Not arousal.

Nature's vampires.

As she smeared the hydrocortisone cream all over the top of her ass, Josie just shook her head and laughed, folding in half as she held her gut, tears streaming down her face.

Laura tried pointedly to ignore her but couldn't help it. "It itches."

"Oh, Laura, that is awful. On your boob."

"I know." She pulled her pants up and went over to the kitchen sink to wash her hands. "How do you think it feels?"

"I don't know how it feels. I've never screwed somebody on the top of a mountain where a bunch of mosquitoes decided to feast on me." She snickered. "If a mosquito bites you in the ass is that some way...is that nature's version of oral sex?"

"Oh, stop it."

"You don't have any on your, you know—on your *hoo-ha*?"

"Hoo-ha? Who calls it a hoo-ha?"

Josie fanned herself and faked a southern accent. "You know me. I was raised in Virginia, I'm a good old Southern lady."

"You're from Ohio."

"I was joking."

"And besides....Lady? Yeah, right. Like *you're* a lady."

"Take some Benadryl for that, you'll thank me."

"But Benadryl makes me sleepy."

"Really? If you don't do something more drastic, you're going to go to work and you're going to look like a hyena who ate twenty-five Mexican jumping beans. You're a lot better off looking like you're just a little sleepy or hung over on antihistamines."

Laura thought about that one for a minute. It's not like she had a really busy work day. Could she just call in sick? Oh, no. The monthly management meeting was today. Shouldn't really have to do anything, but she had to be there.

"Yeah, you're right. Maybe if I take some Benadryl, it'll make it easier to get through the monthly meeting anyhow."

Josie nodded. "So, Laura," she laughed. "Was it worth it?"

Laura reached down her V-neck into her bra and found the offending bite, scratching it furiously, knowing full well that at this rate, she was going to break the skin but at least that would give her some sweet relief.

"Yeah. It was worth it, but next time I'll wear a bug spray instead of perfume."

* * *

Mike sat in bed staring up at the ceiling, counting the little holes in the tiles yet again, for what felt like the thousandth time. Actually, it probably *was* the thousandth time. He'd done it over and over and over ever since Jill died a year and a half ago.

He was doing it because it was something habitual, something rote, something that he could just slip into so that he didn't have to deal with the actually messy emotional aftermath of his date with Laura. The date had gone so much better than he ever could have expected. He never intended to sleep with her. And he certainly never intended to make love to her at the top of that mountain on that blanket.

Yet he had and he was glad.

The last time he and Jill had made love had been right there. While he wanted to reclaim the space with someone new, he hadn't planned to do it in quite that manner. Laura moved something inside of him. Her soft curves, her joyful laugh, the way that she focused

Her Second Billionaire

and her face melted into passion as she came. It all was so overwhelming and too intense.

Mike needed to talk to someone about Laura. How intoxicating. How calm. How lush. How sweet. How—*him*. It was as if someone had hand-sculpted the perfect woman for him and forgotten to tell him that this was what he really wanted.

No, she wasn't Jill. And no one ever would be Jill. That was OK, because it had to be OK. He didn't have a choice.

Always assuming he would never, ever fall in love again, Mike hadn't considered the idea that he might find a different love—one that was no more, no less, than what he and Dylan had with Jill. Could life with Laura be as good? Better? Different? The sex had been astounding, though he could do without the damn mosquito bites. Next time he would take her to his cabin.

Next time.

He didn't care that he was getting ahead of himself. But then...Dylan probably thought he had a next time, and Laura had shut him out. What was that about? He knew Dylan was tormented by her silence, but he couldn't exactly ask her about it, now, could he? Not without blowing his cover.

Cover? This wasn't some CIA movie or FBI plot. He wasn't the center of a sting operation or an undercover drug bust.

He was, however, being deceitful, and that felt very, very wrong. Laura had no idea that he and Dylan were a — *what*? What were they, exactly? Explaining their relationship hadn't been an issue with Jill. They just fell into their life as a threesome, as uncomplicated and easily as any other twosome.

He and Dylan weren't gay. Not quite. But they weren't straight, either. They had tried, before Jill, to each date separate women but what they wanted was the power of three, and it made them both complete.

Dating one woman, sleeping with one woman, was pleasurable. Already, though, he felt a longing for more. He imagined Dylan did, too. The complication now, though, was that Laura was spurning Dylan and deepening her relationship with Mike.

In the short term this was fine, but in the long run...what could he do? How could he mend the relationship between Dylan and Laura to make the triad complete?

Worse, though, was a niggling fear in the back of his mind. His heart. What if she preferred Dylan over him?

Opening up to Laura would be a whole other mess. "Hi, Laura. My partner, Dylan, found you on that dating website and figured you might be open to a long-term threesome. And, by the way, we're billionaires. So...can we keep dating?" The deception was already over the top, strung out too long.

There was no choice here. Whatever Laura decided was final. He couldn't read her—just knew she liked him. A lot. Had she liked Dylan this much, too? If not, why? What had driven her away from him and into Mike's arms?

The only way out was through. Through his heart, and hers. And Dylan's. He would have to come clean to him, and soon, before this spiraled out of control.

It wasn't fear that made him keep his mouth shut. It was exhilaration. Excitement. The secret of *mine*. Mine. Laura was his, for now. Only his. While he knew that wouldn't sustain him in the long run, just as Dylan's dating her, alone, wouldn't do it for him, either, there was a heady confidence that came from scooping Dylan.

He could never have imagined, never dreamed that Laura would spurn Dylan and turn to Mike, but here they were. This was how it had turned out, and now the only concern he had was that Laura would hate him once she knew that they knew each other.

Wait, Mike, he told himself. *Savor this.* After eighteen months of loneliness and pain, it was good to wake up in the morning with a smile on his face.

Even better, though, would be to wake up to two other smiles in his bed. God, the thought made him hard. Rock hard.

And so he found himself counting—879, 880, 881, 882—*counting, counting, counting.* He looked down and saw the tent on the top sheet.

Ah, shit. There's only one way to deal with this. A run.

He left the bedroom and nearly slammed into Dylan, who was coming out of the shower.

"How was that date last night?"

Mike felt his expression shift to complete shock and he tried to cover up his feelings. "Oh, yeah, uh, yeah it was good."

"Great," Dylan clapped him on the back, staring down at Mike's erection. "Thinking about her?"

"Thinking about a lot of things," Mike answered, still stammering on the inside. Fuck—what if Dylan guessed what was going on before Mike could confess it? This was just too much. He spent most of his life trying to craft as simple a life as possible, and now he'd created a huge romantic clusterfuck. *Way to go!*

Dylan said, "I have been too. But, well, anyhow..." He shook his head as if willing away something that was bothering him.

Mike knew he should ask, that this was Dylan's way of reaching out, of being emotionally open, and yet he couldn't. He just couldn't muster the energy to deal with anyone else's emotional struggles right now. Hell, he couldn't even deal with his own.

"Going for a run. I'll see ya."

"Alright, bye."

They were just *so* articulate when it came to expressing their feelings. He could hear Jill's words echoing in his head: "You two are about as good at talking about your feelings as I am at shaving my own balls."

If he could get his feet pounding on the pavement, on the trail, running in the dirt, the trees flying by, the buses groaning— *whatever, wherever, whenever*. Air in, air out, muscles up, muscles down. If he could reach that place within where everything disappeared and nothing was *all*—Mike knew he could figure out how on earth he was going to tell Dylan that he had just stolen his girlfriend.

* * *

Dylan threw on a pair of shorts and some t-shirt from— he looked at the front—middle school? Yeah, middle school. He still had it. In fact, he never let go of any of his t-shirts. He probably had hundreds of them in various states floating around his apartment, everything from the ratty Monsters of Rock his brother had given him when he was just a kid, to the latest cheesy Daily Show shirt.

He opened up his laptop and he tried one more time. Clicking on Laura's profile, he typed in the chat window, "Hey, Laura, are you there?"

Her Second Billionaire

She had completely shut him out. He knew it had been a day, *one* day, that was it. Just a single day since she left his bed. But she didn't answer his texts, didn't answer his phone calls, didn't respond to his chat window—nothing—and she had slunk out of his house in the middle of the night.

Dylan was certainly used to one night stands and having women sneak out—or being the one who snuck out on a woman—but he had felt such a connection with her that this mystified him. And now, the great silence. What was that about? Why was she doing this?

He knew how to find her address. He knew where she worked. He even knew the floor; she had told him. But he didn't want to be a stalker. He didn't want to be *that* guy.

And he *wasn't* that guy. It wasn't his style; he never did that kind of thing to a woman. *This* one, though? Oh, he could actually feel himself drooling, imaging her body, conjuring her touch, the way she shifted her hips, the way that she leaned against him, the way that her hair hung in his face, the way that her lips seemed to—

Oh, man.

He and Mike were a matching pair of tented shorts now.

What in the hell was up with Mike? He was acting awfully squirrelly. That was nothing new, but Dylan was going to all this trouble to find them another person. Not that anybody could replace Jill, but he wanted that closeness, he wanted that sense of family that only three could give him and Mike. And now, now he felt unmoored. Lost.

So he typed again. *"Well, Laura, if you're there, please, I'm trying to reach you. Give me a call, text me, something. I just wanted to talk. I really enjoyed the other night and let's touch base."*

And with that, he shut down, logged out, set aside his computer, and went to join Mike on that run.

As he started to put on his running shoes he remembered, *Oh shit, I forgot to email my mom.* His mom's seventieth birthday party was coming up and he needed to give his dad some answer about some detail. His computer was already off. *I could just use Mike's*, he thought.

So he went into Mike's room and yes, the laptop was open. This would be easy. He clicked on the browser and up popped the same online dating website where he met Laura.

That's funny, he thought, *maybe that's how Mike found his date last night. You would think he would have told me.*

Dylan wasn't sure what he was looking at, but a dull, creeping dread began to fill his veins. As he stared at the computer screen and read the chat windows, the account information, the all-too-familiar picture, and scanned over every detail on the screen, it slowly dawned on him that Mike was logged into his own account and having a lovely conversation about his most recent date.

With Laura.

Her Two Billionaires

Bang bang bang. Fireworks exploded above her, the dazzling pastels blooming before her eyes in a furious cascade of sparks. As the hot coals showered down like burning rain, Laura jumped when one touched her.

Bang bang bang! they exploded, the little pieces hitting her face, her legs, suddenly soft and caressing her like—

"Laura!" *Bang bang bang.* "If I hadn't lost your key I would come in!"

Josie. *Wha?* Laura opened her eyes and fumbled for her phone. 7:22 a.m. She sat upright in horror.

"Hang on!" she shouted, stumbling to the door, unchaining and unlocking it. Josie stood there, petite and jaunty, peering around Laura.

"Is he still here?" she asked breathlessly. "Is that why you didn't answer?"

Josie looked like a chihuahua in skinny jeans.

"Is *who* still here?" Laura yawned and stood on tiptoe, her muscles desperate for oxygen, blood rushing into her extremities and nearly giving her a calf cramp as she slowly went down to flat feet, rolling her shoulders and stretching her neck.

"Whatever hot, eligible bachelor contacted you last night, because you are on a roll, baby! One a day, right?"

She punched Laura lightly in the shoulder and stormed past her, banging and shuffling things as Laura stared at the back of her front door.

For the briefest of seconds she ran a frantic mental check— *had* she gone out last night?— and then cursed herself. This was getting out of hand. No, last night she had stayed home and finished up some quarterly reports, watched a few episodes of *Mad Men*, and gone to bed early. Apparently, she'd needed the sleep. And, apparently, she had forgotten to set her alarm.

Now she would be late for work, though she knew her boss wouldn't mind. Last night she had clocked an extra three hours; flex time and a salaried position made it easier to go in a bit late this morning.

Josie didn't have that luxury. As a geriatric nurse, she needed to be on shift on time, every time. At least she only worked three shifts a week, though. Soon her rotation would take her to midnight shifts, which Josie hated. So did Laura; it was hard to get together when her best friend kept a schedule better suited for vampires.

"I took a break from my busy fuckbuddy schedule," Laura yawned, stretching again.

Her belly felt cold as her shirt hiked up, and when she looked down her braless breasts hung lower, off to the sides, like small, smooth animals with the metabolism of a sloth. Josie had a chest like a boy's, if a boy had tight little breasts you could fit in a headphone cover.

Mostly, they envied each others' figures, though Laura could never understand why Josie would want these boobs. At this rate, she'd need a wheelbarrow by the age of fifty. Or to marry a good plastic surgeon. Or a billionaire.

Ha. Right. Like that would ever happen.

A quick thought of Mike, then a more surprising flash of Dylan, hit her. She couldn't get over Dylan—didn't want to, really. Mike had called her last night. Asked her out again, and this time to his cabin up on the mountain. Maybe they could make love without a million uninvited, biting guests.

That would be a step up, Laura thought, as she absent-mindedly scratched her ass over her flannel pajamas. She needed some arnica for the bites and kept forgetting to buy some.

"Quit scratching yourself and come have some coffee!" Josie called.

How did Josie know she was scratching? It's like the woman was part psychic. Or heard the *scrit scrit scrit* of fabric as she scratched. Or watched her reflection in the hallway mirror. Ah— that was it. She looked and saw Josie's cheesy, overstretched grin as she held up a mug and took a sip.

"Coffee tastes so much better at your house, Laura."

"That's because it's free."

Josie sputtered and laughed. "OK, you got me there."

Laura poured a cup of coffee and sat at her little kitchen table, taking deep breaths. "What am I going to do, Josie? Mike asked me out on a date tonight."

"What did you say?"

"Yes, of course. I really like him." She took a sip. "More than I want to."

"What does that mean?"

Laura said nothing, then started to explain, but thought the better of it. "Nevermind."

"You are stuck on Dylan, aren't you?" Josie's tone was incredulous. "Did you ever figure out who that woman was?"

"Nope."

"And has he tried to reach you?"

Laura blew air out her nose, laughing softly. "I have thirty-four messages from him on the dating site."

"Playing it cool, is he?" Josie laughed. Then she frowned. "I thought you blocked him?"

"He created a new account."

Josie made a low whistling sound of disbelief. "Day-um, Laura!"

Laura smiled wistfully. "Yeah. I just can't go there, Josie. You know how much it hurt when I found out about Ryan..." She had dated Ryan for the better part of a year. They'd shopped for engagement rings. He'd introduced her to his boss, went on double dates, and then one day she got an anonymous message on Facebook. A request to friend.

Someone with Ryan's last name.

His wife.

Funny how he had forgotten that detail.

Laura had a pretty simple morality: don't date people who file taxes with other people as a married couple. Her rule was easy to grasp. Too hard for Ryan, though.

And now she applied the same rule to Dylan: no dating people who were involved with other people.

"If I'm going to be part of a threesome, Josie, it won't be as the invisible third."

"Mmmmm, a man sandwich with Laura in the middle. And those two men..." Josie licked her lips with great exaggeration.

Laura shoved Josie before she could stop herself. "Cut it out!"

Her face burned, though, with the thought. Josie just cackled.

A threesome. Menage. She'd never done it, but she sure had thought about it. As her breath hitched with embarrassment and arousal she shifted in her seat, now painfully aware of the increased heat in her nether regions.

Regions that had seen more activity— and from more men— in three days than in two months.

"Laura and Mike and Dylan, sitting in a tree— oh!" Josie joked, skittering away so Laura couldn't punch her again.

Shaking her head, Laura buried her face in her coffee to hide her expression from her friend, who was about a hair away from figuring out that Laura would welcome the menage.

It was all more than she could even acknowledge to herself, much less admit to her friend. There were lines in friendship. This was one of them. She couldn't take back the words if she blurted them out, and right now she was just too confused and tired to deal with the fallout from admitting what her heart really desired.

Besides, there was that pesky issue of Dylan's girlfriend. Funny how that put a screeching halt to any sandwich fantasies.

At least she had Mike.

"You still have Mike, though," Josie mused. "Poor Laura. Have to settle for a guy who looks like something out of Asgard. Does he have a tongue like a god, too?"

Laura threw the empty half-n-half container at Josie, who chuckled as she walked out the door, leaving Laura to get ready for a torturous day at work, the hours before seeing Mike stretching out like years.

As she dressed, though, she remembered her drive home from their last date. For some reason she still didn't understand, she'd started crying as soon as they'd gotten in their cars. At first, she'd almost jumped out of the seat and run after him, just needing something—more.

More words? No.

More sex? Ah—no.

Just *more*.

By the time she'd arrived home she had been fine, so whatever triggered the tears seemed to have settled and found its place inside her. Could sex with someone she'd only met a couple of days ago unleash emotions *that* strong?

Was it deeper than that? Her earring got stuck as she tried to shove the post through the ancient hole, the back of the earlobe grown over. A few layers of skin had closed up the back of the lobe and she worked to center the end of the post over the spot where the lump of scar tissue was thickest. Gritting her teeth, she forced the metal rod through, the hot sting of newly-pierced tissue evolving into a throb.

Her favorite pearl earring dangled nicely. Was it worth the pain?

Sure. For the sake of wearing something that complemented her perfectly.

Maybe Mike's the same, she thought. You had to date a lot of painful jerks before you found the one who complements you perfectly.

Hot tears filled her mouth and eyes.

Aha. Now she understood.

And yet Dylan—she closed her eyes and full drops poured out of her inner tear ducts and down her nostrils. An ache in her throat spread to her chest. Ignoring his messages had been agony. Sheer, unadulterated pain in the form of restraint.

She had held fast, though she had faltered only once. The (*gorgeous, incredible, irresistible*) idiot had gone and created a completely new online dating account to circumvent her blocking him! How stalkerish and weird and creepy and—

Flattering.

Charming.

Arousing.

She had almost broken down and agreed to meet him for coffee, just to hear his side of the story—which she already knew. It was a cliché upon a cliché, right?

Holding fast, though, she had simply typed:

Please leave me alone.

And, like magic, he had.

The ache that his respect for her wishes created in her was so contradictory yet so pervasive it made her question her own sanity. Why was she so drawn to this guy? What was so special that she would override her own moral code for him?

Ah, but you didn't, her conscience reminded her.

Oh, how I want to, she retorted.

* * *

Dylan stared at the computer monitor, completely unsure and yet paradoxically deeply certain of what he was reading. *Mike and Laura?* Mike was hitting on Laura at the online dating site? What?

He scrolled through the history of the chat window and realized that the first chat took place the morning after his date with her.

Oof. His stomach twisted and his balls felt like lead. Stretching his neck and clearing his throat, he fought back a tearful rage. *Ease up, Buddy.* Last time you let your temper flare you had a $400 door to replace.

He'd been a bit confused when he woke up that morning and she had been gone. But he'd had plenty of encounters where that happened—yet he'd expected her to answer one of his phone calls or his texts. She had plenty of opportunities.

While he wasn't quite ready to stomp over to her house and hold a boom box over his head, with Peter Gabriel's *In Your Eyes* blasting from it, he was definitely in that uncomfortable zone where he expected to have a second date with her, and had been stymied by her refusal to talk to him.

Mike had *sniped* her? This wasn't a rare baseball card on eBay, for fuck's sake.

Even though it had been less than twenty-four hours since he last saw her, and he knew he shouldn't be so eager, it stung. He had an inkling about why she was blowing him off now—some inkling.

A 6'5" inkling.

According to the times on the chat window, it looked like within a few hours of leaving his bed, she was planning a date with—Mike?

Mike? Mild mannered, boring old *Mike*?

This didn't make any sense. Dylan was the one who went out and found someone for them. Dylan had found Jill, who had been their one and only.

Jill.

He sighed, his shoulders slumping, and as he leaned forward, cradling his face in his hands, a wash of nostalgia, of mourning, of *pain* came over him.

And this time he let it.

Normally, he pushed it away, manned up and did what a lot of guys do—went for a run, watched the football game, ate too many wings, pumped iron. But right now he let his feelings sink in.

Watching her die had been the most difficult thing Dylan had ever experienced. The helplessness had nearly killed him, too. Mike had just retreated into his own world. Running tens of miles, half marathons, day in and day out until his shoes wore out within weeks, until his feet blistered, until he put his body into a state of pain that let some of the agony in his heart leak out.

Dylan wasn't like that. Dylan had fought and fought, and *fought*, had argued with the doctors, had argued with Jill. Bargained with God and anyone who could help. Had tried to convince her to try all sorts of alternative therapies that he had read about on the Internet, from vitamin C to certain yoga positions to chelation—and while the doctors said none for it could hurt, none of it had helped.

Jill had gently accepted her own fate after a valiant struggle; Dylan had never accepted it. Ever. Here he was, a year and a half after her death finding someone like Laura, hoping that maybe she could help to repair some of the scars that were still fresh from Jill's fight.

And then Mike goes and turns into a snake.

Why would he do this? This wasn't Mike's style at all. He wasn't the type to poach a girl. Mike was the beta. They joked about it. Dylan was the alpha and Mike was the beta and that was the law of nature and how things worked between the two of them—between the three of them, with Jill. Jill had liked Mike's sensitive touchy-feely, new-agey nature and she'd loved Dylan's arrogance.

Oh, *that* had hurt. She had called him arrogant all the time, as if his self-confidence didn't have a bedrock foundation for his firm grounding. Here he was a firefighter, a paramedic—a former model and he was arrogant? He could wave it away most of the time, but now he just chuckled to himself, thinking about the times she had put him in his place. Frankly, he had needed that, needed her steady, sardonic wit, her—

"Oh, stop it Dylan. She's gone. Just stop it," he mumbled to himself. He looked up stared at the monitor again, and the nostalgia came to a screeching halt.

He narrowed his eyes.

It was time for the alpha to put the beta in his place.

JULIA KENT

* * *

Whistling some Lady Gaga tune that he'd caught in the car on the long drive home from the mountain, Mike was feeling pretty pleased with himself. He had just proven that he, on his own, could catch the same woman Dylan could catch.

And boy, *what* a catch Laura was. Way more than he ever expected. She was absolutely, positively nothing like Jill. And yet, he had a feeling that if the two had met, Jill would have really liked her—and probably would have given her approval.

Laura accepted the fact that he was quiet sometimes. He was able to sit in absolute silence with her, out in a field, staring at the mountain. The two of them could just coexist in peace together. You couldn't find that in many people. Very few, in fact.

Jill had been one of them. Dylan definitely wasn't, but he had other traits that made him worth being with, hard as it might be these days to remember them. As he pulled into his parking spot, his mind was filled with nothing but plans to see Laura again. A niggling irritant scratched deep within his brain, though, ruining the absolute perfection of this new beginning.

Dylan.

He had to tell Dylan at some point. It wasn't going to go well. He and Dylan had been together for so long and he knew him backwards, forwards and upside-down. Even though Mike's intentions were pure, Dylan would view this as a threat, as a challenge—as Dylan put it—an alpha-beta problem.

Mike just rolled his eyes and ignored the alpha-beta crap because he knew that on the surface he looked like a beta. They weren't wolves, though, and this wasn't a pack; they were human beings who were complex and nuanced. And he could show Dylan, and himself, that he was capable of going out on his own and finding a woman.

Okay, that wasn't quite fair. *Dylan* had found the woman. But he could go out on his own and test the waters. Make sure the woman was attracted to him on her own and not as part of some package with Dylan at the lead.

He had just done that today. Quite pleased with himself, that sense of pleasure faded, like a light switch being flipped off, the second he walked in the apartment and saw Dylan's face.

* * *

"You slept with her, didn't you?" Dylan wasn't just pissed. Betrayal was too mild a word to describe his feelings. He was itching for a fight, his fingers clenching against his hot palms.

Mike walked through the door, a cheerful smile on his face, a loose, languid quality to his joints that made Dylan want to throw him against the wall and beat the ever-loving shit out of him for taking his woman.

Their woman.

Funny, how history seemed to repeat itself. Because this is exactly what had happened with Jill almost ten years ago when they'd all first met. Mike would deny it, but the reality was that Jill had been Dylan's girlfriend and Mike had been the interloper then. So, even though Dylan knew that they had this running joke, that he was the alpha and Mike was the beta. Mike was neither—he was really just a snake.

A snake Dylan couldn't live without.

"You son of a bitch, you went and—you found Laura and you—the morning after my date with her, you contacted her and got her to go out with you!"

He couldn't help but stammer, and the sputtering made him feel small and insignificant, reduced to babbling like a lovesick teen. Fury plumed in him, hot and fast, with a taste like blood.

Mike stopped dead in his tracks and shoved his hands in his pockets, staring ahead at Dylan, eyes boring into his.

"Yep."

That enraged Dylan more than anything, because he knew at this point Mike would only give one-word answers. Like a robot, the man shut down and steeled himself, becoming an impenetrable fortress of quotidian bullshit.

"You knew how important this date was, you knew that I was checking her out for us, not just for me, you jerk!" Dylan seethed now, his anger fueled by Mike's withdrawal. "Why in the hell would you go behind my back and contact her? And a few hours after I slept with her!"

"I didn't know you slept with her!"

Dylan cocked his head, rolled his eyes, and made an *Oh please!* gesture. "Right, like any woman I wanna sleep with isn't going to sleep with me on the first date!"

Mike let out a puff of laughter. "Do you know how much you sound like a total douche? *Like any woman I wanna sleep with is gonna to turn me down,*" he mocked, his hands gesturing like Dylan's, chest puffed up and prancing around like a peacock. Animated, mocking Mike was way worse than Robot Mike.

Dylan could feel his heart rate zoom, and, he feared, his skin turn green as he morphed into something so angry he couldn't control it, a firefighter, billionaire Hulk.

And it was all aimed right at Mike.

"What you do or don't do on your dates, Dylan, is up to you." Mike replied. A cold wall, unreadable. Typical Mike.

"When you're poaching women that I find for us, it becomes my business, Mike!"

"I never asked you to go out and find women for us, Dylan!"

"You never asked me *not* to! It's been eighteen months. When are you gonna get over Jill?"

Mike pursed his lips, his nostrils flaring, the affable good guy now morphing into something that Dylan knew was under the surface.

"I think I can ask you the same question, Dyl. When are you gonna get over Jill? When are you gonna get over this idea that there's some perfect woman out there for us. There isn't. There's a good woman for you and there's a good woman for me, but the perfect woman for us? That's..." Dipping his head and hiding his face, Mike's voice faded out as if it were too impossible to voice.

"Then why did you date Laura—why did you go after her? Doesn't make any sense Mike, what you're saying, man."

Dylan's heart rate started to slowly drop. He knew where this was going and he knew that picking a fight with the man he loved was the last thing on earth that he needed right now. And yet he couldn't help himself, because, *son of a bitch*, the guy had just gone and taken away the woman that he was trying to court for both of them.

"You wanna know the truth?" Mike ran a hand through his thick blonde hair and shook his head, smiled ruefully. "The *real truth*, Dylan?"

"No shit, Mike, of course I wanna know the truth. Don't lie to me. Oh, wait a minute. Hey—you already did!"

Mike rolled his eyes again. "The truth is, I wanted to prove that whatever woman you try to find for us is independently attracted to me. I'm sick and tired of getting your sloppy seconds."

"So now Jill was sloppy seconds!"

"I did *not* say that!" Mike straightened up to his full height. Six feet, five inches. A wall of runner's muscle. The aggression was coming out, the anger was reaching the surface, and Dylan could watch it, but all he could do was respond to it, instinct taking over.

"I never said that about, Jill. But you know how that worked. I had—"

"Dylan, you can't just go out and find some woman and throw her down at my feet like a table scrap and expect us to live in threesome harmony. You have to respect the fact that I need to care about her, too. I need to make sure that she cares about me as well."

Dylan had known at the back of his mind that this was true. *Of course* it was true. *Of course* Mike should feel that whoever they shared was in love with him—in love with both of them. Dylan knew it. Dylan had known from the moment he met Jill that she was head-over-heels in love with him and the other night with Laura he had felt something awfully close to that, maybe even the same as that, but he was holding back. Grief had a way of messing with him.

Now here stood Mike, pissed as hell at him. The two of them facing off, the anger tangible, so palpable he could almost lick its bicep.

And then suddenly, both men pulled back. Mike peered at him. "You know, there's only one way to find out where this is going."

Dylan shook his head. "She won't answer my texts. She won't answer my phone calls. She won't—it's like, man, she just cut me out."

Mike frowned. "That doesn't square with the woman I met. Laura's warm, intelligent, she's eager to find someone to connect with to develop a relationship with."

As Mike continued, Dylan screwed up his face, a bit jealous that Mike got that much out of her, whereas Dylan had had more of a surface level experience. More entertainment than emotion.

"Dylan—you listening to me?"

"Yeah, sorry. My mind just wandered."

"What the hell are we supposed to do about this mess now?" Mike asked.

Dylan threw his hands up in the air and made a sputtering sound. "Hell if I know. Then again, I'm not so sure we *have* a situation if she keeps ignoring me." He reached his hand out to shake Mike's. Mike gave him a confused look but grasped his hand. "Then," said Dylan dramatically "the better man won!"

Mike screwed up his face in a grimace. "That's not how this is supposed to work."

"I know. That's not how it's supposed to work," Dylan answered, "but what am I supposed to do? She won't let me say a word to her."

"I think you should go find her."

"Find her where?"

"You know where she works, right? You even know the floor. Can't be that hard. You know her name. You know what she looks like. You may not be the brightest bulb on the string, but..."

"Hey!"

"It's not hard to find her. Go after her, Dylan. Maybe that's exactly what she's looking for."

"Why would she want me to chase her when she's cutting off all contact with me? I mean thirty-four messages is pretty..."

"You sent her thirty-four messages?" He knew it, but the reality hit him, hard, in this moment, with adrenaline making his veins feel like balloons, the steady throb of blood rushing through him like the beat at a Blue Man Group concert. "Jesus, Dylan, are you nuts?"

"What? I was impatient!"

"If I were Laura and some guy sent me thirty-four messages through an online dating site after our first date, I'd run away screaming, too! And I'm a guy."

Dylan laughed ruefully. "Good point. I just, you know..."

"How many texts did you send her?"

"Just three."

"Three?"

"Yeah, and I left a couple...a few...okay." Faltering, he confessed. "Six voicemails."

"Really? You're worried that *I'm* blowing this for us? How about you? Come on, Dylan. It's one thing to be the alpha, it's another to be the nutso!"

"Hey!" Mike was right. He'd gone overboard. "You're saying the only way to make this right is --"

"Go find her."

"Don't you think, if I would have scared you off from all the messages and texts, and phone calls, and voicemails, then won't showing up at her place of employment pretty much guarantee me a visit with the cops?"

"Well, it all depends on how you present yourself."

"What do you mean?"

"Go there with flowers and a latte, make it a double with some vanilla, and you may have a chance."

"How do you know how she likes her coffee?"

Mike grinned.

"Ahhh, geez. You spent more time with her than I did, didn't you?"

"After our date, we ended it with a nightcap. She got hers decaf but I'd imagine that during the day she drinks it straight up. Go find some coffee shop, get her a double latte with..."

"With vanilla?"

"...with vanilla. And show up with a dozen roses and see what happens next. Just don't go all Richard Gere and do the *An Officer and a Gentleman* thing."

"I am a firefighter. I'm used to carrying people up and down stairs and across places."

"Yeah, I know. You're used to carrying people."

A silence hung between them.

"You weren't gonna let me do that this time, were you?" Dylan asked Mike. They stared off at a stand off.

"Just go see her. See if you can fix this."

"But what about...us. The three of us?"

"I don't know. That's a good question."

Mike's answer pissed him off. Dylan puffed up and got closer, in Mike's personal space, his own boundaries barely drawn.

"I don't want to go see her till we've—until *you and I* have settled that."

"Fine. So what *are* we doing here?"

"Um..."

Neither man knew what to say.

Mike's eyes lit up. "I have an idea, but it's really out there."

"How out there?"

"*Way* out there! It's kind of a long shot. I...I don't know."

"Spit it out."

"You go and talk to Laura and see if you can convince her to date you again. Don't bring me up, don't talk about us. Don't talk about our...you know...relationship."

"Our *threesome*." The men spoke in unison.

"Okay," Dylan said "Fair enough."

"Just get the lines of communication open and get her to have a date with you. Not tonight. Tomorrow night."

Dylan scrunched his face up. "Why?"

Mike smiled "Because I have a plan."

* * *

The idea hit Dylan as the elevator dinged and the doors opened on the thirty-second floor of Stohlman Industries. He was holding a giant vase filled with eighteen red and pink roses sprinkled with baby's breath, carrying a double latte with vanilla as well. He could pretend to be the deliveryman—that's how he'd get access to her.

The receptionist made it easy.

"Hey there," he said, grinning madly. "I'm looking for Laura." Pretending to fumble with the card to read her name, he shot the woman his conspirator's grin.

She smiled back, leaning forward on her desk.

"Last name?"

He paused. Let his smile deepen enough for the dimples to show. Flirting with receptionists was one of his finer skills. It helped him with fire investigations. As her face changed from all business to wishful pleasure,

Dylan knew that he was about to get access to Laura in two seconds.

"Michaels."

Her eyes widened. Somewhere in her twenties, she was exactly the kind of woman people assumed was his type. Long, silky brown hair. Big eyes. Great cheekbones. A v-neck top that showed everything but her belly button. If he wanted to, he could take her out for lunch and have a nooner with her in her car. Or a spare office.

Fucking a receptionist, though, wasn't part of the plan. It also wasn't part of Dylan's heart. Dead to the idea, he only had room for Laura right now.

The receptionist perked up, tilting her head and brushing her hair forward, over her clavicle. "Oh, for Laura? What beautiful flowers. I'm Debbie."

He nodded. "Dylan."

Her eyebrows arched as she looked him up and down, appraising him like a piece of meat. Being hit on like this didn't surprise him.

Having zero internal response did.

"Sweet!" He knew she wasn't talking about the flowers.

"I need to deliver them. You know the drill." He leaned on the desk, peering into her eyes. Play it up, man, if it could get him what he wanted. "Somebody must really appreciate her." He eyed the flowers; the spread was gorgeous. The receptionist's could be, too, and from her body language it was clear he could dabble in it at his discretion. "Can you tell me where her office is?"

"You can just leave those here. She's...I don't want to disturb her right now." A look of fake sympathy washed over her face as she created a reason to wave him closer. He obliged, his nose inches from her as she whispered, "She...she actually...well, I'm kind of glad to see the flowers here because she seemed a little upset this morning and we managed to pry it out of her that she was having some man problems."

"Gotcha." He ran a hand through his thick hair, drawing attention to his face, posing just a little. One of his model poses that he knew would show off his biceps.

Debbie practically ate him with her eyes.

"I hate guys like that." Dylan shook his head. "It makes me want to be a better man. Flowers don't solve everything. You can't be a jerk and expect a few roses to fix it all."

Ding. That seemed to get her. All he had to do now was go in for the kill. "If she's had that rough a time, I think it would be better if I just brought these in and delivered them myself and that way, you know, give her a little extra perk up to a crappy day."

He wasn't making any sense at this point, but it didn't matter. He could have been reciting the Pledge of Allegiance for all Debbie the Receptionist seemed to care. She was practically drooling.

"Yeah, sure. Room 311," she said, pointing vaguely down a hallway.

"Thanks so much, hon," he answered. Following her directions, knowing that if he turned back around her eyeballs would be glued to his ass, he sought out room 311. Down a corridor, past the coffee machine, past the bathroom, and then..some tiny little interior office. Poor Laura didn't even have a window. Maybe being a financial analyst wasn't as glamorous as he'd thought.

He knocked softly.

"Just a minute," shouted the voice from the other side.

Yup, that was her. This was going to be one wild surprise. Steeling himself, he arranged the latte in one hand and the flowers in the other, trying to decide whether to smile or not. Too cheesy?

When she opened the door, her expression was not quite what he expected. He thought he would see surprise. He thought he might even see fear.

Disgust had never occurred to him.

"Dylan, what are you doing here?" She glanced around the hallway as if his mere presence were something she wanted to hide from others.

"I'm delivering roses from an admirer," he said, piling on more charm.

"Really? Aren't they better suited for your girlfriend?"

"My girlfriend? What girlfriend?" *Huh?*

Someone at the copier a couple of offices down paused and craned their neck, their ear perked, catching whatever wave of gossip they could grab from the conversation he and Laura were having right here in the hall. He took that as a cue – and an opportunity.

Nodding toward the person, he asked "Do you really want to have this conversation out here?"

Her face changed. She glanced over. "No, I don't." Ice Queen voice. If she could be any colder she'd be a glacial shelf in the Arctic. Ouch.

"Please, let me come in and let's talk, 'cause I don't have a girlfriend and I don't know what you're talking about."

She reached for the flowers, grabbed the latte with a yank, turned around and left the door open. He took that as an opportunity, stepped through and closed the door. She set the flowers on a filing cabinet and took a swig of the coffee.

The room was the most boring office he'd seen—and he was a firefighter, so he'd seen his share. At least the fluorescent lights didn't blink on and off like crazy and trigger eye tics. Everything was beige. The floor was beige. The walls were beige. Nope, change that.

Putty, he had recently learned, was the official name of the most boring shade ever. He'd learned that because he'd had to do some requisition forms for some boring filing cabinets. Replacing some pre-World War II office equipment at the firehouse.

None of that mattered. What mattered was that the dozen and a half roses that he bought were by far the only color in the room other than Laura's perfect lime-green sweater covered by a nice double-breasted suit. She leaned back against the front of her desk, her butt forming beautiful curves against the edge, her arms crossed over her now-swelling breasts. He could tell that she was aroused just by the sight of him, but could also tell that her anger ran deep.

Where on earth had this come from? he wondered. At least he had some explanation for why she'd fled his bed at three in the morning. She thought he had a girlfriend? What the hell had Mike been telling her? Wait, that didn't make any sense, 'cause Mike swore up and down he hadn't said a word about them to her.

"Why do you think I have a girlfriend?" he asked.

"When your bedroom is plastered with pictures of someone who looks like she was part of the Olympic beach volleyball team, it's kind of hard to come to any other conclusion." She gestured down at her belly and hips. "I, obviously, wasn't picked to play for that team."

"My bedroom pictures?" *Huh?* "Oh, my God!" he said, washing his face with his hand, rubbing his eye until he calmed himself down. "Jesus, Laura. That's not my girlfriend. That's Jill!"

She snorted. "Who's Jill? Your wife?"

"Jill is my...man, this is complicated."

"Yeah..." she replied, drawing out the word. "It's *always* complicated. It was complicated with the last guy I dated. Seriously—he turned out to be married, too."

"You think...oh, no, Laura, Laura, *no!*" Dylan shook his head. "Jill's *dead*. Jill's my...my...former lover." The words came out like a mouthful of packing peanuts. How could he describe Jill? She was just Jill. Giving her a label reduced her to so much less than she had been.

"Dead?"

"Yeah. She died of cancer eighteen months ago."

"And so you have pict—*oh!* Oh, oh, no, Dylan, I've made such a big mistake!" she cried. All of the anger drained out of her voice, her hushed tones triggering more hope than mourning in him.

"I didn't bring it up because it was just our first date, Laura," Dylan explained. "But no, those are pictures of Jill. We—" *watch it, Dylan* "I was with Jill for almost ten years. And, she, well...she died. She had non-Hodgkins lymphoma. And there was nothing the doctors could do after trying everything. So, that's...that's my 'girlfriend', as you put it."

He stuffed his hands in his pockets and stared at the industrial carpet for a few seconds, then looked up at her. "Is that why you've been putting me off? Is that why you've been ignoring all of my messages, my texts, my voice mail—because you got up in the middle of the night and saw some pictures of some woman and jumped to one hell of a conclusion?"

All this time, Laura had been blocking him, hiding from him—*running away from him*—and had fled straight into Mike's arms because she thought he had a wife or girlfriend? Damn it!

Leaving Jill's pictures all over his bedroom had been just part of his life; he'd never even considered taking them down.

It gave him pause now. Was he really over Jill? He knew Mike wasn't, had never even begun to heal, but Dylan assumed he was past the worst of it, and that Jill would just remain as a lingering "what if."

The three of them had started to talk about having kids the year before she was diagnosed. That potential had been shut down fast by chemotherapy and radiation and just getting through life day by day. Whatever remained of Jill inside him, though, was bigger than he had realized. If a bunch of pictures were that overwhelming and made Laura think he was a two-timer, then it was time to re-evaluate himself.

Laura's entire demeanor had changed from a defensive, angry countenance to one of apology and self-reproach.

"Dylan, I don't know what to say. I am such an idiot!" She lightly smacked her forehead. He smiled. How well he knew that feeling.

"I see where you made that leap, Laura."

He closed his eyes and inhaled, partly to figure out what to say next and partly because the room was so cold and corporate it was giving him the heeby-jeebies. "We haven't known each other for very long." He took a step toward her. She didn't move back. *Good, good.* "And I can only imagine what it was like to wake up in the middle of the night in my bedroom." *Step.* "Surrounded by pictures of Jill." *Step.* Two more steps and he'd be within range to reach out and touch her.

Gorgeous, long blonde hair pulled tightly back made her look like a cold career woman and less like the Laura he'd fallen for on their date. She seemed remote, but as her face melted into something he recognized—arousal and intrigue—his heart warmed and a little swagger grew in him. He had a chance here. As the seconds passed, the odds leaned more and more in his favor. He glanced at the door. A lock.

Good.

They would need it.

She relaxed against her desk, letting her arms drop from across her chest, and casually unbuttoned her suit jacket. Her fingers fluttered to her mouth, a gesture of contemplation as she seemed to measure what she was about to say.

"I need to say something."

Here it comes. She's going to tell me about Mike.

She pulled on her lower lip with her index finger, then touched a loose strand of hair, twirling it in her fingers, the gesture making her seem much younger and achingly vulnerable.

"Guys like you don't go after women like me," she said quietly.

"Oh, come on, Laura—that's not—"

Palms facing out, she made him stop mid-word. "Let me say my piece."

"Yes, ma'am."

Her furrowed brow made him worry he'd misstepped. "You are a former model. Women pay thousands of dollars to go out on a bachelor auction date with you."

He choked. "You know that?"

"I Googled you. There are more images of you than there are links about you, Dylan."

"Oh," he said. Anything more would seem like he was bragging. The swagger grew. *How about that? Nice.*

Looking down, she stared pointedly at her belly, her legs, and used her hands to flow down her body. "What does a guy who looks like *you* want with a woman who looks like *me*?"

"I—"

"That night with you was unreal. Un-fucking-real. A little too unreal, you know? When I woke up and saw all those pictures of this surf-n-ski bunny all over you—"

"Jill wasn't—"

"I'm sure she was more than that. Really."

She cocked her head and seemed to have a sudden flash of insight, but whatever it was she kept it to herself. This conversation most definitely was not going where he'd thought it would, but it was fine. Laura was sharing. Her willingness to be this open, this real, reminded him of Jill. How lucky was he? And why hadn't other men seen the goodness in her?

They—not Laura—were the true idiots.

"Laura—"

"So I ran." Tears filled her eyes. "It was too good to be true. In my mind, you were just another asshole, like Ryan."

"Who's Ryan?"

"The last guy I dated before we met. He turned out to be married."

"Ouch."

"See why I ran? Why I blocked you? I—we're so different, and I assumed you just wanted a one-night stand. So I gave you one."

Now, Dylan. *Now*. Two more steps and he was there. A hand was all he needed. A hand was all she could handle right now. The soft whisper of his skin against the tightly-woven wool of her jacket's arm sounded like a Greek chorus of chiding. It was good enough, though.

She glanced at his hand but didn't shake him off, didn't step away. Instead, she sighed, a tiny smile on her lips.

"Laura, it's not like that."

"And when you pursued me! Wouldn't stop messaging me and texting me and calling and—Jesus, Dylan, you are persistent!" Her throaty laughter made him harden, his entire body seizing, breath hitching. If he wasn't careful he'd groan, and the sound might scare her off. Oh, how he ached for her.

Easy, boy. Don't overplay this.

Using every ounce of restraint he possessed, he leaned in toward her, his hand now stroking her forearm. "You're worth pursuing."

Indecision flickered in her eyes. Or was it disbelief? Had it really only been a handful of days since their date? And in the meantime, she'd started dating Mike, had *slept with* Mike, and now here he was chasing after her. She wouldn't say a word about Mike; he knew that. And she didn't have to, because what was Dylan to her right now?

Some guy she'd ditched in his bed because she thought he was screwing with her (literally and figuratively) and she had left to protect whatever vestige of integrity and self-respect she had deep inside.

Walking out of his apartment in the middle of the night was an act of courage for Laura; he could see that now. It was her way of stepping back from the last bastard who had dallied with her.

Dating Mike was an even bigger step, and he felt a rush of mixed emotions overpower him, filling his mind and veins and heart. That she liked Mike gave him tremendous hope. That she was willing to talk to him right now gave him more.

Getting her to accept them both and their unconventional relationship would take something greater, though. Something bold. Something that could cut to her core and transmit a very clear, very safe message that she was amazing and adorable and lovely and—everything they wanted.

Never one to back down from a challenge, and often the guy who took stupid risks, he felt one well up within him right now. Without thinking, he stepped back and put his hands on his hips. "I'm really angry right now."

She blinked, her face shifting to confusion. "What?" Then the wall came down hard. "At *me?*"

"No. At all the assholes over the years who have mindfucked you and convinced you that you're somehow less than amazing."

* * *

Breathe, Laura. Breathe.

When Dylan had walked into her office with a batch of flowers she had nearly died on the spot. Died *dead*. The last person she ever expected to grace the halls of the thirty-second floor at the Stohlman Industries building, Dylan had sauntered in like he owned the place. That was him, though—he walked with such confidence, a natural fluidity and power that said *I'm here.*

He really was here right now.

Here. In front of her.

Oh, God. *Mike.*

How could she want both Dylan *and* Mike? In her dreams she wanted them both, all right—at the same time. Threesome fantasies had become all-pervasive, filling her mind during quarterly accounting meetings, code reviews, train rides and coffee runs and hell—even when she clipped her nails. She couldn't get these two out of her mind and had found herself not only enjoying Mike more and more, but pining away for Dylan.

Who she had written off as a two-timing douche.

Boy, had she been wrong. Egg on her face and all that. A dead girlfriend? Could she have made a worse call? The light pressure from his hand on her arm felt like a branding burn, his heat so strong it emanated, rays of warmth and fire pouring through the cloth and onto her eager skin. How could his touch—a simple gesture of compassion—fuel so much arousal and deep yearning within her?

Mike.

And what about Mike? They weren't exclusive, so she didn't have to feel guilty about these reactions to Dylan, yet she did feel tremendously conflicted, because it was *Mike*. Nice, amazing, contemplative, easygoing Mike. Sex with him had been mindblowing, too. She couldn't compare.

Why on earth was she thinking any of this as Dylan's eyes undressed her right here, in this drab office, her body moistening and pooling into a puddle of hormones and cravings under his soulful eye? That familiar tingle between her legs made her nearly groan aloud, for she knew what it meant.

Torment.

She wanted Dylan. Now. On her desk and in her. As she glanced down she saw her sweater, pooched a bit at her belly, right where the waistband of her skirt rested. Did he mean it? She wasn't Jill. Would never be Jill. Couldn't be the chick with legs like a beach volleyball addict. Oh, sure, she could surf. And ski. And maybe run with an inhaler and an ambulance driving two miles an hour behind her. Give her an Olympic bar and some squat racks and she'd do fine with the guys, lifting in the weight room, but they'd outlift her easily.

Call it whatever you wanted—fluffy, zaftig, fat, big and beautiful, plus-sized, curvy, big girl—this was her, and she wasn't changing. Could Dylan (*and Mike! Don't forget Mike!*) really want her? The fat girl?

His eyes changed, softening with a dark intensity, his lips parting slightly, his body moving closer. Unmistakable body language. Yeah. He really was into her.

Right now she wanted him *in* her.

Mike?

Choice A: tell Dylan that she was seeing someone else and ask him to give her a call so they could get together sometime later.

Choice B: fulfill yet another fantasy and have Dylan take her right here, right now, on her desk and behind a cheap lock on her office door, as she bit her hand to keep the sounds of ecstasy quiet enough to avoid drawing sidelong glances and nudges among the gossipers.

"Choice A," she muttered. *Be a good girl. Do the right thing. Don't be that woman.*

"Hmmm?" he asked, the sound hoarse and airy, like he was struggling for control.

Just like her.

His eyes—oh, those eyes, so pure and focused and wanting her. His words were a balm that healed so many wounds, softened myriad scars, made hope spring eternal in her heaving bosoms which, right now, strained against her all-too-silky bra fabric and made her tense and frenzied, her clit hot for Dylan.

That hand on her arm slid up to her shoulder and she reached out, too, the fat girl with the firefighter/model, the swaggering man of muscle and bravado who swept her off her feet and gave her a taste of fun and confidence.

His palm cupped her cheek, slid to loosen her hair, the thick waves pouring down her back and shoulders as he immersed both hands in the strands and brought his lips to hers.

Choice B, after all, it seemed.

Don't be that woman?

Might as well tell herself not to breathe.

The press of his soft lips on hers made her inhale so deeply her breasts compressed against the silk of her bra, the sensation of puckered nipples and taut rib cage band so constricting she felt faint for a second, the room spinning as his tongue found hers, his hands sliding down her back, then to her waist. With a sudden push inward and up he lifted her off the ground and onto the desk, the force of his strength unnerving yet making her grin. He could *lift* her?

He could lift her. With catlike reflexes he slid her jacket off her body and snaked her skirt up, over her thighs, one hand kneading the flesh of her hip like a hungry man grabbing for food.

"Oh, how I've missed you," he whispered in her ear, his breath hot then cold as the spaces between words stood out in stark relief, the air filling the void of his sweet confession.

"I'm so sorry," she answered, her voice thick with apology.

"No." He pulled back and kissed her forehead, then her nose, and stared at her. "I am sorry. Sorry that it took this much determination to reach you. Sorry that so many men before me hurt you enough to make your walls necessary."

Mike. *Don't think about Mike.*

Gulp. "You're different, though—"

"You couldn't know that. I had to show you. Let me show you more, Laura."

The brush of her hair against her neck, the rasp of his stubble against her cheek as he kissed her, the scent of him, a smoky musk with a hint of citrus—she was his.

As he gently leaned her back on the desk, his muscled body over hers, she availed herself of his skin, palms sliding under his tucked-in shirt, the glorious heat of Dylan finally tangible, touchable, tastable.

Taste him. As he hovered over her, she reached up and found the softest spot on his neck, the skin fragile and tender, begging for her tongue. As the tip slid over the nape of his neck, she felt him swallow, his Adam's apple moving slightly, air rushing through his windpipe in a gasp. He was salty and human, the little buds on her tongue feeling the hair follicles, half a day's growth peeking out.

She breathed in his essence and then her legs parted, widening to accommodate his hips as a flash of his groin pressed against hers, his hard rod pushing against his pants.

She knew exactly how he felt right now. Reaching for his waist, she unbuckled his belt, unbuttoned the row of buttons on his fly (*vintage Levi's? How quaint*) and slid his pants over those thick, hard hips, her palms cupping the curves of honed *man* as sinew and tendons, tight from working out and just plain old *work*, gave her a relief map of his body to touch and explore at her leisure.

Except right now, there was *nothing* leisurely about her touch. Molecules in motion increased the frequency of movement until her every pore buzzed, all expanses of skin at the ready, the brush of Dylan against her so exquisite she nearly screamed. His mouth teased and played with her lips and tongue as her hands took him in, his boxer briefs more than she wanted between them, yet just enough to keep him enmeshed and unleashed.

The vibration of his moan on her mouth unhinged her, his hands under her sweater, fingers memorizing her ribs, her waist. Laura's hands made quick work of stripping him nude, the inequity of their states of dress an added thrill. In seconds she could right herself, skirt down, sweater pulled straight and neat, panty status hidden by her clothing.

A naked firefighter, though, would be hard to hide if the mail clerk or the receptionist wandered in.

She chuckled at the thought and he pulled back, questions in his eyes. "The door," she whispered and he cocked one eyebrow.

"You want me," he hissed, biting just hard enough on her earlobe to make her hips rise off the desk, "to lock it?"

"I want you to fuck me," she growled, reaching for his tense rod.

"That's a given, my dear," he whispered. "But first things first."

As he slid off her, she actually whimpered, reluctantly letting go of his hot flesh, the sound so ludicrous she began to pant, sitting up as he walked away. Ah, but the view was worth the added seconds of wait. Dylan glided across the room, his body so full and real she reveled in the pleasure of watching him move, the need to have him in her still urgent yet paused, her appreciation for the perfection of his form like an artist's eye for beauty.

Yet he wasn't perfect. Scattered scars spoke to a childhood and adolescence of outdoor exploration, and she gasped when he turned and she saw an enormous, jagged line running down his back.

"What's that?" she asked as he quietly locked the door. "On your back." The scar was an angry, foot-long keloid welt that seemed so incongruously positioned compared to the rest of him. It stretched a good three or four inches wide, like something had taken a bite out of him. No hair grew on it and the skin seemed alien, a pale white that stood out from the rest of his olive tone, as if it were abandoned by the rest of his body.

"A support beam fell on me during a fire," he answered, leaning over her in seconds, fingers lacing through hers as he eased her back down from her now-seated position. "We can talk about that later. Right now I have a different fire to attend to."

One hand released her palm and slid between her legs, the touch maddening as his fingers reached her curls, then one slid to find her sweet clitoris, the touch making her rasp his name.

"Oh, Dylan." His hardness was there in seconds, her wet, ready pussy practically drawing him in. Her cheeks were flushed and she had a moment of unreality as she imaged the scene from above, Laura and naked Dylan going at it on her desk, next to the state of Wisconsin's quarterly reports, the thrum of her desktop computer the only soundtrack to cover their groans and gasps.

She was never more grateful to have been promoted out of the cubicle farm than right here. Right now. Right—

He entered her, slick and right and full and his hands roamed her breasts, mouth imprisoning her, hair splaying out across the desk calendar, covering half of July, her body tensed and relaxed at once, full of nothing but Dylan. Her body completely fixated on his touch, his taste, his fingers on her clit and in her hair, his lips devouring her, biceps tight as her hands explored his body, the dusting of dark hair that seemed to cover so much of him a braille of consummation.

Of reunion.

His thrusts were gentle but thorough, his ass gorgeous to touch, her palms making love to the twin cheeks, with dimples she could feel. Both knew they needed to be quick; Laura sensed it in his careful attention to her clit, how he knew exactly which skin to touch and when, bringing her higher, to a new level of unfolding and opening, waves of orgasm lining up at the ready as he called them forth.

A thin sheen of sweat covered his chest as he pulled back, eyes intent and staring at her, a brief flicker of self-consciousness making her smile shyly as he drove himself deeper into her.

She almost broke the moment with a nervous word but stopped herself. And then—oh, then—her back arched and his fingers and self were lifting, lifting her as all heat and fire and warmth and wetness zoomed between her legs, into her chest, her heart expanding and blossoming, his voice in her ear whispering, "Yes, come, come Laura, I'm—"

Biting her hand was her only recourse as she twitched and jerked, the sheer force of her orgasm so strong that her body tried to escape it, couldn't run away, had to stay and let the pleasure envelop her, nerve endings straining to grow enough to accept all

Dylan gave her now, his legs working for balance and purpose and then—

"Laura, oh, Laura," he moaned, but she was too caught up in the layered power of her own body's response to reply. Her walls clenched around him, abs tightening in places so deep within her she didn't know she had, Dylan's own climax feeding off hers as her excitement increased, knowing he wanted her, that his body was in hers, that she did this to him.

Her.

Every nerve ending exploded as her hands balled into fists. Her fingers opened and she clawed at his shoulder as he worked to keep his thrusts even, their hips bucking and her ass slamming the desktop, face contorted and primal, her diaphragm nearly spasming, too, as she tried to stay silent, her orgasm cresting and then slowly, too slowly, fading out as Dylan, too, milked his own release.

As reality seeped back into her mind she took in the scene.

Naked, sculpted man slumped over her spread-eagled body on her desk? *Check.*

Spot on beige carpet where their juices leaked onto the floor? *Check.*

Hair balled into a rat's nest at the back of her head from the friction of fucking on a veneer desk? *Check.*

Aroma of sweat and sex in an office that normally smelled like cleanser and coffee? *Check.*

Mike. His name popped into her head as she kissed Dylan's sweet cheek, his breath still rushed as his own orgasm faded, his head resting against her neck.

Guilt? *Check.*

Her Two Billionaires

* * *

As she boarded the train for home, her skin still plastered with the scent of Dylan, she marveled at what had just happened a few hours ago. Laura's mind raced with the implications of what she had just done. Breaking her hard and fast rule about having sex at work had been one thing. He wasn't a coworker, so that didn't really count, right?

Sleeping with Dylan again was exhilarating. Astounding. Fiery. All the good parts she remembered with a hefty dose of danger, making the office sex some of the best she'd ever had.

Even better, though, had been Dylan. The revelation that those pictures had been of a girlfriend, all right—but a dead girlfriend, one he mourned for nearly two years after the fact—had been glorious. There was no hidden wife, no girlfriend lurking in the shadows stealing part of his heart.

The ride home helped her to downshift. She needed to think this through without Josie wisecracking in her ear and without that inner, doubting voice. Sitting on the half-empty train gave her space to think. All the other women her age were reading on their phones, texting, or deep into an eReader device. Hmmm. She needed to get one of those for the ride.

Maybe if she buried herself in a good book she could escape from the clusterfuck she'd created in her real life. Reading about other peoples' foibles and mistakes was so much easier than living through her own.

Leaning her head back against the glass, she sighed, the train's rumble sending her head bobbing forward slightly. Mike. Dylan. Mike. Dylan. Mike. Dylan. The rhythm of the car moving forward on the metal tracks turned the two words into a mantra.

Why couldn't she have both?

Both, both, both, both.

Now that word looped through her mind to the beat of the train's motion. *Both, both, both, both.*

Beep!

Her phone told her she had a text. Reaching into her purse, she pulled it out. Battery was low, too. Making a mental note to charge it when she got home, she checked.

Mike. His text confirmed their date. He was taking her up to his cabin tomorrow night.

You like pasta? he asked.

Who doesn't? she replied.

LOL he texted back. *Can't wait to see you tomorrow.*

You too, she replied.

And then she immediately texted Josie, because right now? She needed her friend, some ice cream, and a lot of talk.

Sorry. Can't make it until morning.

Laura gawked at the screen. What? She needed Josie right now! Why couldn't the woman be free at the time Laura craved a good bitch and moan session?

Why can't you come over? I've got cherry chocolate chip ice cream, Laura texted.

Work. Extra shift. Money. Sorry. Tomorrow morning? Josie answered.

Damn. The train skittered to a stop, then *fwap!* Laura was flung to the side. Too busy texting, she forgot to grab one of the stabilizer bars, and she nearly landed ass over tea kettle on the floor. A quick scramble out the wheezing doors and she was on her way home.

Fine. No ice cream for you, Laura texted as she walked home, her heels clicking on the pavement. A balmy night, one that should be enjoyed outside, drinking margaritas at an outdoor table.

Instead, it was her, Netflix, and Mssrs. Ben and Jerry. Josie could suck it. OK, Josie could come over for coffee in the morning.

By the time she got home, stripped down into her jammies, and grabbed dinner (*the pint had plenty of protein, right? And cherries counted as a fruit...*), she found she was too tired to make it through the monologue on *The Daily Show*. Throwing the other half of the ice cream in the freezer, she padded into the bedroom, plopping on top of the covers. The clock read seven p.m. A nap?

Sore legs pulled up against her belly as she curled into a ball. A nap.

* * *

"Slow down, slow down!" Josie held up her hands, displaying her nails of the week: little tiny campaign posters, alternating on her fingers, five for each Presidential candidate. It looked like a sea of red, white and blue had been vomited up onto her nail beds. What Laura had thought would be a nap turned into more than eleven hours of sleep. She felt like Rip Van Winkle, and this time, Josie made the coffee. Laura must have looked *that* zombified, because Josie *never* made the coffee.

Yet another morning talk with Josie. If she wanted to enjoy breakfast with someone, she wished it could be Dylan or Mike.

Or Dylan *and* Mike.

"So you're telling me Dylan brought you flowers, it turns out the girlfriend in the pictures is dead, and you fucked him. On your desk. At work. In the Beige Room of Pain."

"No, see it wasn't really like that—what? Beige room of what?"

Josie held up one finger. "Uh, uh, uh! I'm just establishing the facts here. Your office is where color goes to die. That's a fact. We'll get to the moral and ethical judgments next. But first: did Dylan, in fact, pose as a flower delivery man to sneak into your building at work yesterday?"

"Yes." Laura poured herself a cup of coffee and sat down. She was going to be late again.

"And did he then come into your office, and you told him that you knew he had a girlfriend or a wife?"

"Yes."

"And he then informed you that the girlfriend was dead, has been dead for almost two years, and then you — fucked him on your desk?"

"Yes."

"Okay, the facts are established."

"Good. So I—"

"Now: *Are you out of your fucking mind?*" Josie grabbed Laura's coffee mug and took a swig, arching one eyebrow and looking more like Stephen Colbert than she had any right to.

"What are you, a lawyer all of a sudden? You're a nurse. You work in an old folks home!"

"I don't work in an old folks home," Josie sighed. "I do clinical research on geriatric patients."

"Same difference."

"No, it's *not* the same difference. Do you design Tylenol bottles for children?"

"What? No, I work in IT for a children's health insurance program!"

"See? Related—but not the same!"

Josie finished Laura's coffee and slammed the mug down, but was considerate enough to get up, pour more, and slide it across the table to her.

"Oh, shut up. That's not what this is about. Why the hell are you grilling me? It's an interrogation, like I'm being cross-examined or something."

"Because—you're—behaving—like—someone—who—has—lost—her—mind!"

"Why—are—you—talking—like—I—am—a—toddler?"

Josie snorted. "I don't know."

Laura squinted at Josie. Stared her down. "You're just jealous because I've had more sex than you."

"Well, *duh!* You slept with Dylan, and then a day later you slept with Mike."

"No, a couple days later."

"And then, like, *a couple days later*, you slept with Dylan again." Josie held up her hands and wiggled them, pursing her mouth in a silent "O." "A couple days makes all the difference when you're fucking two guys at once."

"Not both at once," Laura jumped in. Her face burned. *If only...*

"So, Mike's next on your dance card..."

Laura sighed, "Can we just not do this right now, Josie? I'm confused and tired, and..."

"And you're probably kinda sore, huh?"

Laura grabbed a pot holder and threw it at Josie's head.

"Hey, you almost cracked one of my nails!" Josie made a great show of examining each talon.

"It will match your cracked head. What kind of friend are you right now? You're supposed to be *supportive*!"

"I *am* being supportive. I support you getting your head out of your ass! What are you doing, Laura, sleeping with these two, on and off, on and off?"

Laura didn't have an answer. It was easier to just argue. "Because I—really like them. Both."

Josie plopped down on the couch next to her. "Well, damn, girl, give your poor hoo-ha a little break here and there. It's not the Energizer Bunny!"

"*Jea-lous*," Laura mocked.

"How much did Stohlman Industries pay you during the time that you were being serviced by the fake flower delivery dude?"

Laura laughed. "I don't know. It didn't last as long as you think it lasted."

"Oh, I'm sure it didn't. Quickies at work never do."

Laura punched Josie's shoulder. "How would you know?"

"Have you ever seen the on call room at a hospital? There are brothels in Bangkok that get less action." Josie grabbed a clementine from the bowl of fruit on the table and pierced the sweet, loose skin with one of the same nails she'd nearly cracked when the limp pot holder had whacked her head. Laura opened her mouth to make a sarcastic comeback but couldn't.

Both.

If only there were a way she could have both.

"Too bad you can't have both." Josie elbowed her in the ribs.

Laura slid sideways, giving Josie an evil look. Had she read her mind? Had Laura said something she was thinking aloud? Was Josie baiting her to see if she could get a rise?

"Both?" Laura laughed lightly.

Shrug. "A girl can dream, right?"

A vision of her fantasies in the shower hit Laura, surreal and stifling and shaming.

"Some dreams are just a little too farfetched, Josie."

Plunking the peel in the trash can, Josie spoke through a mouthful of juice wedges. "No such thing."

"What?"

She swallowed, her voice clearer now. "No such thing. That's why they call them *dreams*. If they weren't supposed to be farfetched, we'd call them *plans*."

* * *

"When I said I had a plan, having you go to Laura's office and fuck her on her desk was most decidedly not part of the plan. Not.Part.Of.The.Plan."

Mike stretched his neck, turning it so hard that something popped. Twice. It felt good—he needed to release something other than his foot up Dylan's ass.

"Yeah. I always said I'm a 'pantser.'" At least Dylan had the decency to seem sheepish. Cocky and sheepish. How the hell did he pull that off?

"How about you try working on being a 'keep it in your pantser'?"

Dylan bit his lips and did an "Aw, shucks" gesture, staring at his toes and kicking the floor lightly. *Good try, buddy. Like you're Opie or something.*

"I'm sorry, Mike. It really wasn't planned."

"I know." He softened a bit, knowing Dylan was telling the truth. He never lied; that was one part of their relationship that made sense.

Shoulders relaxing, Dylan perked up. "The good news is that she likes me again!"

"The bad news is that she still has no idea what we really want from her."

"And the billionaire thing."

"Yep." They sat in a stony silence, the weight of too many unresolved issues smothering them. Mike felt a sudden sadness, a depression out of nowhere. Dylan got Laura today, and he was genuinely glad, if conflicted.

Dylan bit his lips.

"Whatever. At least you're back in her good graces now, and maybe we can find our way through this one and not scare her off." What Mike wanted to ask, and what he knew he couldn't ask, was *Had Laura said anything about him?* Because if she had, and still slept with Dylan, that meant one thing. And if she hadn't, and slept with him, that meant something else.

He wasn't sure *what* either option meant, just that it meant *something*.

Dylan was staring at him, head cocked, eyes slightly narrowed, his arms crossed over his chest, bunching up his t-shirt. "You want to know if she said anything about you, don't you?"

The guy really could read his mind. Then again, after ten years together, maybe he could sometimes. "Did she?"

"No."

The silence that hung between them meant something too. *Damn it*. Mike knew it. But knew what? All this meaning and no clarity made him confused, overwhelmed, frustrated.

Time for a run. This one might require a half marathon.

"I'm going to go do a half. Are you in?" *Might as well invite him along.*

"Thirteen miles? Are you *crazy*?" A loose thread on Dylan's t-shirt caught his attention and Dylan played with it, slowly twirling the thread tight, nice and taut, and then snapping it off. He flicked it into the trash can. Then he leaned back against the kitchen counter and stared at Mike. "You're trying to pound the pain out of yourself."

"How's that any different from what you do? You just lift yourself into oblivion."

"No, lifting is different. It builds strength. What you do just saps you."

"Running centers me, it doesn't sap me!"

Dylan thought about that for a moment. "Aw, what the hell. I'll do five with you. But that's *it*, man. You are *not* talking me into doing thirteen."

"Far be it for me to ask you to say one thing and do another."

The look on Dylan's face told Mike that the barb had hit its target. "Come on, Mike. Don't be like this."

"Be like what?" Mike stiffened, steel pouring into his body, making him tight, in control, immutable.

"Look," said Dylan, "we're not competing here. We're not enemies. We have the same goal, and the goal is to find somebody we can both love. Find somebody—"

Mike interrupted him "To replace Jill?"

Dylan let out a big breath of air. "I thought that's what we were doing," he said, shaking his head.

Mike frowned. *Where was he going with this?*

"But it's not about that any more. It's about moving on. It's not about replacing Jill. It's about—" Dylan paused, his eyebrows raised, his body relaxing. "It's about Laura. It's not about Jill, not any more."

Just when he was starting to enjoy his self-righteous anger, Dylan had to go and get all reasonable and introspective. "All right, fair enough." Mike held his hand out. "Truce?"

Dylan grabbed him and hugged him. "No need for a truce. There was never a battle."

* * *

"Oooo, what kind of pasta is that? Spinach? Basil?" Laura marveled at the spread Mike was putting out for this meal. So much food. You would think they were having dinner for more than the two of them.

"It's green." He shrugged.

"Hold on! I'm mocked when I don't know what kind of wine the red stuff is, but you get a pass on green pasta?" She mock pouted. "No fair."

Silly and playful, Laura felt giddy. The giddiness drove out the guilt. Sort of. In many ways, this date with Mike was a test. Sleep with Dylan. Sleep with Mike. Sleep with Dylan at work, sleep with Mike tonight in this amazing cabin. Then everything would be fair and balanced.

What are you, Laura? Fox News?

He stirred the pasta, steam floating up in swirls like magic potion from a cauldron, his white cotton button-down tucked nicely into tan business pants. Shirt sleeves rolled up and the top two buttons undone, Mike looked a little too business casual for her. She liked him sporty. Sweaty.

Naked.

What he was wearing now made her think of middle management. Corporate life. A flash of her beige office and her legs wrapped around Dylan's naked ass made her wince.

"You OK?" Mike peered at her, concerned. "Something wrong?"

Shake it off. "No, just—no."

He bent over the stove, his frame so tall he had to crouch to fit under the hood. It made her feel Lilliputian. No one—*ever*—made her feel diminutive, yet somehow Mike mastered it. She liked it.

Liked his cabin, too. How in the hell did a ski instructor afford this? Four bedrooms, each with its own bathroom, a deck bigger than the house she'd grown up in, and a sliding door at the lower level where you could just ski right up, unbuckle your boots and snap off the skis, and come right in. Decorated in knotty pine and colors that screamed "Ski lodge!", the place was amazing.

All this and an apartment in the city, too? He hadn't invited her there, though. Just here.

Next date?

Why had he just turned the burner off? Laura took a big swig from her glass of Pinot Grigio (*she was learning*) and Mike grabbed the bottle, filling it instantly.

His grin was saucy, a wolfish look on his face. "Like the wine?"

Gulp. Three big mouthfuls and she finished half the glass. Thoughts of Dylan kept invading. The brush of his fingers on her inner thighs. The rasp of his stubble against her ear. The texture of his ass as it tightened under her steady palms as he thrust into her.

Gulp. Enough wine and maybe he would quit invading her brain.

Maybe you should quit inviting him.

"Earth to Laura."

Mike. Oh, yeah. Mike. The back of his hand brushed against her cheek, fingers stroking her face, tucking loose hair behind her ear, then trailing lazily down to her collar bone, one palm cupping her breast as he bent down for a kiss.

The touch of his lips on hers made her swoon. Spinning rooms were never really her thing, but the wine hit her as his warm body crushed against hers and she went limp, his strong arms holding her in place as his tongue provided an elegant rough draft of what it was going to do in, *oh*, about five minutes.

On her clit.

She pulled back, blinked coyly, grabbed the wine bottle from the counter and filled her glass again. This time there was no pretense of gentility; she chugged it like a sorority girl at a kegger, placed the glass down on the granite counter with a click, and grinned like a fool.

"Are you really hungry for something green?" The flooding warmth that covered her was equal parts wine and arousal for what she knew was coming.

Her.

"I'm more in the mood for a pale blond." His fingers brushed her loose, blonde curls away from her neck. She shivered, his touch like an unwinding sigh. Kisses delivered to her neck, her earlobe, then her mouth made her throat tighten, her legs loosen, and the rest of her melt.

"Or," he added, one hand traveling up from her hip to her breast, "I'm pretty sure I'd prefer something pink."

They had both dressed more casually, the intent of the evening clear. When Mike had shyly suggested she bring an overnight bag, he didn't need hand puppets, markers and a white board to explain what he expected from the date. Muscular and wiry at the same time, he managed to look like a gentle giant and a lanky teen all at once.

Right now, though, he was all *man*. Confident, sensual—and very much in command. She hoped he liked what she had worn, simple J.Jill casual clothes, with a flowing mauve skirt and top that hid her bigger parts but accentuated her face. She didn't need to hide anything with Mike (and that was the beauty of him), but she also felt unready to run around in crummy workout clothes or flannel jammies. Not yet.

Someday, though. Just not right now, as his hand burned a hot path on her skin, clit at the ready as if at attention and waiting for its next order. His warm sigh and low growl made her woozy. Or maybe that was the wine. At this point, it didn't really matter.

"Hot pink?" she gasped as his hand traveled under her skirt, flirting with her panties, one finger slipping under and—*oh!*

"Very hot," he murmured, his lips against the corner of her mouth, her thighs quivering as one hand discovered exactly how wet she was for him, the other wrapped around her back, pinning her to him. She raised the stakes, too, by sliding her hand along his inseam, finding him hard and ready for her. Dinner? What dinner. The pasta could be purple with blue polka dots for all she cared.

He pulled back, hand slipping reluctantly from her thong, his face dark and playful all at once, with a mischievous look he pulled his hand to his lips and licked the fingertip, eyes locked on hers. Then Mike cocked his head, held his hand out for her to grasp, and nodded toward his bedroom.

"Shall we?"

I thought you'd never ask.

"We shall," she declared, clearing her throat as he twisted and pulled her gently through the doorway, the room obviously decorated by a guy, with thick leather, unfinished wood beams, and a stark, unlived-in look dominating. *How long has he had this place?* she wondered. It was like he'd just moved in. Too sterile.

A cream comforter with imprints of brown and green bears covered the bed, like something from a B&B that catered to ski people. The backs of her legs grazed it; soft and well worn. Mike reached out for her and, with a neutral, open expression on his face, slid his palms up her sweater, untying the sash where the wraparound stayed together, gently nudging it off her shoulders where it pooled on the floor.

His hands were so warm, his face open and inviting, intent on his actions as if making love in a meditative state. Laura knew that no matter what, one hundred percent of Mike's attention was on her; he was so present it almost hurt, an awareness too deep and painful at times.

Right now, though, she reveled in it, like finding the perfect patch of sunshine after a storm.

His hands moved under her t-shirt and slid up. She pulled her arms into position to take it off easily, his sigh the only reward she needed. Eventually, they would find their way into the bed. This dance of unveiling was worth the linger.

Reaching for his buttons, she imitated his actions, his skin softer than she remembered, the flesh tight and muscles hard beneath. As his arms folded and peeled off his shirt, she watched a concert of twitches and stretches play out before her, like an artist's rendering of male perfection—but real. His tan skin and long torso were achingly hot, looking up into his face as he bent down to kiss her.

Nimble fingers unbuttoned his pants and unzipped him, his sharp inhale seeming to fuel the depth of his kiss, tongue pushing harder against hers and hands pressing her jaw as he tried to get a grip on what seemed like an overpowering urge. Nearly frantic, his hands made quick work of undressing her the rest of the way, leaving Laura completely naked within half a minute, Mike following after.

So much for the linger.

The room was so warm that when he pulled her onto the bed, reclining in each others' arms, she didn't need the covers for comfort—but would have preferred them for modesty.

You don't need to hide, a voice said. It was Mike's. In her head, though—he couldn't have spoken, actually, because right now he was kissing her belly, his route revealing his intentions as he aimed for her womanhood.

A little sigh escaped from her mouth, over her teeth and through her lips like a prayer as his hands roamed up her hips, palms and fingers splayed to take in her skin. She loved how he appreciated her body. Not tolerated—appreciated. Enjoyed.

Owned.

Her own hands were eager for more of him on them, fingers brushing against his neck, palms taking in his shoulders as—

Creak.

The bedroom door opened slightly, then a footstep. She froze. Was someone else here? Mike seemed to hold his breath suddenly, though his hands continued to caress her.

To her complete mortification, Dylan walked into her line of sight.

Dylan?

She squinted, as if her eyes deceived her. Nude, in Mike's arms —or, rather, with her legs in Mike's face—Laura could have named five other people she'd expect to see walk through that door before she'd have anticipated *Dylan*.

"What are *you* doing here?" Laura felt exposed.

He just stared at them, Mike nuzzling her belly and pointedly not looking up. *Caught*. She was caught. She hadn't been exclusive with either guy, so she shouldn't feel guilty, but she did.

And what the hell was *Dylan*, of all people, doing here right now?

He gestured toward the door. "Uh, your front door was open, and I came here to say hi, and when I saw it ajar I was worried about you and came in to make sure you were OK." He shot Mike a dark look. "I see you're more than OK."

Laura choked, not sure what to say, naked on the bed with Mike going down on her, like something out of a bad soap opera. A bad, *kinky* soap opera.

"I don't know what to say." Her face burned red with embarrassment.

And more. It was like her dreams, her shower fantasies, had come to life, as if somehow the universe had read her mind (or, at least, Dylan and Mike had) and decided to make this all come true. But it was too real, too creepy, and she found herself immobilized by the surreal.

Yet turned on beyond belief.

Finally, Dylan said, "I'm so sorry." But he didn't mean it. His face burned with desire. And if Mike could see her face right now, she feared, he'd read her lust on her face, too.

Laura knew Dylan could make her wet. Those perfect, sculpted abs. And the thatch of hair at his waist —*mmmmm*. Those thick, sinewy arms folded across his chest. Smart, gleaming eyes and a smile like molasses reminded her of his sensuality.

Clever eyes, with flecks of gold, read her like a professor studying historic documents. He felt it, too. Everything but Mike disappeared.

A shot of destiny made her want them both, for they were meant for her, as one.

Mike cleared his throat. "Want to clue me in?"

His face rested on her thigh. She almost forgot he was there. The scent of her permeated Mike's skin and there it was again, that wave of guilt, but this time tinged with...possibility?

Something crackled in the air between the three of them, a subtext she didn't understand. Laura was starting to feel like maybe these two complete strangers had planned something that she didn't see coming.

A dog barked outside. Her senses froze. That was crazy, right? Apparently, they knew each other, though. *How did they—?*

Dylan crossed the room fast. Then he stripped off his shirt. "Can we make this a triad?"

Laura's insides clenched and her body tingled. His rippled torso made her drool.

He gave Mike a conspirator's half smile. There it was—a familiarity between them. Both were the alpha type yet they seemed less interested in establishing control and more interested in—*her*?

Laura was caught between the two men. What would Mike say?

Mike cleared his throat. "It's been a while, but..."

"You've, uh, done this before?" she blurted out, the words escaping before she could push them back in.

"You haven't?" His voice carried a sweet, incredulous tone. Her breath disappeared as he traced a lazy circle at the hollow of her throat. This was less an invitation and more a requirement.

"No, I mean—you two know each other?" *Duh, Laura.* Of course they did. "How do you...but I've been dating you both!"

"We know," they said in unison.

Their chuckles made her even wetter, if that were possible.

Mike looked up and caught her eye, one eyebrow cocked.

Cold blood flooded every cell of her body. This was a set up? Dylan and Mike not only knew that she'd been dating the other but they were an...item?

And they wanted a *threesome* with her?

Go with it, her heart said. Maybe that wasn't her heart. Something much lower on her body swelled and pulsated, eager for her showerhead fantasies to come to life with flesh.

She liked it. Laura stared impolitely at Dylan's chest, eyed him up and down, and then turned back to Mike. Staring deep into Mike's eyes, she squinted and sighed in torment.

"Is this really what you want?" *Please say yes*, she thought.

Dylan groaned. "I vote yes!" he purred. His eyes were burning for her.

"Mike?" she asked.

He licked her hip, rubbing his nose on the soft flesh where her belly and thigh met, the nuzzle somehow both playful and sensual.

"I'd say that's a yes," she moaned. A drunk feeling enveloped her, but it wasn't from the wine. Dylan's tan, muscled hands undid his jeans. Meanwhile, Mike resumed his activities. She closed her eyes. She heard Dylan's jeans hit the floor. God, how she loved his ass. Her nipples tightened.

Two more hands roamed over her skin. She shivered, a sharp inhale and a wetness making her nearly come. The tongue Mike flicked drove all thought away. She couldn't breathe now, was just a mass of nerve endings and goo.

Imagining Dylan's cock in her at the same time as Mike's made her moan and tweak her own nipple. A strong hand pushed it away.

"Oh, no, you don't," Dylan's voice cautioned. "That's my job."

She felt Mike's chuckle on her clit as he drove her crazy, soft tongue teasing her skin, bringing her so achingly close. Sliding her hand on Dylan's skin while the other buried itself in Mike's hair, Laura feared she would come this second. They were too much, together, but oh, God, how good it was.

The scent of both men mixed with hers, like the ocean at sunrise. *Man* and nothing but. She needed to taste them, and she pulled Dylan to her. Her tongue poked out and licked his arm.

"Don't waste that tongue there, babe," Dylan murmured.

And just then, Laura lost control. Mike moved up to kiss her. He was the gentle savior, always tender and sweet. Four hands, two men, and she was still ravenous.

"Oh, please, more!" she begged. One hand found her clit and she bucked against it, eager for release. Mike's mouth grazed against her ear. She shivered, making her wetter.

Dylan's other hand traveled up to her breasts, pinching as he rubbed her, keeping her orgasm at the ready, her hips bucking to find a rhythm for release.

"You have the most luscious body," Mike groaned.

Laura wanted to believe it. Years of being teased for her curves had toughened her, but now she found her true partners. All the insecurities she felt, every worry, roared into her mind, and then Dylan sidled up to her face, giving her a gentle kiss.

"Laura, I've wanted you for so long," he said. "*We* have."

The hand on her clit, their words, all sent her over the edge, her cries a prayer as she came. Dylan held her, strong arms feeling the waves as she trembled and twitched, a flood of intensity making her head explode.

She batted at Mike's hand, which still strummed her, the orgasm released, and she lay panting, with two naked, gorgeous men staring at her.

Oh, shit, she thought. *Now what?*

She was so spent already, Laura didn't know what to do next. Two hot men were in her bed. She was about to have her first threesome.

And all she could do was stare back.

"Ready for round two?" Dylan asked, as Mike took her hand and placed it on his rock-hard cock.

She slid her hand from the base to the tip as Dylan pressed her shoulder lightly, Mike moving to the side of the bed. She felt a small drop of pre-cum on Mike's rigid cock, and the fluid made it easier to stroke him, Mike's knees buckling as she groaned.

Meanwhile, Dylan climbed on top of her, his cock soon in her face, and as she took him in her lips she felt two fingers slide inside her soaking pussy. Not what she expected, so soon, and yet her body surprised her with a deep, abdominal muscle clench and a groan that made her vibrate against Dylan's thick shaft, making him groan and he pushed against her, riding her mouth.

As she deep throated him, she focused on giving Mike attention, too. What were the chances she'd found two incredible men like this, hot for her, the girl who was teased when it came to romance?

She knew they weren't lying; she could tell by how they touched her. She relaxed. It made this moment so much more precious, for they appreciated her for who she was.

Dylan stiffened and she knew he was about to come. She wanted both of them in her, though. Was she crazy? The guys weren't touching each other.

"Oh, no!" Dylan shouted, pulling out of her mouth. "No, not like this," he begged, glancing at Mike.

Mike nodded. His hand stopped on her clit, making her cry out. "Oh, Laura, this is going to be so fun," he said, sliding up her body, caressing her, as Dylan walked over to the couch.

Filled with a new sense of confidence, Laura stood and ran her hands over her breasts. "Ah, Mike, the question is: Can you both satisfy me?"

The question emboldened her and turned up the heat a notch, both men puffing out and elongating at her words, their hands and bodies larger and warmer, the air tingling with suspense.

His rough hands claimed her, the force shocking her, the crush of his lips an answer. Dylan pulled them apart gently, cocky and ready, as Mike sat down on the couch. Now Dylan kissed her, exploring and teasing, making her wet and eager for what was next.

Dylan nudged her to sit on Mike's hot, rigid cock; it was time, finally. Sliding down his pole, she straddled him as her pussy walls clenched and held on, Dylan bending her over just enough to make what came next possible.

A slick sensation hit her backside, Dylan getting her ready. His mouth was on her ass, shocking her, the sensation new and aching. Never before had she let her mind go there, the taboo so great that unless she read about rimming in a magazine or story she didn't consider it, pushing it out of her mind like so many other forbidden pleasures. It felt so good, yet seemed slightly wrong.

Right here, right now, though, it felt sooooo right. Her pussy tightened, making Mike groan, and Dylan slipped one finger past her sphincter.

"Ah!" she cried out. Mike was more than enough, but she needed Dylan, too. Dylan poured lube on her ass, then another finger slipped in, both fingers stretching her, soon replaced with the tip of his cock.

Meanwhile, Mike kissed her breasts, his hips keeping a slow rhythm, building a slow climax.

Now, *oh!* a pressured, erotic pain filled her, Dylan bracing himself behind her, the breach of her anus too much, to the point where she almost said no.

It pushed every boundary, leaving her unsure of herself, until Dylan leaned over and whispered, "Relax."

Oh, how she did. That was part of the surprise and delight. Knowing they treasured her, Laura reveled in defying convention, creating a world where Dylan's hands were a sacrament.

Both filled her completely, Mike's slick sweat against her as friction inside made her slippery and hot, all three breaths like a symphony, the sound a special music just for her.

Dylan's calloused hand took her nipple, his jaw tight and ready for more. Mike's eyes were light yet intense, loving her as she felt Dylan's hands slide over her belly, one hand finally slapping her ass, her groan all he needed to hear.

Her thighs were drenched as she rode Mike, all self-consciousness gone, and now Laura enjoyed the tactile sensation. She bit Mike's lower lip, hard, whispering, "I want you both so much."

All flesh and bone and breath.

Mike lifted his hips up, his fingers—*whose* fingers?—now circling her clit and ringing her ass. She tipped her head back, leaning on Dylan's chest, her breasts in the moonlight, body on display, and she felt possessed by herself, unleashed and ready to gush.

"I'm so close," Mike groaned, planting a sweet kiss on Laura's shoulder. Words escaped her, a sudden thunderclap inside her and she answered with a cry. Both men worked to keep up with her, and although she knew inside she should slow down, she felt something greater than guilt: need.

The thin membrane between them became the center of her soul, stretching and turning and sliding and tingling until she felt her arms and legs and fingers and toes curl into one little supernova. Shaking, Laura lost all thought, fingers gouging Mike's chest, slipping on slick sweat, hands scratching and clawing for someone to cling to as the world ended and began all at once inside her core.

Dylan came next, his hands firm and rough and flexing against her ass, his body shuddering as he came, filling her with a hot wetness, throbbing against her pulsing muscles.

She had never been so full, Dylan's cock expanding and meeting a need she never knew she craved. She was pleased with her own boldness. Spent, he leaned against her, making her want just a bit more, as if one wasn't enough.

But just then, Mike's turn came, his eyes unfocused, face tight with concentration, arms bulging as he thrust up, up, into her, making her tighten and see that she had another wave in her to catch. Cool air hit her ass as Dylan pulled away.

"Come here," she said, panting.

"I'm here," he murmured, moving next to Mike and Laura, licking a trail up her ribs, the sensation so luscious as he took one ripe nipple. Sliding her hands over Mike's shoulders, she stretched into the sucking, her hips taking in his thick rod, the simultaneous attention so erotic she felt the new orgasm snap.

She clamped on Mike at that exact moment, milking him as he thrust up and shouted, "More!"

He thrust, then halted, repeating the action, until with one final sigh he finished, leaning back against the couch, eyes closed, chest heaving with exertion.

Laura's orgasm sprang to life as if she hadn't just exploded mere minutes ago, the intensity taking her breath away.

Dylan nuzzled her ear from behind and kneaded her breasts, murmuring, "Let it all out."

He didn't need to say it.

She became someone else—no, she became *her*, the self-confident woman she remembered and the sexy beast she knew was within. From her core, her entire body clenched and heaved, a plane of climax shooting through her, bisecting her being. Dylan's fingers and hands drained every drop from her until she slumped forward, Mike's hands caressing her back, the tenderness a comfort she didn't need but welcomed anyhow.

For now, tenderness wasn't a surprise; it was a right. Her eyes raked over Dylan's glistening body as he walked to the bed, stretching on the sheets, arms over his head, muscles taut and strong. He shot Mike a conspirator's look and the two started laughing.

A cold flush took over her body.

Oh, my God.

This was all a game? Were they really tormenting her? Was she the fat girl again, the butt of some awful joke? Had they recorded this, a cruel joke to show on YouTube in a few days, making her a social media pariah?

They were *laughing*.

All her self-confidence, all her sensuality drained out of her and she buried her face in her hands, hot tears filling the back of her throat.

"Oh, no! Laura, we weren't laughing at you!" Mike picked up on her distress first, rushing to cradle her. How did he know what she was thinking? It was uncanny, but words escaped her again, the pain of what she thought they were doing so great that even if they weren't, its echo remained.

Dylan's hot hands caressed the back of her neck. "We, uh, well...." Dylan hesitated, then blurted out, "we kinda planned all this."

"Nice. When's the YouPorn video going up?" she asked, now pissed but also hoping Mike's arms weren't part of the joke, that his soothing was real.

"What? No, *no*. We planned it because we wanted a threesome with you. We were together, watching for someone like you to appear on that dating site for a long time."

Dylan's voice seemed so earnest. Here she was, naked and covered in their juices, Dylan and Mike and their luxurious flesh before her, and all she could do was cry.

"Someone like me?" Hope bloomed. Maybe she had been right all along. The two men exchanged a glance and Mike spoke first.

"Just like you. Blonde. Perky. Funny as hell. Centered. And with a smoking bod. We're tired of women who aren't real, and who don't have the ability to see beyond convention, outside of judgment, and to just follow their hearts."

"So you decided to put me to a test and see if I'd rise to the occasion?"

Laura searched frantically for her clothes, her vulnerability like a giant shark bite where her heart should be. Exposed, she felt shame pour out of her like an open vein. How could she go from the exhilaration and attachment of what the three of them had created just moments ago to this all-consuming pit of despair?

Why were they doing this? The mixed signals stymied her. A sick joke? A bet? Some kind of weird competition that ended in threesomes?

Those same comfortable, flowing clothes that she had loved wearing here tonight when all she had expected was a date with Mike were the bane of her existence as she struggled to throw them on as fast as possible, her foot getting caught in the yards of ample fabric.

"God damn it!" she shrieked, nearly falling over.

"Laura." Mike climbed out of bed, his naked form stretched out in front of her, her face inches from his crotch as she bent over to untangle herself. Under any other circumstance she would have welcomed the view, but right now his golden flesh just prolonged her agony.

Kneeling with more grace than she could ever possess in three lifetimes, he grasped her foot tenderly, peeling the stretchy cotton cloth off the toes where it had twisted. Her leg free, she could pull her skirt around her waist and shove her arms through her blouse, then fling her oversized jacket over it, all with Mike staring balefully up from the ground. Those giant blue eyes communicated so many emotions Laura just couldn't receive right now.

Her Two Billionaires

Run.

Run away. They're making fun of you, Laura.

Joke was over. She heard Dylan call out her name as she slammed the front door and marched through the dark to her car, the tears spilling over her lashes before she'd made it down the porch steps. She reached into a non-existent pocket for her keys. Keys. Thank God she'd driven here in her own car and could leave, but she couldn't get out of here if she didn't have keys.

Damn. Her purse. It was back in the—

Creak. The front door opened and Mike's long, taut arm came through it, her purse dangling from the end, the porch light making the entire production seem like some rejected scene from one of the later *Friday the Thirteenth* movies. Horror was apt; it's what she felt right now.

Gently, the arm knelt down, resting the purse on the welcome mat. Without a word, he withdrew his limb and the door creaked shut, the glow on her purse like a spotlight of failure.

Was that a message? Don't bother coming back in? Like a pilot light pluming as it is first lit, Laura felt a fireball of rage explode in her. She wanted to ram the front door.

No. The fury snuffed out fast, leaving a deadly calm inside. Mike did that because it was Mike's way—quiet, silent. Deliberate. He knew she wanted to leave and he helped. No judgments, no words, no complications.

What she needed most right now, as she sneaked up the steps and snatched her purse strap, was no complications. No thoughts, no feelings, no regrets, no *nothing*.

Laura stormed back to her car, yanked the door open, piled in and cranked the engine. To her relief, it started fine and off she went, the aroma of sex and Dylan and Mike perfuming the air. Their hands were still imprinted on her, the ache of them inside her stretching and throbbing inside, as if she hadn't quite readjusted to the lack of their stroking, their kisses, their—

Don't think about it.

After her first threesome, she was touched out. The next thing to touch her lips better be named chocolate. Or coffee. Or Xanax.

Hot tears, though, beat them all to it.

* * *

"Her purse? Of all the gestures you could have made, Mike, you put her purse out on the porch for her?"

Although he'd stayed in bed while poor Laura had wrapped herself into a knot rushing to put on her clothes, now Dylan leaped out, pacing like a caged animal. His nude form was less appealing than it normally would be as Mike struggled to make sense of the last hour.

"She needed to be able to leave in peace."

"She's going to think that was a big old 'fuck you,' Mike! Like we were telling her to get out."

"No."

"*Yes*," Dylan replied savagely. He grabbed his boxer briefs and dragged them on.

Mike heard the popping of stitches and bit back a smirk as Dylan untangled himself from having put both legs in the same hole. As Dylan figured it all out, Mike calmly put his own underwear and pants on, desperate to go for a long trail run. Where the hell was his shirt?

"Where are you going?" Dylan shouted as Mike wandered out of the room in search of his shirt.

"For a run."

Where was it? He and Laura had been by the bed, and her fingertips had—Oh. Yeah. Turning around, he walked back in to find Dylan shoving his shoes on, glaring at Mike like he'd just ripped his puppy's head off and eaten it.

"At midnight? Smelling like—uh, us? Are you trying to be bear bait?"

Behind the door he found his shirt in a wrinkled heap. His biceps ached as he stretched his arms and slid them into the sleeves. *Sore already?* He snorted.

"You think something is funny? At a time like this? Man, you're cold." Dylan bounded to his feet, fists curled, itching for a fight. Mike knew he wasn't mad at him; Dylan was frustrated and hurt, and this was what he did.

He got mad.

Mike, on the other hand, got *out*.

Out on the road, the trail, the running paths—wherever his feet took him. Coming right up to him like a peacock ready to strut, Dylan got in Mike's face, his bare chest brushing against Mike's tight-weave cotton.

"What the hell are we supposed to do now?" he hissed, arm pointing toward the front door. "She's gone. Your little plan failed."

"Quit saying 'my plan.' My plan didn't involve a threesome on the spot."

A deep itch, an urge like a tic, swelled up in him from bones to outer skin; the need to flee. To run. To race.

To get the hell out of there.

His throat started to hurt and Dylan looked like a gremlin, yapping about Laura and how it was all destroyed now and who was crazy enough to run in the woods alone in the dark and why hadn't he been there more for Dylan after Jill and then his words went into slow motion, like molasses pouring from his gaping maw, until Mike had to look away.

Acid trips were less surreal than this.

"Laura thought we were mindfucking her, Mike," Dylan growled. "That we were laughing at her, like we planned a joke and she was the punch line." He ripped his hands through his hair and made a keening noise not unlike one he had made when the doctor had come to them after Jill had coded. "And who can blame her? I pop up like I'm stopping by for tea and cookies and BAM! Her first threesome." Dylan collapsed on the bed, shaking his head and groaning, hands clamped on his temples.

"It would be a bit jarring."

Shit, Dylan was right. He couldn't run now. What next? His muscles kept tightening, spasming without conscious effort. The urge to move was too great. This was not going to end well.

Dylan sat up and shot Mike a withering look of incredulity. "Jarring? Who are you—the queen's PR person? Keep calm and carry on is one thing. Keep calm and act like a robot just makes you look like an ass, Mike."

Blink. Mike didn't know what to say. Had nothing to say. He needed to run. His lungs felt like they were collapsing in, his spine curling forward, his knees itching and nerves burning.

Run.

"And then there's the whole billionaire thing!" Maniacal laughter poured out of Dylan's mouth. Now he was just plain old scaring Mike. He plopped down next to Dylan on the bed and watched him.

A grotesquely loud gurgle vibrated from Dylan's gut. "Sorry," he muttered.

"Gotta eat." Mike shrugged. "Laura and I didn't really even get dinner going," he added guiltily. The sight of the unfinished meal made him go cold. Memories of what had transpired a few short hours ago, the promise that held everything—he had to get out of there.

"I don't really—you know, just being here bothers me." Smoothing the bedsheets, Dylan looked around the room. "I just—"

"Yeah. Me too."

"Did we fuck this one up?" Dylan's eyes begged him to say "no."

Mike couldn't. He wasn't a liar by nature, not even a social liar, and right now he didn't have an answer. Whether they could reach Laura or not, on her terms and her timeline, would be key. Trying right now, when she was raw and hurt and bewildered, wouldn't do anyone any good.

"I don't know." Dylan grabbed a shirt, some ratty Rush concert t-shirt his older brother must have bought at a concert in the late '80s, and tossed it on.

Mike wanted to say the exact right thing. Perfect words that would solve this problem. That, however, was the problem with words—he never could use them well enough to make any mess better. In fact, he always seemed to make it all worse when he opened his mouth.

Action made so much more sense.

"What time is it?" Dylan asked, looking around the room for the clock. He fingered a hole in the hem of the shirt, worrying it bigger.

"It's gotta be past two. And good grief, man, you're a billionaire. Buy a new shirt. Hell, buy the entire band. You can afford it."

"Geddy Lee's not my type."

Mike stared out the window and muttered some lyrics.

"What's next, Mike? You gonna rickroll me?"

"Over pancakes?" Mike grabbed the keys to his car, a new Jeep Grand Cherokee. Loaded. Paid cash.

Dylan's eyes lit up. "Jeddy's pancakes? They're open twenty-four hours. I could go for some chipotle maple sausage crepes."

Ugh. "Whatever happened to a simple short stack?"

"You are so vanilla."

Mike arched an eyebrow dramatically in response.

Dylan backpedaled. "OK, OK, not so vanilla. Just boring."

Mike's feet itched to run. Pancakes first. If he carb loaded, he could bang out a good half marathon later. "Jeddy's it is," he agreed.

Dylan fairly bounced out of the house. So easy to please.

"The ride's a good hour."

"Worth it!" Dylan shouted as they ran for the jeep.

If only chipotle maple sausage crepes solved everything.

* * *

"You what?" Josie's voice was as close to a shriek as Laura had ever heard, her face flushed with shock and awe. "You WHAT?"

Laura literally ducked and covered, her face so hot she imagined it would burn her fingers if she touched it. "I know. I really am a slut."

One call to Josie and her friend had come over bearing a large box of Godiva chocolates, a bag of salt 'n vinegar potato chips the size of a third grader, and new fingernails: Beetles album covers. Abbey Road was currently shoved in Laura's face, accusing and menacing.

"A slut? Hell, no! You're a goddamned queen! Holy shit, Laura! You're living every woman's dream!"

That was not what Laura expected to hear.

Not one bit.

"Huh?" She peeked up at Josie from between her fingers, like taking a glimpse of a scary horror movie.

Little Josie was buzzing like a hummingbird, face flushed, upturned nose and pursed lips making her cuter than ever. Laura had hated how Josie was "cute" while Laura was "smart." Josie was "petite" while Laura was "big boned." Josie was "pretty" while Laura had "such a pretty face."

Not that it got in the way of their friendship all these years, but the parents, the adults in their life—everything and everyone had to fit neatly into a category. A word. A phrase. And if you didn't—

You ended up in a threesome with two guys who were still mourning their dead shared girlfriend.

Maybe categories weren't so bad.

"OK, not every woman's fantasy, but uh, most of us..." Josie's voice trailed off and now, to Laura's surprise, it was her friend's turn to be embarrassed. "Two hot guys, both after you, wanting you in their bed and in their hearts—and they're not gay? Huh? So you get two guys' attention all the time. Who wouldn't want that? You fucking lucky *bitch*." Josie spat out the last word with contempt. Not the kind of contempt Laura was primed to hear, though.

This was the sound of jealousy.

"Hold on! HOLD THE FUCK ON! So *you* have wanted a threesome?" Laura leaned forward. Her turn to wag a finger in someone's face. To her surprise, it felt good. She saw the appeal.

"Sure. Ever since that one time in college."

Laura's eyebrows shot up. "You did? You had one?"

Biting her lower lip, considering her thoughts, Josie cringed. "Yeeeesssss. Once."

"AND YOU NEVER TOLD ME?"

"I was too ashamed."

Shame. Was Laura supposed to feel shame right now, after what had happened with Mike and Dylan? She didn't. And didn't think she ever would. Shame might have been front and center in her chaotic bundle of twisted emotion with the two men, but it had faded fast. That shame had been less about the pleasure they'd just shared and more about her worry that she was the butt of some cruel joke. Once she had some distance, her wise mind kicked in. What did she have to be ashamed of? She'd done nothing wrong.

Neither had Dylan and Mike. At least, not in terms of the threesome. Behind the scenes was a whole 'nother issue...

Defiance rose up, welling like a geyser, ready to explode. "I'm not ashamed."

"I never said you should be. Frankly, I'm—impressed. Stunned. Gobsmacked." Josie chuckled, sitting on the couch and folding her tiny legs under herself, looking like a kitten curled up on the sofa. "You amaze me. Laura, you have found it *all*. Are they really as hot in real life as they are in those pictures?"

That brought Laura up short, and all she could do was to slump down on the couch across from Josie and blink.

Found it all. Dylan, with his swagger and zest for life. Mike, with his quiet contemplation and steady sweetness. The two really did complement each other and when you put them together with her they made—

Everything.

"What about the fact that they ganged up on me? Hid their real relationship with each other from me? I mean, I felt so, so—caught off guard. There I was, naked and in bed with Mike, and *oh, hi!* Dylan pops in."

"Sounds like the beginning to every other letter in Penthouse Forum. "*Dear Penthouse Forum, I was minding my own business trimming my rose bushes in the buff when the mailman and the meter reader just popped in...*'"

The pillow wasn't hard enough to knock Josie down, but Laura threw it anyhow. A brick would have been better. "It's not like that."

"Then what is it like, Laura?" Josie frowned. "It was voluntary, right?"

Huh? "What do you—oh!" Laura pressed her fingertips to her lips. "Oh, no, no, no, Josie it wasn't—yes. It was completely voluntary."

Both women exhaled.

"Good." Josie chuckled. "You had me worried there when you said 'it's not like that.' What did you mean?" She played with the loose tassel on a throw pillow as Laura thought for a moment, pulling her feet under her in a mimic of Josie.

"I meant that it wasn't cheap and tawdry, like those Penthouse letters. Dylan shocked me—can you imagine one guy you're dating walking in on you having sex with someone else?"

Josie reddened. "Um. Well. Ah. Uh..."

"Is there anything you *haven't* done?" Laura screeched.

"My situation didn't exactly end like yours!" Josie shouted back. "You ever try to get dressed while crawling out a second-story window?"

Dumbstruck, Laura squinted at her friend and shook her head slowly. "Sometimes I don't think I even *know* you."

"College was a time of exploration."

"Translation: I also slept with a lot of professors."

Josie shrugged. "Can't get through organic chemistry any other way."

An ambulance flew past, the lights spreading a disconcerting disco glow throughout Laura's living room. The clock read three a.m. What kind of friend comes over in the dead of night with one call?

The kind who, apparently, fucked her way to a high GPA. Laura tucked this detail away for later. Right now, she had her own mess at hand.

"I feel like a freak, Josie." Laura wailed, rubbing her eyes. She peeked through her fingers. "Though less of a freak now that *you've* shared."

"I'm a giver."

"You're a—well, that's one word. I guess I'm a giver, too. More like a sucker." Laura straightened her shirt and cracked her neck. Aches began to emerge. Minor pains that reminded her of the contortions she had engaged in hours ago. Delicious twists and flexes. "And I mean it—I feel like a freak."

"No, you don't. You just *think* you should feel like a freak. Deep down, Laura, you don't—not really."

How could Josie be so sure?

"How do you know what I feel?"

"I know you feel like buying me a latte." She sized Laura up. "Scratch that. This is definitely more than a latte conversation. We need us some pancake breakfast at a sugar shack."

"It's July, Josie. The sugar shacks are closed."

"Okay. I'll settle for Denny's."

"Gross." Laura recoiled. She'd waited tables there for three years in college. The only superbird she wanted to see was her own middle finger flipping off her old manager whenever she was in town and drove past.

"Well, excuse me for not knowing the proper gourmet etiquette for what to eat while talking about your best friend's threesome."

"Brie and Nutella, actually," Laura intoned, faking sincerity. "Haven't you read Dan Savage's column on it?"

Ding! Laura's laptop made an all-too-familiar sound. Her Home Page was the online dating site—who could this be?

"Laura! Batman's calling. Or maybe the Green Lantern. Iron Man's taken—Gwyneth got him already." Josie grabbed her arm and dragged her to the door. "No—you can't answer it. We need to talk about the two you already got before you get any more hot guys. Leave some for the rest of us!"

Laura whiplashed her head between the front door and her laptop. "But..."

"Nope—and now you're definitely buying. Hope you have lots of cash, because I am starving. Flash Gordon can wait."

Laura ran back to the table, slammed the laptop shut, and trotted back to Josie, the streetlights outside her door blinding her as she realized she was starving.

The night air whipped against her cheeks, refreshing and cleansing, like a baptism of reality.

Walking a few blocks, she and Josie searched out a good breakfast joint.

"What time is it?" Josie asked.

Laura checked her phone. "3:12."

"Jesus," Josie muttered. "You're getting me a giant stack of pancakes, eggs, bacon, a milkshake—the works. Three in the fucking morning."

"Yer getting old, Josie. We used to just get started at three a.m."

"Getting started at three a.m. with a guy in my bed is one thing. Prowling the town for pancakes with you? I need three shots of espresso for that."

Insatiable. The rush of hunger hit Laura like something sexual, a teeming need for a brownie sundae. Breaded, fried shrimp. Mozz sticks. Apple pie.

They turned a corner and—hooray! Jeddy's was open.

Josie pointed. "Jeddy's?"

"Good old Jeddy's. Geez, haven't been here in...what?"

"Seven months," Josie said, a sour expression on her face.

"Seven mo—" Oh. Yeah. Josie had come here to drown her sorrows after her last fuckbuddy left her. For a guy.

"Let's talk over caramel toffee chocolate chip pancakes. With crushed bacon cooked in." Josie wiped an imaginary line of drool from the corner of her mouth. Or was that real?

"Only if you add in real whipped cream and homemade chocolate sauce."

"Deal."

As they approached the door, Laura's hunger pangs sounded like gongs at a Buddhist monastery, the reverberations filling every void.

Except for two.

Her Two Billionaires and a Baby

Chapter One

The waitress's giant set of balls always threw her off.

Jeddy's was one of those neighborhood holes in the wall that had probably been a breakfast joint since Laura's grandma was a kid. During the height of factory shift work it had been open twenty-four hours and, as a relic to the Industrial Age, had never stopped. Even as the fluorescent lights buzzed and blinked and the streets were empty in that surreal hour between three a.m. and four a.m. when everyone in the world is asleep and you're not, Jeddy's still had the cheap red vinyl bench seats, gummed-shut sugar containers and a few ancient men scratching their balls and chewing on a piece of something from 1983.

And then there were the waitress's balls.

Someone, years ago, had taken a cut-out cardboard life-size person, put a Jeddy's uniform on her, and attached a pair of those truck hitch plastic balls to it.

It had, uh...stuck. So the waitress with balls greeted every customer with a smile, except that the cardboard cutout was actually Julian Sands from the old '80s movie, *Warlock*.

The stuff of nightmares and cheap Netflix thrills. Everything about Jeddy's screamed old, forgotten, ratty and dated.

Except the food.

One of the owners had passed the restaurant on to a family member who had earned a degree at Le

Cordon Bleu in Boston, and this had created as schizophrenic a restaurant as ever there was, for as Josie and Laura greeted the ball-bearing waitress, which involved giving her nuts a squeeze and saying "How you doin'?" in the best Joey Tribiani imitation, the aroma of the restaurant was strictly gourmet. Better than gourmet. Cheesy roadhouse Top Chef Gordon Ramsey Fucking Awesome gourmet.

Chipotle maple sausage. Cinnamon caramel ricotta crepes. Peanut Butter Hulk Smash cake. You name it, Jeddy's had it, including honest-to-God real fried green tomatoes, but with a dill agave tarragon cream sauce for dipping instead of ketchup.

All served on chipped, ancient industrial-grade restaurant wear by an old woman named Madge who'd been working the booths since 1948. And could still walk and talk faster than Josie on three espresso shots.

"Whatcha want, Sweets?" Madge asked Laura, her breath the graveyard where old cigarettes and Chanel go to die. The woman had to be at least eighty but looked fifty—except for her mouth, where smoking lines were grooved so deeply her lips looked more like an elephant's puckered asshole than anything resembling human flesh.

"Let me see," Laura said, amazed at how quickly she downshifted into comfort here. The glare of the overhead strip lights and the cracked vinyl held together with duct tape didn't faze her. Madge's bags under her eyes, though, were mesmerizing, with caked-up foundation in the creases. Who knew undereye circles could have wrinkles in them that would hold enough makeup to cover a small community theater's needs?

China blue eyes reminded her of Mike, and when Madge started tapping her stylus on her ordering tablet, the incongruity hit her.

"You guys use a wireless ordering system?" She pointed to the smartphone-like device in Madge's hand.

"No. This is a chisel and a chunk of marble. Grog back there deciphers it all with hand puppets and grunts. Now what are you two eating? I've got work to do."

Josie craned her neck around, surveying the nearly-empty joint. "It sure is hopping."

Madge smirked. "The silverware don't roll itself."

Those eyes. Mike. A pang of despair hit her—hard. His hands on her. Dylan's tongue on her.

Josie shot Laura a skeptical look and turned to Madge. "What are your specials?"

"At four a.m. you get the fryer and the desserts. And maybe a limp salad. Jeff ain't here now to cook the good stuff."

"Do you have coconut shrimp with that aioli?" Laura perked up. Despair faded a notch.

"Yep."

"Two of those, an order of chipotle maple saus— you got that tonight?"

Madge nodded, not looking at them, hand flying with the stylus.

"With cheesy potato pancakes. One piece of Peanut Butter Hulk Smash cake and a giant peppermint hot fudge sundae," Josie declared.

"And drinks?"

"Just water," Laura replied.

"Watching yer weight, huh?" Madge snickered, walking away.

Fortunately for Laura, she'd looked at Josie when she said it. The last thing she needed right now was a comment on her weight. Eating comfort food—even at four a.m.—no, *especially* at four a.m.—was exactly what she needed.

"What about coffee?" Josie asked.

"I'm not making you any."

"Hah. I'll order some after we pig out." Each booth had an old-fashioned jukebox attached to it. "You have a quarter?" Josie begged.

Laura fished one out of a pocket. Josie slipped it in as Laura wondered how they got away with still just charging a quarter. She remembered long car trips to visit her relatives and stopping at the L&K Diners, the jukeboxes identical, a burgundy red she only saw in ancient Italian restaurants and rest stops in the Midwest.

Back then a quarter got two songs. Now, one. Josie punched some buttons, fingers more accustomed to glass phone screens than analog squares, and soon Gloria Gaynor crooned.

Laura groaned.

"*First I was IM'ed! I was petrified*," Josie sang, using her rolled silverware as a microphone. Seriously? The song was bad enough. Josie's tone-deaf performance would be worse.

"*Kept thinking there was no way these guys would want my backside...*"

What?

"Stop it," she hissed, whacking Josie's forearm. The fork slid out and shot across the room, hitting a table leg. Madge strode by without missing a beat, picked it up, and threw a clean one on the table in front of Josie, her stride completely fluid.

"*And then Thor and Superman, they came to me in the same bed, and now I'm half dead, oooooooh now I am half dead!*" Josie wriggled and thrust her neck out as if singing, her voice a cross between an eight-year-old's earnest choir attempts and something out of Killer Karaoke.

"You have the music ability of William Hung." *And the stage presence.*

"*I will ménage! I will ménage!*" As Josie parodied the familiar chorus, Laura lunged across the table and clamped her hand over Josie's mouth. That was quite enough.

"No brawling," Madge chided as she used a bissel to sweep the tattered carpet a few tables away. "Don't make me call the bouncer." She hooked her thumb over at the old homeless man sucking on a cup of coffee. He looked up and grinned, two teeth total in his mouth, eyebrows shooting up to a bald pate and creased, greasy hand waving. The girls laughed and Laura settled back down in place.

"You are such an asshole."

"But you love me."

"You're buying."

"No way."

Laura reached for the triangle game with pegs. All the writing had worn off long ago, and the wood was a solid block. This was an old stand-by that had probably been original to the place when it opened. The pegs were worn down and the colors faded, but the premise was the same: get down to one peg.

Laura played. Three pegs.

Josie played. Three pegs. "Doo doo doo doo," she teased, like music from a creepy movie. "The universe it telling you something." Laura snatched the damn game out of Josie's hands as Gloria Gaynor went into her second verse.

Just then, Madge appeared with the potato pancakes and a huge, steaming pile of coconut shrimp.

Three cruets of aioli and Laura and Josie dug in before Madge could croak out with "Anything else?"

"Mmmmmmmm," Josie groaned, her mouth nibbling on the end of a fried shrimp the size of her hand. "Uh, yeah." Brow furrowed, she caught Laura's eye. "Did we forget the fried green tomatoes?"

Before Laura could reply, Madge said, "Got it," striding off.

"We are going to be so full," Laura said, using the side of her fork to cut a pancake.

"Is that a complaint?" Josie opened her mouth and panted, trying not to burn her tongue.

"Nope. Can't you wait until it cools down?" She pointed at Josie's mouth.

"Nope." The two sat in silence, the only sound now their masticating jaws working furiously on dissembling the amazing tastes before them. It was a relief for Laura; too many hands, too many mouths on her, too many feelings that didn't have a home.

Eating was easy. Order delicious food. Have it delivered. Open mouth. Enjoy. Repeat ad nauseum.

Food was always there for her. It never changed. Hot fudge was hot fudge. Butter crunch ice cream just *was*. Coconut shrimp were steadfast and tasty, filling time, her belly, and whatever aching hole was in her that needed to be sated.

Cheesy potato pancakes didn't send out confusing signals. Cookies didn't judge her. Peanut Butter Hulk Smash cake would serve her, would be at her disposal, would meet her needs.

With no expectations.

Screw Dylan and Mike. Fuck them.

Fuck them in the eye.

At the thought, she punctuated the air with her fork, imagining poking them with it. Josie looked up from her plate, mouth stuffed now with the cooled-down shrimp.

"You conducting a symphony?"

"Fork you."

"Paradise by the Dashboard Light" wafted through the restaurant, a group of college kids snarking on the old tune and torturing poor Madge with half-drunk requests. She'd probably served their parents. Maybe even their grandparents. Laura rolled her eyes and dug in, her turn at coconut shrimp heaven.

"Ahhhh," she moaned. Josie's impatience made more sense now. Each bite was like something out of a food porn movie, like Coconutty Clit Lovers with Clam Sauce or—no, scratch that. She had just grossed herself out. Did she make that joke aloud? If not, why was Josie staring at her like that?

"Coconutty *what*?" Josie gagged, her face in a confused snarl. Laura could feel her cheeks turn a hot red as the room spun a bit, overwhelmed by what she now realized was nearly twenty-four hours of being awake, the most intense sexual experience of her life just a few hours behind her, and Madge's lined face twisted into a pantomime of smoking, her fingers against those leathered lips and sucking away at an imaginary cigarette.

Her thousand-mile stare bore through Laura, who pulled her eyes away to look down and see the last coconut shrimp on the plate. Grabbing it, she shoved the entire thing greedily into her mouth, only to hear Josie's confusion shift to a self-righteous howl.

"*Hhhheeeeyyyy!* No fair! What the hell is wrong with you?" Josie's sulking face was an after-thought for Laura, who right now felt like an animal in the woods, all instinct and no thought.

"Nothing," Laura muttered. What the hell was wrong with her? "It's just—this is soooooo good." She ate the tail and all, the breading and the crunchy outer shell making her gag.

"Coconutty...Laura, you need some sleep."

Madge turned and nearly ran into the kitchen, then emerged with a still-sizzling plate of friend green tomatoes and more cruets filled with sauce from heaven.

Palm outstretched, Laura flicked her wrist toward Josie, the gesture meant to allow her friend first dibs on the tomatoes. Appeased, Josie dug in, playing hot potato with the breaded delight.

"Hot! Hot! Hot!"

Chipotle maple sausage appeared out of nowhere, followed by an enormous piece of green cake smothered in hot fudge and peanut butter sauce, sprinkled with pistachios and surrounded by two huge scoops of vanilla ice cream coated with a crunchy brown sugar sauce.

"It's as big as your head, Laura," Josie gaped.

"It's bigger. It's the size of my ass."

Madge pointedly peered behind Laura, pulled back, and pursed her lips, contemplating. "Nah. Not quite, honey."

Laura gave her a grateful smile. Madge was Laura's new best friend. "You girls need anything else?"

"No—thanks!" Josie had a sausage on one fork, was spearing part of a potato pancake, and had a spoon attacking the ice cream. Laura dipped a piece of pancake in the aioli and stabbed her fork into the luscious pistachio cake, made green by the nuts.

"Who needs sex when you have Jeddy's?" she muttered, filling her mouth with the cake.

"Hello! Me?" Josie waved her hands like an air traffic controller on an airport runway. "Right here. I'd give all this up for what you just had tonight. Wouldn't you?"

Laura stared plaintively at the spread before her. "Uh..."

Josie stabbed the dark chocolate and mint rose off the top of the cake and ate it. "You don't have to choose. Lucky you."

Lucky. *Lucky?* Here she sat, drowning her sorrows in fudge-covered cake the color of infected snot while her body still hummed from being double stuffed (*note to self: get Oreos on the way home*) and as the sun began to make its first entrance on this glorious day, Laura had to go to work in a few hours. Then there was that pesky issue of needing to deal with the fallout from storming out of Mike's cabin, leaving the two people in the world she most wanted to forget wondering what the hell was wrong with her.

"Madge!" Laura shouted. A quick glance down showed her cleavage covered with green crumbs and an embarrassing number of hot fudge drips. It was a meal unto itself.

For Dylan...or Mike...

Stop it!

Madge didn't even blink, just tilted her head up, painted-on eyebrows lifting up. If she'd been bald she could have given Tim Curry a run for the role of Pennywise. "Whatcha want?"

"Got any caramel sauce?" That shit cures everything, like Windex or Robitussin.

"Nope. How about peanut toffee swirl?"

"You're a good woman, Madge. My new BFF."

"Hey!" Josie mumbled, her face stuffed with ice cream. "Wha' 'bout me?"

"You're my *old* BFF."

Laura heard the door behind her creak and the sound of loud voices. More college guys. Swiveling around, she took a look. Fresh, unlined faces. Wet t-shirt contest-looking tops and running shorts. Sneakers. Backwards baseball caps. Why did they all look twelve?

"Henderson Cross Country" read all the wet shirts. Ah. High school. That's why they looked twelve.

The sound Josie made caused Laura to pivot back, whiplash a distinct possibility.

"You pig! At least try not to burp," she hissed.

"In some cultures it's a compliment, you know."

"In some cultures, a woman who did that would be stoned to death."

Josie stuck out her tongue and stifled another belch. "How can I be your old BFF when that woman is like a thousand years old."

"She's young on the inside."

"She could be the cryptkeeper's mother. Grandmother. Uh—"

The door behind her creaked open again and she heard footsteps. Then a low whistle from Josie, who peered around Laura. "Hot damn!"

Madge slid a cruet of peanut butter joy at Laura, who speared a chunk of green cake and dipped it in the creamy mixture.

"Whuh?" she asked, tipping her face up to watch her friend.

Josie pitter-pattered her fingertips over her heart. "Some day my Thor will come. And this one is mine, Laura. All—" She halted, eyes growing alarmingly huge, her words ending abruptly in a strangle. Mouth dropped, Laura could see parts of Josie's meal in her tongue.

"Jesus, Josie, shut your trap."

Julia Kent

"Hey—I didn't say anything bad." Squinting, Josie cocked her head and flinched, suddenly nervous.

"No, I mean literally. Your jaw is almost on the table. Shut your mouth. I can see what you just ate. We're not in third grade."

"Right," Josie answered absentmindedly.

What the hell was wrong with her? Laura's feeling of comfort was dissipating fast as Josie's distracted body language just added to Laura's feeling of exhaustion and confusion.

As she shifted to look behind her to see what on earth Josie was staring at, her friend shouted, "No!"

"What the hell is wrong with you?"

When she turned around, though, she understood exactly what was wrong with Josie.

There stood Thor, cupping the waitress's balls, with a more muscled version of Joey Tribiani grinning madly at him and saying "How *you* doin'?"

* * *

Dylan hadn't been back at Jeddy's in more than two years. Last time he was here was with a group of guys from work, after a fire, when in the bowels of the night they'd found themselves embraced by soot, dead tired, and starving. No ramen noodles or scrambled eggs back at the station would do, so they'd come here.

His balls greeted him nicely. OK—*their* balls. Because it had been the trio who had invented the famous cardboard, be-balled icon at Jeddy's, a combination of some wicked bad peyote and Mike's college job working at Newbury Comics.

Old Madge had helped, offering up an ancient server's uniform, and the balls had been Jill's idea. Dylan's Joey Tribiani imitation stuck—a little too well, because he was known as Joey until they'd finished college.

"You two," Madge greeted them, shaking her head, lips pursed in an expression that was either pleasure or disgust. Dylan didn't think the difference mattered much at her age. Or with her temperament. How the hell do you serve drunk frat boys, homeless glue sniffers and post-coital munchie seekers for six decades and not become jaded.

Was that? Mike elbowed him. No way.

No.

Fucking.

Way.

From behind, he couldn't quite tell whether it was Laura, but he had to be dreaming. She sat at a booth, hunched over a plate, blond hair in need of a combing, the woman across from her looking like a greasy chihuahua posing as a human dancer. Teeny tiny and hyped up, eager and craning to look at something.

Him?

Them?

"Is that Laura?" Mike whispered furiously as they followed Madge, who threw two menus down on the scarred formica table and walked off unceremoniously. Dylan slid in on his side, ass catching something, impeding his fluid movement. Duct tape. He wiggled his butt to settle down the torn edge, then froze.

"What? You're crazy, man. What are the chances she'd be here?"

"Come to claim your third?" Madge's gravelly voice nearly made Dylan laugh. She sounded like a caricature of an old South Boston woman combined with Harvey Fierstein.

Mike's eyes bugged out of his head, shifting between the blond in the booth and Madge. "Our third?" His voice sounded like Peter Brady going through puberty.

"Someone grab your balls too tight tonight?" Madge rasped, clenching the plastic balls in her hand. She nodded toward the warlock waitress. "You ever gonna cart this monstrosity away?"

"Oh!" Mike groaned. "You mean him?" He pointed at the cardboard cut out.

"What other third would I be talking about?" she asked, incredulous, her hand batting the testicles and shooting Dylan a dirty look. "You two are too old to come in here drunk," she chided.

Mike sighed, his lips buzzing as the air left him and he and Dylan buried themselves in the menu. "God damn, Dylan. We need to figure all this out."

The last notes of some Meatloaf song faded out and then the all-too-familiar first chords of AC/DC's "You Shook Me All Night Long" filled the air. The blond's head began tapping out the beat and the ratty little brunette with her looked like Will Ferrell playing a cowbell.

Could that really be Laura?

Nah.

Why did the brunette keep staring at him? She huddled with the blonde, who fake-scratched her head and tried to do that sly thing where you look behind yourself without making it obvious.

"Chipotle maple sausage and a five-scoop sundae for me," Mike announced. "Fried green tomatoes, too. Double order."

"Swear to God, Mike. Look at her. It's Laura."

Just then, Madge appeared, dragging the warlock waitress with her. Julian Sands seemed to be judging their meal choices.

"The third in your threesome," Madge announced grandly. The frat boys at the other table all did a spit-take in unison, bursting into good-natured laughter.

And then the brunette froze. The blonde turned slowly, the folds of her neck reluctant to complete the motion, her arm reaching back as if through water, her body needing to know.

Yes. It was Laura.

And boy was she pissed.

* * *

"Motherfucker!" she hissed. "They're following me?"

"So that is them? Holy shit, Laura, they're more scrumptious in person than online." Josie actually licked her lips and said, "I wish they were on the menu."

Threesome? Had Madge actually said something about a threesome with them? Were they that open with everyone but her? Why on earth would a dried-up old octogenarian speak openly about their sex life like this?

"Warlock Waitress here wants you to take her home. Have your way with her. Give her the complete sex change she's entitled to," she heard Madge joke, a raspy smoker's laugh rumbling after.

"You mean make Julian into Julia?" Dylan dished back. All three laughed.

They had no right to laugh. Not when everything in Laura's mouth turned to sawdust and Josie stared at her like something in an insane asylum under twenty-four hour watch.

"I'll make a scene and you can crawl out through the kitchen," Josie suggested.

"What?"

"And then I'll go over there and hang with them and we can be besties and I'll," she licked her lips again, "get my own taste of Superhero Sandwich. I can be the meat."

"You are a sick woman."

"I got the fever and they got the cure."

"I know you're joking, but this isn't funny anymore."

Josie dropped the act instantly. "Sorry. You're right. What can we do?"

Crawling on hands and knees was starting to look like a great option, except she would have to abandon the rest of her cake. Was saving face worth leaving this luscious, green-tinted pistachio chocolate mound of salvation?

With ice cream? And the untouched homemade mint whipped cream?

No. She would stand her ground.

For the sake of gastronomical integrity.

Someone had to. And she would make that sacrifice. Determined, Laura took another enormous bite of cake, ice cream, whipped cream and all dipped in peanut butter sauce.

The moan that escaped her body rivaled anything she'd made in bed with those two.

Which is probably why they both turned in unison, staring as she devoured her true love. Thor could have his hammer. Dylan looked enough like a short Christian Bale to be Batman. Right now, though, she was going green, getting her most important hole stuffed by the Hulk.

Peanut Butter Hulk Smash cake allowed her to be the avenger now.

Could those two be any weirder? Following her here to Jeddy's, where she still had their funk on her. In her. In places no man had ever been before on her body. Places she suspected no one except maybe, once, the gynecologist had touched during a routine "Hi! Welcome to twenty-five!" exam.

Was it getting warm suddenly?

"Are you hot, Josie?" she asked through a mouthful of cake.

"No. But they are—hey! One of them is coming over. Thor," she drooled.

"Not funny."

"It is when I'm not you, hon." She nodded behind Laura.

Shit. Mike really was walking over here. Covered in food splotches from haphazardly digging into the delights, she wondered if the rest of her was as disheveled. Barely able to look, she forced herself to anyhow. The ratty old sweats that seemed like a good comfort choice at home made her look like Tori Spelling after giving birth. Her hair was shoved into a knotted mess and makeup—what makeup? It had been smeared off long ago.

Hell, some of it was probably still on Mike's torso.

Her mouth watered. And not from the food.

"Hey."

Why did his voice have to have this reaction on her, like a warm breeze on wet skin, her every pore attending to his presence before she even looked back? Why did his tone make her body inhale sharply, every part of her lungs ready to sigh with pleasure at the very thought of his presence?

And why, for the love of all that is holy, was Josie goggling at them both like this was a side show at a carnival?

Oh. Because it was.

"Grab his balls!" Josie's words made Laura glare, wide-eyed and wild.

"What?" she hissed.

Jumping up, Josie skittered around Mike as if he were a pillar holding up the restaurant. "Grab his balls!" She ran over to the cardboard cutout and began chatting up Dylan. All Laura heard was a handful of words from Dylan's sweet mouth:

"...I know, I..."

"...no, the balls weren't my..."

"...four? No, we never considered..."

and Josie's rat-a-tat-tat machine-gun fire conversation.

Don't look at him, she told herself, though she could feel him, inches away, the hair on her skin like hundreds of thousands of little clitoral hoods, all aching for him, for release, for this yearning to go away.

Especially via his touch. As if on command, his hand touched her shoulder. Involuntarily, she flinched. He pulled back.

This dance? Really?

It sucked.

"Hi, Mike," she said reluctantly. Couldn't ignore him.

Fluid grace poured into his limbs as he deftly slid into Josie's space, his movements belying his size. Hands eager for connection, she pulled them into her lap, then sat on them, her ass pinning errant fingers in place, knowing damn well what she'd do if she didn't.

Wait. No. She was supposed to be angry with him. Them.

Everyone.

"Hi." The shy act wasn't going to cut it tonight. She went for the throat.

"Stalking me? Isn't that Dylan's specialty?"

He flinched and winced, then arched one eyebrow and took a deep breath. Target hit. So why didn't she feel victorious? Instead, her stomach roiled and nausea crept in. Why did he and Dylan have to ruin this? Her one refuge—food and Josie, together—and now what had been the beginning of sorting through threads entangled between the three of them had turned into even more enmeshment, confusion, and hurt.

"No—we—uh—" He gave up, not making eye contact. Eyelids fluttered shut and he splayed his palms on the grooved table top, his right index finger worrying someone's carved name. Jane. Who had Jane been? Could have been Madge's mother, for all they knew.

Or one of Mike and Dylan's lovers.

Using his arms as leverage, he slowly stood, back curling and shoulders flaring, leaning in toward her. When his face tipped up his eyes locked with hers.

"Whatever you think right now, you're wrong. And when you're ready to talk, we'll be there." One hand reached for her, steady and firm, the touch like tissue paper against a rose petal. An apologetic smile twitched in his lips and the skin beneath his eyes softened.

"We won't come after you, Laura." He glanced over at Dylan, who was laughing at Josie, who had removed the warlock waitress's balls and was teabagging in front of an audience of golfers and hungover college boys. Mike rolled his eyes. "OK, *I* won't. Can't guarantee what Dylan will do."

"He and Josie seem to have hit it off."

"Is she twelve inside?"

That made Laura laugh. Bingo.

His thumb stroked the underside of her cheekbone and she went liquid, all muscles melting and everything warm became wet. Mike leaned in and softly kissed her temple.

"When you're ready."

* * *

Was Mike seriously kissing Laura right now? Right *now*, as Dylan was stuck with her friend, who was mouthing the set of balls thousands of people had manhandled for the past decade? The very balls Jill had grabbed and stuck on the warlock in what now felt like another life?

Cool.

Whatever it took to get Laura to believe that they wanted her, that they wanted a *we* that no one else really understood. Hell, they didn't even understand it. Who could blame Laura for feeling conflicted and fearful.

Oof. This Josie chick just whomped him in his very real balls with those fake balls.

"Hey! You paying attention there, Thor's sidekick?"

Thor's what? "My name is Dylan. Who is Thor?"

She laughed, rubbing the plastic testicles against her cheek, like stroking a kitten. "Like I don't know your name. You and Mike are all Laura talks about."

"Really?" *So they call Mike 'Thor'?*

She shot him a look. "Really? Like you don't know. You aren't exactly *conventional*. I haven't seen Laura eat that much food in one sitting since Ryan left her. Some wicked show you two got going on."

Show? "We didn't mean to—"

Placing one long finger with an even longer fingernail against his lips she shook her head slowly. The rest of her fingernails looked like peacock tails.

"You don't get to speak right now. In fact, I hope Mike doesn't try to talk too much."

Dylan snorted. "No worries," he said. Except it sounded like "mo uhwees" with her finger pressing against his mouth. "He's a quiet giant."

She made a face like she was impressed. "Then you might have a shot. Too bad you guys set her up. The last thing Laura needs is to feel manipulated." She glowered. "Why am I telling you this?"

Whack. She smacked him with the rubber balls. "Ow!"

"You deserved it."

She was right; he did. They did. His stomach rumbled and he checked the wall clock. Pushing five a.m. Shit—he started a new shift in two hours. Whatever they needed to do to get Laura to believe that they wanted her—wanted more—and that this wasn't some pervy plot, they needed to do it fast.

Turning on the charm, he shot Josie a warm grin, his arm going up around the back edge of the booth, the gesture intimate and inviting. "You're her best friend. What would you tell some amazing guy—"

"Guys." She turned it into two syllables. *Geye—ZUH.* Which made it all sound rather pervy.

He kept going. "Guys. OK. What would you tell us to do to get her to explore this with us?"

"Explore? That sounds so...eww. Would you say that to someone if you were just in a one-on-one relationship? '*I want to explore this. Explore you. Explore your hoo-haw*'—"

"Hoo *what*?"

Just then, Mike approached. *Thank God,* Dylan thought. He was starting to feel a little too...something.

Flinching, he pulled back from Josie and shot Mike a pleading look. *Rescue me?*

"Hi," Mike said to Josie, extending his hand to shake. She grasped it and Dylan got a good, long look at those weird, long nails. Yep. Peacock tails. Golden, glittering streaks interspersed with some weird, glittery green and a bunch of colors you'd only see in nature.

She smiled *real* wide at Mike, clearly drinking him in.

Mike's return grin was polite. Hesitant. He gave nothing. *Atta boy*, Dylan thought. Josie's face went a bit tentative, the first sign of any social filter in the woman. Mike could do that to people. He was so centered—not self-centered, but grounded—that his openness unnerved people. It was yet another aspect of him that drew Dylan, and probably Jill and Laura, to the giant—

Ah. *Thor*. Studying Mike's features, Dylan suddenly got it, chuckling at the women. Taller than most men, Nordic features, the dark blonde hair and those glittery eyes. Legs like tree trunks and a cobra chest and back.

Thor.

Did that make him Loki?

He shuddered at the thought, his chuckle fading fast. He was *way* more built than that guy. More Captain America than anything else.

"Earth to Dylan." Mike was waving a hand the size of a catcher's mitt in his face. "Josie was just telling us some important information about Laura." Mike widened his eyes and his look said, *Hey dumbass, show some respect*.

"Yeah. Sure." Movement at the other booth caught his eye as Laura stretched her neck from one side to the other, then slid to the right, out of the booth and walked unsteadily to the bathroom. That fine, round, soft ass sashayed away from him, her hips encased in some loose yoga pant fabric that clung to her curves, disappearing around the corner as she opened the door.

It was unsettling when what he really wanted was that ass on him, in his lap, or in front of him, hands feeling every—

"...so I'm not going to sit here and pour out all of Laura's secrets to you two idiots, but you obviously need someone to hit you with a clue bat." Josie held up the plastic balls. "Or clue balls. Whatever. You should have been upfront with Laura and told her that you know each other. And that you're gay—"

"Nope." Dylan crossed his arms over his chest. *Here we go again.* "Not gay."

Mike shook his head.

She smiled slyly. "OK, not gay. But...not *not* gay?"

Dylan pursed his lips, eyes narrowing, face hard. Mike had closed up, too. "We're not having this conversation with you."

"No offense," Mike jumped in, palm up and facing Josie in a gesture that asked her to give them a second to explain. "It's complicated."

"It's *always* complicated."

"Where have I heard that before?" Dylan muttered. Now he was getting pissed, and he could tell Mike could tell he was getting pissed, and he was hard from watching Laura walk away and now this little yippy drowned rat of a friend wanted to tell him *allll* about him and Mike.

Judgment was all fine and good until the other person was just plain wrong.

Then it was torture.

"You don't know us from Adam," Mike said in a soothing voice.

Josie looked at him with rapt attention, her mouth open slightly, lips parted and face softened. It made

Dylan like her a bit. Just a bit. Mike had that effect on women. On men. On dogs, for that matter. He could make almost any living being feel like they were the center of the world.

"And we hope you respect that. We know you're Laura's best friend and we know you know her far, far better than we do. Someday we hope to rival you on that," he added, his grin widening, eyes lasered on Josie's.

She smiled.

Dylan dropped his hands from his chest. Now they were getting somewhere. He couldn't stop surveying the women's room. A glimpse of Laura was what he wanted.

Not really. What he wanted was to storm over to her table, slide in next to her and charm the pants off her. His pants tightened. Damn jeans.

"If you really want to understand Laura, you two need to back the fuck off."

The profanity caught Dylan's attention; her tone was nasty but matter-of-fact.

"You're not asking for anything she's ever experienced. Or that most people have experienced. You lied to her—"

"We didn't lie," Dylan sputtered.

Mike tried to shut him up with a look but Dylan wasn't having any of it.

"We just didn't tell her everything."

"You Catholic?"

"How'd you know?" Dylan asked, bewildered.

"You have the Irish-Italian Catholic look. So you know the difference between lies of comission and lies of omission." She said it flatly. It wasn't a question.

Mike pinged between the two of them, a confused look on his face.

"Yeah." She had him. Omitting the truth was as bad as telling an outright lie.

"Fill me in?" Mike asked, waving at them both. "Lapsed Lutheran here."

"You guys didn't tell her the truth," Josie said, exasperation coating her words. "You have a lot of trust to regain. A lot." She screwed her face into a disapproving look that was a bit too reminiscent of those nuns Dylan dealt with back in elementary school. "I don't see how you ever thought that was a good plan. Date her separately and then assume you could just shift into threesome mode?" Hissing the word "threesome," Josie twisted her head back and forth, making hard eye contact with each. "Not the smoothest of moves. Who came up with that one?"

Both men dipped their heads, suddenly entranced by the silverware, Mike fingering a fork while Dylan polished his spoon with his old t-shirt.

She snorted. "Whatever led you to surprise her like that—don't do it again. Not if you hope to get her back."

"Any ideas?" Mike asked, a half smile trying to coax some allegiance from her.

She shook her head. "Don't stalk her?"

As she stood to walk back to her and Laura's booth, Dylan caught a glimpse of a blonde pony tail, Laura's face down as she hurried back to her booth.

"We didn't stalk her," Mike protested. "We just wanted Jeddy's as much as you guys did."

"Everyone has a big appetite after a menage," Josie joked.

Madge appeared, arms laden with plates of hot sausage and more, just as Josie spoke. Plates delivered, Madge pivoted three steps, stopping.

"Menage, huh?" Madge muttered as she filled salt shakers the next table over, pointedly taking in Dylan and Mike. "I wouldn't mind surviving that." She shot Josie a sideways look. "They must have crushed you to a pulp."

Laughter filled the restaurant as Josie plunked the rubber balls in front of Dylan and Mike and walked back to her friend, leaving Dylan with no appetite and a million questions. Go slow? How do you go slow after what he and Laura and Mike had just experienced?

Madge waggled her eyebrows. "You boys ever need a third, you know where to come."

Ewww. Dylan's pants loosened instantly. "Uh—"

She threw an arm around the warlock waitress. "I meant *him*. Her. It." A choking laugh carried down the aisle as she shouted back, "Sorry, boys. I'm taken."

* * *

Laura hyperventilated in the bathroom stall. Calling it a stall was a bit of a stretch. Years ago, someone had removed the metal door and replaced it with a cheap shower curtain with an outline of an arm wielding a knife and red splotches. All that stood between her and the mess out there was Psycho. Nice.

Crying on the toilet felt like an accomplishment. Hell, just walking down the aisle into the bathroom was a victory, her legs shaking from nerves and anxiety and panic. If her heart rate was any indication of what those two men could do to her, she should be in an ambulance on the way to a cardiac center for immediate surgery to fix...to fix...

Whatever they'd broken in her heart.

This was not how she'd envisioned seeing them next. If at all. She hadn't even gotten to the point where she could think about whether she wanted to see them again after what they did to her. With her. *In* her...

Gah! Now motormouth Josie was out there spilling all her secrets. She knew Josie well enough to know what was happening out there, and that it was useless to try to stop her. The tongue lashing those two were getting from her friend—

OK. Bad choice of words.

The *nagging lecture* Mike and Dylan were likely getting would turn them off her anyhow. She chuckled through the tears. Served them right. They knew each other? Were double-teaming her in every sense of the word? Had planned this big threesome night without telling her the little, trivial detail that *oh! hai! I can haz menage?*

And they were together? But not gay? Neither had touched the other—not once—during their lovemaking. So how did that work? It was complicated enough to figure out one guy's needs, his wishes, his quirks and such in a hetero relationship.

Two guys? Double the fun and double the trouble, and then the dynamic between them that would mean —*what?*—for her? If she were in a permanent relationship with both men, would they always have sex together? Or would they pair off and rotate nights? Would it be like something out of *Big Love* but in reverse—with Laura the one they shared?

If she wanted to cuddle on the couch could she pick one and hang out, or would they always be three? Her head hurt and as she relaxed enough to pee she felt a stinging that took her by surprise. Oh. Yeah. That whole area was still sore from those two.

Who had lied to her.

Lied. Not told. Same thing.

Snot covered her face as she wiped her nose with the palm of her hand, misjudging how full her nose really was. Cheap, scratchy toilet paper cleaned her up but just made everything feel raw now. Would any part of her ever *not* feel raw, so shaky and vulnerable? As she finished up and washed her hands in the sink she found herself staring into the mirror, her eyes puffy and red from crying, the bloodshot whites in great contrast to the shiny color, the stained walls behind her covered in graffiti that probably extended back to Madge's youth.

Big sigh. Inhale. Exhale. Inhale—just as the automatic air deodorizer pushed out a little spritz, filling her lungs with some God-awful fake Lily of the Valley scent that mixed with the stench of the bathroom and made her gag.

Great. Like this couldn't get any worse.

She fled the bathroom, gasping for fresh air, and the sight before her told her that why, yes, Laura. It could get worse.

Josie was whacking Dylan with a set of rubber balls.

Retreat! Retreat! Had they seen her? Ducking behind the coat rack, she crouched, feeling stupid and ridiculous. Mike sat down and introduced himself; she had a full view of the scene from behind someone's cigarette-soaked tan barn coat. He shook Josie's hand and then Josie yammered at him. From afar, the interaction was almost comical, Josie's mosquito-like buzzing a stark contrast to Mike's slow, steady existence.

Dylan sat, cocky and comfortable, arms stretched out behind him across the top of the booth. Josie whacked him in the lap with the balls and Laura giggled. The way he folded in half told her it hurt.

Good.

Tears filled her eyes. Good? *Jesus, Laura—Good? Now you're wishing harm on him?*

No. Not OK. Time to go out there and—what? Confront them? Confront yourself?

Nope. Time to go back and have your cake.

And maybe finish eating it, too.

* * *

The more she talked, the calmer he got. Zen. Focus on what is. Just breathe. Let her existence interfere with nothing. What she said, she said. Who she was, she was.

When she whacked Dylan with the balls, it just was.

And it was funny as hell.

Mike pulled out every meditative awareness technique he could think of, with more than ten years of reading, practice, conferences, and seminars under his belt. Nothing seemed to work very well with Josie, though; she was spitfire and *alllll* reaction. Completely unaware of how she seemed to everyone else kinetically, she just moved through time and space as sheer energy.

He remembered a time when he was like that, years ago, a time when he was so exhausted. So busy searching for something, judging everything, fiercely protective and loyal to his loved ones and scanning, yearning, sorting and journeying to find—what?

He hadn't known. Still wasn't sure, but he definitely understood now that slowing down, acting rather than reacting, and just being present helped him to find it.

All this back patting must be tiring, Mike, his inner voice said, clearing its throat. He sighed.

Touché.

Nothing about the night was going as planned. Plans. *His* plans; Dylan had been very kind back there, not blurting out the truth. Having Dylan surprise them at the cabin had been Mike's bright idea. *Stupid stupid stupid*, the voice said now, a taunting, lilting tone.

It wasn't supposed to look like they'd ganged up on her. He'd envisioned a different outcome, not the threesome they'd enjoyed but more of a quiet talk, some soul bearing, and a gentle discussion about possibilities.

Dylan had changed the plan, coming far later than planned and interrupting them at the most delicate of moments, then broaching the subject like a bull in a china shop. Delicacy and tact were never his strong suits, to say the least.

When she'd agreed, Mike had been as shocked as she probably was. Never in a million years would he have pegged her as someone who would, in the heat of the moment (*and oh, what a hot one it had been...*) make a snap decision like that and just jump. Leap. Go for it.

Have her fill.

The thought made the corner of his mouth shift up, not quite a smile, definitely not a smirk. Washing his face with his hands, he wondered how he and Dylan appeared to Josie. Were they freaks? Jerks? Guys who were somehow mindfucking her best friend?

From the look on her face right now he guessed the answer was *All of the Above*.

He made himself seem like he was paying attention to the conversation that unfolded before him between him, Josie, and Dylan, but all of his focus was on Laura.

Her Two Billionaires and a Baby

She'd gotten up and gone to the bathroom and her skin was still on his lips from that simple kiss. Why had he been so bold? She seemed moved to tears, unable to walk straight.

Maybe that was a result of something earlier. He made a face at the thought.

Dylan frowned, watching him. "What?" he mouthed.

Mike shook his head imperceptibly and resumed paying attention to Josie, who was giving them hints on how to handle Laura.

If being whacked over the head by their own stupidity could be categorized as a hint.

Right now, he'd take any advice if it had half a chance at working. Why did he know when to back off and give someone space, but was utterly clueless when it came to drawing close?

Josie assumed they'd been stalking Laura, coming to Jeddy's at the same time, and he knew trying to explain that it was a weird coincidence—Jill would have called it "the universe speaking to us"—was futile.

Josie and Laura would believe what they wanted to believe, and nothing he and Dylan said or did would make a difference.

So why were they even trying?

Because.

Because.

That's all Mike knew. Because.

Laura staggered back to her booth and Josie walked away. The old waitress made a lewd comment. Mike inhaled. Mike exhaled. Mike inhaled. Mike exhaled.

And then Dylan stood, eyes flashing and intense, body aimed for Laura's booth, and Mike stopped breathing.

*\ *\ *

"Fuck," Laura whispered.

"What?" Josie asked, sucking the last remnants of ice cream from her spoon.

"Fuck me, Josie!"

"I don't do girls. Well, except for that one time in college when—"

Laura grabbed Josie's arm, her fingernails sinking in. "They're coming over here."

"And you're surprised?" Josie looked at Laura like she had three heads.

Three.

As if he owned the joint—no, as if he owned *her*—Dylan slid into the booth right next to Laura, arm stretching across the back of the booth, his chest against her shoulder. Mike had the decency to stand at the side and look awkward. Because he *was* awkward. This much, she knew.

And Dylan was being a strutting ass because he *was* a strutting ass.

This she knew, too.

What she didn't know was why they had decided once again to come after her. One fuck. She had been just one roll in the hay, right? They'd convinced her (*you convinced yourself*) to have her first threesome and she'd reveled in it. Still felt it on her skin, inside her, in her mouth, on her thighs—everywhere.

But this wasn't how she wanted it to go. Her guilt at dating two guys at once was bad enough. Learning they knew each other and were an item (*sorta*) that wanted her to complete them was too much to absorb at nearly six a.m. When she needed to go to work on zero hours of sleep. She still needed a shower, was starting to get a headache, and now six eyes stared at her with expectations that turned into a churning soup of hope and dread.

"Can you people pick one table and stick to it?" Madge croaked, refilling Laura's water glass. "Breakfast rush is about to start and I'll need the table."

"We're over here now, Madge," Dylan replied, winking at her.

"You done with your food?" She nodded at the half-full plates.

Mike gave her a closed-mouth smile and nodded.

"OK," she sighed. "I'll bring your check here."

Laura pretended Madge was the most interesting sight ever and watched pointedly as the old woman cleared the table in about three seconds, delivered the checks, and seated a new group at an empty table.

"Man, how old is she?" Josie asked, admiring her energy.

"She's been here at least since we were in college and put up old Warlock," Dylan joked, nudging Laura. The heat from his chest made her feel like she couldn't breathe, as if the warmth itself, made true from his blood, his flesh, his movement and soul, were a force field that stopped time, stopped her heart, stopped everything and made her want to bathe in him. His presence. His scent.

Wait. What?

She looked up at Dylan, the muscle of his upper arm poking through the thin lines of his cotton t-shirt. Could she lick it without being caught?

Bad Laura. Bad.

"You made the Warlock Waitress?" Laura's hold on reality was tenuous at best. Learning these two had been responsible for a local culture legend would send her over the edge.

"Not quite," Mike chuckled. "It was really Jill's idea."

If Mike had thrown a bucket full of cold ice water on her head, he couldn't have jolted Laura out of her slump any faster. Jill. Of course.

Of course it was Jill's idea. Some part of her that had been churning and unfocused came into play again, sharpened by competition. She wasn't seriously threatened by a dead woman, was she?

Even one who looked like she'd been hand-chiseled by Ralph Lauren?

Dead, Laura. Dead. You can't compete with the dead.

And maybe that was part of the problem here. Two very real, very alive men breathing next to her, both with heartbeats and fingers and raspy stubble and soft smiles. Both in love with a woman who had died not quite two years ago, someone they had spent early adulthood loving. Surfing and skiing and forging a very unique relationship that few would ever dare to try.

They had ten years of this to draw on.

She had a handful of hours. And was competing with a dead woman.

She wasn't feeling stifled for no good reason. And Josie saw something in her face, could read Laura so well, because before Laura could open her mouth to fumble through an explanation, Josie stood, ushering Mike away from the edge, kicking Dylan in the shin.

"Hey! What was that for!" he shouted, rubbing his leg bone.

"Out. Give Laura some space."

"But I—"

Her glare cut him off.

Rolling his eyes, he huffed—but moved. Biceps flexing under that Rush t-shirt, Dylan's body moved away, leaving a vacancy, a coldness where he'd been, that made her feel a little bit abandoned. Ping-ponging back and forth emotionally like this wasn't her style at all, and she was weary. Just wrung out and ready for this night to end.

The sun blinded her out of the blue, the restaurant's windows unshaded. Madge went down the line lowering the blinds. Laura checked her phone. 6:07 a.m. Time to put the night to rest.

Scooching over, she stood, Mike's arm inches from her, his eyes purposefully not meeting hers. She smiled at Dylan and he took it as an opportunity, stepping closer to her until Josie blocked him.

Josie shook her head slowly, piercing him with her stare. "Don't be that guy." She looked up at Mike, tipping her head way, way back. "Those guys."

As the sun radiated through the filthy glass and illuminated Jeddy's, a renewed sense of...*something* struck Laura. She lacked the right word for it, but knew the feeling. Not hope. Not promise. Not quite possibility.

Willingness.

Mike took a microstep toward her. "When you're ready," he said, echoing his earlier words.

"Can we make you dinner some night this week?" Dylan asked, pushing—ever pushing.

She made a mirthless laugh. "Last time Mike did that, dinner wasn't just dinner."

"We swear," the men said in unison.

"Unreal," Josie muttered.

Laura grabbed the rubber balls from the table, where Josie had propped them up against the jukebox. Fishing a quarter out of her purse, she leaned over, giving anyone who walked by a nice money shot of her ample ass. She knew both men were staring and she cared—more than she knew.

Plunking the quarter in and making a choice, she turned and attached the balls to the cardboard cutout's crotch. Giving them a squeeze, she and Josie sauntered out as the opening chords of "Call Me, Maybe?" wended their way through the early breakfast crowd.

* * *

Calling in sick was the best decision Laura had made in the past five days. Not that this was a week for exhibiting stellar judgment, though. As her fingers punched in the number for her boss's personal cell phone, though, she felt legitimately ill. So ill, he just said, "Do what you have to do to recover," and made sympathetic noises.

Off the hook for the day, she stared dully at the back of her front door. "Do what you have to do to recover" was easier said than done.

Josie came out of the kitchen using one talon to peel a clementine. "And?"

"I'm off for the day."

"Cool. I don't work until three, but I need some sleep." Yawn. "For once, I won't ask you to make me coffee."

Laura was too tired to smile. "Help me, Josie. What the hell do I do?"

"You're asking the woman who hasn't been laid for seven months for romance advice?" She shoved a wedge of citrus in her mouth. "I'll tell you what I would do."

"That's what I'm asking!"

"I would hear them out. Let them make you dinner. Spend time with them—together. Don't fuck them, though."

"Josie!"

"You can't blame me for saying that, Laura. 'Cause you did. And it freaked you out. They caught you off guard and I'll bet it was the hot Italian dude who made it all happen."

Laura's face must have revealed all.

Josie pointed and said, "I knew it," as she shoved the rest of the clementine in her mouth, standing and crossing the room to throw the peels away.

"He's a charmer," Laura answered. Not that Mike wasn't, but *Dylan*. He could talk the pants off a prison guard.

"And the other one—Jesus, Laura. Did you need stilts *and* a stool to fuck him?" Josie cringed and held up one hand, fingernails radiating from her palm like a metal sun sculpture. "TMI. Don't answer that."

"Then why did you ask?"

"Because I have no filter. Duh. *You're* my filter. And I have no filter when I'm talking to my filter about her positions when screwing a guy the size of a streetlamp."

Laura pretended to mull that one over, then threw a couch pillow at Josie, who seemed to know it was coming and ducked well ahead of time. "Dinner? Really?"

Josie blinked hard, rubbing one eye. "Yeah. I think you need to get to know these guys. Spend time with them. Not the kind of time where you sit there, all anxiety-filled, wondering when you'll end up in bed. I mean the pal-around, cuddle on the couch, watch a movie and cook dinner for each other kind of time."

"That's called a date."

"Yes. You need to date them."

"Date them. Double date by myself?"

Both laughed.

"Josie, I don't even have a language for this!" she wailed.

"That's the problem, hon. No one does. And I think," she added, pensive suddenly, "I think that's why they care so much about you. Because you may be the first person they've met in a long time who is even willing to learn whatever rare language they speak. So far, most people don't even view it as words. Just offensive gibberish."

"I find it lovely," Laura whispered. Yawn.

Josie laughed quietly, grabbing another clementine and her purse. "I know you do, sweets. But right now, the only language you need to speak involves a lot of zzzzzzzzzzzzzzzzzz. Go to bed."

"I need a shower." Laura sniffed one armpit. "God, that bad?"

"Sleep first. Shower after."

By the time she heard the door click as Josie left, Laura's living room was spinning, the air washing before her like waves of water, her eyes heavy and lids drooping. As she heard footsteps waning down the hall, before she knew it she was fast asleep, vulnerable now only to whatever her subconscious conjured for her in her dreams.

Chapter Two

She knew he was there long before her senses registered him, ears perked and hearing an unspoken need that shouted through the silence. Her neck shifted to the left, open for his lips, and he did not disappoint. As if forged by God for his very shape, the touch of his mouth on the nape of her neck seemed divine, the two parts of flesh melding into one through the sigh that escaped her, unbidden and knowing.

When Mike's hands slid over her shoulders, down to her elbows, then effortlessly transitioned to her hips, the two slipping into a V that traveled to her womanhood and stroked out to her thighs, his cock hard against the cleft of her ass as the shower spray poured down on them, the sigh that came from her was like a prayer.

Spinning around, she took his face in her hands and kissed him, hard, the sudden, fierce uprising in her needing as much of him as possible now, hard and fast and tough and quick and in and out immediately. His tongue matched hers, all fire and taking, as his knees parted her legs, then let her go with a tight nip to her lower lip, turning her around and bending her down.

"You are so luscious," he murmured in her ear, words shattered by the spray and the steam, cut into bits and pieces her overwhelmed, pulsing mind and body could barely understand, the allure of his hands on her breasts, one pausing to shift himself and plunge into

her, then resuming its spot on her overflowing cup, taking her to an aroused madness.

As friction grew, his thrusts timed perfectly, her swollen, red passage seemed tapped into her lungs, her heart, her lips and her everything.

Mike's hands roamed her torso, teasing her clit as his gliding tightened, thrusts harder and more focused, the feel of his body behind her hardening as his own climax surely built. Her fingers clawed at the tiled walls, needing flesh to dig into, to hold on to for the wild ride of an explosive, wet, dripping orgasm that—

Beep, beep, beep.

"Ack!' she squeaked, hand flailing for her phone. An alarm? What? Eyes unfocused and clit in the throes of an orgasm (*huh? In her sleep?*) she fumbled the phone, its ineffectual clunk on the floor making her cringe in horror. Another broken glass screen wasn't going to please the geniuses at the Apple store.

Retrieving it and sighing loudly with relief at its intact condition, she stared dumbly. An alarm for a meeting at work. Jesus. So why was her pussy on overdrive, pulsing as if she—

Oh.

A flash of her dream drizzled into her subconscious —and then a tsunami of tactile and mental dream memories hit her.

Seriously? Coming from a *dream*? Was she that far gone?

As her clit drummed a beat like a bass drum being attacked by a throng of marching band directors, the answer made her weep with frustration.

Yes. Apparently.

* * *

Josie was Dylan and Mike's savior, because it appeared that she had convinced Laura to give them a shot and to come over for dinner. One very, very long week had passed without word from her, and then—a text. A quick phone call. An invitation heartily extended and hesitantly accepted.

Accepted. That's what counted, right? They had a chance.

Mike knew they could blow this so easily, so he had deferred to Dylan as the cook tonight. Admitting he was better in the kitchen was hard, but he had to face facts: something about the Italian in Dylan made his food a little extra...something. Extra flavorful? Extra intense?

Extra *fine*. Like the man. And if that little bit of extra could be the deciding factor between Laura's giving them a chance or walking away, Dylan could cook.

Choosing the wine, though, was Mike's fierce prerogative.

"Oh, a nice red!" Laura teased, taking the glass by the stem from Mike's nervous hand. They were standing in the doorway between the living room and the kitchen in his and Dylan's apartment, the entire place decorated in a slick, cold grey and black scheme he had never liked, but that been a legacy of choosing this place a few years ago. The price had been a stretch for him and Dylan, though Jill had shouldered a bit more of the rent; after her death they'd learned she had paid well over half the real price, the two of them blindly forking over a rent check to her every month, never knowing the true cost.

So he understood—on a more trivial level—how it felt to be duped.

You're really comparing that to this? his conscience exclaimed, riding him. *Not even close.*

"It's a Chilean carmenere."

Fine, he argued with himself. *Not the same. Stop comparing and just stay in the moment.* He took a deep breath, held it for seven seconds, and let it out in four. *Center yourself, man. She's worth it.*

"It's, um, very red," she agreed, drinking half the glass in one long sip. Her hair was down and flowing tonight, framing her face with soft curves that mirrored her body. Casual, in a simple v-neck pink sweater, low-rise jeans that made his hands itch to grab that voluptuous ass, and with a tentative, but guarded, approach that made him want to reassure her, Mike wasn't sure how the night would end but he did know one thing:

He and Dylan were going to pull out all the stops to encourage Laura to take a giant, unconventional leap.

His fingers slid over her forearm, the touch soft and reassuring, meant to get her attention—not her arousal. He nodded toward the living room. "Can I talk to you for a minute?"

Laura had a way of tipping her eyes up first, eyebrows hitching up slightly, then bringing her entire face into the light—Mike's light, that is, given his height—that was so endearing his heart felt like it blossomed, a lotus flower of love.

Love? Where'd that come from? His conscience panicked.

"Sure," she said, eyebrows furrowed now. He didn't want to worry her. In fact, what he was about to say was all about getting her to relax. He compared what he was wearing to Dylan's flour-coated polo shirt, jeans, and bare feet. On balance, he'd done fine after changing three times—a simple blue button down and his most comfortable jeans seemed to fit in.

Spending so much time worrying about little details was, at best, nothing more than angst and nothing less than an exercise in occupying his scrabbling mind.

Either this would all work out or it would fall apart. No matter what, he had to find peace with the outcome.

She leaned against the arm of the deep, scarred leather couch, made shiny from too many hours of his and Dylan's asses being planted on it, watching some sports game (*Dylan*) or a quirky documentary (*Mike*).

Jill's butt had left its considerably smaller imprint, too, for she had tortured them with her Christopher Guest obsession until Mike had finally gotten it—and loved those movies, too.

Shaking his head slightly, he willed himself back to the present, where Laura's perplexed look was shifting, microsecond by microsecond, into wariness.

No, no, no—not what he was going for.

"I just wanted to say that we're really glad you came tonight."

The skin between her eyes wrinkled with something other than a smile.

She looked up and simply said, "Thanks."

"And Laura, I—this is awkward, but I want to say it. There are no expectations tonight."

His words had the opposite effect as his intent, her body bristling, eyes shifting away from his. Damn it! "I mean, Dylan and I—we just want this to be a simple dinner. No expectations."

"You mean no assumptions."

Her voice was hard. Cold. Closed off. She nailed Ice Queen, that's for sure. It made the awkward teen in him come out, his voice shifting up.

"I just—I mean—I," he choked out. Fuck. This wasn't how he meant it.

"Mike," she said, interrupting him. "When you tell me there are 'no expectations' what you really mean is that normally you and Dylan would want sex. *Expect* sex. But you're—what? Being *kind* and letting me off the hook tonight?" She searched the room, looking for something, and then her head froze.

Her purse. She was looking for her purse.

Mike had driven her to leave by trying so hard, with good intentions, to put her at ease.

Once again, his plans destroyed everything. This wasn't really happening, was it? In horror he watched as she handed him her glass of red wine and walked to the couch where her purse sat.

Dylan appeared in the doorway, mouthing "What the fuck?" to Mike as Laura turned her back to them, pausing with her hand inches from her purse strap.

"No," she said, shaking her head. Turning toward them, her eyes widened at the sight of Dylan, who now wore half a pound of flour in his hair and on the front of a bright red apron he'd donned. It even sprinkled the tops of his toes, giving him a disheveled, slightly-nuts chef look.

"Guys, we need to talk."

She picked up her purse and sat down, plunking it in her lap, then cocking one eyebrow at Dylan's appearance, a hint of a smile spreading her lips.

Good. *Good.* Mike let out a rush of air; he'd been holding his breath without realizing it, as if that could stop time.

"I don't have anything to lose here, so I'm just going to say this." She paused, eyes rolling up and to the left, as if rethinking something. "Well, I have plenty to lose," she muttered, "but pride can be rebuilt."

With a frown, she put her purse back down and stood, waving her hand at Mike and Dylan, who both followed her lead. Soon Mike found himself sitting next to Dylan, who plopped on the couch with a poof that made Mike cough a bit, flour now sprinkling his forearm. He gave Dylan a *C'mon, are you kidding me?* look.

"What? I get artistic in the kitchen." Dylan self-consciously wiped his face, looked at his palms, and grimaced at the white powder.

"You cook like a four year old with an Easy Bake oven and a fan."

"Hey!" Laura said firmly. "Me. Remember me?"

Sheepish, they both had the sense to dip their heads before giving her their eyes. Mike suppressed an urge to shove Dylan. Unfortunately, Dylan had the impulse control of Bill Clinton in a room full of interns and couldn't hold back his nudge.

Mike simmered. *Not worth it. Not worth it. Not worth it.*

His eyes settled on Laura.

Worth it.

Dylan blinked, his eyelashes white. "Yes." His voice came out like silk. "Of course we do."

"Then shut up and stop the childish crap and hear me out." She wasn't angry—her voice was preternaturally calm, and it creeped Mike out. Like she was detaching. Detaching not in some Buddhist sense, but detaching from them. From the relationship. From the possibility of what he knew, deep inside, was achievable.

That creepy feeling needed to be respected.

And so did Laura.

"You know that what you did was wrong. You know that you should have told me."

Ah, here it comes, he thought. *Good. Let's get this out in the open so we can deal with it like adults.*

"We don't need to talk about this right now," Dylan jumped in.

Mike's hands twitched. If he strangled him would it be justifiable homicide? Instead he shoved him, hard, and stepped on his foot.

"Ow! Hey! What was that about?" Dylan crossed his leg up and massaged his instep. More flour. Jesus.

Mike gestured toward Laura while disdainfully brushing flour off his arm, carefully aiming it toward Dylan. "Let the lady talk."

A grateful look from Laura was his reward. "We do need to talk about it. Now. So settle down there, buckaroo."

Both men flinched, Mike's entire body turning into a lightning rod during a storm, directing all the electricity in the air through his nose, making his scalp stand on fire.

Dylan just gawked at her, wide-eyed.

Instantly on alert, she seemed to realize something had happened, but Mike knew she wouldn't understand. "Did I just say something wrong?" she asked.

He leaned forward, wishing he could touch her, soothe her. Knowing he couldn't. Not yet. "No, no. Nothing wrong. It's just—that's what Jill used to call Dylan when he was, well, when he just *was*. Buckaroo. We haven't heard it in nearly two years."

That face. Her cheekbones were so perfect, soft curves blunting hard bone, her eyes serene, questioning, and hard all at once, brows knitted in confusion and wariness, in something more—a look of evaluation, of surmising what was critical and worth knowing, to apply to some emotional calculus he didn't understand.

Buckaroo.

Oh, how one word could so easily change everything. Dylan swallowed so hard Mike could feel the click in his throat. He realized *he* had to break the tension, *he* had to make this all make sense, because Laura and Dylan weren't going to do it. All those years of Jill and Dylan carrying the emotional water in the relationship had made him stale. Soft. Lazy.

Time to step up.

Literally. He stood, took two steps and reached for her shoulder. The sweater was warm, she was warm and soft, and she smelled like something sweet, a vanilla-scented perfume that made half the words fall out of his head before he could say them, replaced by a desire to embrace her and just stand there, bathed in her. Warmed by her.

Holding back that impulse was one hundred times harder than not shoving Dylan had been.

"Laura, it's fine." She tipped her face up, head at an angle, eyebrows up and questioning.

Is it really? *h*er face seemed to ask.

"I know," she answered. He froze. She uttered the one answer he'd least expected, the one answer that made his heart swell and his mind nearly crack in half. For Laura knew herself far better than he had ever imagined.

And that made this all the more compelling.

"If there is any hope here," she said, talking to him but also giving her eyes equally to Dylan, who now stood next to Mike, "we need to get two things straight."

They nodded.

"No more lies. None. That doesn't mean we need to spill everything about ourselves into one big baggage pile-up right here and right now—"

"But we could! I could! When I was in eighth grade I set fire to a field that caught train tracks on fire. And my senior year I slept with the new, hot assistant principal at my—"

Laura cut Dylan off with a well-placed finger to the lips.

Mike got hard just *watching* it. He could only imagine what Dylan felt.

"No." She *tsk tsk'd* him, finger now wagging in his face. "But no more enormous lies. You're lucky I am even here tonight."

"We know," they said in unison.

She laughed.

Mike felt a shift in the balance of power, as if she had come in uncertain and questioning and now—she was the one in charge. It made his body buzz a bit more, set his senses on fire, and made him want to rescind his earlier offer of no expectations.

Fortunately, his rational mind knew better. But his body....He'd need to run a solid half marathon to pound this one out.

"What's the second rule?" Dylan asked, his hand running up and down her arm, slow and steady.

"No sex. Not tonight. Not until I ask. Being double-teamed like that—"

Dylan snorted involuntarily. Mike cocked his jaw in irritation and kicked him in the calf. Dylan yelped.

Laura just shook her head and resumed. "Being— fine—*ambushed* by you guys was really destabilizing. I don't regret anything we did. Not for one second."

She took a step back and Mike understood why. It was getting hot in here.

"And yet...I need to just hang out with you. Get comfortable. Understand how this all works. It's not like there are books out there on how to be a threesome."

"Yeah, I know," Mike muttered. "I checked."

Every muscle on Laura's face came to life with laughter. "Me, too!"

Dylan shook his head. "I totally didn't." He stopped rubbing Laura's arm and ran his hand through his hair. A puff of white smoke popped up over his head and his dark hair stood on end. He looked like an adult, human version of a Muppet. The one who cooked with the Swedish chef.

"You look like Beaker! From the Muppets!" Laura squealed, patting his head as the hair sprang back up. "Myork! Myork! Myork!" she shouted, jumping up and down, her sweater climbing up and giving Mike a splendid view of her ass in what looked to be well-loved jeans. He could love them, too.

Being patted on the head didn't seem to suit Dylan; he looked like a dog being poked in the eye by a toddler, begging his master to rescue him, knowing he couldn't bite back.

Tough shit, Buddy, Mike thought. *You get to be Beaker for now.*

Dylan rescued himself, his fingers clasping Laura's wrist the third time she tried to flatten his hair. He led her into the kitchen and handed her a colander. "Unlike the Swedish chef dude, I don't set meals on fire, so let's get this pasta going."

"You do *so* set things on fire," Mike objected, ready to tell Laura plenty of stories about his roommates kitchen screw-ups.

"Not since I became a firefighter."

"Touché. You did nearly destroy a dorm kitchen single-handedly with a toaster and a frosted Pop-Tart, though."

"Not my fault. Do you have any idea how many fire safety seminars there are about Pop-Tart glaze? It's breathtaking."

"Yeah. Makes me gasp." Mike poured a few inches of wine in his and Laura's glasses as she shot him a surprised look. Sarcasm didn't suit him, he knew. It oozed out when he was anxious.

Anxious? Still? Things seemed settled.

Ish.

Ding! The kitchen timer went off. Dylan leaped and ran, leaving a small cloud of white flour in his wake. "The meatballs!" he shouted. Mike and Laura followed, curious.

"What is that amazing scent?" Laura asked, pretending to swoon. Maybe she really was.

Mike was half delirious himself from the smell of whatever Dylan was making. Taking a chance, Mike slid his arm around Laura's shoulders. She relaxed into him, keeping her eyes on Dylan. The press of her body into his felt so comfortable he needed to pause and blink, arm resting against the nape of her neck, across her shoulders, the casual comfort of the gesture so...right.

This was what he missed most. The normalcy of a night of cooking, hanging out, watching movies and just relaxing. Being. Living. As Dylan pulled a meatball out and put parts of it on forks for everyone to taste, something in Mike released. Exhaled.

It felt damn good. Better than sex right now.

*　*　*

Laura snuggled in closer, reaching for the fork, taking it from Dylan, lips closing over the morsel, her ribs expanding against Mike as she sighed. Eyeing the contact between the two, Dylan just smiled. Cool. Everyone was finally starting to chill.

His grandma's magic meatballs cured *everything*.

If not everything, at least they brought them all a little culinary bliss. He tasted a bite. Perfection. A blend of beef, a little veal, some pork, and oregano, basil, pepper, a touch of sugar and some grated parmesan with a tiny bit of mozzarella. Loads of garlic, of course! Juicy and coated in homemade tomato sauce (*was there any other kind? If it came in a jar it wasn't real food*), each bite was like stepping into an Italian restaurant in the North End in Boston, red velvet booths and low light and white-shirted waiters shouting in Italian.

"All that's left is the salad. Give me a few minutes and I'll have everything out." He surveyed the countertop. Destroyed. Red sauce everywhere (*how'd it get on the kitchen ceiling fan blades?*), the backsplash a buffet of splotches, every large pot dirty and stacked crooked in the sink, and zero counter space. None.

"I'll help," Laura offered, peeling off Mike, who looked disappointed. Good.

"Great!" He handed her a decanter of olive oil and a cheese grinder. "Can you put the parm on the pasta and if it needs more oil, add some?"

"What about me?" Mike asked. "Need anything?"

"Set the table?" Mike nodded and made quick work of it, grabbing plates and shuttling to and fro between dining room and kitchen. It all felt so...domestic.

Until Mike put a dent in it. "Hey, Dyl!" he hissed, nodding to the hallway. Laura was tossing pasta and rotating the cheese grinder handle, sprinkles of parmesan snowing on the bowl of noodles.

"What's up?" he asked, drying his hands on a towel.

"That whole no lying thing. Should we tell her about the—*you know*..." Mike made a reluctant face.

"The *you know* what?"

"The billionaire thing. She doesn't want lies, and she considers not telling her something major to be a lie."

Fuck. He hadn't thought of that. If they kept this from her, eventually it would come out. Would she be angry they didn't confide in her? Or would she understand why they wanted a little more time? It wasn't about worrying that she'd become greedy, or view them as sugar daddies, or any of the normal reasons guys with money would hesitate to let a woman know.

They had so much money there wasn't anything a woman could do to drain it anyhow, short of buying an island or a private jet, and even then—he shuddered, overwhelmed by the realization—it would just put a *temporary* dent in their cash flow. Jesus Christ.

They really were filthy, stinking rich.

Next time, he was buying filet for dinner. Why had he made boring old pasta with meatballs? Sheesh.

"No way, man. Not tonight. It'll scare her off," he told Mike. Hell, he hadn't even wanted poor Laura to have to get into talking about what he and Mike had done before. Anything that reminded her of negative feelings about them was off limits tonight. This dinner was about moving forward, not lingering in the past.

He wiggled his toes, feeling flour. Brushing his hand through his hair, he was shocked by the not inconsiderable amount that rained down on his shoulders and chest. Then he took a good look at the counter. Man, he was a slob.

But a slob who cooked some *damn* fine food.

"You don't think we should take the opportunity?"

"I do—just not *this* opportunity." Dylan blinked, struggling to explain himself. Finally, he let arrogance take him where he needed to go. "Look, Mike. She's vulnerable and unknowing right now. What women want at times like this is certainty. She doesn't need truth. Oh—eventually, sure," he said as Mike opened his mouth to protest. "Not now, though. What we all need is a quiet, comfortable, fun night where we get to know each other and—" He winked.

"*Uh uh*. No—" Mike winked back, exaggeratedly.

"OK, fine." He sighed heavily. "I was on the fence anyhow. Not that I don't *want* to, but more that—"

"That she needs time."

"I think she needs us."

"And time."

"Not too much time, I hope."

"We're fucking lucky she's here, Dylan," Mike whispered. No anger. No frustration. Just a matter-of-fact statement.

"Not lucky," he argued.

"Then what?"

Pink. Soft swells. Blonde hair. "Hey, guys?" Laura asked, head peering around the corner. "Ready to eat? I'm starving." She raised her eyebrows, the skin pulling her nose up a tad and making her lips fuller. A cheerleader's face. A *smart* cheerleader's face.

"Yep—ready!" Dylan nearly shouted, almost jumping out of his skin when she appeared.

"What're you guys talking about?"

"You." *Mike.* So blunt.

The three walked into the dining room. Mike had even lit candles. How romantic. How unnecessary, given the cockblocking.

"Me?" she asked.

"How great you are," Dylan jumped in, eager hands slipping around her waist, his lips reaching out to press a kiss against her temple. The way she melted into him gave him more information than one thousand words uttered from her lips.

Mike frowned at him.

She pulled back from Dylan and said breathlessly, "This is one amazing dinner."

Pulling out her own chair, she settled into what would normally be Mike's seat. Dylan grabbed Jill's old place and Mike settled into what they called the "guest" spot. No need for formalities, right? Tradition and habit were thrown out the window now anyhow. Everything they knew, from domestic life to finances to dating had gone out the window over the past two years.

Live a little, he thought. Shake it up. Sit somewhere new.

Ah, Dylan, you wild and crazy guy.

Homemade pasta, meatballs, salad and garlic bread was probably the most stereotypical Italian meal he could have cooked, but it seemed to hit the spot for everyone. Laura ate with great gusto and Dylan admired that. So many women he dated ate like they were competing in American Idol: Anorexia Edition.

She couldn't possibly eat more than Mike, though, who managed to eat the share of a seventeen-year-old football player going through a growth spurt. With a tapeworm. And a hollow leg.

Three plates later, Thor pushed himself back from the table and finished off his wine. "Amazing, Dylan. Really."

"Thanks." Dylan's stomach stretched just enough to make him want to unbutton his jeans. And he would have, if Laura weren't here.

"Oh," Laura groaned, setting down her fork. "I give up." She turned to Dylan and put her elbow on the table, chin resting in her palm. "That was the best dinner anyone has ever cooked for me."

"Ready for dessert?" he asked. They both groaned and put up their hands in protest.

"How about a movie, first?" Mike asked.

"Which one?" Mike liked some really weird shit, like those Christopher Guest movies. Not "The Princess Bride," which was a classic even Dylan liked, but the ones where people talked to each other like they were on some pretentious stage doing improv designed by a philosophy professor at a dog show as filmed by the Farrelly brothers.

"Let's let Laura pick." Mike bowed slightly, in deference to her.

Mike always knew what to say. It made Dylan feel like an idiot sometimes. In retaliation, he totally hogged the spot next to Laura on the couch, grabbed the remote and turned on the television, flipping to an on demand service.

"Comedy?" Dylan suggested.

Laura looked between the two men, reading them. Her cheeks were a bit flushed from the wine and she seemed to have let down her guard a bit, relaxing into the sofa with a patterned throw pillow in her lap.

He loved seeing her like this. Just being. And there went his body, tingling and rising to the occasion.

The occasion Mike had squashed.

Squash this, he thought, wiggling just enough to take the edge off his discomfort. Mike nudged past their knees and took his place on the other side of Laura. She looked to the left and to the right and seemed amused.

Grabbing the remote from him, Laura's soft touch made him close his eyes and exhale. *Garlic*. Elephant amounts of garlic on his breath. Mammoth levels of garlic.

Leaning in toward her, he smelled it on her breath. Mike probably reeked, too, which made him relax. OK. It was all good. If everyone smelled like an Italian restaurant, then there was no need for breath mints.

Laura settled on a comedy he and Mike happened to have watched a few weeks ago. They exchanged a wordless glance of understanding; don't question it. The film was funny enough to enjoy again, and she seemed to be a bit nervous suddenly. Whatever it took to keep everyone happy was what they needed right now.

Even if it meant laughing all over at a movie they'd thought was just OK. Besides, his attention wasn't exactly focused on the television screen, with Laura's warm body next to his, the rise and fall of her chest in his peripheral vision, her fingers worrying the wine glass stem.

She wriggled and settled in place, crossing and uncrossing her legs, finally gulping the last of her wine and leaning forward to place her empty glass on a coaster.

Heat from her body disappeared and left him feeling colder than he'd expected, and then Mike burst into laughter, followed by Laura's surprised giggle. Something funny in the movie.

Dylan could only give it half his attention because the entire room came into sharp focus suddenly, as if he were watching them from above. A quiet night, capped with a decent, funny movie about some modern woman who was insecure, some man who'd hurt her accidentally, some big misunderstanding that needed to be unraveled, supported by each person's best friend as plot devices.

Add a second man and you had, well, *them*. All three.

Here they sat, laughing at it on the big screen.

Mike's legs were stretched out on the coffee table, ankles crossed. Laura leaned back in and slouched a little, head cocked to the left. Dylan clutched a pillow and let the glow of the TV wash over them all. They were just three friends hanging out, watching a movie after a great meal.

The tiramisu he'd soon spring on them was soaking in flavor.

He was soaking in all of *this*.

Self-assured, he stretched his arm behind Laura and rested one hand on Mike's shoulder. A little smile played on her lips as she pretended to be completely absorbed by a movie that really only needed five of your brain cells to compute.

Mike caught his eye. Looked at his hand. Nodded.

Life was good.

Chapter Three

Knock knock. "Wha?" Laura sat up. Who in the hell knocks at 6:11 a.m.?

Bang bang bang.

"Laura?"

Josie.

"What?"

"Lost my key!" came her muffled voice through the door.

I never gave you a new one, Laura thought, shuffling to the door. Daylight was a glaring bitch this morning, sunlight aggressively spilling through her apartment.

"You know, they have these places," Laura said sharply as Josie walked past her, into the kitchen, and grabbed the coffee sack, plopping it next to the coffee machine. "They're called coffee shops. Professional coffee people make it for you and you give them these green pieces of paper and you get to drink it."

"Green pieces of paper?"

"Or silver coins." She yawned. "Or plastic cards."

"But they don't have stories about threesomes like you do."

"Oh, I'm sure if you ask around enough someone will."

Laura scooped the coffee with a slightly shaking hand. Could you have a tiramisu hangover? Jesus, Dylan had used a lot of rum in that delightfully scrumptious dessert.

Pressing a few buttons, she got the coffee going and plopped down in a kitchen chair.

"You're here to interrogate me, aren't you?" she asked, resigned.

"So whassup?" Josie stretched the word out in an annoying mimic of an old beer commercial's frog actors. "You a little sore today? That Dylan might be short but I'll bet he has a dick the size of a coke can."

"Ewwww!"

Close, she thought. But she'd never tell Josie that.

"I just crossed over my own line." Josie held out her palms in a surrender gesture. "Sorry. TMI. I blame caffeine deficiency."

"Blame your genetics. Your mom's way worse. Remember how she announced to everyone in the marching band that you needed to use non-chlorinated tampons because you couldn't bear to experience another rash—and then had pictures to warn other girls away from—"

Josie shuddered and interrupted loudly. "No, yo mama."

"No, *yo* mama!"

Were they really acting like they were in seventh grade? *Yeesh.*

"I don't have a mama. She died that day."

Laura chuckled. "You wish she'd died that day, because when we graduated, there she was at commencement, under the bleachers, banging the band director."

"She likes a little pomp with her circumstance."

"She made it clear to the whole auditorium how much she liked his wand."

"Topic change!" Josie shouted, leaping for the coffee maker.

"Her crescendo, too, was—"

"Oh, my God, *stop!*"

"Oh, dear. Am I going too far?" Laura said facetiously, playing it up. "Have I crossed a decency boundary? Have I made you uncomfortable talking about sex?"

"My mother's sex—"

"I wouldn't want to force you to talk about anything so prurient. That would be *being a bad friend, now, wouldn't it*?"

Josie finally got the hint.

"Was it weird? Being with two guys like that? I mean, and not sleeping with them?"

Laura rubbed her eyes. Why was Josie getting on her last nerve lately? She was still angry with her for pouring everything out to Mike and Dylan. Why not make her walk around naked with a sign that said "Ask Me Anything"?

If your best friend couldn't keep your secrets, who could? That night at Jeddy's had been one of the most stressful and surreal in her entire life, warlock balls and all. When she'd learned, later, what Josie had told the guys, after Dylan blurted it all out in a tiramisu-induced haze, she'd come home and nearly killed Josie.

The morning coffee routine was getting old. What wasn't getting old, though, was this developing relationship between her and the guys. *The guys.* Even that was surreal and weird.

Ah, hell—nothing about this threesome *wasn't* bizarre, so she was getting tired of labeling it all as outside the mainstream. It just *was*. No getting around that.

An internal argument deep within her raged on, one part telling her this was madness and a stronger, more settled part humming along nicely, ignoring the part that screamed "freak!"

Speaking of freaks, Josie was saying something through sips of java.

"If you kiss one of them, do you have to kiss the other?"

"Huh?" Laura poured herself a cup. Might as well benefit from the fruits of her labor. That, and she needed the jolt. Yet another uncomfortable conversation with Josie, though she had to admit that the girl definitely helped sometimes, making her think about things she hadn't considered. Like this?

"Does it have to be 50/50? If you sleep with one, do you have to sleep with the other? Or is it always a threesome? Is there always double, well—you know?"

Freak! "You actually sit around contemplating these things, Josie? Seriously?"

She had the decency to pinken a bit. "Who doesn't?"

"Most of the rest of the world." *Sip.*

If she didn't fill her mouth with something it would soon be full of words she'd regret saying. Please. This was devolving quickly into voyeurism. Laura was surprised by how annoyed she was becoming. Josie was always inquisitive. It was just who she was, and as aggravating as she could be at times, it had never troubled Laura this much.

Josie shot her a wary look. "I just...no, I don't sit around dredging up embarrassing questions to ask you, Laura." Her tone of voice conveyed hurt feelings. "But it's natural to wonder. Most threesomes are one-night-stand kind of deals. What you have is so out of the realm of normal that it makes me think. Philosophize and stuff, about what it means for the long haul."

Aha. And that was it. That was why this bothered Laura so much.

Because Josie was *right*.

"What you're doing, Laura, is fascinating to watch from the outside. Plus, yeah, I am demented. So sometimes my mind just...goes there. And I found myself wondering what it felt like, eating dinner with two guys, snuggling on the couch with two guys, wanting affection—but not sex—and having to, what? Pick? Kiss both? Cuddle in a sandwich?"

That made Laura laugh. "I thought it would be weird, too. It kind of was, at first. Mike made a big spectacle of making sure I knew they didn't expect sex. I knew what he was doing. He really was just trying to be nice and to help me relax." She let out a puff of air. "And it was good and kind and all that, but it pissed me off. I still don't know what they were thinking, hiding the truth about their relationship from me."

"They're not gay." Josie started to unpeel a banana from Laura's fruit bowl.

Laura did a double-take. "Did anyone ever think they were?"

Through a mouthful of banana, Josie sputtered, "Ah, c'mon, Laura. Two guys with one girl? *Gay, gay, gay.*"

"Not gay!"

Holy smokes, not even close to gay. Laura knew gay. Gay men, that is. Her high school boyfriend her senior year had turned out to be gay. He'd come out when they were juniors in college, home at Thanksgiving and hanging out in a piano bar with a group of friends.

Ding! A million little questions had been answered with one big answer. What other hot-blooded seventeen-year-old teenager wanted to cuddle and kiss all the time instead of banging wherever they could get a shred of privacy? Or knew all the words to the disco songs? Or liked to go clothes shopping with her?

And eyed the same guys Laura surreptitiously checked out as they had wandered the mall?

Her gaydar wasn't pinging with Mike and Dylan. No way. It was just...complicated. That's all.

Why was it always so complicated?

Josie swallowed hard, trying to clear her mouth. "I know that. I asked."

"You *asked*?" Laura's turn to sputter.

"They closed right up. That Dylan is one scary dude when he's being cold. Mike, too—but Dylan was worse. I felt like the ice king had just cast a spell over the booth."

"You asked them that at Jeddy's? Jesus, Josie. You have some—"

"Balls. Yeah. I know. I had to ask, though. If you're just some bed toy for them, then I'm not letting anyone do that to my best friend, because that is some fucked up mental shit right there. If two gay guys are just out trawling for a chick they can bang to get off their jollies, it won't be you."

Laura started peeling a clementine. "I'm touched." She frowned. "I guess. In your own extremely convoluted way, you mean well."

"And, by the way, no foursomes. Dylan shut that one down."

The orange wedge in Laura's mouth went flying across the room, landing in the sink as she did a spit take.

"You asked about a foursome?"

Josie winked. "I was just testing them."

"Oh, my God." No wonder Dylan had made a funny face when Josie's name had come up last night. Mike's arched eyebrows without a smile had made her wonder as well. What in the ever-loving hell did they think of her best friend? And how did this reflect on how they viewed her?

The night had been nice. Just nice. And *just nice* was exactly what she'd needed after far too many nights of surprise, shock, passion and boundary pushes. Breaks. Annihilations.

Having a few boundaries in place where affection, banter, food and fun were all that were expected of the night had been refreshing.

And now Josie...

She wagged a finger in Josie's face. "No more foursome tests. Or jokes. Or—*ewww*." She shuddered. "And no more going behind my back to tell them how I feel."

"Someone has to."

"Has to what?"

"Tell them how you feel. And frankly, if you won't do it, I will."

Laura plunked her elbows on the table and rested her chin in her hands. "Why? Who appointed you the keeper of my feelings?"

"Ryan."

Jolt. "You don't see me sabotaging your relationships!"

"I'm not sabotaging anything, Laura! I'm saving your relationship. *S*. Plural. Well, it's one, but with two guys. Where is Miss Manners' Plural Guide to Threesomes?"

This was getting out of hand. "To answer your original question, no. I don't have to kiss one and then the other. I asked."

"You asked!" Josie clapped her hands gleefully. "Did they hand you a neatly printed manual on how to have a perma-threesome?"

Glare. "I wish you came with a user's manual so I could find your off switch."

Smirk. "You're not the first person to say that to me."

Sigh. "And I won't be the last."

Josie reached for her hand, the gesture one of caring. "Laura. Seize this. Accept it. Yes, it's crazy. No, no one has words to describe it. And yes, I did go behind your back and tell them about you—because someone needed to. They're really great guys. You know that. Don't blow this." She released her hand and stood.

"Are you really jealous?" Laura squeaked out, surprised by Josie's tenderness.

"Jealous? Hell, yes. I don't want to take it away from you, of course." She grabbed an apple and headed toward the door. "I just wouldn't mind finding two guys like that for myself."

The door shut on her words. *Sip.* The coffee tasted better than normal. Calming and soothing yet putting her on alert to start the day. Stretching, her arms reached high and her shirt rode up a bit, exposing a thin expanse of belly flesh. Not wearing a bra, her breasts rubbed against the thin cloth of her cotton jersey, her pajamas loose and comfortable. The day was about to start and work loomed large.

Last night she'd left their apartment after watching a stupid comedy she'd picked simply because she'd already seen it the previous week, with Josie. Picking something she'd seen made sense, giving her the mental space to go through an hour and a half squished between Mike and Dylan, trying to figure out how to just be as, well—*three.*

Those ninety minutes, followed by gorging themselves on an amazing tiramisu Dylan had hand crafted, were like living in parallel. Half of her enjoyed every minute, the domestic normalcy easier to sink into than she'd imagined.

The other half was the problem: Judging. Questioning. Analyzing. Poking.

Doubting.

If she could just quell that half of her then this could work. *Really* work.

Where was her off switch? Her user's manual? All she needed was the good half. The half that believed, that turned toward healing and tenderness and love in whatever form it took.

Meanwhile, both halves needed a shower. She had another threesome in mind right now: her, Mr. Showerhead, and Bob, her battery-operated boyfriend. That was a threesome both halves of her could get behind.

And now she didn't have to fantasize about faceless lovers with their hands and mouths all over her. She had a very real memory to draw on.

And a very real promise of so much more. Hers for the taking, in fact, if she just reached out.

She reached out, alright. Turned on the shower, grabbed Bob, and slipped out of her jammies as the water heated up. The first spray of water hit her, tickling her shoulder with little wet pin pricks, and soon her head was under the water, her hair soaking fast as the water wended its way down her body. Ah, how different her hands felt against her own skin today. No sex last night; they'd ended the evening with warm hugs and tentative kisses, each man waiting his turn for a moment with her. It had been sweet. Mellow.

Just right.

As a smile played across her lips and she reached for the shower head, she marveled that something so simple—dinner, a movie at home, a homemade dessert, two kisses—could complete her so readily. She inhaled deeply as the spray tickled her clit, the shower head doing its magic as she balanced it in her right hand, left reaching for good old Bob. This Bob (*ah, she had a drawer full of electronic boyfriends...*) was purple and shiny and sleek. No need for a clit attachment when she had a shower head. And now, she no longer held Bob and the spray nozzle, but instead that was Dylan's mouth.

Mike's hands roamed her back, soaping her as his torso slid along her rib cage, hard muscle hot and wet, the spray bouncing off skin the color of sun-kissed honey, his face wet and eyes intense, mouth reaching down for hers as his fingers slipped between her legs and began to stroke her.

Now Dylan's mouth was on her, kissing her hips, her ass, desire pooling and expanding deep inside, eager to clamp down on him as he thrust inside her, little sighs and groans in need of a reason to be made. Ah, those abs, wet and slick and rubbing against her breasts, lips on hers, tongue exploring as Mike's hands did their magic on her clit, tracing lazy circles that took her breath away again. Again. And again, hitching higher as he built an orgasm from scratch, like a fine artisan plying his trade, infusing the final work with a delicacy and craftsmanship only one, lone man could spin. A lone man with eyes that cut through her flesh like a hot knife in butter, hands melting her skin to a core of need that pulsed, red and eager for more of him. Of them. Of all three as one.

She lost herself in pure sensation, mind and memory and body fused as she came and came and came, alone and complete.

Bob shot across the bathtub and skittered to the drain. She threw her head back as the massive orgasm wracked her body, her legs no longer trustworthy, her arm grabbing the safety bar just in time as her neck tightened with the force of wave after wave of orgasm, anus clenching and opening as her pussy pushed against it, the deep muscles exorcising her pent-up desires.

She imagined the three of them, spent, all sitting under the spray and twitching as the leftover neurological impulses wiggled their way out of their bodies, this drawing of three giving life to fantasies most people could only nurture, well—

like this. The shower head hung on its hose now, the spray aimlessly pointing here and there, Bob resting on its side, half dead, buzzing uselessly against a metal drain circle it could never make come.

She slouched down and pulled her knees against her bare, wet breasts. Hands combing her long, wet hair, she sighed.

When she really could have both Mike and Dylan right here, right now, like this, what on earth was she doing with such pale imitations? Was that part of Josie's point?

Reality was scary. Far safer to whack off in the shower and imagine it all.

Reality, though, had given her this—the most intense shower experience of her life. Drawing on what she knew was real, was possible, was achievable had made her—well, it had made her want the real thing.

God damn it.

She hated when Josie was right.

* * *

The phone rang. Mike's phone never actually rang these days; just texts. The ring tone was so unfamiliar he ignored it the first three times, then realized what it was. A comedic moment of bumbling to fish the phone out of his pocket, then he answered.

"Hello?"

"Mike?" Laura. Ah, Laura's voice. It had been a week and they were trying to find a time they could all get together. Fall was approaching and ski prep was in the first slow, languid stages. Ad campaigns and supply orders and a host of issues he'd never dealt with as just an employee were keeping him busy on the mountain.

Man, did her voice sound nice.

"Hey, there," he answered, voice going low and sultry. Lots of parts of him felt sultry suddenly. Good thing he'd already run a quick six miles today.

"How're you guys doing?"

"Dylan's working out right now. Lifting. I don't know much about his schedule beyond that."

"Where's he lift?"

"At the Y in Cambridge."

"That's not far from my apartment."

He'd never seen her apartment, he suddenly realized. His admin brought him a spreadsheet with a bunch of numbers and pointed to a place for him to initial. Tucking the smart phone between his shoulder and cheek, he listened while he scribbled.

"Yeah? Maybe you can go catch him and outlift him." Laughter greeted that one.

"I'm pretty fair at it, but no way I can match him."

"Can you bench your weight?" Few women could.

"Nope. Close, but nope." She hesitated. He could feel a change in the conversation's tone, from light-hearted and just touching base to something more guarded. Was it something he said? Weightlifting didn't seem to be emotional minefield territory, so he doubted it was that. Why did everything these days have to be so rife with issues?

Breathe, Mike. Breathe. Just wait her out.

His silence provoked her. "I can bench about fifteen pounds less."

Again, that weird hesitation. He ran a frustrated hand through his hair and pointed a delivery guy with boxes on a dolly to his destination. This split attention drove him nuts. Focusing on one thing at a time was key to feeling more grounded, and right now he needed to be centered. Whatever was going on in some subtext he didn't understand with Laura, he needed to be on his game.

"I used to bench double my weight," he added, then stopped short. Weight. That was it. They weren't talking about abstract numbers here. She thought he expected her to say how much she could bench? Which would clue him in to her weight? Women really were that sensitive some times.

"Dylan can bench about a thousand pounds," he said, grinning.

"What?"

"Yep. Carrying that ego around..."

She laughed. Score.

"It's almost a fourth partner," she joked back.

Warmth spread through him, unexpected and welcome, his throat thick with emotion. If she was going to make threesome jokes, this was deepening nicely. Jill had told him a long time ago that she began to really accept their relationship when she could wisecrack about it.

"Hey, Mike? The wax guys are on the line—they said there's a problem with the order," his admin, Shelly, interrupted. Full-figured, energetic, and highly opinionated, she was only nineteen but had been in the back office for three years, practically running the show. She tapped her foot and managed somehow to convey urgency and ignore him all at once as she worked on her smart phone. "Seriously," she added. "They won't talk to me. Only you."

He held up one finger in Shelly's direction. "Damn," he muttered. "Sorry, Laura—I've got a work problem here."

"A work problem? As in, you have no snow and can't work?"

"No, a supplier needs some attention."

"I didn't know you were so heavy into the business side of things."

You have no idea.

"Oh, I help out with inventory sometimes," he explained.

Shelly shot him a *WTF?* look and he started to feel unmoored. This was veering into dangerous territory, fast. He wasn't ready to tell Laura about the money. Soon, but not just yet.

Torn, he paused, wishing he could just take a thirty-mile run and think. Think it all through. Telling her was the right choice, so why not just *say* it? What was holding him back? A part of him feared, deeply, that he would regret this one day. That she would find out the truth and hate him.

That these secrets were eating away at his soul.

"I'll hurry then—I just need a few seconds more. Can you and Dylan come over to my place for dinner tomorrow night?"

The warmth returned. "Of course," he gasped, surprised by the offer.

"I'm not as good a cook as Dylan," she added.

Shelly twisted her wrist in repeating circles, pushing Mike to get off the phone. Hell of a time for this.

"Whatever you make, we'll savor," he said. "What time?"

"Seven?"

"We're there. See you tomorrow."

As he said the words, Shelly reached up and plucked the phone from him, slamming the red button to end the call.

"Hey!" he shouted, pulling himself up to his full height. Who did she think she was?

Shelly didn't even bother looking at him. "Yeah. Right. Like that'll intimidate me." Her snort followed him as he marched away to talk to the wax dudes.

Madge's granddaughter was a chip off the old—well, the *old*.

* * *

What caught Dylan off guard most was how pink her apartment was. He hadn't pegged Laura as one of those pink girls, but the apartment practically glowed. Not in a sickly-sweet Barbie dream house kind of way, but more like IKEA had decided pink was the color of the season and Laura had happened to decide to decorate her entire place that year. Even the bathroom had some shade of pink that dominated.

It wasn't a show stopper.

Chuckling as he dried his hands on a pinkish bath towel with blue and lime highlights, he paused to stare at himself in the mirror. This was really happening. Mike had been wrong. Mr. Doubt Everything had come back this morning from one of his killer runs and declared that the situation with Laura was tenuous at best, and that they needed to pour their hearts out tonight at her place and just tell her about the billions.

"You're nuts," Dylan had told him flatly. He was off for the day and ironing work shirts while deciding what to wear that night. The ratty Rush t-shirt or the ratty Dead shirt? Hard to decide.

"Not nuts," Mike retorted. "Sane. Rational. Reasonable. We're skating on thin ice here by not telling her. And if it comes out before we're the ones to sit down and talk about it with her, all hell will break loose."

"How will it come out, Mike? She doesn't know anyone we know."

"The workers at the ski resort figured it out."

"That's because there are financial people there who had to know who owns the place, and they sniffed the money trail back to you. But they don't know about the trust fund, right?" Mike's uncomfortable silence had sent a chill down Dylan's back. "Right?" he said sharply.

Mike had looked up at the ceiling and shook his head. "Someone there knows. They had to. I couldn't buy the entire resort outright and I needed to give financial statements proving the steady income. I'll finish paying it off next year, but there was no way to do this without disclosing it."

"Damn." Dylan hadn't known that.

"So we need to tell her."

Dylan argued back. "Not yet. We need one night to just...be. Last week was perfect. Tonight can be more perfect."

Mike's skeptical look had nearly broken him. Truth be told, he just wasn't ready to look into Laura's sweet face and declare he was a billionaire. That Mike was, too.

Oh, yeah, we lied about this one little thing...we make more money than most major movie stars do in a career. Only we make it per year. You'll never have to worry about money again with us.

And—*smack*. He imagined the slap. Because it felt like one, in his gut. If roles were reversed he'd feel betrayed and pissed and all the things he imagined she had felt until last week. The roller coaster of their relationship was making everyone queasy, and taking a break was helping to settle everyone into a comfortable place where they could proceed. That's what he wanted more of. Not secrets and reveals and heart-felt explanations and angst-filled pleas.

And sex. He wanted sex.

Letting that be secondary had been hard. Hell, *he* was hard. All the time now. And lavender-scented hand lotion wasn't the best girlfriend these days, no matter how nice it smelled. It couldn't sigh, or groan his name, or dig its fingers into his shoulders at the just perfect moment when—

Damn tight pants. That helped with one clothing decision for the evening—looser jeans.

Mike had accepted that they should wait, though his reluctance was clear. And now here they were, in her homey, pink apartment, ready to take things to the next step.

The second he and Mike had entered her apartment the air had crackled with anticipation, the atmosphere a one-hundred-eighty degree difference from dinner at their place the week before.

Laura had shifted a bit, wearing something loose and diaphanous, a little more sultry and open than last week.

They were all ready for more.

But not Mike's level of *more*. Not yet. Having luscious sex with her and Mike in the next hour, spread out and spread eagle and licking and laving and loving and touching and thrusting? Sure.

Baring his soul and revealing the money and experiencing the unsettling feelings he still didn't know how to cope with?

No way.

"What is that incredible aroma?" he nearly shouted as he walked into her tiny kitchen. White tile floor, white formica counters, a cheap kitchen table and vinyl-covered chairs. Red and pink, of course. It looked like any kitchen in any apartment you'd expect a twenty-something corporate worker to live in, especially someone likely still paying off student loans.

You could fix that, a voice whispered. He quashed it.

"I'm no Italian cook," she joked, pretending to be humble, "so I made chicken satay and pad Thai."

"From scratch?" he and Mike said simultaneously, both with an incredulous tone.

She shrugged. "Sure. Just have to follow a recipe."

Could they have found anyone better? She was already the whole package, but add in the fact that she made her own Thai food and—wow.

"I, uh—you do *like* Thai food?" An alarmed look crept over her features.

"We love it," they said.

Dylan looked at Mike. "Jinx!"

Everyone laughed. The pink shrimp Laura was throwing into the noodle dish matched, exactly, one of the stripes of pink on the dish towels. This was getting to be a bit much. He looked at her and realized she was staring at him, eyebrow cocked.

"What?"

"You keep peering around my apartment as if you were in a museum, surveying it." Her eyes narrowed. "What's going on?"

Caught. "It's nice!" he said, a bit too cheery for everyone's tastes.

Mike grabbed a bottle of red wine he'd brought and began to uncork it, pretending not to pay attention to the interaction between the other two.

"Nice." There was no way to come out of this one on top, was there? He had to fess up.

"It's really...pink."

"Too pink?"

"Just right pink."

Mike interrupted. "Laura, where are your wine glasses?"

She pointed to an upper cupboard. "Up there. The *not pink* ones," she added dryly.

Now he knew this was just a game. Two could play...

So could three. "Next time I'll bring a rosé," Mike muttered.

Dylan and Laura both did double takes. All three burst into laughter.

"It is quite pink. Josie helped me decorate," Laura explained, her smile so deep it made her cheeks look like apples, dimples forming and her eyes lighting up.

Dylan loved that smile. Wanted to make her have it every waking moment.

And in her dreams, too.

As the guys set the table, Laura put the finishing touches on the meal, and the three dug in. "No dessert," she announced.

You can be our sweet ending, he almost said.

The rice noodles were perfect, flavored with the right touch of fish sauce and something spicy, red flakes mingling with crushed peanuts, chicken and shrimp. It was pad Thai like he'd never had—fresh and flavorful, without that bogged-down, MSG feeling. He ate three plates full, giving Mike a run for his money.

"Hungry?" Laura asked, agog at his appetite.

"It's so good!" he groaned.

Mike nodded, working a bit slower through his food. "It could use a nice white, though," he pointed out, referring to his wine glass. "I'll bring some next time."

She grinned. "Rosé would be fine. I have a feeling you'll learn to enjoy my pink."

Whoosh. Dylan felt his eyes go wide. Mike bit his lips. Laura seemed to realize her double entendre and everyone avoided eye contact for a few seconds until Mike let out a little snicker. He poured the last of the wine into their glasses, giving each a few final ounces, before peals of laughter and an uncontrollable folding made Laura slip to the ground in a crouch, her body shaking with mirth and giggles.

Now *that* was the kind of pink he could get behind.

Er...now he lost it, too, until all three huddled on the ground in a cluster of jovial hilarity. Laura wiped her eyes and resumed her gigglefest whenever she looked at either of them. Mike dragged himself to standing and tried to shake it off. Long ago, Dylan had given in, abs aching from laughing so hard.

It was nervous laughter, but from a place of truth. And now was the test, as he slid his hand up her back to her neck, the touch decidedly sensual and a complete change in tone from where they all were, ensconced in chuckles that belied the underlying tone of sex and hope and desire in her innocent joke. Dylan would be the one to reveal it, because Dylan was the only one in this breath who could cut through the worries and the hesitancy and the what-ifs and get to the heart of what they all really wanted.

The only sound they heard was Mike's deep breath as he watched, enraptured, his eyes on Dylan's hand as Laura arched her neck just so, responding to the intensity of this searching caress. Would she? Would she not?

Hers to answer, the question hung in the air like a fourth partner, needing to be included and welcomed, answered and accepted.

Like Laura.

Like all of them, really, for this was what spoke to the center of their beings, the need to find someone else who understood, who cared, who could navigate the slippery emotional landscape of want and love and need that was so fraught with confusion.

In this space, though, as his hand lingered on her neck, now sliding up to feel her cheek, his torso twisting to face her, open and ready, the negative side of it all washed away. They were just three people in an apartment, alone, forging their own reality stroke by stroke, caress by caress, look by look and breath by breath.

That the word *love* was beginning to seep into his subconscious mind when he thought of Laura, when he considered the three of them, made his heart soar. In a few short weeks he had found her, courted her, lost her and won her back—they both had, he and Mike working as the partners they always had been and always would be.

Love wasn't a word they used lightly, and he wasn't ready, consciously, to use it just yet. Instead, it hovered, watching and observing, taking in their new dance, their interactions and hopes and dreams, and he hoped that soon love would join them and help them, too, to create something new and wondrous, as delicious as her hand on his now, on her open face, searching and warm, asking him questions with her eyes that he and Mike could only answer with their hands, their mouths, and other parts that yearned to be used and included.

Laura had to take the lead now—and when she reached over and her lips brushed his, it unleashed a wellspring of *everything* that had been pent up these weeks, of wondering and hoping and assuming and thriving. Her lips were soft and eager, testing and nipping, tongue slipping between his lips and prying more out of him.

She didn't need to ask twice; he used his mouth to take more of her, hands embedding themselves in her hair, stroking the soft waves roaming over her shoulders and down her back, palms filling with hot flesh he needed to squeeze to own.

She pulled back, breathless, eyes dark and serious, and stood, walking over to Mike. A tentative smile from her, a contemplative piercing look from him, his hands reaching out to make the first move, hips leaning toward her as he embraced Laura, their waists touching first, hands almost an afterthought. Dylan halted himself, sensing he shouldn't walk near them just yet, that this was Laura's sequence, her lips and mouth and hands and body needing to pursue, to test both men separately before meshing with them as one.

Just when he thought he would burst in an explosion of craven, overwhelming need, Laura broke away from Mike, reached for both of their hands, and gently led them to her bedroom.

* * *

This was it. It was time. She'd been thinking about their hands on her all day, her body making little sighs, imagining the flutter of eyelashes against her belly, thinking of Mike's blonde hair and Dylan's thick arms.

Before, when they'd surprised her at Mike's cabin, she'd said yes to a pre-ordained situation, one that caught her by surprise and tapped into so many fantasies—dreams she'd never imagined possible but, when suddenly offered to her, she felt compelled to accept.

Right now was different. Right now she was in control, making decisions long before they were pre-destined, assembling her own ideas and thoughts about how the night would go. Before she'd even started cooking, she had let her mind wander to where it needed to go and she'd known that she would invite them into her bed. It was inevitable, but more than that—it was her choice.

Her choice.

Time for them to enjoy *her* pink.

When did my bed get so small? she thought, staring at the queen-sized mattress. *When Mike and Dylan are both on it,* her mind answered as Dylan reclined, lazy and expectant, patting the bed beside him. His smile was impish and open. He was ready for anything. *Anything.*

And she was about to get *anything* as she slid on the bed, still clothed, and Mike laid down next to her. Captured perfectly between the two, she paused, enjoying this—the few seconds before anyone would touch her, before they would start what would end in release, before her brain shut down and nerve endings went into autonomous control. This frozen speck in time was still pregnant with possibility and as she—

Oh. Dylan's hands were so warm as he slipped them under her thin cotton jacket and tank top, the fabric pooling nicely on the bed, like little islands of cloth. Her legs twitched as Mike's hands rested, warm and soft, on her ankles, both riding up her calves, over her knees to the soft, supple flesh of her thighs, her tender clit beginning to pulse already, so wantonly throbbing for them both. She moistened, her wet womanhood ready for what came next.

All three of them.

Four hands slipped her clothes off, her own hands practically useless, the two men knowing what to do and Laura being catered to with an intensity and focus that she found amusingly seductive. They were a well-oiled (*and well-hung*) machine, these two, serving her right now.

As the chill of the air hit her back, her ribcage, and her breasts, her nipples pebbled and she reached for the waistband of Mike's pants, unbuttoning the pants and reaching behind him, hands slipping under to grab fistfuls of ass, his fingers quickly unclasping her bra and making her shudder with the thrill of it all.

By the time she remembered to look at Dylan, he had dispensed with his own clothes, his nude body a welcome and delectable sight. She chuckled and her brow furrowed.

"Something wrong?" Mike's hands slid up and teased her labia, giving her just a hint of what she could come to expect and making her swell and blossom.

"Everything's perfect," she murmured, Dylan's mouth descending on hers again as he pressed the length of his body against her, abs to belly, breasts to chest, rigid rod to pliant pussy.

A quick flash of shower memory hit her, her spray and Bob mimicking what Mike and Dylan were now doing in the flesh, in her bed, very real and warm and wanting. How could she have denied herself this?

The scent and taste of Dylan filled her as Mike made sounds of disrobing, the bed shifting as he stood, threw off his clothes, then knelt back on the bed, the smattering of hair on his chest tickling her back, his fingers tantalizing with promise. He sighed into her neck and his hot breath made her belly clench, the tightening leading up to her throat, the body readying for both of them, for all of them, for explosion and release and love.

So much flesh. Her own, ample curves, which the moonlight streaming through the window between the parted pink curtains illuminated in a muted relief, the same lush handfuls she'd once found embarrassing were now something her men luxuriated in, touching and grasping and caressing and marking with their pinches, their strokes, their licks.

Her men.

And they were, as Mike's finger slipped up to tease her clitoris, giving it a "hello" and then retreating, his mouth dotting her back with small kisses and sighs, his cock pushing against the cleft of her ass as he journeyed across her flesh.

Dylan now stretched before her, leaning her onto her back and carefully positioning a pillow under her hips, the two men exchanging a glance as Mike moved up the bed to Laura's side. Dylan moved down and then went down, his tongue catching her not so much by surprise but by relief. Swollen desire clustered so neatly in these nerve endings made real by vulnerable, pink flesh, her clit screaming out for him, for Mike, for any attention.

Mike kissed her, his hands on both sides of her jaw, his mouth both brutal and pleasant somehow at the same time, her own tongue rising to a threshold of near violence as she tried to take in as much of his mouth, his lips, his tongue as she could without hurting them.

Yes, yes, yes, their mouths screamed, her hips lifting as Dylan slipped two fingers inside her aching emptiness, her wet warmth closing around him as he hooked one finger up to find a pitch-perfect place to call home, tongue zeroing in on her nub and making her tighten, ass clamping down, pussy folding in to a pinprick of pleasure as he slid in and out, finger and tongue fucking her with Mike consuming her mouth, the multitude of sensations making her forget about climax, forget about orgasm, damn near lose all sense of purpose here as she just was—flesh, rolls, curves, tongue, pussy and—*ahh.*

Mike's fingers rolled one nipple with just a tad too much force, the nip enough to make her throat bleat with pain, which he took as encouragement, pinching a bit harder. She couldn't say no, didn't want to say no—between Dylan's lapping at her clit and fingers thrusting in and out, the pain took her mind to a new place. Soon she gasped, unable quite to breathe enough, her hips out of control. Reaching for him, she grasped Mike's cock at the base and he inhaled sharply, the sound whistling through the night and joining her own rasping throat sounds.

He took her hand as an invitation, moving so he straddled her face and she welcomed it, giving her something to do as Dylan's tongue gave her such devoted attention. He was languid and attentive, giving her body the time to warm up, letting her feel the pleasure and live in the layers that covered each other, each bit of arousal building on the next, a warm, wet blanket of pending orgasm. Her mouth took Mike in all the way to the base, tongue flicking the tip and hardening to give him a concentrated point of muscled focus. Shifting his hips, he started to rotate and move in and out of her mouth slowly. Perfectly pinned to the bed, between Mike on top of her and Dylan below, she couldn't move.

Even if she wanted to.

She was trapped, and the thrill of it clouded her mind, because what if she wanted to get up? Get away from the sensuality of Dylan's cunnilingus? Move herself from Mike's blow job? She couldn't.

And, for whatever reason, that fact aroused her even more.

She had to give and had to receive right now, knowing there was so much more coming. Whatever Dylan did he did to give her more, and now she could take without guilt, could give without fear, could exchange these acts of love and lust and carnal knowledge on equal ground and know that it was mind-blowingly amazing and hers.

All hers to take and give.

Tall, long, lean Mike seemed to stretch up to the sky as she took her hands and moved up his ass to the small of his back, then maneuvered to get one finger on his taint, pushing up hard on the spot between anus and scrotum. He threw his head back and groaned, the vibration so intense she could feel it in her teeth, which were currently around the base of his cock, a light pressure but held back by tongue and lips that buffered.

Slowly, he changed position and slid out of her, her hands fondling his balls now and his hands scooping her breasts as Dylan closed the deal.

And then Mike changed places with him.

The sudden shift of men made her lose the rhythm, the near-orgasm retreating now and hiding a bit, though the different technique Mike used quickly coaxed it back into play. Dylan stood by the bed and watched Mike and Laura, one hand lazily stroking himself, waiting for what she knew would be next, the thought sending a shiver down her spine.

Mike's mouth was so different from Dylan's, faster and more demanding, a personality change. He was aggressive and intense and her body rose to it, Dylan sauntering over to mouth her nipples, biting suddenly as Mike's tongue pinpointed and began to apply hard, friction-filled strokes just as her entire body clamped and flushed.

Her hands grabbed fistfuls of pink satin bedsheets, flailing and stretching out like a woman impaled by a tongue.

"Oh, oh, oh!" she cried out, words long gone, her hips now thrusting up and down, seeking Mike's face and tongue, a sudden balloon feeling making her inhibited but too late.

She exploded. Gushed. Squirted, the stream flying through the air as Mike followed her gyrations, seeking to keep a steady pace on her clit as she bucked and groaned and thrashed and turned all animal. Basic instinct was it—that was all she could be right now as she was the climax, was the orgasm, was the fluid that poured out of her, evidence of the drama of what these men had wrung from her.

And this was just the appetizer.

"Oh, yeah, Laura. Let it all go," Dylan cheered quietly, his hand no longer on himself but his shaft at attention and ready for orders.

She gently pushed Mike's head away, the climax still in progress but the touch now almost painful, that post-clit orgasm sensitivity that made her grit her teeth in a not-good way.

He sensed it and pulled back; *ah, good*, she thought. He knew enough to do that. Learning about new lovers' bodies was always a game of *does he/doesn't he/will he/won't he* that was new each time, and never reliably easy to guess. On her back, hips still elevated, she felt an enormous wet spot under the cleft of her ass and panted little breaths, letting her arms go liquid, her legs splay out, her body in some yoga position of complete contentment.

Yet still she wanted more. Needed them both in her.

Rolling over, she chuckled at the sight of the wet spot, bigger than her ass, knowing she'd gushed and not at all shy about it. It had happened once or twice before, typically when she was so blindingly aroused and not looking for it. Squirting found her when it wanted to, and on its terms, and damn if Dylan and Mike hadn't summoned it.

"Well, that's new," Mike laughed, staring at the spot.

"Really?" Dylan puffed up a bit. "Never seen that before?"

Clearly, Dylan had, and viewed it with his typical assertive self as something he had manifested. Proud of it, even. And damn if he shouldn't be, with that magic tongue. Mike's, too.

Their talk amused her. "I have, you know, in videos," Mike sputtered, his body stretched out. They seemed to know to wait, to give this a few minutes.

Laura pulled back the wet sheet and crawled under, cuddling a pillow.

"G'night, boys," she whispered, then pretended to snore. "Thanks for that."

Her passage almost cried out in agony, needing to be filled by something other than two wholly inadequate fingers, fingers that had been fine when they were touching her and teasing out the climax but that needed to be replaced by Dylan's cock, or Mike's or—

Both.

Both in her, the double penetration right there, moments away, the thought of it sending her into spasms that nearly brought her to orgasm from the mere thought.

Dylan climbed on top of her and pulled the sheet back, his cock settling into the cleft of her ass, micro-movements from his hips making him ride her.

"Sure you don't want more, Laura?" he murmured in her ear from behind.

The groan that escaped her mouth came from another layer of self that was ready, teeming with intent right now, her thick throat the only sign of struggle in her. Some part of her knew all too well that she would be completely drained of all passion and sex by the time they were done with her.

Which was her form of nirvana.

Laura rolled herself into a sitting position, completely uninhibited, as if it were routinely part of life to be naked in her own bed, wet spot testifying to an eroticism a few minutes ago she'd never thought possible. Her eyes feasted on the long, lean Mike and the shorter, muscled Dylan, both watching her with expectation and very, very obvious signs that they were eager for her.

Signs pointing up.

It was Dylan who gently nudged her to the side and slid under her, positioning her hips over him, guiding her to straddle. Her breasts, pendulous and full, brushed against his chest as she laughed, her hair falling over her shoulder and tickling his chin. His tip touched her clit, an agony she inhaled her way through, the feelings so raw and exquisite she wanted to plunge herself onto him.

So she did. Angling her hips just so, she rode him effortlessly, his rod filling her slick walls and making her cry out to Mike.

"You, too!" she gasped, ready for the forbidden once more, but this time completely at her call, at her request, as she opened herself up to them on equal footing. No lies, no secrets, no omissions.

The bed seemed to tilt slightly to the left, then right, as she felt Mike climb behind her, his hands on her ass and then his voice.

"Hey." Hot breath on her neck, a kiss. "Do you have any lube?"

"There." She pointed to the drawer next to her bed.

She'd bought a new tube—and cleared out her electronic boyfriends—for tonight. Somehow, he managed to keep his knees in place, firmly planted on either side of Dylan's legs and her ass, and pulled the bottle from the drawer. In seconds she felt the delicious, wet, slippery warmth of fluid on her ass, her walls clenching with greed for all of him in her.

"Oh," Dylan sighed as she tightened. And then Mike's finger sent an electric jolt through her as Dylan sat up and took her left nipple in his mouth, the combined sensations making her buck against Dylan and start to really fuck him.

"*Tsk, tsk, tsk!*" he teased, his words mumbled through a mouthful of her bosom. Coupled with Mike's finger's making slow, snail trails along the edge of her puckered ass, she felt swollen and captivated by the anticipation of what was about to happen, to have Mike in her, both holes full, all three joined by her flesh.

Mike's finger slipped past her over-snug hole, the feeling so thrashingly hot she almost came, though Dylan held her still, anchoring her to the bed as Mike prepared to enter her. His oiled-up hands roamed her ass and hips, a playful slap making her gasp finally break.

"God, Mike, just fill me. Please," she begged, Dylan reaching up with his lips and fingers to bite and twist her nipples just as Mike centered the tip of his cock over her ass.

Tapping at the gates, the feel of him perched on the precipice between in and not-in made her push back a bit, needing him to do this, wanting to be complete with them both.

Burning, Stretching, Fire. Then—*ahh*.

Like pouring something warm and enormous in her, she felt her body seize then relent, seize and relent, the dance almost too much, her throat yielding hitched gasps as she worked to hold both men. Mike's belly pushed against her lower back and ass, his hands on either side of her and Dylan, his balance perfect.

It needed to be. One misstep and what was now a tortured pleasure would just be torture.

Taking Dylan's mouth with hers, she moved so carefully, Mike following her lead, until she felt them all tighten viscerally, as if nerves and pores and skin and need all pinpointed to the perfect climax. It was just standing there, as if summoned, and Mike pressed his stubbled cheek into her backbone and groaned.

"Ready?" Dylan said. It really wasn't a question, his face grimaced with excitement and the barely-held-back release he so obviously wanted.

Her body utterly impaled by both men, thoroughly full and ready for explosion, they slowly moved, awkward at first and then finding their rhythm, the power of three bringing them all quickly to the edge, friction and sweat and slick and mouths and everything.

Her ass burned and hummed, buzzed and clenched as Dylan's thick rod worked in tandem with Mike's hands and his mouth on her breasts and hips and then she felt it—that imperceptible roar that came from nowhere and told her she'd soon burst blood vessels around her eyes, scream until her throat ached, and fire neurons from parts of her that weren't supposed to have them.

Dylan's chest hair was matted with sweat, hers and his and Mike's dripping into a thin sheen as she caught his eyes in the moonlight, his face dark and ready. "God, Laura, I'm—"

Tip. She just...tipped, her ass and pussy and body tightening, fingers digging into Dylan's shoulders then releasing as she drew long, deep scratches, etching some part of her pleasured agony into him, then releasing and grabbing the sheets, ripping them from the corners of the mattress as she howled.

Howled.

The sound was like a rutting animal and then she realized it wasn't just her, Mike's long form pushing against her haunches as he thrust harder, splitting her in two and finding a sweet spot deep inside that made her feel like a dwarf star, imploded and eviscerated, a climax of every muscle and of no unturned sensation.

Hot cream poured into her; she could feel the spurt, the rush, the bubbling overflow as her too-tight passages strained to accept what Mike and Dylan's bodies spat out. No one moved too fast or too hard, afraid to cause too much pain, in fear of ruining this sweet, primal moment as they just...howled.

Laura's panting came first, her body going limp like a rag doll, collapsing on Dylan as Mike seemed to finish with one thrust and reactivated her clit, gently pushing it against Dylan's groin and giving her a shiver of an orgasm that was like a tiny, ice-cold breeze in a heat wave, perfect for a few seconds but never quite enough.

Mike hissed out his own climax, his hands kneading her back and then tensing, the feel of him deep in her wet and viscous. He, too, rested as if turned to putty, and soon Laura really was in a sandwich. The thought made her chuckle, which pushed Dylan out of her as her laughter engaged her abs.

Dylan joined her, and soon all three were amusing themselves with chuckles of comfort, of coming home, of satisfaction and of satiety. This was what Laura had dreamed of all these years. This bliss.

And nothing more.

Chapter Four

Dylan couldn't wipe the smile off his face. Maybe he was a bit biased, but he felt like he had really aligned the planets or pleased the gods or found the secret to the cosmos that day he'd read her profile, her sweet smile and creamy skin almost climbing out of the computer screen and saying, "You found me, Dylan. You found me."

As he sauntered into the fire station and unlocked his locker, he shot Joe, the chief, a look that must have been pretty wild, because Joe frowned and said, "You been hit by the dumb love stick, Stanwyck? Why you smiling like a lovesick dumbass?"

"Because I am a lovesick dumbass?"

Dylan stripped off his Howard Jones t-shirt (*man, his brother must have had a lapse in judgment in 1989*) and slipped his arms into his freshly-pressed uniform shirt.

Joe smirked back. "That explains it. The lovestruck part. You've always been a dumbass, and no woman will change that."

A couple of guys nearby chuckled and Dylan just rolled his eyes. The banter was part of the job. Joe motioned for him to follow into the chief's office.

The station looked like the set of Barney Miller, frozen in 1977 with the exception of Internet service and the computers. Scratched metal desks with cheap, fake-wood tops, battered filing and storage cabinets that were Army green and probably army-issued in the

1940s, or castoffs from the war. The floor was Army-green tile streaked with an off-white marble-like pattern that fooled no one; it was linoleum, cheap, and the second the custodians finished the annual stripping and waxing it was scuffed all over again, making Dylan wonder why on earth they bothered.

The place was clean as a whistle, though. When there was nothing to do the paramedics and fire fighters all had chore rotation, and Joe kept a tight ship. A veteran of Vietnam and the first Gulf War, he ran the place like a military officer and it showed. Response time was lightning fast, employee retention was nearly one hundred percent, and they hadn't had a new hire in four years. The waiting list to work there was dozens deep.

Joe closed the door, but didn't sit down. He pulled out a manilla envelope and said quietly, "Murphy just found out his wife has breast cancer."

Cold descended over him. "Oh, shit." His heart rate shot up. No man should have to go through this. He and Mike had, though, and he closed his eyes and took a deep breath, imagining what Murphy was going through.

"You know how hard it is, Stanwyck. And Murphy's dad has Alzheimer's. His wife's been taking care of him. They need to hire some kind of caregiver to help with his dad now, and they have the kids. If she gets the right treatment they think they caught it nice and early. We're taking up a collection, though." He handed Dylan the envelope and reached for the doorknob. "It's none of my business what you put in—just give what you can manage. No amount's too small."

You have no idea. "Of course."

"Put the envelope in my top drawer when you're done."

He slipped out, face impassive. Dylan stared at the envelope in his hand, full of fives and tens. He'd just been to the money machine that morning and had taken out $300. Reaching into his back pocket he pulled out his wallet and threw it all in there, mixing it in with the fives and tens to reduce suspicion. Not that it would help. It was pretty obvious.

He wondered if there was a way to ask the trust guy to send a bunch of money anonymously to Murphy's family. How many other guys like Murphy were out there, though? He had fifty million a year coming in, and the station was trying to get a few hundred to help with parking, meals, and babysitting for this poor family struggling with cancer and so much more. The weight of his inherited money rested heavily on his shoulders, a new burden to carry. How could he help people with it?

Eh. Three hundred bucks was a good start. He slipped the envelope in Joe's desk and walked out. What a great place to work. At least Murphy wouldn't have to worry about health insurance; their coverage was solid. Thank goodness; one less burden for the family.

It was the perfect job, really. Yet Dylan was thinking about quitting lately. He'd hung on for months after getting the first payment from the trust, not wanting to let go of his life. His old life.

That's what it was rapidly becoming, when he was honest with himself. Unfolding before him was a new life, one filled with more money than he could spend in two hundred years, with two amazing partners, and a sense of hope and renewal that made him think long and hard about how he wanted to spend his time.

Coming to work now had become an exercise in habit, following his schedule and hanging out, working rescues and just doing what he'd done for most of his adult life because, well, that's what he had done.

Had. *Had* done.

He stopped picking up extra shifts—didn't need the money anymore. Some of the other guys were thrilled to pick up the extra, making Dylan strongly doubt why he was there. Was he hogging a job someone else could really use? Desperately needed? In this economy, it was no small matter to find decent pay, good work hours, great benefits and a well-oiled machine like the station run by Joe. Another person who really wanted the job and who needed to earn a living would appreciate what Dylan now considered tossing aside.

He didn't need it any more. What had once seemed so valuable was now only important because of the social and emotional ties he had to his fellow coworkers. But even there, he was changing.

Never before had he realized how much conversation revolved around money. Specifically, the lack of it. People seemed to bond over it, complaining about high prices, student loans, hard-to-get mortgages, spouses and girlfriends who wanted to spend more, and how expensive kids were to raise. He'd once easily joined them, shouldering a crazy-high car payment and his own credit card bills that testified to his spending stupidity.

All debt was washed away a few months ago with a check bigger than his ego. Ah, Jill. Only Jill could orchestrate something like that.

Jill. As his eyes scanned the assignment chart and found his name, he realized he hadn't thought much about Jill these past few weeks. He wondered what the smile that elicited looked like, for it twisted his cheeks and lips into something unhappily nostalgic, not really pleased but marginally amused. Wistful.

He wasn't the wistful type.

His finger drew a line to what he needed to do. Cook. Ah, nice. That he could manage. A mess of meatballs and pasta and the guys would be full and appreciative. He made the same damn meal every time and no one ever complained.

And that was part of the reason he couldn't leave just yet. When he knew exactly how to act, how others would react, and exactly what to do, it was so easy to check his feelings at the door and just deliver on life's fixed expectations.

What he and Mike and Laura had, though? Totally uncharted territory. You couldn't blame a guy for hanging on to the familiar when so much was uncertain, no matter how wonderful it promised to be.

He heard the television droning on, some morning show with two female and one male co-host creating reasons to open their mouths. He needed to get started for lunch. Whatever he made needed to be dropped on the spot if an alarm went off and he needed to go on a call, so he reached for the crock pot and started a routine he could almost do in his sleep.

The bustle of the other guys working the same shift coming in, the outgoing shift leaving, the flash of freshly-showered guys toweling their hair dry as they came out of the locker room, hungry for bagels and cream cheese and whatever they could find—he knew it well. Ten years here and he knew it *all*.

Until silence descended, like someone shook a blanket and settled it across the room, smothering the sound and turning it into a muffle.

"Hey, Stanwyck! You're on TV again!" someone shouted. He turned, puzzled. On TV?

The morning show co-hosts were showing a clip of his appearance in a charity bachelor auction a couple of years ago, shirtless and wearing a fireman's uniform, a red bow tie around his neck. The guys hooted.

"Did you oil your pecs? Holy shit!" someone crowed.

Ah, geez. *What now?* he wondered. Wiping his hands, he abandoned the cooking and walked over to the television to join the curious crowd.

The clip ended and the camera focused on one of the women, a blonde in her forties with a perfect, sharp bob and a symmetrical face that looked like a surgeon had crafted it.

"Boston's most eligible bachelor just got a whole lot more eligible! 1.1 billion times more eligible, in fact."

The guys laughed and shot him looks.

His legs went numb. *Oh, fuck.* He tried to turn away and walk but he couldn't, rooted by horror. Mike had been right. Oh, how Mike had been right and *oh holy fuck* how he wished Mike had been wrong.

Laura.

"Records show that Dylan Stanwyck, firefighter extraordinaire, former model, and one of Boston's hottest bachelors, is the heir to shipping tycoon Richard Matthews' daughter's estate. Matthews' daughter, Jillian, died in 2010 and left Stanwyck, her longtime lover, a trust fund of $1.1 billion, with an annual income of more than $50 million."

If the room could have turned into a black hole it would have saved him the agony of living millisecond by millisecond through this. Half the guys were fixated on the television, but the guys he knew best stared openly at him, their faces morphing slowly from shock to disbelief and, unfortunately, to anger in some.

"Sources confirm that her $2.2 billion estate was split between Stanwyck and Mike Pine, a local ski instructor who recently used his inheritance to purchase the struggling Cedar Mountain Ski Resort. Here's to the lucky lady who finds her way to either man as the billionaire bachelors become the hottest dates in town and Stanwyck can buy himself many times over now in whatever charity auction he pleases."

Someone cut the power to the television, everyone turning and gawking openly. Murphy's eyebrows were in his hairline and he shook his head, muttered something under his breath, and left the room.

Finally, the chief took two steps toward him, inhaled slowly, then planted his hands on his hips, shifting his weight to one leg. His jaw flexing with tension, he said, "Stanwyck, you got something you wanna tell us?"

* * *

"I thought you'd been promoted. Not that you're the new owner!" Shelly stormed into Mike's office with spit and vinegar, looking like a younger version of Madge. It was unnerving. Being yelled at by a teenager wasn't on his list of expected experiences this morning, so his response was stunned silence.

"Hello? Going to say something?"

"What are you talking about?" Damn. Had someone in the CFO's office finally leaked the truth? He reached for his travel mug and took a long sip of coffee, buying time.

"The television show. All about you and some hot firefighter bachelor auction dude being billionaires. It's all over the morning talk shows and even on the radio."

Spew. He shot drops of coffee all over his desk, choking, the coughs racking his chest as he set down the mug. *Oh, my God. Oh, my fucking God.* Dylan had been so wrong. Why hadn't they told Laura? She was going to kill them.

No. Worse.

She was going to *leave* them.

He jumped up, tipping the travel mug on its side, a pool of tan coffee inching its way to contaminate the papers, the stapler, the tape dispenser. Shelly grabbed the mug and uprighted it, plucking tissues from a box on the desk to mop up the mess. He was out the door as she shouted, "Where are you going?"

Getting to Laura before she heard the news was his only rational thought. If she heard before they told her...

Sprinting to his jeep, he frantically searched his pants pockets for his keys before he realized he'd left them back in the office. By the time he got back there, Shelly was finishing her cleanup of his desk. The words "thank you" were about to exit his mouth as he searched for his keys, eyes methodically cataloging the desk's surface when she tipped her face up with a dismissive expression.

"Looking for these?" The keys dangled from her finger.

No words.

He grabbed the ring and left as she screamed, "You're welcome!" to his disappearing back.

Unlock car. Climb in. Insert key. Turn. Reverse. Gas. Thank God for autonomous responses, because he was working on muscle memory right now, the jeep racing down the mountain to go to the city, to find Laura, to—

To what? He had no plan. Punching the steering wheel, he flipped the radio to the channel most likely to be chattering about him and Dylan, a stupid DJ show known for caustic comics and nasty, biting commentary on local sports and characters.

Traffic report. Great. Now he knew everything was backed up before exit eighteen eastbound because a tractor-trailer jackknifed. How critical. And now the sports report. Another football player with CTE. Yet another arrested for abusing his wife. And now someone accused of doping.

The miles passed as he balanced speeding with getting caught.

Ding! His phone notified him he had a text. He was guessing it was Dylan. Ignoring it, he just...drove. Wasn't sure where. Just needed to get closer to Laura.

Ring, ring! If Dylan was using the phone then he must know.

Mike reached into his shirt pocket and answered. "Hello?"

"Shit, Mike. Have you watched the morning news shows yet?" He sounded as panicked and sick as Mike felt.

"No, but Shelly just told me everything. Fuck of a day to be there super-early for inventory."

"We need to get to Laura."

"Where is she?" The clock read 8:12 a.m. "At work by now?"

"That's what I'm guessing, too." The radio DJs started saying something about firefighter billionaires. Mike's brain couldn't process driving, talking with Dylan, and their banter. Situation fucked up, though, if this was all over the morning commute. *Fuck, fuck, fuck.*

"I told you we should—"

"You can chew me out later, dude. Let's work on fixing this." Steel edged his words, filling in the spaces where panic receded. *Don't fuck with me right now, Mike,* he seemed to say. *I don't have it in me.*

"Fair enough." Silence.

"She works at the Stohlman building downtown. Thirty-second floor. Meet me at the reception desk. How far are you?"

Mike ran a quick mental calculation. "Twenty minutes?"

"I'm a little closer. Probably beat you by five."

"Just get there and try to explain it before she sees it plastered all over the fucking television or hears some disc jockey cackling about it."

Click. He pressed End and found himself practically throwing the phone out the window. His ears perked and zeroed in on the DJs' conversation.

"So this guy is some muscled firefighter who oils up for these bachelor charity auctions and gives some rich cougar a nice night while underprivileged kids or AIDS patients or earthquake victims get an extra grand to spend on help. And now it turns out his girlfriend dies and leaves him a billion? Where can I find some rich, young woman to leave me a billion?"

Mike's knuckles turned white against the tan steering wheel as he gritted his teeth and sped up.

Different voice, higher and more derisive. "OK, sure, I can see that. It's like 50 Shades of Fire, right? But why'd she leave another billion to the other dude, the ski resort guy."

Pause. A woman's voice. "Maybe she was livin' the dream?"

Derisive DJ: "The dream?"

Woman DJ: "You know. Two guys."

First DJ: "That's our dream!"

310

Derisive DJ: "Your dream is two guys?" The radio spilled over with giggles and full-throated guffaws.

First DJ: "Haha, no—two women! Two chicks for one dick, man. For a billion bucks, though, I might do two guys. (Laughter). Girls don't fantasize about threesomes with two guys—"

Woman DJ: "In what universe? Of course we—"

Mike cut the radio off with a sharp flick of the wrist. *Fuck, fuck, fuck.* Laura was about to be completely devastated. She had openly asked them to tell her their secrets, and Dylan had told him they should wait. Dylan. God damn it! He'd listened to Dylan and this—*this* was the end result.

How had anyone found out about the trust? And of course the news station would use the whole firefighter bachelor angle. What a great lead. He knew the brouhaha would die down within days, and soon people wouldn't talk about it, but that didn't help him to get through this minute, the next hour, the next day—and he couldn't predict Laura's reaction here.

She may already be lost. But he had to try.

The highway was packed with the tail end of the morning commute, the turnpike thick but moving at about forty miles per hour. Better than nothing.

What had they been thinking, keeping the whole billionaire thing from her? That night in their apartment, dinner and a movie, everyone coming clean and her open, honest request that they not keep secrets —why had they, then? Her openness had been so damn appealing and they'd flung it in her face (*behind her back*), still hiding like creeps with a secret that, now that it was out, really wasn't that bad.

How many women wouldn't like to date someone who could buy their hometown? Who could make it so they never had to work again? What was so shameful about the money that he and Dylan had pretended to be working class saps while cashing trust fund checks?

Their stupid fear. That's what it all boiled down to.

Dylan would never in a million years call it fear, but that was the word for it. He could posture and preen and flex and be Mr. Macho all he wanted and claim he was waiting for the right moment, wanted Laura to get comfortable, wanted the three to bond more before dumping such big news on her, but in the end he was just a big old wuss who didn't want to confront the emotional landmine the money created.

And it had just exploded in their faces.

Construction held up traffic near downtown, making him change the channel to AM radio to hear the news report about alternate routes. Ten more minutes of inching through a mile of traffic and he was free. He hadn't been downtown that often and was unsure; Boston wasn't exactly laid out in a grid like his hometown in Pennsylvania, but he was able eventually, with two different circlings of Laura's financial-district building, to find a parking garage and park.

$35 for a few hours? *Doesn't matter, stupid*, his conscience hissed. Oh. Yeah. All his old ideas about life and money didn't apply any more. Ski Instructor Mike had pinched pennies to buy time and freedom. Billionaire Mike needed to pinch himself and wake up from his stupor of denial. He and Dylan had fucked up so badly by not telling her the truth. And she wasn't going to handle this well. It always the lying. Not the actual truth itself.

And Jill never bothered to tell you guys, either.

Taking the stairs two at a time, he raced to the skyscraper's main lobby, then searched for the right set of elevators to take him to the thirty-second floor. If

Dylan had beaten him, he was upstairs already, hopefully with Laura.

Time was their biggest enemy right now.

No, he thought. *We are our biggest enemy*.

* * *

The murmurs coming from down the hallway were loud enough for Laura to come out of her office and poke around. She only shut her door when she needed to make calls or just had to tune out the drone of corporate life to get some actual work done on reports or code. Her half-open beige door allowed sound to travel easily from the reception area, and she heard Debbie, the receptionist, gasp and say, "Oh, that's Laura's delivery guy!"

Huh? She fast-walked down the hall to see what on earth the ruckus was about. Her delivery guy? What delivery guy?

Then her face flushed hot. Dylan? Did Debbie mean Dylan? He'd posed as a flower delivery dude that day when he'd come to her office and they'd—

She flushed even more. Then her nether regions swelled with heat. Oh, my. Just thinking about hot monkey office sex was getting her wet.

Laura came to a screeching halt at the sight before her in the reception area, where ten or so coworkers were crowded around the lobby television. Normally set to news, this time was no different, the morning chat show that masqueraded as "news" barking out into the open area.

Except this time, Dylan was the feature of a video clip, dressed in—*my, my!*

Shirtless Dylan, with an oiled chest and red bow tie, wearing the bottom half of a fireman's uniform and carrying an ax? While strolling down a runway at a charity bachelor auction. She laughed; she'd seen the same clip on YouTube. But why was he being featured on a morning news show?

"Laura, that's him, right? The guy who delivered flowers to you a few weeks ago." Debbie nudged a woman standing next to her. "I could never forget that, uh...face. Yeah," she said with a low whistle. "That face."

"With a chest and abs like that, who needs to look at his face?" someone said, her voice older and smoky. The women in the group laughed. The video ended and the scene cut to the co-hosts on comfy couches, two women and a man doing that chat thing that was designed to keep people watching.

"Records show that Dylan Stanwyck, firefighter extraordinaire, former model, and one of Boston's hottest bachelors, is the heir to shipping tycoon Richard Matthews' daughter's estate. Matthews' daughter, Jillian, died in 2010 and left Stanwyck, her longtime lover, a trust fund of $1.1 billion, with an annual income of more than $50 million."

Laura's stomach turned to acid. Debbie's eyes were as wide as saucers as her head bounced between gawking at Laura and staring at the television. One of the men in the room walked away quietly.

"Holy shit," someone muttered. "A billionaire?"

"What's he doing delivering flowers?" Debbie squeaked.

"Sources confirm that her $2.2 billion estate was split between Stanwyck and Mike Pine, a local ski instructor who recently used his inheritance to purchase the struggling Cedar Mountain Ski Resort. Here's to the lucky lady who finds her way to either man as the billionaire bachelors become the hottest dates in town and Stanwyck can buy himself many times over now in whatever charity auction he pleases."

Ohmigod ohmigod ohmigod, her mind screamed. Rooted in place, she couldn't move. Couldn't inhale. Couldn't feel her fingertips or her lips or her eyelids. Dylan and Mike? Jill? Billions? Money? Why hadn't they—? What were they doing—? *Wha?*

Her phone buzzed in her pocket. Like a robot, she reached in and mechanically looked. Five texts.

Dylan: *Laura, please call me now.*

Mike: *Laura? Call me.*

Dylan: *I'm coming to see you at work.*

Mike: *On my way to see you.*

and Josie: *Those assholes. I am so sorry. Come to my apartment to hide.*

"Laura!" Debbie squealed, pulling on her arm. "He wasn't just a delivery guy, was he?" Her expression showed she was very proud of herself to connecting the (*obvious*) dots. "Oh, my God, you were dating him! Are you still dating him? Holy shit, you landed the most eligible billionaire bachelor in Boston? You're, like, Anastasia Steele!"

The room broke out into a mixture of nervous laughter and derisive murmurs. Debbie's long, perfect, chocolate-brown hair shimmered down her shoulders and her creamy skin made Laura want to claw her.

"If I had a billionaire boyfriend I sure would quit in a heartbeat!"

Debbie couldn't—*wouldn't*—shut up, and Laura was quickly growing faint, her heart rate through the roof and brain spinning out of control. Air. She needed air.

"Do you know the Mike guy? Does he have a girlfriend?"

Shut up, Debbie! Her mind screamed. She opened her mouth to say the words when her boss touched Debbie's elbow lightly and pointed to the phone, which was lit up like a Christmas tree with waiting callers. Mercifully, Debbie sat down and plucked her way through call after call as her boss mouthed the words "go home" and made a shooing gesture.

She needed to escape the Red Lobby of Pain right.this.minute and a flood of gratitude overwhelmed her. "Thank you," she mouthed back. Shaking Debbie off, she fast-walked back to her office, grabbed her purse, and fled down the back staircase. Thirty-two flights of stairs in a spiral pattern of nausea would take her mind off whatever was coming, right?

Those bastards. *Step, click. Step, click.* She'd forgotten how hard navigating stairs could be in heels. Tears pooling in her eyes didn't help, the grey, institution cinderblock walls floating as she descended carefully. *Step, click. Step, click.*

Billionaires? *Billionaires?* Really? Seriously? Could they have kept something bigger from her? It had been bad enough that they'd never told her they knew each other, that they were in a committed threesome before meeting her, that they wanted her—and had set up that night in the cabin as a test.

She was still raw from that—and had just started to heal from it, allowing herself to trust them slowly, giving herself permission to believe deeply that this was going to work, and that they could overcome convention and find their own, unique path to happiness.

Just. Just barely.

She needed more time, more experiences, more of everything to understand how to function as one woman with two men, to be so wanted and craved that she could satisfy them both.

The tears flowed freely now, her nose filling, and she fumbled for a tissue. *Step, click. Step, click.* She stopped, searching her purse. No luck. Ah, fuck it.

Her skirt felt too tight, restricting her calves as she worked the stairs, and finally, in a fit of desperation, she slipped off her heels and walked in her stocking feet, the hose snagging within half a flight and making her foot cling slightly to each step. Nothing was going right today.

She snorted, snot pouring out of her nose, and using the back of her hand she wiped the bubbles as best she could. Who cared what she looked like now? The billionaires? What a spike to the heart that thought was as she reached the twenty-seventh floor. She remembered how Dylan had casually grabbed the check, how she'd wondered how a firefighter could afford such a fancy place.

Hah! Joke was on her! He was a fucking billionaire, made stupendously rich by Jill.

Jill. Of course she was a wildly rich heiress. Of course. It wasn't enough to look like she was chiseled by people making a model of beach volleyball players. And it also wasn't enough that she was this dead, perfect girlfriend Laura could never measure up to.

She was also ridiculously wealthy and had made Dylan and Mike filthy, stinking rich, too?

Sharp, bitter laughter echoed up and down the stairs as Laura cackled, mad with overwhelm. She just couldn't win, could she?

"I give, Jill! I surrender!" she shouted, her voice carrying like crazy through the stairwell. "You win! Uncle! Uncle! I can never be you. Dylan and Mike can't even tell me that you left them more money than God.

You are perfect from the grave! You even made the balls on the warlock waitress at Jeddy's! You're a fucking legend!"

Laura's arms outstretched as she screamed the word "legend," her shoes flying out of her hand and tumbling down the metal railings, *plink, plunk, plonk* as they rattled and rolled, landing who knows where.

As she rounded the twenty-fifth floor, retrieving her shoes, a security guard poked his head through the door, then entered the staircase. The older gentleman reminded her of her grandfather, a beer gut and kind eyes crashing through her overwrought sensibilities. "Excuse me, Miss?"

She didn't stop her slow trek. "Yes?" she called back.

"Are you OK? We're hearing reports of someone yelling in the stairwell."

"Oh, I'm fine. Just getting some exercise." Her voice had that shaky hitch to it she got when she was upset, but she tried to cover it up by acting winded. "And boy, do I need it."

He followed her, and as she passed him on the spiral one floor down, she saw him pat his stomach. "I'm with you there," he chuckled. "I'll walk down behind you if you don't mind. Just making sure it's safe here and that there aren't any troublemakers."

Great. Just fucking great. She couldn't even vent without having it ruined.

Fuck you, Dylan. Fuck you, Mike.

Why would you lie?

She thumped and skipped her way down, moving faster now that she had an audience, hoping she could get to the bottom without making herself dizzy. She'd been a tad lightheaded these past couple days and didn't need the added dose of unreality from spinning around and around as she descended thirty-two floors.

She was somewhere around floor eight when the old man gave up. "See you!" he shouted, waving from five or six flights up. Waving back, she sped up, eager for sunshine and a flat walking surface. The balls of her feet were scraped up from the no-skid surface at the edge of each stair, and her hamstrings and IT bands were screaming. Tomorrow, she'd pay for this.

Today she just needed to get to Josie. If she fixated on that, she'd be OK. Falling apart at Josie's apartment would be the best possible solution here. Fear that Mike or Dylan—or Mike *and* Dylan—would get to her first drove her. Dylan was likely on his way to her office to explain. *Explain, explain, explain.* She huffed as she hurried around floor five. Of course he had an explanation. She could just guess.

"Um, well, it's *complicated.*" His tone of voice, the little sidelong look with a half-smile, Mr. Charm turning it on to cozy up and sweet-talk his way out of discomfort.

Well, Dylan, have fun snuggling up to those complications, because that's what you'll be fucking. Not me.

And you, too, Mike.

Anger seeped in, like an old friend who was a lousy house guest, but you forget every time he leaves how much you wish him gone, and welcome him heartily when he reappears. Anger was so much easier than hurt, or heartache, or regret, so anger it was.

Welcome my old friend.

Bursting through the street-level door, the morning greeted her with hot, sultry air and a brightness that made her squint and cringe. She balanced herself on one foot to put on one shoe, then the other, and took a moment to rebalance herself. Ouch. Her feet felt like raw ground beef right now, but that was fine. Anger would keep her going, dull the pain, make it *alllll* better until she could collapse at Josie's.

Hailing a cab was easier than usual; maybe she looked as pissed off as she felt. She knew it would be a quick, cheap ride, and as the cabbie raced to deliver her she massaged her feet and ignored the increasingly-active smart phone in her purse. If she looked she knew she'd find a ton of messages.

Ring! Ring! A quick peek showed Dylan calling. Nope.

She turned off the phone; five minutes from Josie's meant she didn't need to worry about missing a call from her. The cab was stinky but clean, carrying the residue of countless cigarettes, the stale odor of nicotine and coconut air freshener giving her something to gag on. Something other than sheer anxiety and panic. A quick nudge of the window button and she gave herself an inch of fresh air.

The cabby shot her a look and turned up the air conditioner, then looked again. *Sorry, Bud.* Whatever he saw in her return look made him shift his eyes down and keep his mouth shut.

Within minutes he screeched to the front of Josie's building, a triple-decker that she'd lived in for years that melted into the neighborhood, a gentrifying section of Cambridge that was always on the verge of "up and coming" but, thankfully, stayed under the radar and kept reasonable rents. They'd toyed with rooming together and renting a big place, but neither could give up their neighborhoods, Laura enjoying Somerville more than she really ought to.

She threw some cash at the cabbie and ran to Josie's first floor apartment. Her friend was already on the porch, a look of crumpled compassion on her face, and she embraced Laura without words, holding her and stroking her hair as the tears returned.

Pulling back, Josie put her arm around Laura's waist and guided her into the sunny apartment.

"Let me make coffee for you this time," she said, sighing hard. "It's the least I can do."

If Laura's apartment looked like a Scandinavian designer with a pink fetish had decorated it, Josie's was pure '60s hippie Buddhist funk. It looked like Carole King and the Dalai Lama shared the place. Decorated in thrift shop finds and Tibetan boutique splurges, the perpetual scent of sandalwood and lavender was comforting, though it generally covered up other odors that were finally legal in Massachusetts, as long as one kept it under an ounce and in the privacy of home.

Laura slumped down on an overstuffed monk-red recliner covered in a funky silk throw, vibrant mustard yellow and rich steel blue competing with little reflector things. She could see Josie in the kitchen, the apartment a converted single-family home. Doorways were random and seemed to have no meaning, just plunked here and there. Aside from the bedroom and bath, it was open concept but with walls and thresholds, making the fairly-large place seem smaller.

Josie used a Keurig, and shouted, "Glazed donut or Breakfast blend?"

"Scotch!"

"I have Bailey's." Her voice said she didn't have scotch, though.

"Good enough! Breakfast blend and Bailey's!" It wasn't even nine yet. Who cared? It's not like she was really into following social conventions lately, anyhow. If a girl couldn't get drunk the day *both* of her threesome boyfriends were outed as a secret billionaire on local television, when could she?

"How did you hear about them?" she called out to Josie. A hiss and gurgle told her the first cup was brewing.

"That stupid morning TV Show. I had it on and heard Dylan's name and, well—I texted you right away. I'm guessing they did, too?"

Bzzz. Her phone hummed in her pocket and she pulled it out. Squinting, she read the screen. "Jesus." Low whistle. Josie wandered into the room and handed her a steaming cup of coffee, tinted tan by the Bailey's.

"Let me guess. Dylan's texted you seventy-six times?"

"And Mike's a close second." *Sip*.

The alcohol hit her taste buds like a tsunami of flavor. It felt weird to drink this early. Weird was becoming her default *waaaay* too fast for comfort, but if that was her reality, she'd embrace it. Especially if it tasted like Irish crème.

"Fuck 'em. I can't believe they—man, Laura. Billionaires? I mean, they aren't gorgeous enough, but they have to be secret billionaires, too? Your life is like a cross between *General Hospital* and *Desperate Housewives* with a touch of *Fifty Shades*."

She knew it was funny. She should laugh, right? Instead, she swallowed too much scalding liquid too fast, making her nearly scream from the burning pain. If she coughed, she'd scald her throat and mouth even more. The alcohol tasted weird, anyhow—a little too...something.

As she gagged and choked, poor Josie ran between the living room and the kitchen, shouting, "Are you OK?"

"Ice," Laura hissed.

Josie returned with ice water, which Laura eagerly sucked into her mouth, keeping her lips closed and pooching out her cheeks to retain the cold balm against her torn, raw mouth. Great. Just great. She couldn't even drink a fucking cup of coffee without something going wrong.

Don't try to walk and chew gum at the same time. Might break a leg.

Finally, she swallowed, refilling her mouth with the ice water as the sting abated somewhat, little ridges on the roof of her mouth throbbing horribly. That raw, scratchy feeling that comes from a good scalding started to sink in, and she knew she was in for a good two to three days of this. The universe could stop shitting on her. Seriously.

Cut it out, God, she thought. *My middle name isn't Job.*

"...well, now, he can bring his fire hose to my garage any time..." a voice said, wafting into the living room.

"Fuck!" Josie shouted, sprinting for her bedroom. The sound cut out fast.

Laura's eyes filled, less from mouth pain and more from life pain. This hurt. This was going to hurt for a good, long time. And the hurt was like Ryan times a thousand.

No.

Times two billion.

Laura nursed her ice water, Josie drank her coffee, and the two said nothing, comfortable the way old friends could be, knowing that friendship meant that silence was sometimes the best form of support. She needed someone there, someone to witness her pain but not to comment on it, or judge it.

A few years ago she would have needed Josie to join her in spewing rage about her being betrayed and lied to, but that wasn't what she needed today. Instead, Josie's calm, steady presence gave her the room to let reality fill in the cracks of her heart and to come to her own ready place for processing it all.

One of Josie's cats, an old calico named Dotty she'd adopted from a local rescue shelter a few years back, settled on the couch next to Laura. Her own cats weren't nearly as social, hiding away and largely independent, three puffs of fur who had come to her the same way, two of them Persians that had been owned by an elderly woman who had to go into a nursing home.

No one had wanted cats the ages of teenagers, so Laura had taken in Miss Daisy and Frumpy. Snuggles had come to her from an abused animals rescue network, her ears clipped in jagged wrecks and part of her tail mangled. Snuggles liked patches of sunshine and to be left alone. Somehow, Miss Daisy and Frumpy respected that, and all three coexisted nicely.

Too bad other threesomes couldn't be so smooth.

"How's Snuggles doing lately?" Josie asked. "I never see her when I come over."

Laura laughed, petting Dotty, who tipped her chin up as if granting permission. "I never see her, either. I only know she's real because I see a tail under the bed and she eats her food."

Josie nodded and finished off her mug. "Like a teenage boy. Needs sleep and food." The joke fell flat. Laura was done talking.

"More coffee?"

"God, no."

Josie winced. "Sorry. More ice water?"

"Yes, please." She was starting to sound like Mike. Two word sentences weren't her style but right now, it was all she could manage. Maybe this "woman of few words" schtick was something she should try on, see how the other half lives in a world of low verbal output. Was there something to not spilling every thought out of your mouth? Could Mike be on to something, being the quiet but steady type who was a deep presence without contributing to the non-stop flow of words that filled modern life?

Why was she even thinking about this? Her open mouth called out to her hands to fan cool air inside her, her tongue drying out quickly. She couldn't even drink a cup of coffee correctly. Why mull over esoteric ideas?

Because it was easier than facing the fact that they had destroyed this burgeoning relationship yet again. And, most likely, once and for all.

"So," she and Josie said in unison. Startled, both laughed at the other, the nervous tension that filled the room making Laura's stomach turn again. She'd been queasy all day, her stomach bearing the brunt of the stress.

"You first," Josie deferred.

"So, it looks like I managed not only to find two amazingly hot, wonderful guys who happen to be in a secret, *complicated*—" Josie snorted as Laura emphasized that word "—relationship and we turned it into a great threesome. Oh. Yeah. And they happen to be billionaires and never bothered to tell me because—because—" She faltered there. Why in the hell hadn't they told her about their money?

Josie seemed to have the same thought, scrunching her face in a weird expression. "Huh. What a supremely odd thing to hide from you. I mean, their whole knowing each other and double-teaming you secret was strange, but I can at least understand it. It's really out there, and they didn't know how to approach it, and in typical clueless man style they butchered it."

Laura's turn to snort.

"But this? I mean, wouldn't most guys consider being a fucking billionaire something to gloat about?"

Laura swallowed. Hard. "Maybe they're embarrassed?"

"Why?"

"Because it's Jill's money?"

Josie considered that, tipping her head from one side to the other. "Mmmmm, maybe." Skepticism filled her voice. "You think they were ashamed of coming into the money because she died and left it to them?"

Laura shrugged. "I'm as stumped as you are."

As she shifted, Dotty sniffed the air, stood, and transferred her loyalties and attentions to Josie, who absent-mindedly stroked her multi-colored head.

Josie sighed. "Wouldn't you share that kind of thing pretty soon in a relationship? I've never had that kind of money—any guy who dates me gets Taco Bell, not trips to private islands in Mexico—but I'd think it would be something you throw out there to clear the air right away."

The two sat in silence for a minute, thinking this through. Laura's rage was suddenly tempered by thoughtfulness and pensive considerations on the money issue. Dylan and Mike weren't flashy about it—though this explained Mike's amazing cabin. They both drove new cars, but they still shared a sleek apartment. It wasn't a billionaire's life, by any means. Dylan even kept his old job. He must wipe his ass with his paychecks.

Exchanging confused glances with Josie, the puzzle became more intriguing as she thought about it. If the news channels were covering this, it meant it was all recent. So perhaps it was too recent—they just didn't know how to explain it?

Too much benefit of the doubt. She yelled at herself mentally. *They still should have told you!* Of course they should have, and they damn well knew it. She'd given them every opportunity over the past few weeks, and she was most hurt not that they were billionaires—which she actually found to be pretty damn awesome—but that they hid it from her.

Why?

Josie stood, dumping Dotty unceremoniously from her lap, the cat landing gracefully on the small, shag carpet and surveying the room, eyeing her options. Laura, a throw pillow, the carpet. She chose to leave, clearly displeased with her sudden displacement.

"This calls for some breakfast. You hungry?"

Without waiting for the answer, Josie went into the kitchen and started the Keurig up again. The sounds of rummaging floated toward Laura, and in two minutes Josie returned with a box of frozen donut holes and her new cup of coffee.

"Martha Stewart," Laura sighed, hand over her heart.

"I'm more a trashy version of Rachel Ray. But these are yummy pumpkin donuts."

"Already? Isn't that a fall flavor?"

"It's August."

"August isn't fall."

"In retail it is."

Josie threw up her hands and grabbed one of the dough balls, carefully biting into it. Laura did the same, surprised by how hard and soft the donut hole was. It was a cakey consistency and dense. The half she managed to bite was absolutely delicious. Without being asked, Josie grabbed Laura's glass and returned with it full. A girl could get used to this. She was the one who tended to cater to Josie; it felt nice to be taken care of like this, even in the smallest of ways.

Dotty returned to the room at the entrance of the donut holes, sniffing the box until Josie shoved her off. Offended, she strutted into Josie's room and out of Laura's sight. Although the pastry tasted great, her stomach just didn't want anything.

Why? Why hadn't they told her?

"Maybe they're just assholes," Josie said slowly, answering Laura's internal question. "Maybe they thought you were a gold digger."

"How could I be a gold digger if I didn't know they had so much money?"

Her phone buzzed again. Turning it off completely seemed like a perfect solution, her finger holding down the off button with so much force it left a red imprint in her fingertip. Too bad you couldn't slam a phone down in the cradle like you could when she was a kid. That satisfaction was one area where smart phones just didn't measure up.

"They keep calling?"

"They keep *something-ing*. Calls. Texts. Hell, they may have resorted to email."

"Not email! Only our parents use email." An old joke between them.

"I expect Dylan will find a passenger pigeon's corpse and resurrect it."

"Or worse—use MySpace."

Bzzzz. Confused, Laura looked at her phone. It was definitely off. "That's me," Josie explained. Leaping across the room, she foraged in her giant purse and found her phone.

Slide, tap, tap. Her face! The look on her face made Laura want to administer oxygen and call 911.

"Josie?"

"Dylan!" She shouted his name like she was screaming the word "fuck!" Flailing her phone to and fro, she added, "How in the hell did he get my number?"

"I never gave it to him or Mike. I swear!" Laura answered. He was this desperate? Really?

"*At Laura's work. She's not here. Is she with you? Is she safe? We'll keep searching.*" Josie laughed, a barking horsey sound that registered extraordinary disgust. "Is that a promise or a threat?"

Sigh. "He's persistent."

"He's a whackadoo."

"Well..."

That he would somehow track down Josie's cell phone number meant he was serious about finding her. She had zero desire to see either of them right now. Zero. They really had shredded her life, and what she wanted most was to turn the earth backwards, like in that old Superman movie, and make all of this go away.

No. What she *really* wanted was two men who could be honest and open and tell the truth about themselves so they could all live happily ever after. Was that too much to ask? Jill had died and turned out to have gobs of money that she passed on to the guys. They hid that information from her because—

Her blood ran cold, stomach twisting.

Because they didn't trust her.

"Oh, God," she muttered. "Josie." Her friend sensed the shift in her voice and came closer, curling her legs under herself on a small, faded, orange velvet chair.

"Yeah? What is it."

"They—they," she stammered, her chin quivering now, eyes filling with hot tears and throat salty and thick. "They never trusted me. They wanted the money and a woman but couldn't tell me because they didn't trust me. They just—I don't know!" she wailed, her volume increasing as her pulse raced and her mind raced even faster.

"Oh, honey," Josie replied, reaching for Laura's hand. "You are so trustworthy and so not into money."

"I know, right?" Laura screeched. "It's laughable." Maniacal laugh. "They couldn't have picked a worse thing to be worried about, right? I'm the girl who shops as much as possible at vintage and thrift shops to save money. I drive an older car and I put money in my stupid 401K every paycheck and I pay my student loans on time and I follow all the rules." Her voice rose. "*All* the fucking rules, right? I do *everything* right. Everything! And this is how the universe repays me? Seriously. I feel like I got a galactic shit dumped on my head this morning."

"You did."

"A billion dollar shit!" Her voice was like a gospel preacher, the intonation more revival than revulsion.

"Yes, ma'am!"

"And if those two fuckers thought they could have the best sex ever with me but couldn't bother to tell me the truth about something this big, then they don't deserve me!"

"Indeed." Josie sat back down and leaned forward. "Billionaire bastards."

Laura shot her a harsh look, wondering if she was poking fun, but she wasn't. The words mattered, and they were true. Both men were such steaming assholes she couldn't believe it, the urge to start hyperventilating competing with the desire to punch them both in the face, even if she'd need a stool to reach Mike.

"I can't believe Dylan tracked you down like that," Laura chuckled.

"Should I reply?"

Blinking, Laura came to a screeching halt in her mind, the question jarring. Should Josie reply? What would she say? What *should* she say? No etiquette manual was designed for this. Dan Savage needed to write one. How should your best friend reply when both of your threesome boyfriends turn out to be billionaires and one stalks you to try to make up?

That would be popular.

Laura smoothed her sweater over her belly, which pooched out enough to send a cat invitation to Dotty. She plopped down on Laura's lap and turned into a furnace, which was great in January but horribly warm in August.

Get used to it, Laura, her mind said. *It's the only touch you're getting for a long time that doesn't involve plastic and batteries.*

For some reason, *that* made her finally break down and sob. Not the sheer humiliation in the work lobby. Not the rage that claimed her so easily on the staircase, her feet still aching from that howlingly stupid move. And not the thought that once again, as with Ryan, as with so many guys in high school and college, as with Dylan and Mike the first time they made love, she felt tiny and cheated and shamed and grotesque because nothing had turned out as planned, and her own blind naivete meant that here she was sobbing and racked with grief, her best friend stroking her shoulder and nothing had changed.

She was the same Laura this happened to, time and again, a decade and more of falling for guys who cared less for her than she cared for them, respected her in a way that made her queasy with doubt, and who managed to give her just enough hope such that when it all came crashing down what hurt most was that they ever gave her any.

It would have been easier to become a cat lady who never bothered, and she was about to do just that. As soon as it was safe to go home. If Dylan was hunting down Josie's number and texting her, then she damn sure couldn't go home right now.

Weak and addled, her mind might play a game of sabotage on her, believing whatever smooth line he came up with to try to convince her that she should get up once more, strip naked before them, and let them ridicule her pure, loving heart.

Nope.

Done.

"Josie," she announced, her voice sounding like a drill sergeant's. Wiping the tears with the bottom hem of her sweater, careful not to get cat hair in her eyes, she sniffed and demanded, "you are going to text that motherfucker back."

"Yes, ma'am!" Holding her phone, Josie looked expectantly at Laura.

Hmmm. Now what? What could she possibly say to Dylan that would make him stay away? That would make him just evaporate, with Mike, and let her go on and live a life that didn't have so much pain and wonder in it? Were there magic words she could fit in a text that would do that?

She had to try. "OK, so type, '*If you say it's complicated I'll cut your balls off and put them on the warlock waitress.*'"

Josie choked and clapped. "Fucking brilliant!" *Tap, tap, tap—*

"No! Don't do it. Changed my mind."

A pout from Josie, then a quick change to a neutral face. "Sure." *Tap, tap, tap* as she erased it.

In her heart, what she wanted was an apology from them both. A long, drawn-out pleading and self-flagellation filled with regret and recriminations and sorries and kisses and flowers and all that crap. More words than things, though, more affection than promises, and more attention than empty phrases. At the center of it all was a ball of pain that now lived in her stomach, hot lead and napalm and poison that leaked and festered in her, planted there by Mike and Dylan because *this*?

This was a bitter pill to swallow. And swallow it she had, whole and dry and without any awareness of what it meant.

Her dream world was about her, about people caring what she felt, what she thought, what she needed and wanted. Fantasy.

The real world involved self-centered men who didn't trust her enough to tell her their second-biggest (*or first!*) secret and who let her learn about it from a fluff-chick morning chat show cougar who had the self-awareness of a bottle of nail polish remover.

If that wasn't a big sign that their respect for her was in the crapper, nothing else was.

Add in the little detail that they clearly didn't trust her to be anything but a money grubber and she was, well, she was still struggling to sum all that up into one pithy text.

"Try this," she ordered. Josie's finger hovered over the glass keyboard. "*Don't chase me. Give me that one shred of respect. Why? Because it's complicated.*"

Josie typed it in and looked at her, eyebrows raised with a question.

Laura nodded and Josie tapped Send.

Laura took a deep breath through her nose and let it out through her mouth, making a weird vibrating sound with her lips.

Bzzzz. "Man, he's fast," Josie muttered. Dotty made a hissing sound and arched her back. "It's just a phone. Not a predator," Josie chided the cat. "She does this all the time," she explained, squinting at the screen.

"He replied, didn't he?"

"Yep. Wanna hear it?"

No. Yes. No. Yes. No. Ye—"Yes."

Josie made a disgusted sound, complete with a slow shake of the head that Laura interpreted as not good. "He says, and I quote: '*It's always complicated.*' With a little smiley face."

A slap across the face would have shocked her less. A rising numbness took over. What on earth had possessed Dylan to think that that—*that?*—trite and flippant response would somehow be perceived as funny. Or endearing. Or clever.

If the intended effect were to charm her, he'd failed miserably. If his goal was to piss her off and harden her resolve never to see him—or Mike—again, then he had succeeded wildly.

Yay, Dylan.

"Am I crazy for thinking he's a fucking asshole for sending that piece of shit text?" Laura railed.

"Not crazy." Josie seemed to be keeping her face as still as possible, watching Laura with a wary eye. "It's insulting, really."

"Thank you. Thank you! Because it is, isn't it?"

Bzzzz.

"Don't you answer that! He had his chance. One. I gave him one. And that's more than he and Mike deserve."

"OK. Whatever you want."

Thank God for Josie, because right now she was rising to the occasion in a way Laura had never thought possible. Of course, they'd been there for each other over the years, through heart breaks and break ups, through angry, gritted-teeth conversations where they'd tried to convince each other to DTMFA, as Dan Savage would say.

Dumping the motherfucker already, though, was easier said than done in most cases, and this was another one of those, *ahem*, complicated situations.

Not really, she argued with herself. Its simple. DTMFA. Both of them.

Because the lack of respect they'd shown her told her everything she needed to know, even if that feeling of "fuck you" went against everything her heart was crying out right now, its words pleading with her to give them at least a quick meeting to hear why they hid this from her.

Why she had to learn about it at work, in a lobby, on a cheap television while two women who knew more about anal bleaching than world affairs got to prattle on and drool over Dylan and make comments that made her feel tiny and small and—

Ashamed.

That really was a huge part of this, wasn't it? It had taken so much effort to overcome her feeling of discomfort at owning her own desire for both men, and here she was tentatively growing and accepting who she was and what her authentic self really needed and wanted. And it was Dylan and Mike, together as a trio that would make everyone so happy.

Her shame, now, was overflowing. Shame at thinking she could really have it all. Shame at wanting something so unconventional. Shame that they couldn't trust her.

Shame that she had trusted them.

And, worst of all, shame that she had something inside her that made her feel so much shame. She couldn't win.

She just couldn't win.

"You've got Netflix, right?" she asked Josie.

"Yup." Josie's face changed, shifted to something softer. "Ooo, I know what you want to watch."

Laura sighed. "Let's do it."

* * *

"Oh, my God! It's the billionaire bachelor!" the receptionist screeched as the elevator doors parted and Dylan stepped out onto Laura's floor. The lobby at Laura's work was more crowded than it had been when he'd delivered flowers to her last month and heads turned. Then more heads.

Then every.single.head.

Oh, geez. The last thing he needed.

"You remember me, right?" the receptionist crooned, walking over and extending her hand. "Debbie. I was here the day you *delivered flowers* to Laura." Wink.

The absolutely last thing he needed. He didn't shake her hand. "Where is Laura?" he asked, not caring that he was being blunt, pointedly ignoring all the eyes on him.

"She went home sick." A deep male voice answered, to Dylan's left. The man was middle-aged, greying temples, a bit of a paunch. Nice suit. Her boss? He nodded to Debbie, who skittered over to her station and began answering phone calls, eyes glued on the two men.

"Oh. Is she OK?" He frowned, concerned.

"I won't comment on that, but after she watched the news report featuring you, she clearly wasn't doing well." Ah. This guy was a straight shooter. A little angry on Laura's behalf. Dylan could understand that.

And respect it. Even if it pained him deeply to have caused her pain.

"Thanks. I'll try to catch her at home."

Debbie's eyes widened and she reached for a smart phone, texting furiously. Gossip. Great. Poor Laura.

Poor Laura? He was the cause of what made her poor Laura. Holy fuck. He'd never considered that the fallout could do this to her.

A hand on his arm. Firm. Unyielding. His hackles went up and a thin thread of fight grew in him. The boss's eyes were cold steel, pointed directly at Dylan like a weapon. "I wouldn't do that if I were you. If she wants to see you, she can contact you." This wasn't advice.

This was a veiled threat. Or, at least, that's how it sounded to Dylan's hypersensitive ears. Who was this tool to tell him how to handle Laura? He shook the man's hand off him roughly and got right in his face.

"I'll talk to her if I want to." His face was inches from the boss, who stood up and matched Dylan on height. This guy was twenty years older and out of shape, but he was a fierce dude who wasn't backing down, even in the presence of a very muscled fire fighter.

"If she wants to talk to you. Otherwise, you're just an angry stalker."

There was that word again. Stalker. "You don't know anything about—"

Ding! The elevator behind Dylan slid open and he heard two heavy steps, then Mike's breathless voice. "Is she still here?"

Debbie just about had a heart attack, her jaw dropping so low her mouth could have been a dustpan. "Thor," she whispered.

Dylan nearly barked out a laugh, the comment shaking him from his stand off with Laura's boss.

"No. She's gone," the boss said, then looked at Dylan. Hard.

A new hand on his arm, this time Mike's. "Let's try her apartment." He jabbed the Down button for the elevator as Debbie removed her telephone headset and stood, smoothing her tight skirt, then sauntering over.

Mercifully, the doors opened before she got to them, Mike practically dragging Dylan in. With a pneumatic hiss his last view of Laura's work floor was Debbie's disappointed voice and the back of the boss's head.

Good riddance to both.

Mike stared up at the ceiling and blew out a huge breath of air. "Has she answered your texts or voice mails?"

"Nope. You try?"

"Once, for each. No luck."

"Where were you when that stupid television report came on?"

"At work."

A low whistle from Mike, whose eyebrows shot up, made Dylan wince. He took in Dylan's uniform and cringed. "Yeah. It was bad. Let's just say I am no longer gainfully employed."

"Joe fired you?"

"No. I resigned peacefully."

"Peacefully?" Mike smirked. Damn it, he knew him too well.

"It's complicated."

"It's *always* complicated," Mike said bitterly.

"I'm getting really tired of hearing that."

"I think you started it."

"Do we really need to go there right now?"

"No. We need to go to Laura's place right now. But tell me what happened with the chief." Mike didn't seem to care on an emotional level; he was just asking out of voyeuristic curiosity. The difference in tone and demeanor was starting to freak Dylan out.

Dylan laughed, a cold, harsh sound that hurt his own ears. "He said there was a waiting list out the door for the jobs, that if I was a billionaire I sure didn't need the pay, and that I was welcome to join the volunteer force."

"Ouch."

The volunteer guys were welcomed by the regular staff, but often considered weaker contenders when it came to running calls. There was more to the conversation he wasn't going to tell Mike right now, how the chief had looked in the envelope and found all the cash Dylan had stuffed in there, how Dylan asked about sending a much larger amount directly to Murphy, and how within the course of a painful fifteen minute talk he'd managed to lose his only career but gain some insight into how his future could unfold, using Jill's money for good.

"Yeah. So I guess I'm free now."

"Free." Mike snorted. "If this is freedom, I think I prefer...ah, I don't know what I'm saying any more."

Definitely not the time to tell Mike anything.

Ding! The elevator reached the main lobby and they walked out of the building, the August heat hitting them like a wall of soup. "You drive here?" Mike asked.

"No."

"Good—I'm over here," he nodded, "so let's get to Laura's. You remember her address?"

"Yeah. In Somerville, over near Tufts." They walked down the cold, concrete staircase, descending two levels to the underground spot where Mike's Jeep sat, patient and still. In silence now, they were perfunctory. Get in car. Turn on car. Screech tires on painted concrete to exit. Pay. Leave. Dylan hoped like hell she was at home.

"Wait. What about Josie?" he asked as Mike made a tough left turn.

"What about her?"

"Maybe she'll know where Laura is. Or maybe Laura's with her."

"Let's get to Laura's and see what's going on. Josie's kind of..." Mike made an inscrutable face.

"Batshit crazy?" He didn't relish seeing her under these circumstances. Getting whacked with the plastic balls at Jeddy's had been bad enough. Now that they had fucked up even worse, what would she use to arm herself? Ugh.

"Not what I was going to say. My words would have been 'fiercely loyal'." He paused, then added, "I don't think she's truly crazy. Just a little unbalanced."

"She whacked my real balls with the fake ones and teabagged them in the restaurant while you were talking to Laura."

"Says the man who actually fucked a blow up doll."

Mike's droll delivery didn't surprise him. The words did, causing him to choke with shock.

"How did you know that?" He didn't deny it.

"Who actually names a blow up doll? You were so bizarre that first year of college."

Dylan laughed. "That's true."

"Besides, I didn't know you fucked it. You just confirmed it, though." Smirk.

Shit! "Oh, please. It was a dare and we were drunk and I was stupid enough to want to be in the fraternity and they...just. *Ugh*. Let's drop this."

By his judgment they were five minutes or so from Laura's place. Parking would be a problem, until Mike pulled into a "Permit Only" spot and turned the car off.

"What are you doing? We'll get a ticket."

The look on Mike's face was so out of character as he said, "We're billionaires, Dylan. Who gives a fuck about a $25 parking ticket? That's like losing a penny now." The same wolfish look, a deeply-ingrained expression of cold, brutal action, that he'd seen only once before on Mike's face, when...when...

When he'd told Mike about Laura.

Bounding up the steps to Laura's landing, Mike poked the buzzer over and over, like a little kid calling on a friend for a play date. No answer.

Dylan reached over and rang the bell, too.

"Right. Like it didn't work the twelve times I just pushed it," Mike practically growled.

What the fuck? "So sue me," Dylan scoffed, rapidly getting pissed. He grabbed his phone and tapped rapidly. Search, search, search—there. Her last name was Mendham, he remembered that much, and she said she lived in Cambridge, and—

Score! Josie Mendham's phone number. Some charity thing she organized in Allston for old people, the number and email were posted on a web page. He furiously tapped out a text and hit Send.

"I just texted Josie."

Mike pushed the buzzer *again*. Like it would magically work now? Laura clearly wasn't home. Gone from work. Not at home. She must be with Josie. He tapped on his phone.

The look on Mike's face made Dylan freeze, a preternatural instinct putting him on hyper alert. "You *what*?"

"I found her phone number on a web page and I just texted her. Let's see what happens. Maybe Laura's with her and we can figure this all out. And if not, I'm searching now for her address."

Tapping his foot, Mike leaned against the metal railing on Laura's stoop. "You can stalk the fuck out of women and find eleven billion ways to try to contact them, but we can't have an open, mature conversation with Laura about the money? You're such an asshole, Dylan."

Bzzz. Someone, hopefully Josie, texted him. The word "asshole" hovered in the air between them, like a drone seeking a target. And it had found one. He was the asshole here? He's the one who found Laura in the first place. Mike's the one who had lied to him.

He squinted and read aloud: "*Laura says to tell you Don't chase me. Give me that one shred of respect. Why? Because it's complicated.*"

The sound that came out of Mike was like an animal that had just been hit and wounded by a well-placed, though not fatal, arrow. "Jesus Fucking Christ," he groaned, hand over his heart as if pierced there.

A huge lump formed in Dylan's throat. They'd really blown it, hadn't they? *No, you did*, he thought. *You, Dylan*.

Without thinking, he typed back: "*It's always complicated. :)*" and hit Send.

Mike didn't seem to notice, his back turned to Dylan as his arms flexed, gripping and releasing the metal railing, shoulders hunched over and tight with grief and fury.

"Josie lives nearby. In Cambridge. I found her address."

Mike inhaled deeply, his shoulders spreading like a cobra rising up to strike, then descending as he exhaled. Five long, deep breaths later he turned to Dylan, blinking rapidly, his blonde hair a complete, wavy mess and his eyes shadowed and cold.

"Let's go before this gets any more complicated."

Too late, thought Dylan, but he wasn't going to argue. He'd done enough damage as the leader. Time to let Mike take over.

* * *

All those years Mike had spent sitting meditation, going to retreats, reading books by Jack Kornfield and Pema Chodron and the Dalai Lama, all the time he'd invested in breathing techniques and the miles pounded out on his feet, in skis, swimming and biking in triathlons to maintain a sense of inner centeredness was a waste.

A complete, fucking waste. Because the rage that rose up in him, like a megamonster coming up from the sea in some cheesy B film, was very real, rapidly growing, and so quick to activate that he wondered how he had fooled himself all these years into thinking he had tamed it.

Control? Hah. Control was an illusion. Awareness? Fuck that.

The ache that grew its own voice and began keening within him was what hurt most. Why had he listened to Dylan? Why hadn't he blurted out the truth to Laura when he'd been ready? Trusting Dylan had been such an enormous mistake.

Stupid, stupid, stupid, he berated himself as he drove the quick hop from Laura's place to Josie's, her triple decker near a baseball field and a large playground, the typical setting for dogs off leash and an impossible parking situation.

Rules? Who cared. They'd broken most of them already. Why not add a ticket? When Dylan objected to the parking job he'd shut him down fast. It felt good. Whatever made Dylan go silent, Mike needed more of *that*.

As for anger, there was an unlimited well inside him, as if he'd struck the rage vein, uncharted territory as he became a fireball of pure instinct, driven by the need to fix this, to go back in time, to have been honest and open with Laura and to—

To have Jill tell the truth.

That thought came out of nowhere, whispered in his mind like a snake hissing secrets. He stopped as they walked toward the three-story house Dylan said was Josie's, as if struck in the face by a falling acorn or a random stone. What? What did this have to do with Jill?

"Hey. You ready?" Dylan's voice was clipped and nervous as he worried a button on his work shirt. Work? Joe fired him? Mike wanted to know more about what had happened, but didn't have the bandwidth right now to listen. Without warning, his hands began to shake, the feeling deep and visceral, his chest bones rattling. Completely out of his control, his body seemed to be releasing emotions he didn't know he possessed.

"Uh, uh, um," he stammered, feeling like an eleven year old asking for a first kiss, giving a first speech, talking to his new teacher and realizing she couldn't stand him. "Sure," he chirped out, the sound pushed between his teeth by an ever-expanding tongue, his body feeling like it was swelling and shriveling all at once.

The bell on Josie's door made a buzzing sound. He heard an "Eep!" and then an old calico cat appeared in the bay window right next to them. A flurry of curtain movement, then a face that was unmistakably Josie's.

"Shit," Mike heard, her voice muted but discernible. Then whispers. He and Dylan exchanged looks of rolled eyes.

"Hah!" Dylan hissed, then pumped his fist.

Don't crow too much, Mike thought. *We are still so screwed.*

Ding dong! Dylan pressed the buzzer again and stepped back on the concrete steps, which were fairly shallow. He almost fell backwards. A flurry of scuttling sounds and whispers, and then Josie's voice through the door.

"Go away."

S h e *hollered*. That woman could project. Who knew such a tiny body could hold such a mammoth voice?

"Please," Mike said loudly. "We want to talk to Laura and explain."

Please say yes. A massive wave of déjà vu hit him. How ridiculous this all was becoming. Inheriting this money wasn't his idea. All it had brought was problems.

"Dylan already said everything. He was quite clear in his text." Josie's voice was caustic, like battery acid in voice form.

Mike just blinked, over and over, trying not to react to everything, and as he turned his head toward Dylan all he could think was, *Don't kill him. Don't kill him. Don't kill him.*

"What did you text back to Josie, Dylan?"

He could feel the threat in his voice, like lead and cyanide, and knew his poisoned tongue would morph into pounding fists soon.

"I just texted back 'It's always complicated' and a little smiley face."

Holy shit! "And you thought she wouldn't take that the wrong way?" He enunciated, every word spat out through gritted teeth, his jaw aching with tension and his mind reeling. *Stay calm.*

Deadly calm.

Clearly shaken, Dylan flinched. "I was being light-hearted."

"You have the instincts of a drunken frat boy when it comes to anything emotionally delicate."

"Is that supposed to be an insult?"

Instead of beating Dylan by ripping out his ego and dropping it on his head, thus flattening him to a pancake from the sheer mass of it, Mike stepped forward and pounded on the door. "Please, Laura, we just want to talk."

"Go away," Josie warned, even louder. The woman could do a decent imitation of a foghorn.

"Only when we hear it from Laura," Dylan shouted back. "Otherwise, we're going to keep trying until somehow you let us in."

"God, Dylan, don't say that," Mike groaned.

Two dog owners at the park across the field turned and looked at them, their animals playing on the baseball field. It was a hot August day and already his shirt clung to him. The dogs frolicked and the owners were talking to each other and pointing at them.

"Don't say what? I mean it." Dylan plucked his work shirt away from his body. He was sweating profusely now, running one hand through his hair. The sweat made it look slicked back with gel, the sun shining off the blue-black highlights in his thick hair.

"You don't have any power here right now, you dipshit."

Dylan bristled. Good. The truth hurt.

"Quit calling me names."

"I'm not calling you names." Mike leaned in, pulling himself up to his full height. "I'm calling you out."

The door opened and Laura appeared, eyes red-rimmed and puffy, hair askew, her skirt wrinkled around her belly and covered with white cat fur. Her shoulders were set and one hand clung to the doorway, the other on the doorknob, body language aggressive and dismissive all at once.

Mike's heart exploded with need and fear. "Laura, I—"

"Go.Away." Her voice got louder on the second word, cracking a bit, as her eyes narrowed and bored into him and Dylan, her chest heaving and throat choking out her words. "I texted you," she said, accusation infiltrating every word, anger focused on Dylan, "and asked for one fucking thing. One! Respect. You couldn't even manage that."

"But I—" Dylan's smile warmed and softened as he tried the charm thing.

Mike could tell it wouldn't work. Hell, it pissed *him* off to see it. He could only imagine what it triggered in Laura.

"You smug son-of-a-bitch," she said in a cold voice, chin tipped down and eyes tipped up, the look nearly evil in its perfect composure and composition.

Dylan's neck craned back and he took a step away, which rattled Mike. No holding back, she was showing them everything right now, and he loved her for it. Raw and broken, she was peeling back to show her true self and he was torn inside, knowing he'd done this to her —*they* had done this to her—because they had been too afraid to reveal their own true selves to her.

So had Jill.

"All I asked of you—both of you—" her eyes burning through them, making Mike's body go cold as she alighted on him "—was honesty and respect. You gave me neither. No—worse!—you withheld both from me. I guess you didn't trust me? Thought I was some kind of gold digger?"

Huh?

"Why would we think you were all about the money when we were the ones who found you?" he asked gently.

She relaxed visibly, suddenly, as if he'd said what she'd been thinking. As she closed her eyes and screwed her face into an expression of pain, he wanted to take every action, every touch, every word, every breath where he'd hurt her and make it all dissolve and disappear.

Nothing would make their betrayal go away, no matter how much Dylan wished it away with his charm and sweet talking, no matter how much Mike's earnest tries came from a place of authenticity.

They had betrayed her to the core.

"You tell me!" she shouted. "Oh. No. You can't." Her voice went sarcastic. "You can't ever tell me anything. Anywhere." She made a strange, dismissive sound. "Except in bed. Right, boys?"

The smirk that formed after that was Mike's personal embodiment of despair. He was dying inside, and just wanted to pull her into his arms, wanted her arms around him, wanted to lose himself in her lushness, her soft, warm self.

That was gone. Long gone.

He and Dylan had driven it away.

"You're right," he said, his voice shaky. "I can't tell you."

Not the answer she expected; her face fell.

"I can't tell you because I don't even know. If I knew, I'd pour it out. Whatever explanation I could give you, other than blaming Dylan for saying it wasn't time yet, would be so weak you'd just get angrier."

She just stared at him with contempt, cheeks red and eyes bloodshot. How had they come to this moment? How could all three of them be standing within feet of each other and be so blindingly miserable?

"You can't tell me?" Indignant laughter seemed to strengthen her.

"But please, Laura," Dylan crooned, "invite us in and we can talk. Out here," he gestured at the staring dog owners, "we have an audience."

Thirteen different emotions shifted in her face in rapid succession, most of them negative. She slowly stepped back and shut the door, saying, "No. Just go away" as Mike's view of her narrowed and then disappeared in a line of metal and wood.

"Laura, I want to come in and talk!" Dylan begged.

"You want to come in?" she screamed through the door, her seething so clear it was like a high-pitched tone that crippled, a dog whistle of heartbreak. "Then buy the fucking building, Dylan, and walk in like you own the place."

Mike saw Josie appear in the window, shaking her head slowly.

"I told you," she mouthed, and whatever shred of function that remained in him snapped.

"You can afford it!" Laura screamed.

And with that, Mike threw the Jeep keys at Dylan and began to run home. It was a good ten miles.

A good start to pound out the pain.

* * *

The sight of Mike's back as he began to run away was unbelievable. Dylan stared, mouth open, the keys loose in his palm. The guy was running home? It was at least ten miles, which was nothing for Mike, but he was dressed in jeans, a polo shirt, and Merrell shoes—not exactly runner's clothing in August in Boston. He'd turn into a puddle of goo by the time he crossed the Charles River.

Maybe that was the point.

Right now, though, he didn't have a spare ounce of caring in him for anyone but Laura. How could he have been so callous? Man, he had totally misjudged how she perceived him and his every move. The "It's always complicated" joke not only fell flat, it seemed to have been the nail in the coffin of any chance they may have had to rewind their botched attempt at waiting for the right moment to tell her about their money. Ego be damned; he could admit when he was wrong. He was man enough. And boy, *oh boy*, was he wrong.

Mike didn't even want to be in the same car with him. Laura had just told him, in so many words, to go fuck himself. aNow Josie stood in the window shaking her head, mouthing words in an exaggerated way, as if he should be able to lip read.

"She's done" was all he could read, and then Josie pulled back the curtain, replaced by the old calico.

Done.

He didn't want to give up, didn't want to get in the Jeep and head back to the apartment because *there?* There he'd have to face Mike. Eventually.

Once Mike got home from his run, they'd have it out. They didn't *do* fighting. No one had ever put them in this position.

Wait. *They* had put them in this position. He had to be fair to Laura. Hope died a quiet, soulful death as no one moved, he heard no hushed whispers, and the cat began licking its privates.

Time to go home.

Standing on Josie's front stoop, withering in the heat, the object of ridicule from the two hipster pet owners who now held little grocery bags of poop hanging off their thumbs, Dylan made his way slowly down the steps to get in the Jeep and just go home.

Home? Where, exactly, was home anymore? Laura was home, where he felt comfortable and important and where the three of them, together, could do or be anything.

Including a billionaire.

Driving Mike's Jeep made him appreciate his Audi, the Jeep too high, the steering imprecise. He managed it, driving without thinking while on autopilot, not even bothering to turn on music. The route he chose took him past Jeddy's, ironically, where he and Mike had inadvertently been successful in getting Laura to look past their clumsy error and to give them another chance.

If only he could have another accidental meeting with her. Maybe if she weren't on her guard he could talk to her openly, apologize profusely, and at least tell her how much he loved her.

Good thing he was at a red light and at a full stop, because the words *loved her* made his brain smack against his skull. Love? Where did that word come from?

He didn't throw it around lightly. Being a charity auction bachelor and a bit of a cad meant he had his share of women, and he liked it that way—having his share. His slice. His percentage.

Love? Love was something he'd saved for Mike and Jill.

And now, apparently, for Laura.

The woman he'd just driven away.

The rest of the drive was a blur until he parked the Jeep in Mike's spot, then made his reluctant way to the apartment. When he walked in, he found the last thing he ever expected to see.

Mike. Beet red, veins bulging, shirt completely soaked and arms flexing, neck expanded as if he'd just been doing deep squats with twice his weight on the bar. Huffing from exertion, Mike wouldn't look him in the eye. Pacing, he walked back and forth down the entrance hallway, a hulking mass of nervous energy.

"How did you beat me home?" he asked, puzzled. At best, he was twenty minutes ahead of Mike's top marathon speed.

"Cab."

"Why'd you take a cab? I thought you were running it out."

Silence. *This* Dylan could handle; he knew what to expect when Mike withdrew. But walking into the living room gave him a scene he was wholly unprepared to encounter.

Glass. Shattered glass everywhere. On second thought, it wasn't nervous energy Mike emanated.

That was *rage*.

The smoked-glass coffee table was a heap of shards and broken footings. A fifty-pound dumbbell lay cock-eyed in the middle, books piled on it from the collapse.

"Mike, what the fuck—"

Sheer terror consumed him as he turned to find Mike holding the other fifty above his head, not pointed at Dylan but rather at a small end table next to the leather couch. The crash was splinteringly deafening, the sound of Mike's grunt as he exuded enough effort to pitch the dumbbell in a perfect, parabolic arc combining with the breaking glass to create a noise that made Dylan's teeth rattle.

Jumping back, he avoided getting hit by shrapnel. His mind raced. Was he in true danger from Mike? *Mike?* His partner for more than ten years, the gentle man he'd admired and respected, who was always so compassionate.

Mike stormed out of the room and started throwing objects in his bedroom, the sound of drawers opening and closing, loud thumps and thick cracking sounds making Dylan follow him, wary and ready to protect himself if needed.

Entering Mike's bedroom, which has always been minimalist and sparse, the sight before him was jarring. Everything he owned was everywhere—clothes spilling out of drawers, his closet ransacked, candles rolling in jars on the floor and pictures face down. Mike was standing near his bed, wildly shoving items into a hockey duffel bag, head down and muttering to himself.

"What happened? Were we robbed?"

Mike snorted but didn't look up, robotically grabbing a blue sweatshirt, a pair of torn jeans, then flip flops, all going in the bag by rote movement.

"Yeah, Dylan. I was robbed. Of Laura. By you and your stupid, fucked up ideas."

"Hey, man, you can't pin this entirely on me." His own rage swelled inside, ready to match Mike's molecule for molecule. "You're the one who primed her not to trust us in the first place."

The look Mike shot him was pure evil. His heart sank as his ire rose. That wasn't a look you give to someone you care about. That was a look you get when someone you love turns cold. Turns off. Views you as no one.

It was worse than indifference.

And it was a look he had only received once before, from an old girlfriend. It had made his balls crawl into his throat, his soul shrivel into a shrunken mess, and he had resolved never, ever to let anyone inside his heart who could do that to him.

So far he hadn't.

Until now.

"I fucked up," Mike huffed. "I own it. But dammit," he shouted, smacking his dresser top for emphasis, his wallet and change cup falling off the right edge. "We fixed that! She took us back in! And you—you! You wanted to waste all that because you're so fucking afraid that taking Jill's money means you accept her death or that you loved her less of whatever fucked up emotional process you have buried deep in your ego. I can't even *look* at you.".

Stunned, Dylan couldn't form a coherent thought to respond. Who was this man? He looked like Mike but might as well have been some psycho twin, come up from the dead to steal Mike's spirit and destroy their relationship.

Mike was never mean. He could be firm, and he could be sarcastic (though rarely), and he knew how to take a stand and hold firm, but he was never, ever an asshole. Had losing Laura really driven him to some sort of psychotic break?

Mike strode angrily to the front door, then stopped cold. "Where are my keys?"

"Here." Dylan tossed them in an arc, Mike's hand reaching up to catch them. Palm facing Dylan, the movement precise and clipped, like an athlete who had done it hundreds of thousands of times to reach perfection.

Grabbing the doorknob, Mike was halfway out the door when Dylan called out. "Where are you going?"

"My cabin."

"What about this?" Dylan shouted, sweeping his arm out, indicating the mess.

"Hire someone to clean it up and replace everything. Bill me. I can afford it," he scoffed, then slammed the door. "I'm a fucking billionaire!" he shouted, and then all Dylan heard was the fading sound of footsteps.

Chapter Five

"Wakey, wakey, sleepyhead!" Josie shouted, yanking open the curtains in Laura's bedroom, the pink cloth swaying in a pattern that made Laura's stomach queasy. Ugh. Bad enough she was exhausted; did Josie really need to make her nauseated, too?

The coarse sun blinded her with too much, the glare off the world striking her as so harsh, too unyielding. Give her a nice, grey day with white cloud coverage so she could dip herself back into life.

Let her suckle her depression, for it gave her so much comfort. Being a victim meant never having to think through your own actions, not reflecting on regret, and it definitely gave her ample excuse for eating entire pints of ice cream and wallowing in *It's Always Sunny in Philadelphia* marathons.

It had been a month since the guys...well, there wasn't an easy word for what they'd done to her. The Big Reveal? The Big Not-So-Reveal? Laura's Public Humiliation? Whatever you called it, a month had passed and somehow she'd survived, each day an exercise in how not to fall apart.

Grabbing as many sick and vacation days as her boss would allow had given Laura the time she needed to sit with everything that had happened with Dylan and Mike and process it all. She hated how confusion and hurt made her bitter, had made her scream like that at the very end.

Not enjoying food troubled her; her stomach seemed to hold all her tension now, a shift she'd never experienced. Reading novels over the years, she'd always been jealous when a character lost her appetite, wishing that were a by-product of her many heartbreaks.

Now she understood. It really wasn't all she'd thought it would be. The grinding nausea that worsened with any stressor—and who didn't have stress?—made her curl up in bed and sleep when she could.

"What are you on? The all-orange diet?"

Josie had found the remnants of Laura's dinner, all she could manage these days. Baby carrots, cheese enchiladas and oranges.

Depression really wasn't the word for what she had been feeling for more than a month, but she didn't have a better phrase that conveyed how deeply sad their actions had made her. All of the support at work certainly helped, with her boss providing her with plenty of leeway, and friends coming in at times for pep talks.

More than anything, she appreciated their steady guidance, with various women running interference with Debbie, who kept finding new ways to ask her to help her hook up with "the other one. You know, the one who looks like Thor."

Sigh.

"Look, Laura, you can't keep doing this." Josie was giving her the hairy eye. "I know you have the day off, but staying in bed and doing the sick thing isn't helping. And the orange diet is just disgusting. What's next? Circus peanuts and Cheetos?"

Her stomach decided to swivel a hula hoop around it. "Oh, God, don't," she begged, holding her hand over her mouth.

The hairy eyeball got hairier. "You never get sick like this."

"Sure I did. In college. Hangovers."

"Yeah, but you didn't get drunk last night."

"Maybe it's the flu." Laura really didn't have it in her to argue. The sunshine felt like little daggers scraping against her eyeballs, and her brain was dulled down. Lately, she couldn't watch real television, her brain only capable of reality TV shows. If she watched another season of *The Biggest Loser* she was going to start dreaming about Extra Chocolate Mint Ice Cream gum and Subway.

"A month-long flu?"

Laura sat up, propping herself with pillows and holding her breath, wincing as a wave of nausea made her feel like she was puffy and drained at the same time, the sensation so damning she wanted to die. "It can happen."

"Um, no."

Josie went into Laura's kitchen and she heard her rummaging through the fridge. *Please don't bring me food,* she thought. A quick glance at the leftovers from her dinner made bile rise up in her throat. Scooching back down, she reclined again, flipping her pillow to let the cool side touch her sickened face.

Carrying a tall glass of water with bubbles, Josie reappeared.

"Drink this."

Laura didn't want to obey, but she did anyhow. There was a tone in Josie's voice, the professional nurse giving medical aid and taking no shit.

Do this because it's good for you.

Because I said so.

With crossed arms, Josie watched guard over her, as if Laura's not drinking the sparkling water would constitute a personal affront. The first sip was almost painful, then the next easier. About halfway through the glass she felt an enormous bubble fill her throat, the resulting belch so unladylike she might have roused a standing ovation from a group of truck drivers in a roadhouse bar.

Josie's polite golf clap didn't quite cut it. "Feel better?"

To her surprise, Laura said, "Yes."

And she did. The nausea wasn't gone, the exhaustion was still so all-pervasive she could feel it in her bones, like poured, wet concrete seeking a low point. But the cloud of doom and sickeningly sour stomach was alleviated, even if fleetingly.

The look on Josie's face gave Laura pause. Her friend looked ten years younger, more like when they'd met, hair pulled back and face scrubbed of make-up, though her long fingernails remained, this time designed to look like hot dogs.

"Hot dogs?" she said, pointing to Josie's hands. Even saying the name of the food made her stomach lurch.

"I saw the Oscar Mayer Weinermobile and got inspired."

"Is that a nickname for the guy you're dating?"

Smirk. "She feels better!" Josie announced to Snuggles, who poked his head out from under the bed and popped it right back, terrified.

Sip. Deep breath. Squint. "Yeah. Just barely."

"Some flat ginger ale and saltines might help, too." Wary and watching, the words poured out of Josie's mouth like a string of curses, the words foreign and unreal.

"You think I'm—what?—you're crazy—no way!" Nausea returned in a giant tidal wave, her body twisting to the side to retch into a strategically-placed bowl on the ground. Orange. Everything that came up was orange. It made her vomit more, blood vessels bursting on her face, the rolling contempt of the muscles needed to empty her stomach making this all-the-more difficult.

"How long have you been doing that?" Josie asked dispassionately, stepping closer to pull Laura's hair back as she blew chunks.

A box of tissues nearby were within reach; Laura grabbed one and furiously dabbed her lips.

"On and off for the past week. I swear, Josie. Flu."

"You have a fever?"

"No."

"Muscle and joint pain?"

"No."

"When was your last period?"

"I am not your patient!" Fear and dread crept through her, giving her chills. She hadn't let herself go there. It's not that the idea hadn't occurred to her—it most certainly had, especially when the nausea became so middle-grade and pervasive, lifting only late at night. She was on the pill, though, and while she'd stupidly gone bare, not asking the guys to wear condoms, she'd never worried about this. She was on the pill, right?

But there was that one day, Laura, a voice whispered, low and mean. *One day.*

No! It hadn't even been twenty-four hours! She'd just forgotten. That wasn't enough, right?

Her Two Billionaires and a Baby

"No. You're not. You're my best friend in a shitty situation with those two assholes and now it looks like it's taken a turn no one expected."

Kind and restrained, Josie's voice was simultaneously soothing and frightening. The implications of what she was suggesting were appalling. If she were—if this was—should she actually be—then this was like combining a Jerry Springer show with a Maury Povich paternity episode, all written by Dr. Drew and Judd Apatow.

In other words, a clusterfuck of unimaginable proportions. Because who was the father?

"It's not what you think," was all Laura could croak out. Josie handed her the sparkling water. Each sip seemed to renew her. "Can we talk about anything else?"

"Oh, like the royal baby?"

"Shut up. Where's Nice Josie? I'd like her back."

"Nice Josie is about five seconds away from running to CVS for a few pregnancy tests."

"NO!" Her harsh tone shocked them both. "NO! I said it's not that."

Nice Josie made an appearance, sitting on the bed and taking Laura's hand in hers, kind eyes measuring her. "OK, OK, I'll respect whatever you want. But maybe I'll appear and make you pee on a stick."

"You can't make me," Laura laughed. The feeling was foreign. It felt good.

Josie arched one eyebrow. "I am a nurse. *Vee haf vays ov maykeen you ooorinate*."

Laura laughed again. "I'll bet you do, you kinky bitch."

Josie pretended to be offended, playfully hitting Laura's feet with a pillow. Laura kicked back and growled. A cat hissed and sprinted across the room, out into the hallway.

Closing her eyes, Laura leaned back against the pillow. *Sip.* Exhaustion seeped in again, the room spinning slightly, her eyelids now full of lead weights.

"Go ahead and nap," Josie crooned. "I'll be back later."

"Mmmmkay." Laura was almost asleep and barely heard her door click as Josie left. Snuggles nosed his way up onto the bed and settled next to her hip, his quiet purr singing her to sleep.

Three seconds later, Josie woke her up. The sun was different—not so stabby—and she heard music in the background. Indigo Girls? No. Adele. How could she get the two confused? Dry mouth made her taste cotton and Snuggles practically fell off the bed as she stretched.

"Josie?"

"Yep." Gurgle. Ah—making coffee. Just the thought of having to smell it made her inside turn. It was like vomit in the form of an odor these days.

"You making coffee?"

"Yep—want some?"

"God, no!"

"OK," she answered, her voice a sing song. "I'll drink it out here while you shower."

Shower? Laura pulled her pajama top out and sniffed her skin between her breasts. Eh. A bit oily. Sniffed a pit. Whoa! She was ripe.

That cotton taste wouldn't leave, so she finished off the flat sparkling water on her bedside table. Wait. How could she have dozed off for a few seconds if the water was flat?

"How long've I been out?" she hollered.

"Three hours."

Three hours? Damn. She padded into the kitchen and stopped, the wall of java in the air stabbing her sinuses. "How do you drink that shit?" she accused, closing off her nose and breathing through her dried-out mouth.

"This?" Josie said innocently, pointing to her coffee.

"Ugh." Laura turned away and shouted back, "Just get rid of it by the time I'm out."

Years ago, her grandma had told her she knew she was pregnant when she woke up in the morning and didn't want coffee or cigarettes. Maybe it ran in the family?

No. Don't think that way. Just...don't. Turning on the shower took so much effort. Moving her arm to take off her shirt felt like a Sisyphean task. Sliding out of her pajamas made her feel like she'd run a marathon. A small cup of water stayed down.

Damn flu.

The shower's spray washed away a fair amount of fear and a considerable amount of nausea, thank God. Wash, wash, wash everything away, all the pain, the exhaustion, the confusion, and the grief. Grief for what she'd wanted with Mike and Dylan, for what they could be doing right now, for losing Mike's shy smile, Dylan's jaunty one, for missing out on the New England fall with them, for what could be.

Tentative, she let her hands move the soap where it needed to go, her hand grazing her belly below her navel. Could she—really? She and Ryan had just started to talk about having a baby when she'd discovered he was a fraud. Both had been pleased to find the other willing. A few more years, they'd agreed. It wasn't time. He had asserted that they needed to bond as husband and wife, first, before bringing in a third.

She snorted. Funny how there already was a third.

The lie mattered, but what also mattered was that she had been ready to think about kids, to imagine pregnancy and birth and babies and toddlers and all the roly-poly love that came with them. If she was pregnant —she allowed herself to think in hypotheticals, her hands mechanically shampooing her greasy hair, the feeling of rinsing like a baptism, washing away the past month of dysfunction—then it would be OK.

Everything would be OK. To be more precise, it would all work out in the end because she absolutely, positively, undeniably was not pregnant. And couldn't be. It wasn't true, and as long as she willed it to not be true, she didn't have to face any of the long term consequences of having a billionaire baby daddy.

Or two.

A quick rinse was all she could manage as her legs and arms felt like jelly, her body shivering no matter how much she turned the shower faucet for more hot water. Time to get out. A quick toweling and new pajamas, plus a robe, helped with warmth. By the time she wandered out, combing her hair, she still felt the underlying tiredness and a smaller blanket of nausea, less intense but more pervasive, like a layer of fascia within her body, ever lurking but not always obviously felt.

Greeting her in the kitchen were Josie, a freshly-washed coffee pot, and three boxes on the kitchen table. Pink, white, and purple.

Damn it.

"Josie!" she wailed.

"You're really glowing," Josie replied in a tone of flattery.

Snuggles was in Josie's lap (*how had she managed that?*) and the cat turned and gave Laura the stare of doom. *You're pregnant!* its eyes said. *And I don't care.*

"That's anger, you idiot."

The boxes stood there, judging her. Who came up with the names for these things? Early Pregnancy Test was fine, but First Response? What was she, a 911 call?

Little cardboard soldiers of doom, ready to deliver a message from the front lines that she had lost, and it was time to surrender to the truth.

Never surrender!

And now she was quoting cheesy 80s songs in her mind. This was how far she had fallen.

"Water?" Josie poured more sparkling water from the green bottle and handed it to her.

"You just want to make me pee."

A sweet smile. "I just want to make sure you're hydrated. It reduces nausea."

"And makes me need to pee."

"Does it?" Josie asked, overly innocent and disingenuous. "How convenient."

Resentment kicked in with a healthy side of sour stomach. "Why are you so determined to prove I'm pregnant?"

Josie leaned in, blinking rapidly, her face serious and relaxed, the look jarring to Laura. She hadn't seen her friend this still and composed since...well, never.

"Because if you are pregnant, ignoring it can only hurt you and the baby. I'm a nurse, Laura. I know how important prenatal care is. I've worked labor and delivery and I've worked the post-partum wing. I want to make sure you don't do anything you might regret."

"Like what?" A shadow of something sinister crept into the room. What did Josie mean?

"Like ignore the reality of being pregnant and not get early care. Once you know the truth, you can do the right thing."

"The right thing?" She peered at Josie, wondering if she was implying what Laura thought she was implying.

"I mean get the care you need. Whichever way you choose. Early treatment is best no matter what."

Whoosh. Laura sighed deeply. Whew. "For a minute there, I thought you were saying I should get an abortion."

"Not my decision to make, or to influence." Josie shook her head, her vehemence a little unsettling. What if Laura needed to bounce ideas off her bestie? Isn't that what BFFs were for? Another round of nausea made her close her eyes and breathe slowly, deeply, as if she were getting through a contraction.

Staying perfectly still, Laura took in Josie's response, her body a bit more grounded after the breaths. No judgment. "Right," was all she could think to say.

Josie's face was neutral as she picked up the pink box and began opening it. "This one doesn't need first-morning urine, so you could do it right now, if you want."

Oh, God. A cold wave of *everything* washed over her. This was real. Her entire fate was in the hands of a thin stream of pee and a little plastic stick with chemicals on it that would measure her future in the form of one, or two, pink lines.

The floor seemed really close, the walls closing in on her. Josie's face went from the look of a professionally neutral nurse to that of a concerned friend.

"Breathe. Just breathe."

"Easy for you to say," Laura gasped, hands white-knuckling the back of a chair, her kitchen screamingly pink. Now she understood Dylan's reaction to all the color—it really was dramatic, wasn't it? Viewing her life through an outside lens had become the new norm.

And now through the lens of *baby*.

Laura reached for her water and took a sip. "OK. But you have to be the one to read it and tell me what it says."

"No problem." The concern that had crept into Josie's eyes freaked Laura out. This was the most mature conversation they had ever had in their entire friendship. Somber. Deliberate.

Bring back flaky Josie, *please*.

"Here. Just fill the cup and I'll handle the dipstick."

"That's what she said," Laura joked.

Josie cracked a toothy smile.

She looked at the little cup. Seriously? Her entire life rested in what the pee told them? Josie was now the Pee Whisperer?

Disassembling. "Laura?" Josie asked, nudging her gently to the bathroom.

Memorable pees came to mind. Straddling a Big Gulp as she raced down the Pike to make it on time to a concert. Peeing on a Bush in 2000 on election night (her mom's idea). Peeing in a trough at the outdoor amphitheater while visiting cousins in the Midwest.

Peeing for a stick that would determine her fate? This was #1 on that list now.

What an honor.

Filling the cup was easy, some of the stream missing and hitting her wrist, warm and cloying. Her own urine never bothered her but right now everything bothered her, stomach a barometer of stress and hormones. Hormones that could be detected by the reactions the chemicals in the little cloth-line end of the pregnancy test's stick.

Urine-filled cup in hand, she emerged and shoved the warm container in Josie's hand.

"Thanks." Josie made a flowery production of dipping the stick, waiting the appropriate amount of time, then setting it on the table.

"*Do, do, do, do,*" she hummed. The music to Jeopardy, the little ditty they play while the contestants wager as much as possible to win final jeopardy—where some people bet everything and fail, and others bet everything and succeed in ways that exceed their wildest dreams.

No final jeopardy for Laura, though. The only way out was through.

Through *pee*.

"How long does this take?"

"Three minutes." Josie stared at the stick as if it were a chess opponent in check.

Laura forced herself to go and wash her face, then brush and floss. That should kill three minutes, right? She wandered back into the kitchen to find Josie frozen in place, face serious and scowling. She looked like a chihuahua doing an impression of Grumpy Cat.

"How much more?"

"Fifty seconds."

Laura let herself remember Mike's hands, those gentle, enormous fingers that laced so effortlessly, so eagerly, with hers when they walked together. Dylan's eyelashes. The scent of both when they—

"How much longer?" Laura asked, her foot bouncing a mile a minute as she sat down at the kitchen table, legs crossed, her fingers drumming on the top.

"Thirty seconds," Josie answered. "Twenty less than the last time you asked."

"Shut up."

To her surprise, the smart ass went quiet. Damn well she better. This was no time for jokes. Josie's fingernails caught Laura's eye. Each was a rotation of a positive and negative pregnancy test. She inhaled sharply.

"Jesus, Josie, your fingernails! Have some compassion!" Did she seriously go out and have the hot dogs changed to *this*?

"I thought they were cute." Josie shot Laura a sideways glance and rolled her eyes. "Someone's lost her sense of humor completely. Besides, the hot dogs made you puke, so I changed them."

"Yeah, well, I must have puked up my sense of humor along with my lunch. If it means so much to you, go find it in the toilet."

Ding! The oven timer beeped and Josie met her eyes, both of them scared shitless, Laura moreso. It was her life in the balance, after all, and while her best friend could be the most empathic person on the planet, she couldn't give birth for her.

Laura covered her eyes. "You look. I can't."

"Okay." Silence.

"Josie?" Laura could feel the sandpaper in her voice, could hear her unacknowledged truth, knew exactly what Josie was about to say but needed her to say it. To make it real. Her stomach roiled and that full-body flush—not the good kind—flooded her senses again. She willed herself to take deep breaths. Three of them, to be exact, before Josie finally said:

"It's positive."

"It—*what*?" She snatched the stick away from Josie and forced herself to look.

Pregnant.

Belly swelling, hands growing, her face and skin felt like a sheet of someone else's cells. Something was growing in her. And it wasn't an infection or a crush or an idea or anything else she'd fostered or cultured or spawned.

It was *spawn*.

She knew that was one of the options. Hell, there were only two. Either she was pregnant, or she wasn't. No third choice here. No threesome to deal with. This was binary, baby.

And, apparently, it was *baby* all the way.

"Oh, holy mother of god fucking shit damn whoda*thunk*it?" Sprinting for the bathroom, she hit the toilet at just the right moment, projectile vomiting straight in the bowl, the water splashing up in ricochet as if to slap her out of her panic.

"I'll make some peppermint tea," she heard Josie shout, her voice weak and uncertain. "No—ginger. Ginger is good for morning sickness."

Ah, God. This was *real*.

She was pregnant. *Pregnant!* Her best friend was talking about morning sickness strategies. That meant this would happen again! Being sick day in and day out for weeks meant that this wasn't going away. Wasn't transient.

Permanent.

Heaving into the bowl, the contents of her stomach scrambled to evacuate, to flee the situation, to get as far away from Knocked Up Girl as possible.

If she could, she would, too. Except she couldn't.

Because she was the mommy.

Puke. Hurl. *Blargh*.

Pregnant. She was *pregnant*. Mommy. Someone would call her *Mommy* soon. At twenty-nine, she felt old enough. Inside, she felt seventeen sometimes, though. Could she really do this? How would the whole single mother thing work? Planner-brain kicked in. Look over maternity leave plan. Learn about onsite child care center.

Hot and sweaty, her face inches from discolored toilet water, her stomach wouldn't settle down.

Tap tap tap. "Laura? You need anything?"

"A time machine," she answered weakly. "I have something to undo."

A soft laugh. "I'll leave some fresh water for you to drink right here. I hate to say this, but I have to get to work." Pause. "Call me later?"

"Sure." Pressing her cheek against the underside of the toilet bowl brought conflicting relief. Who prayed to the porcelain gods without having gotten drunk the night before? Pregnancy debased her already.

"I'll come back after my shift and bring some ginger beer and stuff to help your stomach."

Click click click went Josie's shoes, then the soft sound of the front door closing.

Alone. When did life get so complicated? The cold toilet felt like a mother's loving touch, which made Laura laugh at how this was all unfolding.

It's *always* complicated.

And she was utterly alone.

A hand fluttered to her belly.

No.

Not quite.

Chapter Six

__Three months later__

"I can't believe you still haven't told them!" Josie hissed from the corner of her mouth as she sat next to Laura in the waiting room of the nurse-midwife's office. Half the pregnant women seemed to be called to the midwife side, and half to the obstetrician side.

Josie was so out of place there, like a toothpick in a sea of Teletubbies.

Laura compared her growing belly to those she saw. At nineteen weeks, she was almost halfway there. That first trip to the doctor three months ago had yielded a complete shocker: she was seven weeks along. One missed period and *bam!* She was nearly one-sixth through the pregnancy without knowing it. All the prenatal vitamins and pregnancy yoga and morning sickness remedies helped her to get here, but Josie was harping on the one, pesky little detail she couldn't deny her way out of for much longer.

The past twelve weeks had been a blur, and now she was about to meet her baby via ultrasound, go home with a picture of an alien baby that people would pretend was beautiful, and here she sat after drinking a liter of fluid, her panties moist from a bladder that gave up control right around the time her shoes stopped fitting. A light breeze could make her pee at this point. A sneeze would unleash a tsunami.

"Am I as big as her?" she whispered quietly, surreptitiously pointing to a woman who looked ready to drop any day. The shirt she wore looked like something a tent rental company made for her. She violated the laws of physics when she stood.

"Close," Josie guessed. Her face reddened and she *tsked*. "Quit changing the subject! When are you telling Dylan and Mike?"

"Soon. After this," she replied, pointing vaguely toward the midwife's office. Today she would have her first ultrasound and, she hoped, learn the baby's sex. She squirmed horribly, and not from Josie's nagging. Her bladder was rapidly in need of its own, separate bladder. A kegel would help, but damn if she could isolate and squeeze *anything* down there right now.

"You've been putting it off for three months, Laura! And you always say 'soon' but it's never 'soon.'"

"It's complicated." Laura threw her a glare to stop a truck. *If she said it...*

"We're inducing next week, when I hit thirty-eight weeks," she heard the enormously pregnant woman say. A creeping dread seeped through her skin. Or was it a hot flash? She honestly couldn't tell the difference any more. Holy shit! That woman was twice as far along as Laura? How could they be close to—

"Laura Michaels?" A medical assistant appeared, chart in hand. The drill was simple for her normal appointments; go on in to the bathroom, pee, dip the sticks in, and if anything came back irregular, report it to the midwife. Then sit in the waiting area again until called.

For an ultrasound, though, she went back through the maze of medical equipment and desks to a tiny room with an exam table crammed in. The platform seemed unusually high. Climb? Dude, she could barely wipe herself these days, the stretch a, well...stretch. Climb?

"Climb on up," the male technician directed, his voice pleasant and his demeanor kind.

"With this exploding bladder, I'll squirt like a firehose if I lift my leg."

Josie laughed. The tech seemed amused. "Nothing I haven't seen before."

All these baby people kept saying that to her. If it was supposed to put her at ease it did, but also left an unsettled feeling, as if her birth experience weren't unique, as if everything she was going through and that seemed so special were just...ordinary.

Being ordinary didn't trouble her, in general, but the sensations and blossoming of this new life within her were so special, so life-altering, that she wished everyone around her would give a little more "wow!" when they interacted with her.

Or, maybe, what she really wished was that she had a partner to go through all of this with her. Resting her hand on her belly, she wondered when she'd feel the baby move. Hopelessly eager, every pocket of gas, tweaked muscle, you name it—she braced and held her breath, hoping...

And wasn't that something she should share with the baby's father?

Fathers, an evil voice whispered in her mind.

Somehow she managed, with Josie's help, to get up on that torture table. Reclining on her back pushed her womb against her bladder, making her instantly homicidal.

"Oh, man, can't I pee? Please?"

"Just a few minutes," the tech said, then explained the procedure. She hiked up her maternity shirt, a cute print from the Gap. Shopping for maternity clothing had turned out to be liberating, because the designers expected you to have breasts and a belly. Her shirt was covered with hippie swirls of pinks and turquoises, with lots of white thrown in. The panel on her maternity jeans was a pale blue, stretchy jersey added where the zipper and button normally would be.

She wanted to wear these clothes forever.

Maybe you will, if you can't lose the baby fat, that same voice said. Gah. She couldn't win.

The cold gel made her kegels clench, helping keep in her urine but adding a sensory overload to that general region. The ultrasound wand the tech used went on the gel and soon she could see her little peanut, all bones and beating heart, floating upside down in an an enormous sea of black.

"There's the baby," the tech said in a neutral voice, taking measurements. From the start, Laura had decided to have a low-technology birth, so this was the first ultrasound. Meeting her baby visually brought tears to her eyes, her heart swelling, and even Josie was overcome with emotion.

"Oh, Laura," she whispered, voice choked. She squeezed her shoulder.

Her *child*. That womb pressing hard against all that water, making her eyes cross and her ribs ache, contained a little growing human being that was going to come out in twenty-one weeks and be her little, precious baby.

"Boy or girl?" Leave it to Josie to get to the point.

The tech laughed, obviously accustomed to the question. "First off, do you want to know?"

"Yes!" the women answered in unison.

"Then give me a few minutes to do the required measurements, and then I'll try to see. No guarantees—

it's all about whether the fetus is in the right position, and what we can see with the machine."

Laura nodded and Josie seemed already to know that. The room was so tiny that Josie had to jockey for space with the tech. And it was getting warmer in here. Plus, she felt like an overstretched balloon that would burst if anyone breathed hard.

Loving warmth coursed through her. *Baby.* Her body, which she'd despised most of her life for its inadequacies, for letting her down time and again with men, was now ripe with purpose and growing a human being. How could she hate it right now? It was building, layer by layer, system by system, a whole 'nother human who would be part of the next generation.

She was a goddess.

Finally done with measurements, the tech stopped, frowned, and said, "Excuse me. I'll be right back."

The click of the closing door felt like a death sentence, the air sucked out of the room as Laura's entire body switched into panic mode.

"That can't be good? Why would he leave? Do you see anything?" Oh, God, no. Just *no*. Nothing could be wrong, right? She hadn't planned for anything to be *wrong*.

Josie peered at the screen. She shrugged. Nonchalant and cool, she made a questioning face and replied, "I don't see anything obvious, but I'm not an ultrasound tech." Her hand on Laura's felt reassuring. "I'm sure it's nothing. Maybe all your talk about peeing made him need to go."

"Don't make me laugh or I'll give you a golden shower, Josie."

"Now you're turning me on." The laugh did make her nearly pee, giving her a few fleeting seconds of amusement, shifting away from worry. A knock, then her midwife came in, followed by the tech.

Damn.

"Sherri? What are you doing here. They said this was a routine screening and I wouldn't see you."

What she wanted to say was *Go away! Nothing's wrong Nothing can be wrong so go away and let me not hear what you're about to say!* but something in her knew that wasn't the case. She gripped Josie's hand like she was drowning.

Josie gripped back.

Sherri's eyes were kind but guarded, wrinkles forming everywhere as she smiled. She had a relaxed, natural look to her, with dark brown eyes, tanned skin and long, gray hair braided in a thick rope that stretched over her ass. Today she wore a loose, flowing jacket over a tank top and a long skirt, an outfit like many in Laura's closet.

"The tech just asked me to take a quick look at something." Her voice was smooth and practiced. Josie nodded, eyes on Laura, her professional nurse face in overdrive. They were all hiding something from Laura, and she did not like this one bit. Sherri introduced herself to Josie and they shook hands in a perfunctory way.

The midwife and tech put their heads together and murmured medical terms Laura strained to hear. She really was about to explode, her vagina starting to pulsate—and not the good kind of pulsating.

"I need to pee!" she whispered to Josie. How banal, to have such an insignificant need in the middle of what could be the worst news she'd ever heard in her life. Yet nature called.

The tech and Sherri pulled back, the tech leaving the room. Sherri's hand was warm and gentle on

Laura's shoulder. "First, the baby is healthy according to our basic measurements."

A huge, loud sigh poured out of Laura, like a yoga breath. "Thank God."

"But it's a bit complicated."

No.

"Right now, you're on the high end of amniotic fluid. There's a condition called polyhydramnios—it means excessive amniotic fluid. Your measurements show you are at the low end of having this condition, which means the fetus is floating in all that fluid, like an overstuffed balloon."

"Are you sure that's not just my bladder?"

Sherri laughed and reached out to grip Laura's hand. "Why don't you go and empty *that* poor, overstretched balloon and we can talk more. All the images we need are done."

Laura started to get up and stopped. "The sex?"

Sherri cocked her head and made a face of surprise. "Oh! James didn't get to that before he found me. You want to know?"

"Yes!" she and Josie practically shouted.

Chuckle. "Well, then, if you can bear it, lean back again and let's look."

Groaning, Laura complied, the pressure to urinate overwhelming her mind and body. This was crucial, though. Boy or girl? She'd wanted to know since the day the test said PREGNANT.

More gel. Wand. Gouging (*not really, but it felt like it*). Jiggle. "Why are you jiggling?" And then she knew, as the baby moved and shifted, trying to get away.

"This is not an exact science." Josie snorted. Sherri made a self-deprecating gesture. "I am, though, ninety percent certain it's a girl."

Girl.

"I don't see the telltale penis I'd expect to see. Just the umbilical cord. The only time we're certain is at the birth."

Girl. Laura had imagined the baby was a girl since day one. She was right. It really was. Mother's instinct always knew, right?

"Are you OK, Laura?" Sherri asked.

She shook herself out of her own thoughts and grinned. "I assumed it was a girl. I was right." She stuck her tongue out at Josie, who had teased her she was wrong.

"You and Josie are having a baby girl," Sherri said, looking at them both with great joy.

Hold up. "Me and Josie?"

"Awkward," Josie said out of one side of her mouth. She addressed Sherri. "Um, we're not—" she said, pointing between her and Laura.

"Oh, no! No, we're not a couple!" Laura added.

"If I were into women, Laura's totally not my type," Josie added helpfully.

Hey, now. "What does that mean?" Laura cried out, indignant.

Sherri cut them both off, her face red with embarrassment. "I certainly did not mean to start an argument, and I apologize for my assumption. And Laura, you did mention that the father isn't part of the picture—"

"Fathers," Josie muttered.

Laura cut her a glare that would kill Medusa.

Sherri clicked a few buttons on the machine and printed some pictures, handing them to Laura. On slick fax paper, they were the most beautiful photos she had ever seen in her entire life, even if her baby did resemble something from a government archive in an episode of *The X Files*.

"So I'll leave you with this: your chart looks strong; All the lab work is perfect, and while you are overweight, and could technically reach obesity during this pregnancy, depending on total weight gain, you don't have gestational diabetes, your cholesterol and other lab values are well within range, and frankly, Laura, you're healthier than many average-weight women I see." Picking Sherri had been smart.

"Does this mean I can still birth in the hospital with a midwife?"

"For now, yes. We can't predict what will come next, but given the information we have now, you're not risked out of a hospital midwife birth."

Pleased as punch, Laura simply said, "Thank you!"

Josie appeared suitably impressed.

The feel of the paper in her hands gave her a happiness she hadn't felt in months. Not since her last night with the guys.

"This does, though, explain some of your added weight gain, some of it excess fluid. At this point, we'll have you come back in three to four weeks and do another measurement to check fluid. You may find that as you expand, your mobility is a bit limited; if the polyhydramnios continues, it makes you look and feel as if you are further along than you are."

"Is that why I look seven months pregnant but I'm barely at five?"

Sherri nodded. "It explains some of it. So call if you feel like anything is off, or if you have any fluid leakage or spotting. Right now, in the second trimester, measurements can change, so for this month we wait and see. If it persists, we'll do some tests to see if we can find an underlying cause."

Each word made sense. Understanding the basics of this polywhatever wasn't hard. But the screaming voice in her head that kept shouting *wrong wrong wrong wrong* made it hard to fully digest what Sherri was saying.

"I don't feel well," Laura blurted. Josie and Sherri closed in.

"Go empty your bladder. We'll help you."

"The day I need help peeing is the day I—"

"Give birth," Josie interrupted.

Nasty glare. "Go find another woman. I'm so done with you. And you're not my type, either."

Sherri seemed more amused now by their banter as she and Josie followed Laura down the hall to the single-stall toilet.

"I don't need help," Laura announced, opening the door and stepping into the same room she'd peed in for months now. Tears filled her eyes in the silent little tile-filled space. Something was wrong. Too much fluid? Sheri's explanation made sense, and the baby was otherwise healthy. She. *She* was otherwise healthy.

A little girl.

Daddy's little girl.

Which daddy? Her bladder groaned in ecstasy as she released its contents, the entire process taking about four times longer than usual. Ah, what pregnancy did to the body. Never before had she considered how nearly-orgasmic going pee could feel.

Thoughts of Mike and Dylan flooded her as she allowed that tiny little sexual thought to creep in. The pregnancy books talked about the magic second trimester, morning sickness gone and hormones aplenty making the mother horny. Laura got too much amniotic fluid and—*bonus!*—too much libido. Overdrive libido.

The kind that can only be satisfied by two men.

Leaving the bathroom, she was greeted by Josie. "Sherri had another patient. Said to schedule a follow-up in three weeks and not to worry."

"Yeah, right."

"Easier said than done, I know. Let's check out and get some lunch. How about Jeddy's?" Josie asked as Laura approached the desk.

"*Pfft.*"

"What? It's good food?"

"First I'm not your type, and now you want to drag me back there?"

The receptionist interrupted them, quickly scheduling Laura's next appointment. Josie held the door open as Laura exited. "Good food! Peanut butter cake..."

Any other day and Laura would have been all over it, memories of Mike and Dylan there be damned. The weight of the appointment's news felt like a lead burden spread through her body. Sleep was what she needed now, much more than good food.

"I'm really tired," she said, handing her car keys to Josie. "Can you drive?"

Josie grabbed the keys, climbed in the front seat, and moved the seat forward a good foot. Laura carefully twisted to settle into the passenger seat, moving it back a foot or so.

Deep breath. As Josie maneuvered the car from Wellesley to Somerville, she perked up, energy came back. Suddenly, Jeddy's sounded really good. Besides, if she went home it would be her and the cats, and they just hid and wanted food. Josie was a marginally better conversationalist than Miss Daisy, anyhow.

"How about Jeddy's?"

"You bit my head off when I suggested it."

"I changed my mind. Blame the hormones."

"You never had pregnancy hormones before when you couldn't make a decision."

"I'm milking this pregnancy for as many excuses as I can."

"Does that include excusing why you're depriving this baby's father of the right to know about it—excuse me, *her*—and be part of her life?"

Ouch. Josie hopped on the turnpike and flew through the EZPass tollbooth. The little green light mocked Laura. Green for go. Go tell them. Tell them now.

They have a daughter.

Daughter.

Uh, no. *One* of them has a daughter. One.

"I don't know what to do, Josie. How am I supposed to tell them I'm pregnant?"

"You say 'I'm pregnant.'" They had been fighting about this for the past three months, ever since that day in her apartment when the test was positive. Josie insisted the men had the right to know; Laura insisted she needed more time.

"You don't understand." Tall wooden retainer walls lined one side of the pike, while the commuter train moved in the opposite direction on the left, making Laura a bit disoriented.

"Understand what it's like to be pregnant? No. Understand that you are lying to them? Yes."

"It's not..." Laura couldn't even cry about this anymore. Waiting had made it harder, each day, to consider telling them. She wasn't heartless. At some point she'd let them know. Then they could face the question of which man was the father. Cringing at the thought, she turned away from Josie and pressed her forehead against the cool window glass.

Silence. Laura tried to explain, her forehead flattening and the pain of pressing it, hard, somehow helpful. "After what Ryan did, I figured I was damaged goods. That I send out vibes that draw demented jerks. And then here come Dylan—and Mike!—and it seemed too good to be true."

Traffic slowed suddenly as they drove under the hotel that stretched, literally, across the pike. "So when the guys double-teamed me at Mike's place, and then seemed to laugh about it, it felt like I was being suckered. I ran away, then I let them back in. God, they were so convincing."

"Laura." Josie's voice was so mature and wise it made Laura close her eyes. She knew what came next. Josie moved over into the left lane to get off the pike at the split. "You are Ryan right now."

OK, *not* what she expected. "What?" she shrieked, outraged.

"Ryan kept critical information from you about a life-altering fact that made moving forward impossible." Josie stayed left and kept her eyes on the road, though she sighed. "And you are doing the same thing to Dylan and Mike. They have no idea that one of them is going to be a father. And you are making it impossible for the father of your daughter to go forward, to step up and do the right thing, to have a role in raising her."

"I'm not Ryan!"

"You are *totally* Ryan."

Laura knew they were close to Jeddy's; she started drooling at the thought of their asiago cheese foccacia with chipotle maple sausage.

"Ryan," Laura practically screamed, "lied about having a wife for nearly a year. He talked about marrying me. He created an entire relationship with me that was permanently hopeless and never, ever possible." How dare Josie compare the two? In fact, she was the one who had been lied to again by Mike and Dylan.

"Look," Josie said flatly, pulling into a parking space and rummaging for quarters. Laura opened the glove box and pulled out a roll, the paper unraveling from earlier parking jobs.

Josie interrupted herself. "Jesus, you're organized!"

"How hard is it to go to the bank and get a roll of quarters?"

Josie got out of the car and shouted, "How hard is it to tell the two men you were sleeping with that one of them might be the dad?"

"Uh, not even close?" Laura sputtered, grabbing the edge of the car door and hauling herself up and out.

Two women walking a golden retriever stood, staring at her belly, mouths forming perfect little "O"s, one with short salt-n-pepper hair, the other with a shaved head and the wilted look of recent chemo treatments.

Laura wanted to crawl into a hole. Josie looked over, saw the scene, and came to her rescue. As well she should, since she'd dumped her into this fiasco.

"What are you staring at?" she snapped at the women, throwing an arm around Laura, guiding her to the Jeddy's entrance. "Haven't you ever seen lesbians go to desperate measures to conceive?"

"Isn't that what sperm banks are for?" one of them muttered.

"Hater," Josie threw over her shoulder, spiriting Laura in.

"Lame-o," Laura said, shaking her head. "You're losing your touch."

Josie growled at her, baring her teeth. Madge appeared, looking older and shrunken, as if she possessed no fluid whatsoever under her skin.

From Laura's face to Josie's face to Laura's stomach, Madge took them in. Pointing to Laura's belly, she said, "Fat or pregnant?"

"Alien baby."

Madge hacked out a laugh. "Which one?"

"Which alien?" Now Laura was confused.

"No—which guy? The Italian Stallion or the viking?" She led them to the only clean table in the place. It was slammed.

"Actually, the baby is mine," Josie interjected. "New technology."

"Yeah?" Madge rasped. "If any woman's got balls, it'd be you."

"Can't be yours," Laura protested. "I'm not your type, remember?" she said with a bit more snap than she'd intended.

Madge spun her hand in a circular gesture. "I ain't got all day. Same thing you ordered last time?"

"I want that foccacia. And everything we ordered last time."

"Eating for two," Madge mumbled as she poked her handheld device and sped away.

Josie looked around and seemed to take in the crowded place.

"Nothing like it was in the early morning."

"You can see how they stay in business," Laura marveled.

"How does that old woman work midnight shift and lunch?"

"Not human." Laura's stomach jumped as some odd muscle spasm took hold of her abdomen.

"You OK?" Josie asked, leaping to her feet. "You look like something ripped inside."

"No, no, I'm fine," Laura gasped. As she looked down to examine her belly she felt it again, a little spasm and then it was as if something in her moved.

Kicked.

"Oh, my God! Josie! The baby. She's moving!" Laura pressed her hand to her belly and felt it, a little kick, a somersault that made the uterus feel slick and weird inside, as if a pocket of gas spirited itself from one side of her hips to the other.

Fluttering. Nothing. A flimmer, like tiny swimming flippers inside her, moving slowly.

Josie sat down next to her and planted her hands on either side of Laura's belly, frozen in place and staring at nothing, just anticipating.

Then she shrieked, "I felt it!", eyes wide and amazed. From a proud grin to tears, her face morphed into a mask of emotion, gasping and overcome.

"It's *real*." Her eyes met Laura's and she flung her arms around Laura's neck, the two separated by the baby.

"It's been real for a while," Laura cracked, her voice filled with emotion.

"Not for me. I'm not living it. This?" she said, touching Laura's belly, palm flat against it, waiting. "This makes it real." Grinning like a fool, Josie wouldn't let up, her hands pressing to catch another movement.

Madge appeared with their coconut shrimp. She stared at their position. "Get a room, you two." And off she went, speed walking.

Josie shouted, "That's what got her in this condition in the first place!" and abandoned Laura's belly. Coconut shrimp vs. feeling baby move? No contest, apparently.

And Laura had to agree. The shrimp was about as mouth orgasmic as you could get, and lately this *was* as orgasmic as she got. First trimester nausea had depressed her sex drive, but lately she'd emerged, scathed and emotionally battered by morning sickness, so grateful it retreated that she didn't dare complain about anything else. The horndog impulse had just kicked in.

She needed to buy stock in Duracell. The baby's college fund would go to batteries at this rate. There were moments she weakened and wanted to call Dylan and Mike just to fuck them and then send them home, needing the satiety of having these urges and constant arousal expunged, even for a few brief hours.

None of the pregnancy books warned her that she would be engorged twenty-four/seven, that she would want to be touched and manhandled and fucked and to come and come and come until drained, then bounce right back up and be ready for more, face flushed and tissues eager.

Even in her late teens she'd never had a drive like this; if pregnancy turned her into the female equivalent of a sex-crazed eighteen-year-old boy, she was going to have a crater where her clit should be by the thirtieth week.

Or it would secede and go join one of the cat's bodies, claiming sovereignty and a new pussy. Fucking anything that walked wasn't what she wanted; most nights she spent an hour after masturbating thinking about Dylan and Mike, wondering how it had all gone so very wrong, and brooding over what she knew she needed to do.

And now? It really was time to tell them.

Her fingers sought out the photos of the ultrasound, stuck carefully in the outer pocket of her purse. Josie was right—this was real. Reality meant being the stronger, better woman she had deep within and doing what was best for her daughter.

Her daughter deserved a dad who knew her.

Knowing this time to wait a few minutes before biting into the piping hot shrimp, Laura sat and took a few deep breaths. The scene outside was a lovely autumn New England day, sunnier than usual and unseasonably warm. Christmas decorations were already in some shop windows. Her lightweight maternity shirt had lasted since August, when she'd bought it. Soon it wouldn't fit, and the weather would turn to snow, perfect ski weather.

Ah, Mike. She sighed. Half hoping last summer that come winter he'd teach her how to ski, her eyes filled with tears yet again for what was lost. Stupid to think of that when she was holding back the most important news the guys had ever had in their lives. She assumed. Maybe Jill's death had been more important.

Both seemed pretty significant. What was she doing comparing them, anyhow? Ridiculous. Bottom line, though, was that after this meal she would go home, take a nap, and prepare to call them both tomorrow and face what she'd been putting off for months.

"Mmmm," Josie groaned as she munched on her coconut shrimp. Laura plucked one off the plate and took a bite, sinking her teeth in. Instant pleasure. The next ten minutes were a feeding frenzy as Madge brought out their sausage, foccacia, and the grand peanut butter cake.

"You eat more than a high school football team these days," Josie said, incredulous, as Laura asked Madge for another plate of shrimp.

"I have the sex drive of a high school boy, so that's not inappropriate." Munch, munch.

"TMI. I *sooo* did not need to know that."

"My batteries need batteries."

Josie shoved her fingers in her ears. "*Lalalalalalalalalala.*" Laura laughed maniacally and started to feel full. One more shrimp on the plate, she speared it and dipped it in the aioli. Heaven. Pure heaven.

"You're going to talk to them now, right?" Josie asked quietly, prodding without being negative. Pushing her plate of friend green tomatoes away, she smiled at Laura, an encouragingly sympathetic look.

Laura pulled her unfinished plate into her zone of consumption. *Mine now.* Stabbing a tomato, she tried the tiger sauce. Horseradish. Was it worth the reflux? Yes! *Mmmmm.*

"You're right. I'll talk to them. The baby is one of theirs and it's time."

Cupping one hand over her ear, Josie leaned across the table. "Say that again."

"I'm telling them."

"No—the part before that."

Laura made a sour face. "You're right." Time for dessert! She dumped all the caramel and hot fudge all over the peanut butter hulk smash cake and sneered at Josie. "And no cake for you!"

"You think I'm going to try to take a bite of that from a horny pregnant woman? I'm not suicidal."

Laura's laugh carried through the diner, turning a few heads and yielding bemused smiles. Ah, it felt good to laugh, deep belly chuckles that came from relief and calm and goodness and light. The baby kicked again.

"She likes the cake," Laura said, shoveling in another piece, following it up with ice cream.

"She's a gourmand. What are you going to name her?"

A long look at her plate. "Hulk Smash. Hulk Smash Michaels."

"Oh, that's totally a porn name."

Laura threw a wadded napkin at Josie, who ducked.

Finally full, Laura pushed her clean plate away. If she overate, she'd regret it later. Pregnancy was no different from non-pregnant life, with the exception of evil reflux. "I don't know. Whatever we name her it needs to be a collaborative effort."

"Like the conception."

Laura snorted. They were shifting into uncomfortable territory. "Yeah. Except no matter what, it's only one of them who is the father."

"Happy paternity testing." Josie shot her a sardonic grin.

"Go ahead," Laura sighed. "I know you're itching to say it."

"What?" Josie batted her eyes innocently.

"Just do it in a whisper." Laura reached for her purse and fished around. Her bladder announced its presence and she stood, hips clicking and left leg screaming in pain.

"Maury, Maury, Maury," Josie obliged, looking particularly pleased with herself.

"I'm suffering from sciatica and you're chanting baby daddy cultural references."

"And you still love me."

Laura flashed her a middle finger as she waddled off to the bathroom. "You're totally not my type!" she called back.

Madge happened to walk past. "Not my type either," she said, frowning at Josie.

Josie sighed. "I get that a lot."
"I'll bet you do."

* * *

He wasn't a stalker. Really. No—*really*.

Mike kept finding creative—and not so creative—reasons for driving past Laura's apartment building and Jeddy's. If he had to meet with the resort's tax accountant on some issue that went beyond what his onsite CPA could handle, he routed himself through Somerville, because—why not? And sometimes he found himself really craving those fried green tomatoes and a toffee caramel peppermint sundae from Jeddy's, so no harm, no foul if he stopped by—right?

Right?

The past few months had nearly killed him. So finding himself on the road right in front of Jeddy's stuck at a traffic light, neck craned to the left to stare in the restaurant's main window wasn't out of the norm. He made this drive once a week or so.

What was out of the norm was the sight of Laura and Josie in a booth, eating and laughing. All the air in his lungs froze in place, the red light now the only entity keeping him here so he could gaze upon Laura's face. Glowing. She literally glowed. The restaurant's facade was a split set-up, the bottom half of the outer wall wood, the top half glass, so he could only see her and Josie through the window, her chest and arms and face animated as she threw a balled-up napkin at her friend, her mouth open and head tipped back in giggles and fun.

Relaxing, his entire body went liquid, the first time in months he felt grounded, the incongruity of keeping the Jeep running, foot on the brake, and counting out the seconds before the light changed somehow ignored by his nervous system.

All he wanted to do was to stare at her from afar. She looked so, so happy. Being apart from him and Dylan seemed to have done wonders for her, red cheeks and dimpled smile deeper and fuller. His own face stretched into a loopy grin, the first in far too long.

Beep! Shaken out of his moment of joy, he realized the light had turned green. With great reluctance he took the left turn, watching for as long as was safe, her face a beacon of hope.

Then gone.

That day at home months ago, after leaving Josie's apartment, after Laura had screamed—*screamed*—that they should buy the building if they wanted in had been the coldest, hardest day of his life, like watching his own death in slow motion, his heart torn out and thrown to the wolves.

What had they done to her? How had he and Dylan taken such an open, gentle soul and turned her into a screaming banshee? What evil lurked in them that this could happen?

His run home had been fruitless, his need to escape Dylan at all costs greater than the desire to pound it out. All he could think of when he'd arrived home was a great red wall of anger within, and destruction made more sense than trying to be good.

Everything he had worked for went to shit that day —*everything*—so shattering the glass in the room was like shattering his bond with Dylan.

It made sense through the pure hatred he felt for himself at hurting Laura so deeply.

Now? Not so much. For months now, he'd lived apart from Dylan, his cabin a refuge that slowly had turned into a prison. An entire adulthood spent living with Dylan could not be undone so easily; in his rage, he'd missed that point.

He felt as if he were missing a limb, the phantom remains of a leg or an arm feeling real and visceral, yet truly gone. Mike had banished himself from Dylan's life, ignoring the text messages and voice mails that had been plentiful that first week, then tapered off in the second, finally ending with a plaintive, *"When you're ready, I'll be here."*

Mike hadn't been ready. Not yet.

Maybe not ever.

Seeing Laura like that, though—a gut punch. Flooding memories of her, of Dylan, of the three of them—and most of all, of the great promise they'd represented, of a lifetime together. *Double* gut punch. He maneuvered the car into a parking spot at the skyscraper where the tax adviser's office resided and put his forehead on the steering wheel, taking time.

Breaths.

Awareness.

So full of life! Laura had never been so *radiant* with them. Perhaps she'd really moved on, finding a new person—persons?—to be happy with. The way the pink and white and green of her shirt had highlighted her hair, her eyes shining and bright, and how Josie had even seemed happier than her normal self all made Mike wonder if he and Dylan were just poison for poor Laura.

Maybe not telling her the truth, though vicious and unfair, had somehow been the right thing in the end. Beating the steering wheel with one fist, he let himself feel. Not react. Not withdraw.

Feel. *Damn it*. How had his life come to this? Alone in his enormous cabin, designed to be filled with friends and laughter, it was now inhabited by Mike the Monk. Mike the Idiot.

Mike the Lonely.

And he was, for the first time in his adult life. Not alone—alone he understood. Alone he could handle, could even enjoy.

Lonely? Lonely was a form of self-abuse he couldn't escape.

Not that he hadn't tried. Running ninety miles a week, though, didn't get him any further from his messed-up self. How had he turned into such an animal that last day at the apartment? What was buried deep within and unleashed at that moment, so all-powerful he'd gone into a near fugue state and been so violent? It had scared him. Badly.

Maybe he should stay away from Laura. Even Dylan.

Perhaps being lonely was his new normal. What he deserved. Because whatever was going on in Laura's life, from the looks of her countenance in the window glimpse, she was swelling with glee and enjoying life.

Without him.

Screech. A BMW took a corner too close in the cement-floor garage, tires filling the cavern with too much sound. The clock told him he was late for the meeting with the tax attorney. Climbing out of the car and grabbing his briefcase, he smiled at the memory of her. Once his, once Dylan's, once theirs, she had morphed into just Laura.

Which was, all along, what she'd really needed.

Tears choked his throat. He ground a fist into his thigh, willing the unexpected rush of very unprofessional emotion away. Tax attorneys weren't therapists. He was here to talk numbers. As he cantered to the elevators, though, one number rang mournfully in his head, buzzing.

Three.

* * *

"You see that? Mr. Money strikes again." Dylan flinched but didn't say anything. The guys working the night shift were all crowded around the television, the same local morning news show that had featured his doom...er, his billionaire status a few months ago.

"Some guy with more money than he can *burn*," Murphy added.

The morning anchors were babbling on about some unnamed philanthropist who had come to the aid of burn victims from a local warehouse fire, then mentioned another incident last month where the same donor may have contributed $100,000 to help victims of an unexpected October ice storm.

Every head in the fire station turned to stare at Dylan.

"What?" he hollered, trying to get the attention off him. He was here as a lowly volunteer, looking for something to do.

Murphy laughed, the first good belly chuckle anyone had heard from him in months. Dylan had recently, quietly, funneled a substantial five-figure sum to him to pay for a caretaker for his wife and father. With good care, she was expected to have a strong chance of survival. His father, though, was fading fast. The money bought some peace and space for the family, and isn't that all anyone could ask for?

"A torn AC/DC shirt and jeans? You are the strangest fucking billionaire I ever met, Dylan," he said.

"Only fucking billionaire you ever met, Murphy. You probably don't even know any thousandaires," Joe cracked.

Everyone chuckled, Murphy included. The chief shooed them off to do work.

"You slumming?" he asked Dylan.

"Nah. Just covering a volunteer shift."

Truth be told, he was bored and lonely with Mike gone. But he couldn't say *that* at work. The guys might be good at heart, but a few were as enlightened as a lamp post.

"You can do that from home, you know. Scanner."

"Mine's broken."

Joe's eyebrows flew up. "And you can't afford a new one?"

"So sue me. I want to hang out here."

"Poor little rich firefighter?" Joe's voice wasn't mean. Just inquiring. It put Dylan on edge, made him ball his hands into fists, temper rising.

"Something like that."

"Grab one of the scanners from here on your way out, then. There's a big training going on in New York and a bunch of guys are there, so we can use all the volunteers we can get tonight. You OK with being on call through the night?"

A warmth spread through him, making him stand taller. He remembered this feeling. Happiness. Purpose. Power.

Action.

"Hell, yeah! Thanks, Chief."

"Let's hope it's a quiet one."

He always said that. Superstition. If he didn't, one of the guys would jump in and say it. You don't fuck around with bad luck in a station crowded with firefighters. They need every drop of help from whatever forces in the universe help out, from God to Jesus to the Flying Spaghetti Monster to Mother Nature. Even Mayor Menino, who wasn't divine—yet. One more election win and he'd be damn close.

"As quiet as a church mouse," Dylan answered. Secretly, though, he wanted to do some good. Help someone. While he'd never actually hoped for a fire or a medical emergency, the thrill of the run was always in his blood. Helping people was exactly why he'd gone into this business, and it gave him purpose.

If someone needed him tonight, he'd be there.

* * *

Stuffed like the turkeys that had popped up in grocery stores everywhere, Laura lurched into her living room and plopped down. In a few months, she wouldn't able to get up on her own. Time to start training Snuggles to offer her a hand getting out of deep, overstuffed chairs.

No one else would.

"Oh, stop," she muttered to herself. After dropping Josie off, she'd thought long and hard on the drive home. Picking up her phone and texting Mike and Dylan would be the hard part. Months. Four long months since she saw them last. This wasn't a reunion outreach, though.

It was business. The business of, well, *this*. Her hands cupped her belly with pleasure, willing love through her palms to the baby. So much love. Little Naomi—no, Claire—no, Elizabeth—no, Caitlyn—ah, *whatever!*—was part of her heart.

This child was a Michaels-Stanwyck, or Michaels-Pine, creation. Time they knew about the baby. Guilt settled in as her sciatica flared up, the painful nerve running from hip to toe making her rub her muscles to no relief. Walking helped, so she grudgingly lifted herself up and hobbled to the kitchen.

No need for food, but a glass of water and her prenatal vitamin would do for an excuse to move. Sheri said hot showers sometimes helped. Waddling down the hall, she turned on the spray to warm and grabbed a towel. On second thought, she also grabbed a new toy, a sleek little vibrator that couldn't go too deep, but that had turned out to be just enough to take the edge off her horny second trimester.

Too bad vibrators couldn't slap your ass and tug your hair. If someone made one, they'd be filthy, smutty rich.

Undressing wasn't too hard, though she was rapidly losing the ability to bend down and slide pants off. Plucking each leg out was becoming the norm, like tying shoes by bringing her feet up and crossing one leg at a time, leaving the laces tied on the insides.

Lifting one leg carefully, balancing herself, then lifting the other over the small bathtub lip, though, would be a struggle in a month or too. Damn. This single-mama-pregnancy crap was bad enough in terms of a libido the size of Montana, but if basic self care was going to be a problem, she might have to resort to taking Josie's offer and letting her move in.

Hot jets instantly relaxed her neck, the warm wetness a relief. Closing her eyes, she soaked quickly and sank into her well-grooved fantasy about Dylan and Mike. For as much as she barricaded herself against them in real life, in her dreams they were very much present.

Overwhelmingly so.

Mike's strong hands were eating up every inch of her skin, his mouth on her ear. "Your belly is so amazing," he crooned in her ear. "My daughter. You're growing my daughter." His fingers slid down over her navel, delicately stroking her swollen front, then diving down to tease a much-abandoned, very-needy clit that begged for release.

He turned her around, hands creating a trail of caressing love on her back, her hips, her breasts, all leading the way, a map to her mouth, his palms clasping her jaw and bringing his lips to hers, the first kiss a communion, the second a ravaging.

Every part of her that could swell, did, from breasts to lush nipples, swollen folds and rosebuds that screamed out Mike's name. As their tongues danced and he used his to convey a secret message, hands raking her hair, lips bruising hers, her hip pressed hard against his thick rod, wanting it in her, now. Four long months of new hormones and bursting, flush desire made this, made her—

Her own hands turned the vibrator on; no more shower head, in case it pushed water or an air bubble up inside her. The tingling was enough, along with her Mike, his tight hands, his wet chest hair scraping against her sensitive breasts...

More hands. Dylan.

Ah, there you are, she thought. The vibrator tip made quick work with her, getting her so close, so fast, that Dylan had little time to make his case, his body pressed hard against her back, lifting up, riding friction in the cleft of her ass as she thrust backward, Mike's fingers going straight to her intense heat, the—

"Oh, oh, oh!" she gasped, tipped over so fast as Dylan lunged for her, tongue lapping fast, Mike's fingers in her, the vibrator plunging at her entrance, only in a few inches, though, the clamping and contractions of her pussy walls nearly torpedoing it into the shower wall. Huge spasms made her hips ache and howl, her body squirting now, the effort enormous compared to non-pregnant orgasms, the release four times harder than she was accustomed to experiencing.

Climaxing was anti-climatic, though—what she wanted now were strong arms to slump into, and preferably four of them. Someone to rub her feet. Another someone to get her favorite ice cream.

Instead, she got to finish her shower, towel off, somehow twist her way into her jammies and climb into bed, her cats curling up against her. They didn't quite count as those four arms, but as the day faded into sunset and she patted her growing belly, she whispered, "Good night, sweet baby girl," resolved to tell the guys in the morning.

It was time to be a grown up about this. To act like someone's mom.

To stop being Ryan.

Chapter Seven

Wah wah wah wah 345 wah, Somerville, Dylan heard, his ears ringing as he sat up fast, the cold night air hitting his bare chest when the down comforter slid to his waist. The dispatcher's words sounded so familiar.

When she repeated the address again, his blood ran cold. Then the words: *multi-unit fire*.

If you had told him even a year ago that he could move that quickly, shove on pants and boots and a jacket, be down God knows how many sets of stairs and out the door and in his car in less than two minutes, he'd have told you were a fool.

Tonight? Not tonight, though, because that was Laura's address the dispatcher just announced, followed by the words *multi-unit fire*.

Blood pumping hard, he fumbled for his phone (*thank God it was still in his pants from yesterday*) and as he peeled out of the garage he tapped through his Contacts list to Mike.

Multi-unit fire.

Weaving across two lanes, he sped to her place, the drive inching by so slowly. The dashboard clock read 3:11 a.m. Shit. Mike might not answer. Mr. New Age sometimes turned the damn phone off for peace and serenity and all that shit that he'd surely left behind the last time Dylan saw him.

Please let him answer.
Please.

Multi-unit fire.

"'Lo?" Mike's voice. Dylan shot through a red light and prayed, making a sudden turn on a one-way street that might buy him an extra minute. Or kill him. Either chance was equally possible.

He put the phone on speaker. "Laura's apartment is on fire." Not the time for preliminaries.

"WHAT!" Mike's voice went up an octave.

"Sorry to be so blunt. Get over to her apartment. You remember where it is?"

Mike's voice had a weird quality to it. "Oh, yeah. I do. Just—shit! Save her, Dylan." *Click.*

Multi-unit fire.

You ask for so little, buddy.

He took a right so hard he thought the Audi might flip, but damn if that fine European engineering didn't come in handy when you're doing 77 mph on Mass Ave. If a cop saw him, he was toast.

No cops yet.

Two minutes.

Multi-unit fire.

In a multi-unit fire, two minutes could mean death. *Block that thought, Dylan,* his mind shouted at him.

One minute. He heard sirens, ears perked, discerning the direction. Going away from her part of town. Damn it! He might beat them all at this rate. He shot through four different stop signs, hoping like hell no one was walking an unleashed dog in the middle of the night, and slammed on his brakes, halting in the middle of an intersection, running for her building.

Smoke poured out of the basement windows. That could make the first floor—literally, the floor itself—a structural nightmare, depending on where the actual fire was. Firefighter mind battled with his lover's (*ex-lover's*) mind and love won out as he sprinted up the steps and felt the front door using the back of his hand. Cool.

Red lights and his all-too-familiar siren sound caught his attention, the truck making its slow turn. "Stanwyck!" someone shouted. Murphy.

Dylan waved as felt the locked doorknob, then kicked in the door. A mother with two teens ran past him, followed by a young woman, college-age, carrying a cat and dragging her bike.

Laura. His mind raced, plotting out the scene. No heat—yet—but tons of smoke. Crouching, he found clear air on the ground and began feeling his way to her front door. Just feet away, he felt it; cool. Locked.

"Thank God," he muttered, two bodies moving past him as he heard the steady *thump thump thump* of firemen making their way cautiously upstairs. A loud clanging from below; a different crew was sourcing the fire, figuring out the focal point to work on containment and the level of danger.

Kicking in his second door in less than thirty seconds, his heard the splintering of the threshold, bent down again and shouted "Laura!"

No answer. Some memory gnawed away at him, how horrified she'd been (*but had tried to hide it*) when he'd mentioned fire safety in her building on that first date. Her unease, a pained look in her eyes. Fear? A victim?

Bullhorn. Dylan couldn't make out the words he heard outside, but he knew the crew worked to remove everyone from the building. He guessed six units, but it could have been more. As he crawled through the tiny apartment he felt a wave of adrenaline, then gratitude, that she lived in such a small place. Finding her would be easy.

But what if you find her dead? a voice crept in.

He shoved it away and felt, hand by hand on the wall, along the perimeter of her place. Living room, kitchen, no dining room, a bathroom, and then—bedroom.

"Laura!" The smoke was rising up through vents in the floor, especially near the forced hot water heaters against each wall. As he moved, eyes closed, he cursed himself for not grabbing a mask.

Stupid stupid stupid, violating ten years of careful work. Emotions put people in jeopardy, the fire chief had taught them, and now he was caught in his own emotional turmoil, the blaze endangering them both.

Mike would kill him if he couldn't save Laura. He half blamed Dylan for Jill's death anyway, irrational as it was. If something happened to Laura...

Something brushed against him, too small to be human. Cat? She had three cats, right? In the darkness he coughed, then shouted her name again, the cat long gone. "Laura! It's Dylan!"

"Dylan?" a little voice cried out.

Left. It was to his left. Moving away from the wall, he violated what he'd been taught, disorienting himself. The bed, thankfully, was close. Instinct surged within him as she came into view, huddled under the covers, two cats guarding her.

"Get off the bed now, Laura," he ordered, steel in his voice. The cats scattered. She was trembling and likely half in shock.

"I can't," she mewled. How could a grown woman's voice be so tiny? Something was off, but this wasn't the time for psychology. He stood, grabbed her, and pulled her off the bed roughly. No time to be kind. Her body fell in a funny way, more awkward and bulkier than he expected.

"You can and you will," he said gruffly. The smoke was thicker now above, and he could feel the heat from below. They had a minute here, maybe two.

"Stanwyck!" someone shouted. Murphy. "You in there?"

"Back bedroom. One female. Still conscious. I got her." His arms were on her shoulders and she was struggling to stand.

"Don't stand. We have to crawl out now. The smoke is too thick."

Murphy shined a bright flashlight in the room, illuminating what little could be seen in the two feet above the floor. "This way out!" he shouted. "Two minutes, max!"

"The cats! And grandma and grandpa!" Laura cried, trying to stand and walk toward Murphy. He could see her shins and knees and then nothing—grey.

Yanking her hand, hard, he made her fall. "The cats are probably outside by now. Don't stand!" he warned, nearly growling. "Follow me!" Fear made him a lousy leader. And what did she mean by "grandma" and "grandpa"?

"Are your grandparents here, Laura?"

"No!" she wailed. "They *diiiiied.*" Her voice took on a keening tone and she began to rock. Oh, shit. No time for this.

"Crawl!" he ordered. Murphy started toward them on all fours, the line of light bobbing and weaving in his hand.

"I can't! The baby!" She sat on her ass and began what looked like an agonizing crab walk, her ass dragging.

Baby? *Baby?*

Murphy's flashlight ray landed on her belly in that instant, illuminating a very obvious mound. She was *pregnant?* A zing of every emotion he'd ever felt, from joy to agony, flashed through him.

Grabbing the covers off the bed, he thew them on the ground and spread them out. "Get on," he barked. Somehow, her addled state cleared enough for her to comply.

"Murphy! Help!" he begged. Crawling, he dragged Laura a few feet using one hand. The hardwood floors were a godsend right now. "Clear the way—remove the area rugs!"

"Done!" the gruff man shouted.

Two more pulls and Dylan barely had her in the living room. He was doing this wrong. Murphy came in and planted himself in front of Laura.

"I'll pull, you push," Murph suggested. Within seconds they had it figured out, blind and coughing, freeing her into the hallway which was blessedly more clear. Dylan stood, slid his arms under her, and ran out into the fresh air, hefting Laura delicately.

"Here!" A paramedic from a nearby ambulance company waved him in. Out of the corner of his eye he saw Mike, then Josie, but couldn't say anything as Laura coughed and mumbled.

"Shhhh," he said as he laid her down on the gurney. "Twenty-nine year old caucasian female, pregnant. How far along are you, Laura?" he asked.

"Nineteen weeks." Her voice was getting smaller, her breathing more labored. Shit—how much smoke had she inhaled? He could see Mike and Josie trying to come over, a cop behind yellow tape blocking them, Mike arguing and gesturing wildly.

Then Josie slipped under the tape and sprinted, screaming "She's pregnant!" Mike's arms stopped in mid-air, his face agog. Dylan would have to deal with him later.

"I'm so sorry," Laura rasped. "I was about to tell you, but..."

Dylan kissed her forehead and smiled, sniffing as he cried tears he didn't know he was capable of. "It's complicated," he whispered.

She choked out a very weak laugh and said, "It's always—" before losing consciousness.

Mike broke past the cop and shouted "Laura!" as the paramedics worked on her, loading her into the ambulance, Josie seamlessly climbing in for the ride. "Brigham" she mouthed to him as the lights turned on, the sirens roared, the back of the ambulance shrinking, then turning left, out of sight.

Of course they would take her to Brigham and Women's Hospital. That's where all the high risk pregnancies—

Fingertips touched his soot-covered arm tentatively. "Dylan? Is she—" Mike stood there, wild-eyed and shirtless, flip-flops on his feet and running shorts thrown on. He'd clearly raced here from the cabin. How did he get here so fast?

"She's breathing. They're taking her to the Brigham. How'd you get here so fast?"

"I'm at a meditation retreat here in town." He shook his head impatiently. "The Brigham? Why would they take her there? You always said that's where..." Mike's voice faded out. "Oh, holy fuck."

Dylan slipped to the ground, his own body coming into sharp focus. Lungs were a bit wheezy, his body covered in black, feet floating in sockless boots, brain hurting. "She's pregnant, Mike. Nineteen weeks."

"That means—" Mike sat down next to him, elbows on knees. "We gotta get there. Now."

One of the firefighters shouted "Clear!" and Dylan knew from the response that he wasn't needed; so many guys were here he'd just get in the way now.

"Yeah, we do. Can you drive?" A lump formed in Dylan's throat at the simple request, so casual and assumed, like old times.

Mike looked down at his attire. It was November. "Can we stop by the apartment and let me grab something? Or—" Mike's question carried so many layers of meaning. Four month's worth.

Maybe a lifetime's worth.

"Yeah. Sure. I'll drive, then, and park the car at home." They walked quietly toward the street until Mike grabbed Dylan's arm. "Hey, Dyl?"

"What?" Exhaustion was creeping in. He didn't have it in him to argue.

"I'm so sorry." The embrace was the last thing he expected. And then—"Thank you for saving her."

"*Them.*"

Mike pulled back, confused. His face cleared and he raked his hair, shaking his head. "Them. Right. Hoo boy."

"Hoo boy? Hoo girl?" Dylan responded, the knee-jerk joke so inappropriate he cringed. Couldn't turn it off, even in crisis.

Mike's answer came as an afterthought as the two split to their respective vehicles, both running, seeming to communicate without words.

"Who knows?" he shouted, the joke capturing Dylan's heart and carrying him forward, hopeful, as they raced to their future.

Chapter Eight

A fireball was in her crotch, pushing hard, so hard, to come out. Laura couldn't breathe, scratching at her neck, trying to claw open her trachea to get air, air, air. Oxygen was gone, her throat spasming as her vagina split open, divided in two, and out came an enormous, glowing-orange sphere, shooting across the surgical room and catching the wall on fire.

Screaming, she opened her eyes to find a nurse pushing buttons on a box, a man in scrubs holding her arm down, and six very worried eyes watching her from a few feet away.

Eyes she knew.

She was on her left side and the nurse had her face in both hands, eyes boring into her. "Laura! Laura! I need you to breathe slowly, to focus. We can't find the baby's heartbeat—"

Baby! Heartbeat!

"—and the more you panic, the harder it is to get the monitor hooked back up."

Inhale. Exhale. Inhale. Exhale. The nurse took her through the motions, and Laura calmed down. *Inhale*—and she heard more breaths. Her eyes slowly focused and found Josie, Dylan and Mike standing in a line behind the nurse, all expanding their diaphragms when she inhaled, and whooshing out air when she exhaled.

It was kind of creepy.

Buh bum buh bum buh bum buh bum buh bum buh bum, the machines spat out, the sound of little horse hooves a huge relief to everyone in the room.

"There she is!" the nurse crowed, reading the numbers. "One forty. Right where we want her."

"Where am I?" Laura asked, her condition sinking in. Hospital? IV? Baby monitor? What had happened? Oh, God. The fire. Her apartment. Sitting up, hearing the alarms, people thumping and the rush of fear that made her just hide. She had just started to slide out from under the covers as Dylan shouted for her, remembering the baby and overriding the bizarre panic she'd been stuck in.

Freezing, just like she had when her grandparents had died in the fire in their house the summer she lived with them—

"The fire!" she shouted, then coughed uncontrollably. The horse hooves ramped up suddenly, nurse frowning.

Dylan came to the end of the bed and rested a hand on her foot. "It's OK. You're safe now."

She struggled to sit up, the nurse's hands going to her shoulder and hip, pressing. "Please stay where you are, Laura. We're still not sure why you lost consciousness and we need to make sure you rest on your left side."

"Why?"

"Better blood flow throughout your body," Josie piped up. One look of assurance from her was all Laura needed; Mike added his gentle touch to Dylan's, taking the other foot, and the horse hooves went from a racing gallop to a steady canter.

"Much better," the nurse said, soothing voice meant to praise. "You guys have a magic touch."

Yes, they do, Laura thought, her belly tensing suddenly. "What's that?" One of the monitors began beeping.

"A mild contraction," the nurse answered. "You've had a handful since they brought you in a few hours ago."

"Contraction!" she rasped. "I'm only nineteen weeks along! I can't—" Why had she frozen? What kind of mother doesn't get a fight or flight response the second her baby is in danger? Fear had kept her in hiding in her closet that night more than twenty years before, staying until it was too late for grandma and grandpa, a firefighter finding her and carrying her down a long ladder from her second-story window. Of all the nights to have a sleepover with them; her mother had never been the same and, in some ways, it had killed her, too, to lose her parents like that.

What kind of mother could Laura be if she just...froze? Instinct should have made her leap out of bed and out the door. Old trauma made her useless.

The pillow was wet before she knew it, silent tears rolling from both eyes, pooling at the bridge of her nose before spilling over. Josie came closer and took her hand.

"You did a great job, Laura," she soothed.

Mike and Dylan shared a puzzled look.

"I froze!" Laura wailed.

"Hey," Josie said, gently forcing Laura to stare directly into her eyes. "You did nothing wrong. It was totally understandable that you froze at first, but you did get started. You were trying to get out. And you did what Dylan said and you're safe now and the baby is fine."

"Is she? Are you sure?" Laura turned her attention to the nurse, who was now writing rapidly in Laura's medical chart.

The nurse looked up and smiled. "So far, so good. We need to monitor you for another day and make sure you didn't inhale too much smoke. Plus, the polyhydramnios puts the baby at risk in general, so we're running some basic tests to check on that."

Laura could see Dylan and Mike exchange a worried look. So much to tell them. A flood of overwhelm hit her, hard, like a wave of exhaustion. How could she unravel this mess? Why had she waited so long?

Was this what they felt like when they waited to tell her about them—and about their money? One day seemed to have blended into another and now here she was, both men staring at her with plenty of questions—as if she had all the answers. A flash of sympathy for their delay in confessing the truth—both times—coursed through her. Maybe she'd been too harsh. Perhaps she should have put herself in their place and tried to see their choices through her own eyes.

Or, maybe, she was a wimp who felt trapped, now, and could only feel empathy when she experienced the torture of making a similar bad decision. She didn't like to think of herself like that, but if the baby shoe fit...

The nurse looked around the room, first at Dylan, then Mike, then Josie. Finally, she jotted something in Laura's chart and looked at her patient.

"I'm going to leave now so you can rest, but a medical assistant will be in within an hour to check on you and take a few stats."

Laura caught a good look at her now; almond-shaped brown eyes, dark hair, kind, plump face. About her age. Short and full-figured, fast walker, quick wrist for writing. Her name tag read "Diana."

"Rest is what she needs," Diana declared. "The cops and firefighters want to interview Laura."

Her heart began to race. Why would they want to interview her?

Buh bum buh bum buh bum. The monitor sped up.

Diana chuckled. "It's a mood detector, isn't it?"

Really? Every emotion Laura felt was going to be tracked by the baby's heart rate? Oh, wow. That was going to be *sooooo* awesome as Dylan and Mike confronted her. Really. Might as well strip her naked and—

"I promise we won't stay long," Mike said gently, sitting on the edge of the bed, eyes tracking back to Laura's belly over and over.

"Me, too," Dylan added, shooting Diana a charm-filled look.

It worked; the nurse wasn't immune to his smile, and frankly, neither was Laura.

A warmth, a hope, began to grow in her. Deep breath. Maybe she and the baby would be safe and fine and the three of them—

Uh. The four of them—would be OK.

Whoa, there. Getting ahead of yourself. You still have to face the music. The baby monitor made a series of strange sounds, like skittering bumps.

"What was that?" Mike asked, eyes filled with fear.

Laura's turn to laugh. "She's moving all over the place."

"She?"

"The baby."

Mouth open, his expression shifted, then closed off. What he had been about to ask was clear as he stopped himself, mid-reach, hand pulling back.

"You want to feel?" she offered.

Tears filled his eyes suddenly, which made her own pool just as fast, and as Mike's strong palm rested on her sheet-covered belly, it felt like being welcomed home after self-imposed exile. A bit awkward yet familiar, regret tinging everything good but hope a steady presence.

"Oh!" His eyes danced as the baby shifted, the feeling tangible through Laura's stomach. "Was that a kick? It wasn't very strong."

"I just felt her first movement yesterday, so I know that was a movement, but I don't know what she's doing. A kick, a roll, Gangnam Style—who knows?"

A tear trickled down Mike's cheek and landed on his t-shirt, staining the light-blue fabric dark. In that moment, she felt a tearing horror of regret, of pain, of shame for keeping this from him. From *them*.

"I'm so, so sorry," she choked out, voice hoarse and raw from breathing in smoke, but more from her own remorse. "I should have told you a long time ago, but I was being stupid. I didn't know how to handle it and now I get why you didn't tell me about everything. Once you don't say anything it just...snowballs."

Dylan blinked hard and maintained his distance; unlike Mike, he seemed hardened. Which was weird, because she would have expected the opposite, that Dylan would be easier to reconnect with. "Why did you freeze?"

She didn't expect that question. More tears. "You mean in the fire—Oh! My cats!" Panic filled her again, the baby's heartbeat racing. Damn it!

Staring deeply into her eyes, Mike inhaled slowly, her own body instinctively following. The act of being this connected made her heart slow down, his kind eyes extending an olive branch of forgiveness, of love and understanding.

It almost made her feel like this wasn't hopeless.

Almost.

"The baby is telling us something, Laura," Josie said, her voice pinched and worried. "This really isn't the time. And your cats are fine and peeing all over my apartment right now. I grabbed them from the bushes and threw them in my car and took them home for Dotty to terrorize."

"Dotty'll have them in line in no time," Laura murmured. *Yawn*. What time was it?

"Laura?" Dylan asked, his voice gentle but firm. "What happened to your grandparents?"

Josie grabbed his bicep and pulled him aside. "Would you shut up about that? It upsets her."

"No, no, it's OK. I can talk about it. A little." The horse hooves picked up their pace but not too much. Man, she had missed these guys. Even now, here in a hospital bed, her home probably destroyed by the fire, her cats becoming subs to Dotty's dom, it felt so...right to have Mike and Dylan here.

"They died."

"In the fire?"

She nodded.

"Is that why you freaked on our first date when I talked about fire procedures in skyscrapers?"

Her stomach dropped. He remembered that? She'd been nervous enough, and then he'd casually talked about how to handle fires in enormous buildings like hers. What were the chances he'd pick the one thing that terrified her the most?

And what in the hell kind of world made a fire break out in her apartment while she was pregnant?

Wait. Why had Dylan been the one to rescue her? Her turn to ask some questions.

"Why were you the one who rescued me? You live across town."

Mike and Josie turned their attention to Dylan, who blushed. Blushed! She'd never seen anything so adorable before. He looked like a bashful eighth grader. "I was on call. I woke out of dead sleep and heard your address. Ran for it and called Mike."

"In good traffic it's fifteen minutes to my house from yours, Dylan!" Laura exclaimed.

"I made it in six."

Mike made a low whistling sound. Dylan grinned, proud of himself. "And that's why I have that Audi," he crowed.

Josie rolled her eyes. Men.

Exhaustion seeped in some more, making Laura's eyelids feel heavy. Too much to talk about, too little energy. "I'm sorry."

"You keep saying that." Dylan held a finger up to his lips. "Shh. No need."

"One of you is the father," Laura whispered. "I had this one day where I missed my pill. Not even twenty-four hours! But it must have been enough."

"Or maybe I have super sperm," Dylan joked.

Mike's glare was like a laser.

Josie's, too.

Laura smiled weakly. "We need to do a paternity test and then we can—"

"No!" Mike and Dylan shouted in unison. The confused look they gave each other shifted to a strange understanding, their faces animated with shifting expressions even as they stayed silent. It was like watching two mimes have an entire, deep discussion without saying a word.

"No?" Josie said, incredulous. "What do you mean, 'no'? You have to know who the father is, for the birth certificate."

Protective and defensive, Josie stepped closer to Laura, as if ready to shield her from whatever the two men had in mind. Laura, though, knew what was going on.

"You really don't want to know, do you?" she asked quietly.

* * *

Barely four hours had gone by since Dylan's phone call, and Mike had to absorb his first encounter with Dylan since their fight four months ago, watch the two loves of his life endangered by fire, and now he had just learned that Laura was pregnant with their baby. Their baby. All three of them. He didn't want to view it as his, or Dylan's. But he had no idea Dylan felt the same way.

Pointing at Dylan, he said, "You, too?"

The smile on his partner's face was so telling, impish and serious all at once in a way only Dylan could pull off.

"Me, too. She's *ours*. Not yours. Not mine."

Would Laura agree? Mike wasn't sure. Seeing her there, on her side, radiant and scared, made him want to bar the door and protect her from whatever the world threw her way. Radiant! Hah! Now he knew why she seemed to be glowing when he saw her yesterday at Jeddy's, through that window.

A happy pregnant woman, full of life.
Full of his child.
His daughter.
Their daughter.

"I hate to break up this lovely Hallmark moment—where do I get a card for *this?*—but as wonderful as the sentiment is, it's not practical," Josie announced.

Like poking a pin in a balloon, Mike felt deflated, burdened and weighed down by something he couldn't name.

"Why not?" Dylan threw back at her. The opposite of deflated, Dylan seemed emboldened. Cocksure.

"What if something happens to Laura? You need to know who the legal father is for custody. For raising her. I've seen too many really screwy situations in hospitals after parents die to know that you do not want Child Services to be the one who takes your daughter away to a foster home while the legal system sorts all this crap out. Plus there are issues of inheritance." She made a face and rubbed her fingers together. Money.

Like a bucket of ice water pitched on them, Josie's words made him feel stone-cold sober. Crackpot idea, right? Some calm, internally-focused part of him thought it might work—not knowing. Once they knew who the dad was it would shift everything, make him and Dylan competitors, not collaborators.

"I like it." Laura's voice was small but strong. "If they both want to be her dad, I'm fine with it."

Josie looked at them all as if they were aliens. "But you have to know!"

How had they gone from just learned about the existence of this tiny being to having a fight about her already?

"Maybe we can both go on the birth certificate?" Dylan asked.

"What—like you each contributed half a sperm? Biology doesn't work that way," Josie wisecracked.

"I know how—"

Buh bum buh bum buh bum. They all turned to look at the monitor. A large wet spot grew around Laura's eye on the pillow, her chin quivering and chest shaking a bit.

"Out!" Josie ordered. "All of us! We can come back and fight another time when Laura's stronger."

She was right, as much as Mike was loath to admit it. He looked at the clock; was it really not even 7:30 a.m.? Man. He'd lived five lifetimes in four hours. He walked to the head of the bed and bent down, stretching to give Laura a kiss on the temple.

"You have nothing to be sorry about. I'm the one who is so, so sorry, Laura. We should have told you."

"I should have told *you*," she whispered back, reaching for his hand.

The joy of this moment made his own heart grow, and his fingers reached down to stroke the baby.

"We'll be back later. We're here for you." He knew he shouldn't speak for Dylan—that was a bridge he still needed to cross—but the words were reflexive, born of years of knowing he could speak for two.

Dylan came from the other side of the bed and kissed her cheek. "Me too. I'm sorry, Laura, for letting you down."

A smile. "It's all good." Yawn. The baby's heart rate settled back down.

Click. The door opened and Mike saw Josie leading the way. By the time he and Dylan had stepped out, Laura was snoozing, as it should be.

Buh bum buh bum buh bum.

Her Two Billionaires and a Baby

* * *

A dad. Daddy. Dylan fumbled with the idea that he might be someone's daddy. Images of his own father, still strong and hearty at seventy, flipped through his mind. Fishing and hiking and swimming and camping. He knew how to parent a boy, all rough and tumble and energy.

A little girl? He wasn't exactly the princess tea party type. A lump in his throat seemed to push on his tear ducts and make his eyes leak a bit as he and Mike and Josie left Laura's room.

"You're covered in soot," Josie marveled.

He looked down at his forearms. Yep. Nothing new. After a year on the force he had found that his cuticles always had a few flecks of black in them. Professional hazard.

"You literally carried her out and saved her life." Hair wild and eyes tired, she smiled at him, a genuine, earnest look that made her quite beautiful, transformed. "Thank you. You saved them both."

Both. A baby girl. He washed his face with his hands, kneading the skin, willing his brain to focus, as if he could massage it into place.

"What are we gonna do?" Open-ended question. One that no one had an answer to, but he had to ask it anyway.

"This is a start."

For the first time, he got a good look at Josie. SpongeBob pajamas and sockless, with flip flops. What a fashion plate. Then he remembered—three a.m. She had sprinted like they had, and he felt a combination of extreme fatigue and gratitude. Too bad he'd been too stupid to take Josie's advice when she'd flung it at him that night at Jeddy's. Thank God Laura had a good friend through all this.

A look at Mike, who was looking at him. A shared smile. *Maybe this would be OK*, he thought.

How were they going to raise a child? Nausea settled in. Or maybe that was hunger.

Josie rubbed her eyes and took a good look at herself, head tipped down. Chin on chest, she started laughing, a coarse, harsh sound.

"Man, I gotta get home and make sure those cats haven't destroyed everything. And I need to sleep. My shift starts at three."

"You work in a factory?" Dylan asked.

She had a hard look to her, like someone who was streetwise. Yet when she softened and smiled, she seemed delicate and intellectual. What a chameleon.

"I'm a nurse," she said flatly, as if she were offended he thought her working class.

"Cool. I'm a paramedic."

"No—you're a *billionaire*," she said slowly, as if speaking to a child.

Deadly stare. "And you're a—"

The rest of his sentence was cut off by Mike, who wrapped an arm around his shoulders and steered him away from Josie.

"We'll be back in a few hours to check on Laura and talk about our daughter," he said, soothing the simmer that threatened to bubble over in Dylan. Another hand on his shoulder, then a matching one on Mike's.

"Hey." Josie's voice was clipped and edgy. "You two blew it, and if she lets you back in, let me make one thing perfectly clear."

Dylan's temper rose somewhere in his throat, floating like bile.

One long fingernail pointed at their crotches, one by one. "The warlock waitress will be wearing very real balls if you mindfuck her again. And that baby, too."

Holy shit. "You really have some nerve," he nearly shouted, letting his voice rise, feeling it like an old friend.

The nurse, Diana, looked at them from behind a large desk, eyeing them warily.

"Me? I'm not the one who—oh, fuck this. I'm done trying to help you two."

"Offering to chop off our balls isn't my idea of help," Mike added, his voice flat and dry.

"It's seven thirty in the morning. My best friend and her baby nearly died in a fire. Now I have to help her not feel guilty after I've spent the past three months trying to convince her to tell you two assholes."

Josie *what*?

"You two lied badly enough—twice—to crush my best friend's heart. The best friend I've been with now through the first half of a pregnancy." Her voice rose. "Were you there when she cried her eyes out over you two? When she started to get morning sickness? How about when I went out to get the tests and we went through them, one by one, and they all read positive—where were you?"

"We didn't know—"

"I know you didn't know, Dylan. Why do you think you didn't know?" Nostrils flaring, hands on hips, she looked like a miniature Joan Jett doing a SpongeBob imitation, all yellow fury. "Because she thought you didn't tell her about your money because you didn't *trust* her. She was fucking overwhelmed and confused. And by the way—use a damn rubber sometimes, you two!"

She had him there. He should have. Mike didn't? A side glance at Mike, who imperceptibly shook his head. So it really *could* be either of them.

"Forgive me," she said bitterly, as if asking for anything but forgiveness, "if I seem overly protective. Someone has to be, though, because the greatest threat to Laura—and her baby—so far has been fire, and *you*."

Wham. As if struck between the eyes by a hot ball of lead, Dylan nearly sank to the floor. The wince on Mike's face said she'd struck his target, too. Bullseye.

Double bullseye. She walked off, fast and efficient, like a nurse. Except they weren't her patients. Quite the opposite. They were her wounded, her words meant to hurt, to get the point driven home.

And she had succeeded.

Shoulders slumped, he sighed. He had to get back to the station to do reports and go through debriefings.

Mike looked at him and pointed to the hallway toward the parking garage. A slow walk to the elevators was rote enough that he just kept moving forward, brain turned to mush.

"What now?" Mike asked as they waited for the elevator.

"You'll drive me back to my place?" They'd left Dylan's car in the apartment garage and come in the Jeep.

"I'll drive us back to *our* place."

Dylan closed his eyes and leaned against Mike, nodding.

Sometimes it didn't have to be so complicated.

Thank God.

Chapter Nine

Mike held the smartphone's camera up and surveyed the soot-covered room slowly. Laura's apartment building had just been opened for him and Dylan to come down, the fire investigation completed enough that they permitted residents to remove vital items. The conclusion: an electrical fire that started in the breaker box in the basement, directly under Laura's place.

She was damn lucky. A few more minutes and...well, he wouldn't be holding a camera streaming live video to her on her smart phone, her sweet face asking questions and giving directions as she rested under a down throw on his couch, looking relaxed and healing nicely.

His couch. At the cabin. When the fire investigators told her she wouldn't be able to go back to her apartment for weeks, if not months, the structural damage too great for people to live there, the news had seemed to crush her.

Quick to offer help, he and Dylan had both tried to get her to move in. Cabin vs. apartment?

She'd chosen the cabin. Who knew why, and he didn't care. Josie was with her, helping to acclimate her, and now he and Dylan were on a mission to bring back whatever she wanted.

Life as he knew it was over. Not just the past four painful, grueling months, but the time before that as well. He and Dylan would never be the same again. It was less about hiding the truth from Laura (*twice*) and more about what seemed to be a strange role reversal, with Dylan calmer, more reserved, more mature and Mike more emotive, charismatic, and, well—

Alpha.

"Not my circle chair!" Laura groaned as Mike pointed his phone at it. Black. "That used to be a really nice mauve."

"It's toast now," Mike muttered.

"Laura, a restoration and cleaning company should really get in here before you take anything home," Dylan interjected, arms crossed, brow furrowed, voice uncharacteristically stern and bureaucratic. "You shouldn't inhale any of the soot from the fire."

"Mike said he'd wash everything three times before I wear it," she answered, voice echoing from the tinny speaker.

Dylan shot him a look of pure evil. Mike's saucy grin was his only answer.

"Suck up," Dylan hissed.

Mike thought that over for a second. "I'll own that." Deeper grin. Dylan's eyeroll felt like a victory.

Two hours later he and Dylan were straining to carry out a slew of choices Laura had made, from clothing to heirlooms to the cat beds, although he had repeatedly offered to buy her whatever she needed.

"Why does she want all this?" Mike asked Dylan as they crammed it into the back of the jeep. "Her coconut shampoo? Seriously?"

"It's comfort. Control. Fire victims need it, so it's good to do this for her. I've seen people cry over a dirty seventy-nine cent can opener. When your house catches fire and you survive, things take on more meaning."

Mike eyed a hand-knitted lap throw Laura had screamed about when found intact. Her grandma had made it. She wanted it for the baby's crib.

"*Her* things, you mean."

"Right. It's not the same if you swoop in and replace it all with a four-figure trip to Target." Surveying the load, Mike started to understand. Laura hadn't asked for appliances or expensive electronics. She wanted photo albums and video cartridges and clothing. Personal stuff you couldn't really replace easily.

And the damn gallon jug of coconut shampoo.

"Gotcha." Mike relished the drive back to the cabin, knowing she was there. Dylan had put dinner in the oven before they left, a slow-cooking roast, and tonight would be the first night they would all spend together.

As a family? The thought went through his mind so fast, like a blink, that he didn't dare dwell on it. If he did, it might not happen.

Please let it happen. For the first time in months, the drive up the mountain felt like he was really coming home, Dylan singing along to some '80s Christmas song, the late-autumn sun warming his skin as the prospect of creating a true home with Dylan, Laura and their baby warmed his heart.

* * *

"I still think you are nuts. And not warlock waitress nuts. Crazy. *Cray cray.* The baby needs to have a father on the birth certificate."

Laura sat on the sectional sofa, butt sinking deep into the soft leather, a warm red down comforter keeping her toasty. Getting up would be harder than getting comfortable, but she had Josie to help. And, soon, Mike and Dylan. Snuggles moved a foot along the top of the sofa, chasing a patch of sun.

"Well, hello to you, too, Miss Merry Sunshine," Laura cracked. She gratefully accepted the cup of decaf Josie offered.

"They'll be here soon and this is the first chance I've had in a week to talk openly with you. Those two seemed to have had a schedule for making sure one of them was always there in the hospital."

"They did."

Josie's face was agog. "All so I couldn't talk alone with you?"

Sip. "I don't think that's why." *Sip.* "Just, you know, because we're—"

What words were supposed to come out next? Together? Were they back together? Laura didn't know where they stood, actually. Five days in the hospital had been long enough to learn that she was fine. The baby was fine. The polyhydramnios had actually improved a bit, though it wasn't gone. She would need constant monitoring for the rest of the pregnancy, but they hadn't found any problems with the baby that explained it. Being extra-big with added fluid would make it harder to move around, and could make the delivery a bit risky, but they'd ruled out birth defects.

Which had been the best news Laura had received in—well, *ever*. Diana had reviewed her chart with Sherri and the supervising obstetrician, Dr. Kalharian, and they'd agreed on a schedule for follow-up care.

Her orders: go home, rest, hydrate, recover.

Easier said than done, because she'd had no home. Until Mike and Dylan had offered her one. Josie, too. Deciding had been hard and easy at the same time.

Josie was the easy choice, and her friend seemed to assume Laura would pick her.

But her heart, her gut—her *womb*—told her to go heal in the mountains.

She figured out pretty quickly that the guys would respect her, would treat her like a queen, and would wait on her hand and foot if she stayed at the cabin. Dylan had told her, with a quiet serenity and troubled demeanor that was so unlike him, about his and Mike's...fight? Breakup? What word do you use when there isn't one to describe the relationship in the first place?

So many strands of the relationship between the three of them had been snapped by someone deciding not to tell a simple secret, the kind of information that really wasn't a deal breaker, but that can become one if withheld for too long.

Dylan and Mike really cared about her—she knew that, and knew that by screaming at them that day at Josie's months ago, she'd created a rift that needed mending.

And yet she absolutely was not the only one with some guilt to work through. The guys hadn't told her they knew each other, and she was still uneasy, in a tiny place deep inside, about how they had come to her, orchestrated that wonderful first night. Getting over that had been hard, but not impossible. Could she find a place for their other secret?

Staring around the room, she suspected she could. The vaulted ceilings, the knotty pine, the startling view of the snow-covered ski trails, and the cozy fire burning in the fireplace all made her feel like she could—

"—eat shit?"

"Huh?"

Josie stared at her. "I still don't get why you didn't tell Mike and Dylan they could go and eat shit, but I respect your decision." Her tone of voice made it clear she did not. "How's little Josie today?"

"You mean little Laura?"

"Whatever."

Bzzzz. Laura found a text from Mike: *Need anything at the store? Ice cream and pickles?*

She read it aloud. Josie softened. "That is really sweet."

Laura typed back: *Nope. Thanks! <3*

"You're going to regret that at midnight when you want salted caramel ice cream." Josie stood and reached for her purse.

"You're leaving?" Panic fluttered in her chest. Or was that the baby kicking again? Touching her belly, she shook her head slightly, to herself. Nope. Panic.

"Four—er, *five*," she pointed to Laura's midsection, "is a crowd."

Reckoning. This would be it. Mike and Dylan would come back and they'd wash her things and she would need to find a rhythm here as she recovered, the three of them settling in to—what? What, exactly, were they to each other? And then there was the issue of—

"—who the father is." An expectant look covered Josie's face.

"Huh?"

"The baby is sucking your brain right out of your head, Laura." Josie laughed. "It's like you're not listening to anything I say."

"And that's new because..." she joked.

"Ha ha." Josie shrugged into her leather coat. She looked like Captain America when he was little. "You'll talk to the guys about the birth certificate issue?"

They'd cooked up a scheme they thought the guys would accept. Even Laura realized that as sweet as it was to share the baby, and for whichever man wasn't the bio dad to act as if he were, the practical legalities needed to be respected. Someone's name needed to be on the birth certificate.

"I will. I promise." The two hugged, Laura clinging a bit longer than she normally would. As if crossing over into a new life, a new world, she felt unmoored, time starved, and unsure. The baby grounded her in that moment by kicking her, hard, in the cervix.

"See you tomorrow." *Click.* The front door closed and Josie walked out on the porch, the same porch where, nearly five months ago, Laura had slunk out, Mike bringing her her purse, her fear so overwhelming it had almost crushed her heart.

Almost. And then...why hadn't they told her? Why? They were billionaires. Her baby's father was a billionaire. Josie had joked about child support (*"You could get more than you make in a year. Hell, in a decade, per month. Can I get the other one to impregnate me?"*) and Laura reeled from the implications of all.that.money.

Some dish Dylan had in the oven simmered and filled the cabin with a luscious aroma that made her belly start to eat itself. She was hungry.

The guys were on their way. Her stomach dropped. Because this time she'd be alone with them and it was time for some long overdue conversations.

Why was it always, indeed, so complicated?

* * *

A palpable tension sat between him and Mike on the car ride up the mountain, a third partner who wasn't nearly as appealing as Laura. Unresolved emotions, unspoken words, and a sense of uncertainty made the air thick, kept Dylan's nerves on edge, and finally forced him to blurt out, "I was a total douche. I should never have made us wait to tell her about the money, and I almost blew it, and now here we are with maybe—kinda—sorta—a chance with her, and I don't want to fuck it up again."

Cringe.

"If you're a douche, I'm a bigger one. Mega douche. Thor the Douche," Mike bantered back, his voice jovial, but his face serious. Eyes on the road, he seemed to feel the change in the car.

They were talking. *Really* talking, once again.

"How do we make this right with her?" Dylan's words had an urgency, a plaintive tone he could hear in his own voice and hated.

Mike shrugged. "I think this time we actually listen to her and Josie and do what Laura wants."

"That easy?"

Mike picked up Route 2 and they prepared for the long drive. "If it were easy, we wouldn't have fucked it up."

"Twice."

"Yeah. Twice." Mike blinked, revving up to sixty-five mph. "Dylan, I'm sorry about the glass and all that."

"It's OK. You sent that cleaning crew and replaced everything."

"That's not what I mean." Mike's jaw flexed and twitched, his stubble glinting in the sunshine.

"I know. And it's OK. As long as we're OK."

Mike laughed, a sputtering sound of surprise. "We're fucked, man."

"Yeah. We're about as far from OK as you can get."

That made Mike swallow and blink hard. "True. But as long as we're not OK together, I think we'll be fine."

"What if it's not your baby?" Dylan said rapidly, as if saying the words fast would somehow make them less provocative.

"What if it's not yours?" Mike's answer was a growl.

Silence. A dark cloud of confusion and suspicion, with an undertone of something sinister he'd not felt with Mike, ever, slithered about in the Jeep.

Dylan decided to let down his defenses and simply said, "I don't care. I care, but I'm not invested in *whose* she is. I'm invested in loving *who* she is."

Mike's head jerked back in surprise. Shoulders relaxing, he drew in a deep breath. "Same here." He took his eyes off the road for a second and gave Dylan a look that made him fight to hold back tears. "I don't want to be left out of the greatest love I can imagine."

Nodding, Dylan tapped him on the shoulder with a gentle fist and said, "Impossible. Because that love can't exist without all three of us."

"Four. Four now."

Four.

* * *

Laura woke to the sounds of laughter in the kitchen, deep men's voices guffawing and teasing, the room's light telling her it was past sunset and somehow she'd fallen asleep in place, curled up and warm. Her stomach growled and her mouth felt like cotton, parched.

A glass of water on a coaster, inches from her hand, was a pleasant surprise. A few quick gulps and she finished it off, yawned, stretched and—ouch!—sciatica flared up, necessitating that she stand and stretch more.

Little muscles in her hips and along her ribcage needed to be treated with kid gloves, stretched slowly and with great care, or she'd have a stitch in her side and a major spasm. Pregnancy really wasn't for wimps, all the blessings aside.

Walking with a slight waddle, she made her way into the kitchen. Mike was making a salad, Dylan checking on a roast, and both turned to her, smiles at the ready, so amused and playful she almost burst into tears at the hope it all inspired.

"She rises!" Dylan exclaimed, drying his hands on a dish towel and planting a kiss on her cheek. Mike kept his space, reaching for the empty glass in her hand. Without asking, he filled it from the water dispenser on the fridge door and handed it back, full.

"Thanks," she said, looking around, blinking. Both men kept stealing glances of her belly. Obvious and trying not to be. She did a shimmy and said, "Lap dances, $25."

"You undercharge," Dylan said, mirth in his voice but something more sensual in his eyes.

Her pulse quickened and blood flowed to places that had been deeply neglected by a man's touch.

"OK. $50. I'm lap dancing for two, after all."

She wiggled her belly. Mike groaned and Dylan winced. Topic change.

"Whatcha cooking?" She nosed over Dylan's shoulder. A big slab of delicate meat surrounded by carrots, potatoes, onions, and something unidentifiable. "What's that?"

"Celeriac."

"Sell airy what?"

"Celeriac. It's kind of like the root of a celery plant. Sort of. It's really savory and complements the meat nicely."

"Mmmmmkay, Rachel Ray."

He looked offended. "I'm Gordon Ramsay all the way, babe." Arms reached around her, his face nonplussed as he couldn't make it, the belly in the way. "Don't you forget it," he joked, pulling back, bemused.

"More like the rat in *Ratatouille*," Mike said, droll and patient.

"You two are getting Kraft Mac n Cheese if you don't stop."

Her stomach growled audibly. Dylan pointed at it and said, "The baby speaks! She defends me!"

"Are all audible bodily functions a commentary on you, Dylan? If so..." Mike bit his lips, holding back.

"Let's eat!" Laura declared. Her stomach growled again. "I'm starving!" No one had cooked her a homemade meal in, well—not since Dylan's meatballs. It felt good to be pampered, cared for, taken care of.

And the food was divine.

So was the company. Somehow, the three of them fell back into an easy banter, talking and laughing with abandon, yet comfortable with silence. So much to say. So little pressure to say it. Time might heal all, she thought, if they never said a word. Just living and being and coexisting might do the trick.

Not really. She could hope, though. Food, though—food had a universal language that said, "Dig in. Eat. Relax. Enjoy."

And she did.

Beep! Something that sounded like a clothes dryer went off.

"Oh! Your quilt!" Mike said, jumping up from the table and walking down the hallway.

"My quilt?"

"Your grandma's quilt. Mike's washing it a few times. Part of your stuff we hauled home."

A grateful warmth filled her. Blinking back tears, she said, "Thank you."

"Don't thank me. Thank Mike."

She reached for Dylan's hand and squeezed. "No. Thank *you*. You saved me. Saved *us*."

He shook his head, eyes serious. "I almost ruined us. And I hurt you deeply."

Hearing it from him made a difference; she had tried to convince herself it didn't matter, but it did. Mike returned to the table, a look of puzzlement, then alarm, on his face.

"Everything OK?"

"We're getting serious," Dylan muttered.

Mike's face shifted to dawning understanding. "Oh. Got it." He pushed his plate back and leaned forward on the table, chin in hand. "Is this the part where I get down on my knees and beg Laura to forgive me for being such a ridiculous, cravenly afraid asshole?"

"That's my role!" Dylan protested. "I look really good eating humble pie. Lately, it's my specialty. Shows off my good side." He tilted his face to the left, a sad smirk coloring the discussion.

"You can both play that role," she joked. Except she wasn't joking. They all knew it. "No," she added, shaking her head. "All three of us can play that role, because I did to you what you did to me." She winced. "With higher stakes."

No one argued. That made her feel even worse. *Here we go*, she thought. Cards on the table. Hearts on sleeves. It was now or never, and clichés aside, if she wasn't brutally honest with herself and with them, she could never, in good conscience, forgive herself.

Which was the most important person she needed to extend forgiveness to.

"Can I say something, Laura?" Mike interrupted. He stood slowly, with great deliberation, inch by inch rising to stand over her and Dylan, the table miniscule and unimportant, the air filled with intent.

"Sure," she squeaked.

He looked at Dylan. "I need to say this to you, too." Dylan looked askance, uncertain and a bit worried, mirroring Laura's own internal state.

Mike sighed. "I love you both." He bent down and touched Laura's belly. "And I love her, too. We have lots of words we could utter and exchange, decode and expunge, but none of those words matter as much as these: I'm sorry." He looked deeply into her eyes, then Dylan's. "I love you." Again, at both, careful and measured, meted out equally. "I love this. I've missed *this*."

His hands swept over the table, gesturing at the room, trying to capture the love and laughter and comfort in his hands. Laura knew he couldn't, because it wasn't a thing. It was something the three of them created when they were together, an alchemy they couldn't force. It just *was*.

"I want it all, for the rest of my life." He bowed his head, releasing Laura's swell. "I don't have any better words."

"There aren't any." Dylan's voice was thick with emotion as he stood. He and Mike moved to Laura, who volleyed between them, head bouncing left and right to take this all in. With one on each side of her, she struggled to understand what was going on as they both knelt down.

"I don't know what to say," she admitted. And she didn't. Nearly five months of wants and needs and luscious thoughts poured into her now, less from passion and more from a knowing love. A place of goodness and completion, of welcomed desire, of being treasured and assured not by words or by touch but by presence.

"Say you'll stay. Say you'll let us take care of you." Dylan touched her belly. "Both of you."

She frowned. "Take care of?"

"We have more money than we can spend in ten lifetimes. Quit your job. Be a full-time mom. Start a business or a charity or whatever your heart desires, Laura. Hang with us. Help me run the ski resort. Become a gym bunny. Open a bakery. Hell, buy Jeddy's and fire Madge," Mike laughed, his face wide and open, body tense but eyes serene and raw all at once.

"In other words, let us take care of you, because we need you to take care of us," Dylan said, getting to the point.

Oh, guys, she thought. Her heart should be racing, temples pounding, face flushing and heart swelling, right? Instead, all she could feel was a diffuse calm. An acceptance. An understanding.

And the baby did a somersault right then, her little foot practically poking a hole in Laura's belly.

"Holy shit!" Mike shouted. "I could see the outline of her toes on your shirt!" She'd chosen a fairly tight, "slimming" light pink maternity shirt, with a little spandex, and it was pulled snugly over her belly.

"I saw it, too!" Dylan joined in.

"Maybe she was answering for me?"

"Was she?" they asked in unison. Laura closed her eyes, shoulders dropping, her breath even and mature. Yes.

Yes yes yes yes.

In later years Laura would try to remember the exact moment she leaned down and took Mike's face into her hands, kissing him gently and with great passion, but try as she might she could never pinpoint it, would never find her recollection precise enough to discern when she made the decision. Like so many other moments in her years with Dylan and Mike it just *was*, a delicious shift of molecules and energy that moved her body, compelling her toward what her heart wanted.

Regardless, Mike's response was keen and matched, lips connecting, arms wrapping about her waist, sliding up her back as he stood, pulling her to standing, the belly making an awkward chaperone that separated them.

Dylan stood back and watched, smiling. He wasn't left out for long, as Laura pulled back from Mike, breathless, and reached out.

The little, doubting voice inside her, the one that whispered insecure comments in her ear at inappropriate times, the saboteur of all that was good and whole in her life, tried desperately to wiggle its way to the surface as Dylan's arms wrapped around her, as his lips touched hers, as his mouth explored hungrily and apologized with little movements and sighs, hands saying "I'm sorry" in ways words and looks could never convey.

Laura found herself not only not caring what that voice said, not actively pushing it away, but instead just not listening. Tuning it out like static, like traffic, like the sound of something so insignificant it becomes white noise after a while. You know it's there but it blends in with the rest of the world and takes its rightful place as something you don't need to attend to.

What she needed to give her attention to was right here, standing before her, both men here, now, for her. And she was here for them, all three together and hopeful and trying to find their way to a new truth.

A new honesty. A new vow.

As she warmed to Dylan's caresses, their bodies awkward and accommodating, the reality of their earlier coming together very real—regardless of whose baby she carried—desire roared forth, a huge ball of need and hormones rushing to the surface, her mouth aggressive, hands not backing down. Wanting them both, needing time and pleasure, her skin's memory of the fear of nearly dying now straining for an expression of life, to conjoin and co-mingle with Mike and Dylan, to renew something deep and unspoken as they unveiled a commencement. A beginning of something unspoken but cherished.

Dylan's touch became tentative, hesitant.

She pulled back and asked, "You OK?"

Mike's eyes held the same conflict that Dylan's reflected as she looked at them both.

"Can we...are you...is this -- " Dylan stumbled.

"Oh, God, yes!" she nearly cried out. "Do you have any idea how much I've missed this?" She stroked his arm. "Both of you." A sigh. "All of this."

"No, I mean, the doctors—can you, you know?" Mike jumped in, hands clearly itching to touch her, but keeping a respectful distance as she was in Dylan's space.

She blushed. "I'm cleared for 'intimate relations,' as the nurse put it, but I don't think they were thinking of what we do," she laughed. Pointing to her belly and hips, she added, "And I think we have to do this the old fashioned way this time. No room for two at the inn."

"I like old-fashioned," Dylan sighed in her ear, nuzzling her neck. A zing of pleasure made her inhale slowly, savoring the heat of his cheek on hers. Mike stepped back, sweeping his arm toward his bedroom, the same room, same bed, where they'd first been together, what seemed like a lifetime ago.

In a way, it was. This world was theirs to forge, social and emotional rules that they landscaped, shaping it as they wished. No doubting voice, no righteous screeds, no one else could dictate how or whom she loved. This lifetime that she embarked on felt like her real life. Time to start it.

Start it off right. Nice and slow and easy and luscious. Taking Mike's hand, holding on to Dylan's with her other, the three walked with languid grace, her body hot and ready so soon, so fast, she nearly burst as Mike reached down to kiss her, Dylan stroking her shoulders and back, hands wrapping around her from behind and loving her belly.

Sinking back into him, soaking up Mike's skin, the taste of him, how his mouth was lush and present and fully aware of hers made the scene less surreal.

Just...real. As if all of the other moments in her conscious life were somehow a preparation for this, and that all her worries and concerns were useless, unnecessary.

Discarded.

The sound of Dylan's long inhale, then his deep exhale, hands reaching under the hem of her shirt and warmth, made her smile.

Mike's hands cupped one breast, his hip grinding into hers, back curled over her, shoulders lifted, one hand stroking her ample, swelling nipple as the other kneaded her hair, little kisses interspersed with great, deep, wet explorations. Her clit pulsed, abs tightening and elongating, body primed and ready for *everything*.

And it looked like that's what she was about to get.

Four hands slid up her ribcage, across her shoulders, down her legs, everywhere, like tentacles made of honey and wine, slipping and caressing until she stood in panties alone, their flesh ripe and clear, her own hands busy and red-hot from sliding cotton and threads off six packs, glutes, biceps, and flesh that now stood ramrod straight, as if tipped up to say *thank you* for the coming feast.

Mike's bronzed chest, with a sprinkling of sun-kissed hair, felt familiar and foreign under her finger tips, his hands lifting up under her thickened breasts, face gazing down and marveling, as if looking at a work of art for the first time. When his eyes met hers they were smiling, and he touched her lips with one finger.

"I do love you." His hand migrated to her belly. "And her."

A lump in her throat made it hard to speak, Dylan's hard, muscled form behind her, leaning against her back and ass. Heady from the touch of both, she tipped her face up and drank in Mike's words.

"I love you, too."

His smile, his mouth, their tongues touching as she was enveloped by manflesh, manskin, the two men who completed her—it made her feel truly, madly, intensely loved.

Cherished.

Dylan's words were a trigger for so much more as he nipped her ear and whispered, "I love you, too."

Mike released her and she spun around, arms lifting over his shoulders, his muscled forearms on her back and hips, their embrace less sexual and more a homecoming.

Until his mouth found hers, telepathically transmitting everything they couldn't say but felt, as if he thought and emoted for her through a long, wet stroke, or fingers that trailed a line down her neck to her breasts, pausing to turn a soft areola into a pebbled nipple.

"And I love you," she replied, smiling into the kiss, feeling his mouth shift, too, into a grin. Ah, she really was home. Love. They'd all said it, felt it, *meant* it. The sweet taste of it was nirvana, a light, delicate—but hardy—flavor that they would relish forever.

She moved to the bed, climbing on carefully, the only one wearing anything. Slipping out of her panties, she became self-conscious of her body for the first time —how it had changed, how she had gained weight, how her breasts were fuller, more sensitive, her hips wider and more lush. Would they like it? Was she too big?

Mike's hands held an answer as he reached for her, eyes tracking his own hand as he moved it along her side. She propped her head with her hand, elbow holding at an angle, breasts and belly pulled down by gravity and one leg bent.

"You're so..." He sighed, his hand opening where her ribcage met her breast, smoothing and sloping to take in more. "Voluptuous. Glowing." Bending in, muscles rippling and arms tight, he kissed her and then slid into bed, arms warm and chest pressed against her, molding himself around her. "Amazing." She relaxed into rippled muscles on his thighs, his long, lean body surrounding her, mouth kissing her neck.

Oh! That was Dylan, who had taken up residence behind her, her back warmed instantly by a wall of hot skin and hard flesh that started with her ass, then her thighs, gliding up her sacrum, back, and shoulders, a strong blanket of sensuality. His hands cupped her breasts as he kissed her neck, erection pressed into the cleft of her ass, ready for her bidding and whatever they all chose next. Delicious. They had all the time, all the *choice* in the world, to do as they wished.

The feel of them against her body made her abs tighten, the flesh above her clit buzzing, her hands eager and needy, touching Mike and Dylan with an urgency she didn't have to possess any more. No rush. No scarcity. All three had made the decision to move on, to redesign the world, to make their love so much more.

Mike trailed kisses down her breasts, looping one nipple into his mouth, tongue teasing with circles of benevolence, making her walls clamp and the air in her lungs rush out. Base instinct guided her hands to his hair, hoping—oh, hoping!—he was headed where she needed that mouth most right now. It had been long, long months without, and her body tingled with anticipation for that first cool touch of tongue tip, as the warmth of her flesh would mix with his wetness and make her gasp.

"Are you OK on your back?" Dylan asked.

She hadn't considered it.

"I can be creative," Mike answered, his voice muffled.

For some reason, it made her giggle. She got a case of the sillies, right here in this incredibly sensual moment. Laughing so hard tears filled her eyes, Dylan watched her, eyes dancing with amusement.

Mike paused, then crawled up her body, dragging his chest along her skin.

His head popped up, face curious, as she quivered and shook, overcome with laughter. "I've been laughed at in bed before," he said, "but never while doing *that*."

Oh, God. That made her giggle even more, great whoops surprising her, Mike glancing at Dylan, Dylan's shrug, both sets of eyes watching her. Contagious, the laughter got them too, deep voices rumbling with chuckles until finally Laura settled down, flapping her hands in front of her face to cool down and calm herself.

"What was that?" Dylan asked, finger circling her nipple.

Mike dipped his head back under the covers and moved down. A kiss on her hip. "Was that funny?" A kiss on her knee. "Funny?" A kiss on her mons. "Giggling now? How about I make you gasp." The last word came out as a low growl, so predatory and primal she filled with a blooming wetness, all heat and low thrumming, body fully ready.

And gasp she did, for as his hips moved, Mike folding his extended body into position between her legs. Although she was on her side, he simply moved one leg up, balanced it on his shoulder gently, and leaned down, tongue touching the exact place she needed it to. Like a butterfly in slow motion, his tongue lapped and licked in a perfect, slow rhythm that took her from ready to gone.

Dylan's scent, all musk and smoke and salty, filled the air as he lowered his mouth on her other nipple, keeping symmetry.

She didn't care, transported to a frenzied near-climax by a few touches of Mike's tongue. When Dylan rotated slightly, calves brushing against her hip, his body hovering over hers, her mouth was open, breath coming out in pants, his lips taking hers as his hand reached for her ass, pulling her closer.

What she wanted, though, was more. Urging Dylan to slide up, she reached for him, fingers lacing around his thick erection, guiding him to her mouth. Knowing she would soon come—hard and furious, crazy and tilting—she wanted to give, to make someone else feel as good as Mike made her feel now, to spread out her own intensity, delay her climax, to make it all the more incredible and vital and *liquifying* when it did come.

At this rate, she didn't have long, with months of pent-up frustration and need and arousal waiting to be unleashed. Mike's hands spread up her hip to take in what they could, as his mouth worked wonders, exploring the full, pink flesh of her labia, one finger sliding inside her—now two—the added sensation giving her a gasp, indeed, as she tongued Dylan's mushroom cap, his body tensing, all of this energy traveling like a physics math word problem.

If Mike's tongue flickers at a rate of 69 beats per second while Laura's mouth licks Dylan's enormous cock five times per minute, as her hands dig into Mike's golden waves and Dylan groans at 200 decibels, when will they all come?

About...now, apparently, Laura's body twitching, removing Dylan from her as he eased back, her face turning to the pillow, unable to do anything but experience this, biting the sleek cotton to keep from screaming. Didn't work.

"Oh, God!" she shouted, her body convulsing, neck muscles stretching and pulling at the same time, her body stretching like a cat's, then shaking, stretching, then shaking, hands curled into fists in ecstasy.

Beyond words, she came and came, exploding as Mike rode the wave, following her as her clit bobbed and jumped, hips out of control, her eyes open and then shut, occasionally catching glimpses of Dylan's transfixed look, watching her with such passion it nearly made her come again.

"No, stop!" she begged. "I want you in me!"

"I'm here," said Dylan, smoky and sensual. He slid against her, from behind, as Mike straightened up, slipped out from under the covers and rested on his knees, a delicious drink of water her eyes soaked up. How could he have so little fat, pockets of muscle etched into his ribs and abdomen? Unreal.

Dylan's hot skin married hers, hips resting behind as Mike's mirth-filled eyes acknowledged what he'd just given her, and waited patiently for so much more, lips flush and red, blue eyes growing serious and sultry.

Now it was Dylan who nudged against her, her own passage eager to be filled, nudging back as he centered himself, then the tip of him touched her outer lips, eliciting a sigh that turned into a moan, her body responding with such fierce arousal she was grateful for two men.

They might not be able to satisfy the tiger inside her, the one that had prowled for the past few months through her erogenous zones, pacing and searching, but they damn well could try.

As he entered her everything split and she felt nothing but slick, her body welcoming and warm, his erection pushing hard from behind as she rested on her side, trying to get him deeper, needing a fuller feeling of man, of Dylan. He began to thrust, slow and tender, and she whispered, "I love the feeling of you in me. I need you so much."

"I need you, too, babe," he answered, the hissing musk of his breath enough to put her into a cocoon of this, of nothing more or less, his abs pushing against her ass, his knee between hers, his cock inside her as rough palms massaged her breasts, wet lips kissed her earlobes, and then—there it was.

Explosion. Implosion. Screams—hers, of pleasure and orgasm and release and pluming and of complete annihilation of the mind.

Hands and fingers and mouths and cocks and ass and pussy walls all worked in concert until everything was a pink and red void, panting breath and hot, wet flesh and a gritty, guttural groan of fucking and being fucked, of having her body pushed to its sensual limits and over the line, of crossing something that expunged all worry, all fear, all timid nature into a ball of greedy desire and lust and—

Dylan. His neck muscles pushed against her ear; she could feel the strain as she came down from her own high, could sense the creaming inside her as he came, could hear the little sounds the back of his throat involuntarily made as he thrust, then froze, thrust, then froze, squeezing every drop from this masterful movement.

He slumped against her, spent, as her energy roared to life, her appetite for sex and skin and being fucked a thousand times stronger than it had ever been in her life, the roar of want so great she feared she would devour them.

Mike. Could Mike be enough now? As Dylan slid out of her, kissing her shoulder, Mike moved like a lion, slow and sure, owning the land and the bed, her body and his, knowing what she needed without her saying a word. He didn't seem surprised when she took his mouth with force, a maniacal power driving her to kiss him, to use her tongue to nip, to suck, to measure the terrain of him.

"I want you on top," he murmured, stretching out on the bed, his tall runner's body going on and on. Dylan had rolled over and watched, an open, friendly face that seemed more wistful than voyeuristic. As she climbed on Mike's hips, straddling him, she unceremoniously plunged down on his rigid cock, the tip hitting her cervix with a push of pleasure that made it seem as if she hadn't just made love with Dylan, hadn't just come from Mike's mouth and Dylan's cock, hadn't just been satisfied and catered to in every way possible.

Because she needed more.

More, more, more.

Mike obliged, pulling her down for another kiss, her own taste more evident now, her lips spreading in a grin at the mixing of their juices, their bodies, the ease of so much sensual abandon. She leaned down and changed the angle of her hips, now in control of the thrusts, her ass lifting up, pussy lips encasing him, her shifts imperceptible to him but giving her clit more friction, making her so, so close.

"God, I love your body," he gasped, hands full of her breasts, throat tight as she milked him, plunging down as hard as possible to feel so full, so real.

Moonlight spilled into the room and she took in the scene, Dylan's gaze of love and enjoyment, Mike's body filling hers, his chest and face below her, eyes concentrating on her, absorbing their lovemaking, the love in the air palpable.

Tipping her head down, she inhaled slowly, primally as she pulled up, the room filled with moist heat and the scent of three, the thought combining with her faster movements, her body fucking him now, the one who maintained the pace, who took the rising ball of lust inside her, which expanded and grew until—

Starbursts. More screams. An emptying and a completion that she couldn't name.

"Laura! Laura!" Mike shouted, his face twisted in torque and thrust as she raked her fingernails over his shoulders, his hands kneading her hips and ass, fingertips pressed hard into her luscious curves. They thrashed and vibrated, her pussy climaxing less from her clit's frenzy but more from the deep pushing, the perfect pitch of flesh against flesh, of the supernova of juicy sex.

Her hips ached, forcing her to rest her head on Mike's shoulder as she came down, down, down from a high she didn't know was possible, much less achievable in the arms of anyone—or any two.

Mike murmured love and whispered loyalty in her ear as Dylan snuggled up to them, helping to ease Laura onto her side, her body limp with the feeling of being wrung out, a joyous song of satiety humming in her head.

As their breathing returned to a normal pace, Laura looked first at Dylan, then at Mike, then at the window, moonlight smiling in on them. Finally.

Finally she had what she wanted. Exactly what she wanted.

Almost.

"OK, boys," she commanded, arms folded up under her head, the gesture one of authority. "Which one of you is going to give me a foot massage, and which one of you will make the salted caramel ice cream run?"

Mike looked out the window with a forlorn look on his face. "But it's snowing! And a twenty minute drive to the nearest store." The look he shot her said *what are you talking about?*

She pulled her hands out from under her head and clapped twice. "Then get to it!" Settling back down, she let a deep, satisfied sigh flow through. "Now I see why I need two men."

Cold hands touched her feet, Dylan already at her bidding with the massage, laughing at Mike. "Too slow!"

"I don't wanna—it's cold—are you kidding?" Mike pleaded. Even so, he seemed to know the argument was lost, reluctantly standing and throwing on his pants.

She pointed to her belly. "Does it look like I'm kidding?"

"Fine. Salted caramel? A pint?"

She nodded, then stopped. "No! Make it two. It's going to be a long couple of days and I don't want you leaving for one second longer than you need to." She batted her eyelashes as Dylan worked on her feet.

"Anything else?" Mike held his smart phone, ready to type. "A list? Because I don't want to have to leave again."

A lascivious smile consumed his face. Laura liked it.

"Nope! Simple list. Ice cream."

"Easy," Dylan said, nodding approval.

"That's right," she sighed, winking at Mike as he shrugged on his coat. Mike kissed her forehead and shot Dylan a promise of future revenge as Laura lay in bed, stretching.

The baby kicked in agreement as Dylan laughed.

"A girl could get used to this," Laura said, feeling dreamy.

"That's right," he said, working on her arch. "It's never complicated—anymore."

THE END

Sign up for my New Releases and Sales email list at my blog to get the latest scoop on new eBooks, freebies and more: http://jkentauthor.com

* * *

Don't worry—the story isn't over yet!

Readers often ask me what order they should use when reading my books. Now that you've read *Her Billionaires*, I'd recommend you move on to *It's Complicated*, the book that includes the birth of Laura and Dylan and Mike's baby, and where Josie finds her own love...

And after that, there's *Completely Complicated*, which looks at life after Mike, Laura, Dylan and Josie and Alex all find each other.

Please join my New Releases email list to get a notice when new books come out, when books are on sale, and so forth: http://jkentauthor.com

OTHER BOOKS BY JULIA KENT

SUGGESTED READING ORDER

Her Billionaires
It's Complicated
Completely Complicated
It's Always Complicated

Random Acts of Crazy
Random Acts of Trust
Random Acts of Fantasy
Random Acts of Hope
Randomly Ever After: Sam and Amy
Random Acts of Love
Random on Tour: Los Angeles
Merry Random Christmas

Maliciously Obedient
Suspiciously Obedient
Deliciously Obedient

Shopping for a Billionaire: The Collection (Parts 1-5 in one bundle, 670 pages!)
Shopping for a Billionaire's Fiancée
Shopping for a CEO
Shopping for a Billionaire's Wife

Other Books by Julia Kent

Shopping for a CEO's Fiancée
Shopping for an Heir
Shopping for a Highlander

About the Author

Text JKentBooks to 77948 and get a text message on release dates!

New York Times and *USA Today* Bestselling Author Julia Kent turned to writing contemporary romance after deciding that life is too short not to have fun. She writes romantic comedy with an edge, and new adult books that push contemporary boundaries. From billionaires to BBWs to rock stars, Julia finds a sensual, goofy joy in every book she writes, but unlike Trevor from *Random Acts of Crazy*, she has never kissed a chicken.

She loves to hear from her readers by email at jkentauthor@gmail.com, on Twitter @jkentauthor, on Tinstagram @jkentauthor and on Facebook at https://www.facebook.com/jkentauthor . Visit her website at http://jkentauthor.com

CPSIA information can be obtained
at www.ICGtesting.com
Printed in the USA
LVOW12s2017010318
568342LV00002B/605/P

9 781682 307380